PLAGUED
BY BAD
BELIEFS

PLAGUED
BY BAD
BELIEFS

JERRY DEAN PATE

ISBN: 978-1-955119-27-6 (Paperback)
ISBN: 978-1-955119-28-3 (eBook)

LCCN: 2022901607

Published by: Write Publish Sell
Cover Designer: Kevin D. Pate
Photo Credit: Michelle Fairbanks
Editor: Jodie Caine Smith

Publisher's Cataloging-In-Publication Data
(Prepared by The Donohue Group, Inc.)

Names: Pate, Jerry Dean, author.

Title: Plagued by Bad Beliefs / Jerry Dean Pate.

Description: [Columbia, South Carolina] : Write Publish Sell, [2022]

Identifiers: ISBN 9781955119276 (paperback) | ISBN 9781955119283 (eBook)

Subjects: LCSH: Women journalists--Southern States--Fiction. | Disinformation--Southern States--Fiction. | Southern States--History--Fiction. | Truthfulness and falsehood--Fiction. | United States--History--Civil War, 1861-1865--Fiction.

Classification: LCC PS3616.A86646 P53 2022 (print) | LCC PS3616.A86646 (eBook) | DDC 813/.6--dc23

DEDICATION

This work is dedicated to Aunt Bill who had to go to work in a cotton mill when she was eight years old. It is also dedicated to her daughter Sallie who loved me, and to the thousands of textile workers, sharecroppers, and African Americans who struggled against a political system that held them back by keeping them distrustful of each other.

"*They . . . will turn their ears away from the truth and wander off into myths and man-made fictions.*"

—2 Timothy 4:4 AMP

CHAPTER 1

THE UDC - HAIGLER'S CROSSING, SC

E very community has customs and beliefs. Some are good as they ensure the normal behaviors of daily life. Some may be just quirks, harmless in their effect.

But then there are beliefs, grown out of lies, that lead otherwise good people to join in or stand aside and watch . . . as great harm is done.

Some Boy Scouts didn't believe the weather warning one night and went to the pond anyway. One of them slipped on a log, hit his head and drowned just as a bad lightning storm blew in. His playmates, afraid of the lightning, were too scared to jump in after him, abandoned their encampment, and ran home for help.

Days later his mutilated corpse was found among a thick growth of cattails and lily pads some distance from the log. The sheriff said it looked as if some animal had dragged it toward the shore and ate on it. Some believed it was an alligator, but duck hunters and fishermen swore there were no gators there. That's when the rumors started about the boys, their scoutmaster, and Lura Mae McCutchen's ghost hacking at the body with her butcher knife.

1

When the truth came out it was found that the boys had disobeyed their scoutmaster who had called off a campout due to reports of a bad storm headed that way. Instead of going home like the rest of the troop, the boys hiked to the pond, set up camp, and were playing near the water when the storm came.

Now those were the facts. But by this time, the rumors and speculation of loud-mouthed opinionists had grown too big for truth to overcome. At the barber shop there were three men waiting and one in the chair when the local tough-talker came in. The barber said "Take a seat" then returned to clipping and looking at the guy's head he was working on. The others grunted hellos and nodded. Tough-talker sat in a chair he tipped against the back wall and asked "What y'all up to?"

"They been talkin' bout them boys," the barber said without changing his focus or pausing his clipping.

"They need to do something about him," Tough-talker said.

"Who?" somebody grunted.

"That scoutmaster. He was responsible. Somebody oughta teach him a lesson."

Tough-talker never served in the military, but he sure spent a lot of time trying to get people to think he did. He talked a lot about wars, and combat, and guns, and how things should be, or, by God – must be. He believed men leading boys must be manly. They must talk manly talk and work manly jobs instead of doing sissy women's work like teaching grammar school as did the scoutmaster.

When the men in the barber shop sat silent, although some smiled, Tough-talker thought he had permission to teach the scoutmaster a lesson. A few nights later he and a couple of his buddies got drunk. "That damn sissy needs his ass beat," one of them slurred.

"Yea, let's get him," Tough-talker said.

They parked their car on the street back of the boarding house where the Scoutmaster roomed with his sister. They drank encouragement from a whiskey bottle then got out in the dark where the trees shooed away the streetlight. With Tough-talker in the lead, they rang the doorbell and were in luck when the Scoutmaster opened the door. Tough-talker was smiling real friendly like when he said, "We got something your Scout Troop will like. It's a big rock with old painting on it. We dug out of the Indian cave."

"Where is it?"

"It's in the trunk of my car. Come 'round back and we'll show it to you."

Tough-talker led the Scoutmaster into the darkness. His two buddies trailed close behind balling their fists. One of them hit the unsuspecting man with a kidney punch and his companion grabbed ahold to keep him upright as the man's legs buckled. Tough-talker wasn't smiling now. He growled, "you sissy-queer son of a bitch," and beat the helpless man with left and right roundhouse punches until he gave out of breath. Then he panted, "One of you want some of him?"

"Yea, hold him up. You son of a bitch this is for lettin' that boy drown."

The blows continued until a real mean Jack Russell terrier ran from a house and put a stop to it. His owner was yelling "no," as the little dog flew at the man swinging away. He bit the man hard on the butt and held on fast while growling something fierce. Tough-talker slung the Scoutmaster to the ground and ran for the car with one of his companions running too. The third man was screaming, "get this dog off me." The man spun and swatted and spun and swatted until he heard the car crank and then with a hard chop, he sent the dog flying and ran to the car. By this time the whole neighborhood was out, one of them hollered, "Call the cops" and the three men drove off as a neighbor wrote the license plate number in the dirt.

Tough-talker and his buddies spent a night in jail for what they did. But that gave him something to brag about. Besides, he enjoyed the smiles he got from his manly pals in the barber shop. A couple of weeks later the school weighed-in on the rumors too. They fired the scoutmaster because . . . *well, there was just too much controversy about to let him continue teaching children.*

Now, despite the scoutmaster getting run off and an abundance of plausible stories, there were those who thought the boy's body was chopped up by the ghost of Lura Mae McCutchen. They swore they heard Lura Mae crashing through the underbrush and going after people stupid enough to go back out to those woods near the pond.

This Lura Mae story got started after her husband came home one evening and caught her in the woods . . . having sex with her own cousin. He killed the cousin, heaved Lura Mae down a well and stuck a butcher's knife in the bucket. As he lowered it, he told her she should use it to kill herself. Then, he ate the barrel of a shotgun, closed his eyes, and blew his head off.

Lura Mae stood in the cold water with a foot tangled in the bucket hollering all night, the next day and the next night. On Tuesday, her husband's boss came to the place to see why his man was missing work. He found the dead men by the well and got the sheriff. One of the deputies looked in the well and found Lura Mae's body dangling by the foot.

Her throat was cut.

Ever since then folks had believed Lura Mae's ghost left signs that she was moving about the woods, and she would cut up any man or boy who came near.

*   *   *

Betsy McCall never believed the Lura Mae nonsense. And—she knew the truth about the scoutmaster—he was her teacher. Betsy was in the sixth grade back then and got her classmates to sign a letter asking the principal not to fire him. But he fired him anyway.

As she drove past the pond that morning, the last thing on her mind was what happened there twenty years ago. She was the speaker at a meeting of the United Daughters of the Confederacy and was running late. It had been years since she'd been in this part of South Carolina, the roads and trees had changed, and she worried she'd made a wrong turn.

The only person moving about was a man over in the mill village, a clerk sweeping the porch and setting out wares at the company store. She turned onto the dirt street, gunned the car then slid to a stop which had the clerk swatting at the dust and squinting to see who was fouling his setup. She hollered for directions, he pointed, she spun the car around, and raced off. The clerk cussed, shook his fist, and brushed from the porch the very dirt he just swept away.

Betsy was heading to the Hastings McDowell chapter of the United Daughters of Confederacy, that Southern ladies organization formed after the Civil War to help defray costs for re-internment of Confederate soldiers. She was unaware she was headed for trouble by sharing a document she hoped would qualify her to join the chapter. Membership in the UDC required ladies to provide evidence a relative had served in the Confederate military.

Betsy had been raised on the myth of "The Lost Cause," which the UDC promoted. And she and other southern school children had been taught from UDC endorsed textbooks based upon misleading and dubious rewrites of southern history. It claimed the War Between the States as southerners now called it was fought over State's Rights, not really about slavery and it was Yankees who destroyed South Carolina and other southern states.

The McDowell house where she was headed was near the cotton mill out from Haigler's Crossing. When Betsy got there Sarah McDowell, a nervous brooding thing, fretted, "Oh dear, you're late please come quickly, I must start the meeting." She ushered her into the parlor and pointed for Betsy to sit and made no introductions. The rest of the women gave Betsy a glance then returned to their animated talk of those "trashy mill people." She heard someone say, "and that Yankee Lemuel Webster, you know he married Amelia just to get her daddy's mill."

Sarah McDowell cleared her throat and called the meeting to order. Although somewhat shy, she loved playing hostess for the event as it gave her an opportunity to flaunt her family's history which she did with the only gusto she could generate. She had repeated the introduction so often most chapter members knew it by heart.

"Ladies, please settle down. We have a candidate for membership today, who has just arrived. In a minute we will hear her report. But first, I want to again welcome you to McDowell House for this meeting of the United Daughters of the Confederacy. Great, great grandfather Ellis *Seastrunk* McDowell—his mother was a Seastrunk—would be pleased to see so many lovely ladies representing the finest families in this lovely home he built nearly two hundred years ago."

"We will again serve from a royal-china tea set great grandmother Hastings McDowell saved from the Yankees. She hid it in a croaker sack, put in the bottom of the well before Sherman's horrible soldiers found their way onto our family's property. She personally oversaw the recovery of this tea set and the silverware although Sherman's thieves confiscated all her trays and a silver kettle dating back to the Revolutionary War.

"We are thankful Hastings Le Grand McDowell had the ingenuity and courage to protect these historic possessions from Yankee soldiers. You know the Yankees were nothing more than common thieves."

Sarah finished, then introduced the new candidate.

"Betsy McCall here is the latest to seek membership in our organization. Now please tell us about your relative who served in the glorious cause."

The women looked at Betsy as if she smelled. She was informally dressed: no hat, no gloves, no lipstick or rouge. Betsy worried about that when she first sat down.

Crap, now I gotta be a magnolia blossom so they'll believe me.

"He was David Jenkins my great grandmother's cousin," she cooed in a pretentious Southern accent. Some ladies smiled and nodded, some didn't.

"He was a private in General Kershaw's unit at Gettysburg. I have the letter he wrote his mother after the last battle."

"Oh, do please read," Sarah encouraged.

"It's dated July fifth, eighteen sixty-three. It's not pretty. It sounds like he was still scared when he wrote it. But here goes:

'Dear Momma, we got to this place called Gettysburg and fought for three days before pulling back. It was horrible. We fought one day from early in the morning until ten o'clock at night.

'My friend Virgil was trying to run when a cannon ball exploded square against him. He burst into pieces so tiny, there was nothing left of him to bury."

The ladies began whispering. Betsy paused, looked at them, then slowly resumed her reading:

'Virgil … was … a good friend. Since then, I've asked myself why did he have to die? What are we fighting for? It ain't right for me to have to fight when you and papa don't own no slaves.

'Several in my company have been talking about that long before we got here. Some of them say that since we're retreating, they might as well leave for home. I might go with them, but I might not. They are shooting deserters now so I don't want to get shot by my own men and I wouldn't want to bring no shame on you but I'm—'"

"That's enough!" a lady interrupted.

"Those words are lies, outright lies. Where did you get that?"

"I got it from my grandmother. It's real."

"I don't care what that letter says, I know for a fact our men served bravely and with honor. They didn't desert."

Women nodded. The timid ones stared at the floor hoping unpleasantries might be avoided. The arrogant ones clinched lips and flashed censorious looks at their guest.

Betsy stared back open-mouthed. She looked at the letter, then back at the women, mystified by their reaction and explained again, this time without the accent, and a bit defensive. "My grandmother *gave* me this. She got it from her sister. It's real." She stood and held up the letter, "see, it's dated July fifth, eighteen sixty-three . . . after . . . he fought . . . in Gettys . . . burg."

More silence. The clock in the hallway chimed eleven times. The leader of the bunch stood, pointed at the door and ordered, "Miss McCall, leave—right now."

The UDC didn't tolerate facts disproving their beliefs. They romanticized the Civil War as a noble cause. They promoted dubious explanations of dirt-poor southern men *gladly* taking up arms to protect their beloved homeland in the hopes they too could someday become planters and live in luxury.

Poor farmers had little choice. The Confederate States had conscription laws drafting southern males and paid gunmen to scour the country for those trying to avoid it.

In South Carolina, Greenville County was so filled with draft dodgers, it was called The Black Hole.

Even with evidence to the contrary the Lost Cause narrative described draftees as honorable men willingly serving under the leadership of gallant knights, those of finest families born to lead the southern states. Confederate Generals, regardless of ability or outcome, became gods venerated in statues the UDC helped erect across the South.

"Is she a Yankee?" a lady asked.

"No, she told me her family was from Jefferson. I'm sorry, I thought with her working for that newspaper she would have brought us some good information and not that. . . and . . . well, I should have known better when I saw how she dressed."

One of them harrumphed, "A newspaper woman, that figures. I bet she doesn't like men. Probably sleeps in the same bed with a woman in some apartment." Other ladies nodded.

"Next thing you know people like her will be trying to tell us we're wrong about the war."

The leader of the bunch cleared her throat and warned, "Sarah, we need to be careful about who we let come to our meeting. We have customs and traditions to maintain. And we certainly don't want common white trash coming here thinking they are as good as we are."

The ladies nodded as if their leader had recited some Nicene affirmation. All they needed now was to sing a doxology. They had run off someone who disrupted their sacred assembly with that most foul of things . . . the truth.

Why, these ladies *knew* what was and was not true, they had the bloodlines, coats of arms and family ties to prove it.

Outside the house Betsy was so stupefied by what they'd done to her she didn't hear her shoes crunch the gravel walk or feel the cold of the door handle when she reached her car. It was stuck. She tugged and jerked and laid a good "you son of a bitch" cussing on it as if it were alive and defiant. After several moments the door apparently tired of this and went *hell, if you want it that badly, here!* and popped off the handle tumbling Betsy onto her butt—*Shit!*

Now, this was a good thing because it pulled Betsy away from the well of self-reproach she was about to fall into and brought her back to the present. It also set off her sizable temper as she struggled to get up. *Damn women. I was right. I told them the truth and they didn't believe me.*

Getting run off by uppity ladies was bad enough, but now this rattle trap was screwing with her plans for a dramatic *kiss my ass* departure. She slid in from the other side, put the handle on the seat and cussed at the motor which grumbled at being woke. After several quivering gyrations and Betsy cussing it finally started.

She popped the clutch—*take that pretentious bitches*—slinging gravel into the flower bed. But, instead of roaring off with the great flair she wanted, the Model-A could only wheeze, and spit, and buck no matter how hard she stomped the gas.

Betsy McCall was tough, she had to be. An orphan from early years, she was tossed around family members depending on who had food and clothes and a willingness to put up with a precocious smart aleck. These stays ran about two years until they tired of her. Usually the aunt mysteriously got sick, or the uncle got lame from some weird accident, the story of which changed every time Betsy asked, *how?* Finally, she was taken in by a widowed uncle who had two boys her age. He grew tobacco and made good money off it.

It was here she learned to cuss, drive a tobacco sled, smoke cigarettes on the sly, and pee standing up. This latter skill mastered while poking her head above tobacco stalks and hollering back at her "you can't do it" cousins three rows away.

Betsy and her special gift became legends the day she pushed against the *men only* barrier at Clemson Agriculture & Military College in the South Carolina upstate. The Dean admitted her tobacco farm cousins but turned her down despite her protesting she could do *anything as good as any man.* Betsy stomped out Tillman Hall into a crowd of incoming students who roared and applauded as she flipped the finger at the Dean's open window and hollered, "You son of a bitch, I can pee standing up!"

A week later her uncle took her to the University of South Carolina where she got upset again as the admissions office there tried to steer her into courses for women. "I'm not gonna be a schoolteacher," she glared, "I'm gonna be a newspaper reporter."

Betsy was tired of being told "You can't." She'd heard that most of her life. And now these snobby UDC ladies were saying it. They accused her of lying and refused to accept the letter she read, because it said things that went against their beliefs. She was still cussing them and the car as she drove away. At the mill village, that store clerk was back out, yelling and shaking his fist at her again. *What the hell?* She stomped the gas, flipped him the finger and lit a cigarette.

Fussing between self-reproach, and *I did nothing wrong* she drove back into North Carolina and headed to Wadesboro. Her stormy thoughts didn't stop when the car bumped the curb in front of the newspaper where she worked. She tramped into the lobby and slammed the door. *Damn women.*

The noise interrupted her boss's nap. He hitched his pants and walked out fumbling to get the curly ends of his glasses over his ears. Grinning as he leaned across the counter, he watched his new employee light a cigarette and sit at her desk.

"I take it your UDC meeting didn't go well."

"Hell, they ran me off."

"For what?"

"For telling them the truth."

"Oh god," he laughed, "I told you those people over there have their own ideas about what truth is."

"Yeah, but you didn't tell me they were magnolia blossom dawtuhs of the sou-yuth, bat-shit-crazy." She took a drag and huffed, "They yelled at me, Mister Sweat, and told me I was wrong. Look at this and tell me if I was wrong."

"Your great uncle wrote this just after the first battle at Gettysburg?"

"Yessir, my grandmother swears this is the letter she got from her sister. I tried to show it to those UDC women, but they refused to look at it. Said it was all a lie."

Sweat chuckled, "The people over there are still fighting the Civil War." He passed the letter back. "They keep changing what really happened into tales of what they wish had happened. We got people in North Carolina believing the same lies, but not with the fury of those Sandlappers." Arthur Sweat liked Betsy. She was a good writer, but what he really liked about her was she didn't take crap. "Here," he handed her a note, "I need you to call Mrs. Davenport. Her daughter is getting married next week and wants us to do an article with a bridal picture."

As he walked away Betsy looked at the number, took another drag and jabbed the cigarette in the ashtray. She exhaled, *Shit, so now I gotta write another, glorious wedding account of—The bride wore a traditional wedding gown of ivory peau de soie featuring a fitted bodice and portrait neckline.*—"Yuck!"

She had argued the newspaper would draw more readers if it published wedding articles more realistic with less fluff. Arthur Sweat laughed then told her *No!* when she grinned "C'mon boss, wouldn't it be more truthful if we said, 'Dressed in virginal white, the bride married *this* man—after screwing through the entire trombone section of her high school—and on her wedding night would tell her husband—'As a matter of fact, I'm not—*surprise!*'"

When she got the job, she realized Arthur Sweat was taking a chance letting her in the door of a business marked men only— even if she was stuck in it writing puff-pieces of *who visited whom* and *bridge club guests* known in the trade as women's news. Betsy was determined to work on real news.

Okay, straighten up, she told herself and dialed the number. Her desk mate Vernon Covington walked in. She waved him a hello, and he removed his jacket and cap and hung them on the clothes tree behind his desk.

The newspaper was on main street in an old building, which had been the Coloreds' waiting area of a doctor's office. It sat empty for a couple of years after the previous owner hastily left town amid folks giggling and elbow poking over the scandal he wrought.

Seems the doctor's wife took exception to her husband, *the doctor*, and her sister, *the nurse*, doing late night medical exams on each other which somehow by-accident and "we weren't doing nothing," left the sister pregnant.

When Arthur Sweat bought the place, he didn't do much to reconfigure the front. His office was in what had been the reception area, a cubicle of glass panes atop fading white wainscoting. He had a counter built near the door with room for customers to stand. That was to give space behind it for his two reporters to work facing each other across desks jammed together.

The area was so small, during phone conversations Betsy and Vernon had to turn away to keep the distractions down. Even then eavesdropping was unavoidable.

When she heard "hello" Betsy morphed into magnolia blossom and cheerily spoke, "Mrs. Davenport, Betsy McCall from the Wadesboro Press. I understand your precious Anita is getting married next week."

Vernon's eyebrows flicked. He grinned but kept his head down and thumbed through some copy. She frowned at him and turned away.

Betsy was a crusader. She disliked that, even when they were permitted to work, women got paid less than men for the same job. She was single, kept her curly hair short, preferred wearing pants but thought better of it. Instead, she wore solid skirts and plain blouses with pockets crammed with pencils behind a pack of Lucky Strikes. She pulled her reading glasses off her head and bent to jot notes about the wedding guests and the bridal gown and bridesmaids' dresses. When they got to the floral displays, she chuckled as Mrs. Davenport mused, "My cousin Duzon is preparing the loveliest of flowers for my daughter."

"Oh," Betsy asked, "is he the one who owns *Floral Beauty Creations by Duzon?*"

Vernon's eyebrows jumped again.

"Why yes," Mrs. Davenport continued. "Of course his real name is William Eddings Henry Frampton the Third but Little Willie, as the family knows him, prefers we call him Duzon— although sometimes we forget."

Betsy turned, took more notes, cooed another "Oh, how lovely," into the phone, then flipped Vernon the finger for patting his hands and pursing his lips at her like a schoolboy. The Davenport woman droned on. Betsy rolled her eyes, and clumsily fished the cigarette pack out her pocket. Her nicotine receptors were tapping again. She debated then tossed the cigarettes onto her desk. Mrs. Davenport was still at it. Vernon was on the phone typing an obituary.

Betsy made more notes. The craving tapped harder. She pulled out a smoke, lit it, took a deep pull, and exhaled. Finally, the phone call was over. "Thank you, Mrs. Davenport. You will need to get the bridal picture to us by Monday. Okay, yes, thank you, thank you Mrs. Davenport."

She took another drag, exhaled loudly, and was enjoying the cigarette's taste until a dull ache throbbed in her lower abdomen. *Shit, I've got things to do and now this.* Her period was coming on.

She headed past her boss's office for the rest room. Still puffing the cigarette, she got mad at herself for wasting her time with the United Daughters of the Confederacy. *I should have quit looking for that place and come back here, but oh no, I had to keep going.* Betsy enjoyed working with Vernon and her boss. Arthur Sweat was a stickler for reporting the truth in a land where newspapers often looked the other way to satisfy local customs and beliefs.

Sweat was from West Virginia and came here to buy the paper off a bankrupt owner shortly after the stock market crash. His stubbornness for printing truth was underwritten by coal barge money from his family's estate. He used it to fend off screaming threats of advertising cancellations for printing stories which were true but ran against common beliefs. That was another reason Betsy liked working for him, even if she was stuck writing *Women's News*.

She stepped in her boss' doorway.

"Mister Sweat, Vernon says you know about Mildred Turnage."

"I didn't know her, but I read about her, why"

"She was my aunt."

"Mildred must have been some kind of woman. Vernon published stories about her during the strike at that cotton mill near Haigler's Crossing."

"And those people were the ones who put Vernon out of business?" Betsy asked.

"It was Dupre Merchant who did it, but it might as well as been the whole town. Dupre owns the only bank in Haigler's Crossing and he was the one who called in Vernon's note. Dupre's daddy and granddaddy ran things in that town for years so Dupre thinks he and his buddies on the bank board still have a right to tell people what to do.

"Vernon made the mistake of siding with the workers at Crowell Mill during the strike. Vernon is a big Roosevelt supporter and FDR said folks can join unions and negotiate better work conditions. When the workers got killed, Dupre stormed into Vernon's newspaper and tried to strong-arm him into publishing articles that the strikers were Communists. Dupre hates the mill and the Yankee immigrant who owns it.

"Vernon gets mad and yells, nobody is gonna tell him what he can put in his newspaper and ordered Dupre to get out. Vernon called me about it. He's my brother-in-law, you know.

"I sez to him 'Vernon you know better than writing spite stories when you're drinking.' He tells me to mind my business and he'd only had a couple of drinks that day. Then he writes this big screaming headline front-page story about how cotton mill workers had a right to join the union. He said the Labor Board ought to investigate the shootings and how old man Webster kept them locked out of work 'til they nearly starved to death.

"That was on a Thursday and by Monday Dupre Merchant had called in Vernon's bank note. Then he told the banks in Cheraw and Bennettsville not to lend Vernon any money either. That put Vernon out of business. That's why I brought him up here.

"You need to talk with him about your aunt. I never met her but read the stories he wrote about her. There are copies of them out in the warehouse. Talk with Vernon, he interviewed her."

*   *   *

Despite being busy all day, Betsy's brain would not let loose the UDC's dismissive *Miss McCall, leave right now.* All her life she struggled with feeling good enough. Her thoughts permanently set on standby; ready to record and play back every slight, big or small. It ran in a never-ending loop of *see, you're not good enough* that she could never shut off. Then she'd get mad at herself for thinking that way. She had been naïve in believing her letter would qualify her to join the UDC. But no, they rejected her letter and . . . her.

Late the next day she asked Vernon to take her to the warehouse and show her his newspaper's back issues. She wanted to know more about the strike and the Civil War and also hoped it would give her an opportunity to know more about Vernon. Outside of work they hadn't talked much in the few months she'd been at the office.

Vernon Covington met Arthur Sweat when they worked at a newspaper in Fairmont, West Virginia. He married Vernon's sister and took to drinking when she drowned in a mill pond during a church picnic one cold Sunday. After that Vernon didn't have much use for churches.

He came south, bought the weekly newspaper in Haigler's Crossing thinking the change in locale would keep away the sadness. It didn't. Besides losing his wife he was struggling to understand the people in this new community. He was frustrated by their demands to report things according to their version of truth rather than his explaining that colored men taken in by police on questionable charges of vagrancy always had some mysterious accident that left their faces swollen or lips busted. For months he drank to unconsciousness to push away the memory of his wife's death. The drinking got so bad Arthur took Vernon to a clinic in Lancaster to get him dried out. It worked for a couple of years, then the mill workers got killed, and Dupre Merchant foreclosed on the newspaper and Vernon started back.

Vernon had struggled for so long and so often, he thought having problems were supposed to be his normal state. He got uncomfortable when it wasn't. If things were going too good, too long, he'd get angry and jittery until he worked himself into a full-blown case of the heebie-jeebies. That was his excuse to go on a roaring drunk, get in trouble so he could add another thing to hate himself for, then life would be returned to the way it was supposed to be.

He wasn't at the heebie-jeebies stage yet, but Betsy noticed that lately he *was* getting angry more often. She worried he was headed for a drunk when they went out back to the warehouse. He began cussing the warehouse door as if an evil spirit possessed it.

"This damn thing keeps getting stuck . . .there, now let me get the light." Vernon pulled a chain overhead then snapped on a goose-neck lamp bolted to the table. An old typewriter on rollers was in the corner with a chair against it.

The room was filled from floor to ceiling with dusty cardboard boxes on wooden racks. They formed a narrow passage requiring them to walk one behind the other. There was barely space to pull boxes out and to see what was inside. You had to open them on the floor or wrestle them along the walking space to the standing-height table in front of a side window.

Vernon coughed from the dust. "How 'bout opening that window and I'll get the boxes with my papers about the strike."

They spent some time flipping through articles and talking. Betsy looked at a headline. "Vernon, those people over there put you out of business for this? You got run out of town for telling the truth?"

"Yep, and you got kicked out of the UDC for the same. Those people have their own version of what the truth is. If you want to see what they're like, go through those old newspapers the original owners wrote about the Civil War."

Vernon nudged and handed her a worn book. "You need to read this, Arthur brought this with him from West Virginia. It's a truthful account of the Civil War and Reconstruction, not the false stuff you and the rest of the people in South Carolina were taught. Read this then compare what it says to what's in the newspaper accounts."

They walked back to the office. The newspaper had closed for the day. After putting the door handle back on Betsy's car, Vernon left for the pool hall and beer with his drinking buddies. He thought beer would hold off the bout of heebie-jeebies coming on.

Vernon may have his flaws and internal demons, but Betsy knew he believed newspapers should tell people the truth. She put the Civil War letter in her desk, took the book then left for the boarding house where she shared a room with another woman but not in the same bed. As Betsy drove home, she got mad at the UDC women again. *Why is it those people over there want to believe things that are just not true?*

CHAPTER 2

THEY CAUSED THE CIVIL WAR.

The next morning Betsy was standing behind the counter drinking coffee when the door opened. A short, middle-aged lady stepped inside, paused, and looked down. "Oh dear," she mumbled and brushed her shoes on the mat as if she'd stepped in something. It was the Home Demonstration lady from the extension service.

After checking her shoes, she smiled then walked forward with an envelope in her hand.

"Betsy, here's this month's article, Mister Sweat told me he was reserving space for it in this week's edition."

"Okay, thanks. I'll set it up."

The lady left. Betsy went back to her desk, opened the envelope, and muttered, "Oh, for Christ's sake."

Vernon looked up. "What."

"They want us to run this, this *Women's Fashion News*. Listen to this." Switching into magnolia blossom she purred, "'Yo-wuh clothes speak for you before you can speak for yo-se-yuf. They tell others how you think and more importantly . . . *what* . . . you are'"

"Oh God, Vernon, I'm gonna be sick."

"Please, Miss Women's Editor, don't leave me in suspense."

"It gets worse," she continued. "'With the way you dress you reveal yourself to others as a lady or . . . as a careless woman. You must be mindful of this and dress properly regardless the occasion. When going to church, for example, a simple suit or softly tailored dress is appropriate. For church you must be fully dressed. This means a hat, gloves and a clutch purse of fabric.'"

"Oh, thank you Miss Scarlett, thank you," Vernon laughed.

"Damn Vernon I must be a slu . . . no wait. I must be, what'd she call it? a *careless* woman. Why do we put shit like this in the paper?" she asked.

"Well, I been talking with Arthur about that, Vernon said. "We need to write stories about people doing things important, like your aunt Mildred leading the strike. It's happening in the mills up here in North Carolina too and we need to be writing about it."

The door opened again and a lady from the Baptist church came to the counter. Betsy greeted her and took a draft of the bulletin for next week's service. The newspaper printed bulletins for most of the churches in the town.

The phones started ringing and the typewriters clacked all day. Late that evening Betsy went back to the warehouse and flipped through old newspapers on South Carolina's role in the Civil War and Reconstruction. The newspaper accounts didn't match those in the book Vernon gave her. The more she read, the more upset she became. *So, those early newspaper stories were made-up tales about what folks in Haigler's Crossing wanted them to be.*

She flipped through more pages and cussed loudly when she read that three men from Chesterfield County started the Civil War. "Shit, why didn't they tell us this when we were in school." *I gotta write about this. I'll talk with Vernon and Arthur about it maybe we can do something.*

A couple of days later she tried to get Vernon to tell her about the Civil War. He didn't want to talk. Vernon had a day-long set of the shakes from drinking. The heebie-jeebies had grabbed a hold of him. He spent the day cussing himself for drinking beer with the boys in the pool hall last night then going home and slugging straight whiskey to shut off the blame for his wife's drowning and the loss of his newspaper.

Arthur could see Vernon struggling and kept an eye on him all day. Fearing he'd start drinking if he got loose, he sent Betsy for sandwiches at lunch. Later that afternoon Vernon still had the shakes when Arthur directed him, and Betsy to close up at the regular time as he had to leave early to call on an advertiser.

As soon as he left Vernon stood to go. Betsy stopped him and pulled out a pint of Old Grandad.

"I got this at lunch. Sit down, this might help."

Vernon grabbed the bottle, started to turn it up, then realizing how undignified it looked, he poured himself and Betsy shots in paper cups. He gulped three quick ones and wiped his mouth as he quivered, "now what is it you want me to tell you about?"

"The Chesterfield County men who caused the Civil War."

CHAPTER 3

THE PLANTERS MEET

Vernon poured himself another shot, set the bottle down and looked at it. "The Civil War," he quivered again, "that's all those people at Haigler's Crossing talk about Betsy, and they are proud of it.

"Back in 1859, about a year before the war, Cyril Merchant bamboozled Gedney Crowell and other planters to attend a meeting they were told was about runaway slaves. In fact, the speakers that night would talk the men into doing something that would destroy their state."

The meeting was held at the slave market hall across from the courthouse. It stood on a corner lot with a grassy area surrounding it. It looked like a small house stuck on top of tall white columns built high enough to allow room for people to walk about underneath. The lower half was open at the front and sides with benches set on a floor made of paving bricks to accommodate buyers and sellers. The market was better maintained than the city hall courthouse across the street. Slave merchants believed if buying and selling human beings were conducted in a formal setting, they could demonstrate that slavery is a natural, even noble activity engaged in by the very-best-people.

The place was filling quickly when Gedney Crowell got down from his carriage. He saw a half-dozen slaves, big, sweaty field hands, spaced about the grass around the building. They were holding torches to light the event and swatted at bugs with rags. As he moved through them, he wondered if the organizers had thought through what they were doing. Here were slaves standing outside to light the meeting for wealthy white men who would talk about slaves in front of slaves and make decisions affecting slaves in a place used for selling slaves.

Gedney shook hands with a couple attendees, then removed his hat, stepped into the open area, and sat. He nodded at a couple men across from him and looked around, estimating the group at about twenty.

They were all wealthy. Crowell thought there wasn't a dirt-farmer in the bunch. These men dressed in fine clothes and were driven to the meeting in nice carriages by slaves dressed in formalwear. Gedney had slaves, but not as many as these men.

On the back wall two small colored boys stood on each end of a stage holding torches. The youngest one scratched his nose, and too young to understand what was going on, was more interested in the black smoke curling up from his torch than the men below. The other boy stood impassive, looking out in the distance, avoiding the faces turned his way. He must have hated what was going on but minded his momma's warning: *You be respectful. Don't show them you upset.* He stared at a spot across the street as the red-faced white man down front yelled, "Three of my bucks ran away to Pennsylvania and were taken in by some Quakers."

The boy swallowed hard but otherwise didn't move as the man continued.

"I sent a warrant up there to get them back, and those Quakers are refusing, claiming it's against their religion. What good is the

Fugitive Slave Law if states up north ignore it. If I can't get them back, I'm gonna lose nine thousand dollars' worth of slaves."

Cyril Merchant stepped onto the platform and said, "Gentlemen, that's why we brought you here tonight. These men from Cheraw have a good idea about how we can fix this problem. The first one is Henry McIver, an attorney from over there."

McIver took the stage to stir the crowd. "This mess was created by Yankees in Congress. They're passing laws that threaten our very way of life. We have a plan to fix it."

"How?" a man asked.

"We'll withdraw from the United States and form our own country."

"We tried that back in fifty-one and lost the vote. Why do you think it will work now?"

"Because now there are more men in favor of it, especially in the upcountry. The federal government exists only from the power granted it by the states. So, we can choose not to be a part of it when it does things harmful to us. That's what John C. Calhoun argued during nullification of Andy Jackson's tariff. My law partner John Inglis has written a document that will do just that. John, come up and tell them how we can do it."

Inglis took the stage. "This time, there is enough sentiment to get this done. We'll get the legislature to appoint a state secession convention and get them to adopt the referendum I've drafted. Then we get the voters to vote for it. I'm certain we can get the votes this time. We'll declare South Carolina is no longer a part of the United States, but a new nation free to establish its own laws and government."

"Are you *sure* that'll work?" a man criticized.

"We're positive. We've already run it by a couple of judges. We need all of you to help us convince other planters in the state to get the legislature to do this. There are only a few hundred of us, so it should be easy. Other slave states might want to join us, too. We must do something to stop Washington."

Gedney Crowell thought the idea was harebrained. He frowned as the man near him gestured, *Maybe, why not?*

When Inglis finished speaking, Stephen Jackson stepped in his place. He worried there might be some who would oppose the idea, since it already had been tried and failed. Jackson was confident he could win them over and needed only one thing to do it—fear. "You want Washington letting runaway slaves hiding in free states and you can't get them back?"

One man said, "No."

"You want Washington telling you what to do about your field hands?"

"No." The crowd stirred.

"You want Washington telling your slaves they're no longer slaves, but free, free to leave your fields and houses?"

"No," the crowd got louder.

"Well now, you better do something about it, because it's coming. Think about this. Do you want big bucks free to roam the countryside at night, free to steal your stuff, and free to rape your women?"

"No!" the crowd yelled.

A tall man jumped up, "I just beat a nigger boy for telling my daughter she was so pretty he could kiss her."

"Hell," another man said, "I had to beat one of mine for looking at my wife. She said he looked at her like he was gonna hump her right there at the well."

"You listen to me," Jackson said, "if you don't do something, there will be raping and plundering. None of us will be safe. Why, coloreds at your place and mine already outnumber us ten to one.

They outnumber all the whites in the state almost double. We can't have them take over. Help us out. We have a plan. Judges have already told us it would work."

Jackson brought into open the fears these big planters had uttered for years on hunting trips and in lodges away from their wives and children . . . and their slaves.

John Inglis stood and said, "Go to your neighbors, and tell them to get their legislators to do what's necessary for our state to leave the Union. It's all legal. We can form our own country. Then nobody in Washington can tell us what to do. We'll have our own sovereign nation of South Carolina."

The crowd stood, the men angry and telling each other, "He's right, we gotta do something."

Gedney Crowell was silent for a long time as he rode back to his house, troubled by what he heard.

Finally, his driver asked, "Boss, is we going to succeed?"

"I hope you're right, Elijah. I hope we succeed. But first we must secede."

When he got home and sat at his desk, Crowell was still muttering, "Secede? Would they let us do that? I remember daddy telling me the referendum didn't get enough votes when I was a boy. Maybe now it'll be different."

He frowned as he looked at his accounting books and confirmed what he'd realized years before his father died, and why the slavery talk in Washington was troubling. He wasn't so much a cotton farmer; he was more like a cattle rancher.

Eighty percent of his wealth was based on the market price of his slaves. Like other planters, he used their inflated value as collateral to borrow money to buy more land and plant more cotton. But his wealth was mainly in slaves.

Now, people up North wanted to outlaw the thing that made him rich, and his crazy talking neighbors wanted to form their own country to keep it going.

The Atlantic slave trade evolved from the early 1600s into a sophisticated business arrangement between African tribes and Europeans. For hundreds of years slavery had been practiced around the world. In Africa slavery was a benevolent form of servitude to pay off debts or time served for crimes committed with the enslaved in some cases ultimately set free. This was far different from the brutal Chattel Slavery of the Americas. While the benevolent form may have continued, tribal leaders in Dahomey, Kanem Bornu, Allada and other African areas had no problem capturing fellow Africans and selling them as property out of African-owned slave markets. Usually these tribal leaders arranged deals with Europeans to exchange their slaves for goods, especially guns. Portugal, Spain, and Britain bought and shipped, most of these slaves into the Caribbean, Central and South America. A smaller number were sent to the American south.

By the time America came to be, opposition to slavery was such a big deal there was fierce debate over it at the 1787 Constitutional Convention. Delegates wrestled two months before a compromise was struck. Slave importation would continue for a while but by 1808 would cease. At that time, ninety percent of slaves in America had come from African-owned slave markets. With no more imports permitted American slave holders anticipating the ban had for years claimed ownership of their slaves' children as a means of maintaining a labor supply.

Even though the practice continued in Africa, western Europeans outlawed it in the 1830's. This put pressure on America to eliminate it altogether. Over years slave state legislators threw up every argument they could to try to stop Congress from outlawing the practice. They argued states had a right to set their own laws, even slave laws, and the federal government had no right to interfere. Besides, if America wanted to outlaw slavery, then why not make the Africans stop capturing and selling their own people? Abolitionist Fredrick Douglas argued against this approach:

> *The savage chiefs of the western coasts of Africa, who for ages have been accustomed to selling their captives into bondage and pocketing the ready cash for them, will not more readily accept our moral and economical ideas than the slave traders of Maryland and Virginia. We are, therefore, less inclined to go to Africa to work against the slave trade than to stay here to work against it.*

Gedney Crowell saw no way to fix it. That was Washington's problem. He was concerned about his problem. He flipped through his ledger and saw that over the last decade, his riches tripled, not so much from the cotton he planted, but from the market value of his slaves. And now under the threat of abolition, his fortune was at risk. He needed to get out of the slave business.

His neighbors said he was crazy. He was going against norms. But Crowell made up his mind. He stopped planting huge stands of cotton and began selling his slaves at highly inflated prices. Then, worried what would happen if this secession idea took hold, he began depositing his slave profits in British banks.

This caused problems at the next secession meeting. Cyril Merchant ran up to Gedney's carriage yelling, "You just stay right where you are. You're not welcome here you traitor."

"For what," exclaimed Crowell.

"For sendin' your money overseas."

A crowd formed. "You Crowells have always been up to no-good tricks and now when we need the money in the South, my bank's not good enough. You'd rather those nasty British have it.

"I oughta call you out Gedney Crowell, but the gentlemen's code prohibits me from desecrating the sacred field of honor with the blood of a swine like you."

Men stepped between Merchant and the carriage. One of them grabbed Merchant and cautioned, "Cyril, this is not the time," then pushed him away. Several men followed to insure there was no more arguing.

Gedney told those remaining, "I'll be joining our local army unit tomorrow. I'm no traitor. Cyril is upset because he can't get his hands on my money, that's all he cares about." He turned to his driver, "Elijah, let's go," and rode back to his farm.

*   *   *

Vernon leaned forward in his chair, reached across Betsy's desk for her cigarettes and said, "You need to know the bluebloods over in Haigler's Crossing never liked Gedney Crowell or any of the Crowell's for that matter." He pulled a cigarette from the pack. Thanks to the whiskey his voice no longer quivered, and he was smiling. His eyes had the gleam of a man lost in alcohol's warmth. Betsy asked him why the Crowell's were disliked.

Vernon took a big puff and spit away tobacco stuck to his lip. "Gedney's grandpa took advantage of one of their kind over there, that's how he got the Crowell fortune going. "When I was at Haigler's Crossing the folks told me that the man Gedney's great grandpa hoodooed was a drunkard with sloppy behavior, and philandering. But to the bluebloods he was still a treasure because he was from one of the better families in town," Vernon smirked. "According to them Edmund Crowell stole prime acreage from this beloved in a big-stake poker game one night and the bluebloods never forgave or trusted him or any other Crowell after that."

By the time Gedney had taken over the family estate, it had grown to large tracts of land farmed by hundreds of slaves down near the river. Gedney was a young man at the time and wanted to be accepted by the important people in the town. It didn't work because he was a Crowell.

After getting cussed at by Cyril Merchant for putting his money overseas, Gedney tried to join the local Confederate Army unit but was rejected by men Cyril Merchant influenced. So, Gedney rode into the next county, joined the unit there and was elected Captain.

Despite the Southern hubris they'd whip the Yankees in six weeks, the Civil War trudged along for four horrible years and ground the South into ashes and bare fields.

The slaves representing nearly eighty percent of the fortunes of old southern families just walked away, plunging most big planters into bankruptcy. Banks failed. Plantations shriveled up. Fields lay fallow. There was no money.

"Gedney Crowell's planning paid off—he had money and the others hated him for it. Gedney bought stands of timber and began operating a lumber mill and turpentine distillery west of the county seat. He spent years focused on his work until he felt his business was big enough, he could marry and start a family."

As Vernon finished his tale, Betsy sat amazed. "Has anybody written about this?" she asked.

"Not about the Crowell's. Plenty's been written about the Civil War but most of what the South wrote about it is embellished or flat-out wrong. After the war, rather than admit *they* caused the destruction of their homeland, Southern leaders blamed Yankees and the Federal Government for it. They worked hard to see that their message was promoted by preachers, teachers and newspapers until all the white people believed them."

"Vernon, nobody told us about the men starting the Civil War being from Cheraw. We were told the Yankees caused it by their horrid taxes and tariffs."

"They didn't fire the shots, Betsy, but they wrote the articles of secession. The articles were used for South Carolina to leave the Union which, when you think about it, that ultimately led to the firing on Fort Sumter, which started the war, so I guess in a way, you could say they caused it."

"Do you think Arthur might let me write about this Civil War nonsense? Something is bad wrong with what I was taught."

"Write it up and show it to him, he knows the truth. But don't expect him to agree to publishing it right away. He'll probably want to gauge community attitudes before printing your story. Thanks for the whiskey Betsy, I feel better now."

"Vernon, come with me to the boarding house, they have a good supper most nights."

"Naw, you go on. I'll lock up."

"Well, promise me you won't drink anymore tonight."

"I promise. Oh . . . leave the bottle, I'll put it away for us."

CHAPTER 4

Two House of Representatives

The next day, when Betsy brought up the subject, her boss told her she'd have to research and write a story on her own time. He'd take a look at what she wrote and would consider running it, *if* it were good enough.

When she closed the paper for the day, Betsy locked the door, and returned to her desk. Everyone knew the Civil War happened and had their views, right or wrong, on how it started and who was to blame, but Betsy had never heard what happened in the years immediately following the war. That was the part of the story she knew she had to tell. Betsy fired up a Lucky and began typing hard.

Columbia, SC, 1876 . . . After starting and losing the Civil War, South Carolina had an honest-to-God real representative democracy—for about ten years.

Freed slaves got the right to vote and used their population advantage to flip South Carolina politics from Democratic to Republican. Over a decade, they elected coloreds to Congress and the state legislature. Keep in mind, this only worked because coloreds had federal soldiers and officials on hand to protect them.

That all changed after the 1876 elections. That was when the big-name white families rigged things to take back political power.

Angus Merchant was with that bunch that day in Columbia. They were inside the Capitol, arguing over election results, and the Yankee soldiers posted there weren't happy about it.

*   *   *

The first sergeant was red-faced, frustrated at trying to organize a crowd of civilians. He yelled, "Didn't you hear the captain? He said a column of twos." He grabbed a man by the shoulder and shoved him. "Here! In a column of twos, you stand next to only one person, dumbass."

A voice cut in. "Lay off him, Sergeant. He's a member of the House."

The sergeant's eyes blazed. *A civilian corrected me?* As the people in the crowd grinned, he yelled, "I don't care if he's Jesus Christ! The captain said for them to get in a column of twos. Don't you people understand what a column of twos means? Shit, no wonder you lost the war."

He stomped down the stairs and yelled some more. The crowd had screwed up his line. "Dammit, I told you to give way and let these men through. Now, get back. You House members keep moving, two at a time."

He was frustrated at having to keep the peace between white Democrats and mainly Negro Republicans inside the Statehouse. Hell, he didn't want to be in South Carolina anyway. "Damn rebels," he muttered. Then he yelled, "Keep in line!"

The first sergeant was part of a military contingent President Grant had ordered in after gunfights among black and white groups broke out across the state. A hundred federal troops were in the Statehouse that morning to maintain order.

"Corporal," the sergeant yelled, "get up there and open the door!"

Republican legislators were already in the chamber when the white Democrats filed in. One of them yelled, "You can't come in here!"

"Try to stop us, Sambo!" someone yelled as the whites filed down the middle aisle and took their seats.

Then it started. Republicans began yelling, "Hey, hey! You can't go up there!" as three Democrats climbed onto the dais reserved for the Speaker of the House.

"My name is William Wallace," a tall white man announced, and he held up a document. "General Ruger, with Governor Chamberlain concurring, has determined that we have been duly elected members of this body, and this paper here, signed by the general, says we are permitted to sit in this chamber, just as you are."

"Yeah, but you can't sit there. That's the Speaker's chair."

The chamber door opened, and a voice announced, "All rise for the Speaker of the House, the honorable E.W.M. Mackey."

The Republicans stood. The Democrats sat. One of them muttered, "Ain't no nigger my Speaker." The sergeant-at-arms set the Mace of the House in place, signaling the House was in session.

The Speaker and his clerks ascended to the dais. Mackey walked to his chair and said, "Mr. Wallace, you're in my seat."

"No, this is my seat. I was elected Speaker earlier this morning."

"By whom? The full House of Representatives?"

"By a vote of fifty-seven to zero," Wallace said, smiling as his fellow Democrats laughed.

"Well, I was elected by the House fifty-nine to zero just last week," Mackey said. "We outvoted you, so I am the official Speaker of the House. Now, get out of my chair!"

A few Republicans ran up, and one of them yelled, "Get up, white boy! You in his seat."

Wallace grinned and then slowly turned his head and mouthed, *Nooo.*

One of the Republicans pointed a gun at Wallace and hollered, "Get out his seat, cracka!"

At this, a white man ran to the dais, pulled out *his* gun, and warned, "Nigger, I'll blow a hole through you."

Other whites ran up, and all the commotion sent the corporal out of the chamber, yelling, "Get Captain Henderson, quick!" as blacks and whites pushed each other on the floor.

At the dais, the standoff continued.

"Boy, put your gun down," the white man said with a glare.

"Both of you," ordered Speaker Mackey, "put your guns down now. This is getting out of hand."

Wallace looked up at his man. "Do as he says. Put it down."

Men from each side stepped between the gunmen and took turns warning them to holster their pistols and return to their seats. As the black man left and started down the aisle, a white man yelled, "Point a gun at my Speaker!" and *wham,* knocked him to the floor. That did it.

Both sides emptied and began punching and swinging away. A Democrat was hit and fell behind his desk as his assailant yelled, "White motherfucker!" Then, *wham,* he was hit with a trash can swung by a white man yelling, "Take that, yard ape!"

The headlocks and kicks and cussing had spread around the room in five or six heaps of flailing combatants when the captain ran in. He ordered his sergeants to send soldiers to the balcony. Then he and his first sergeant tossed and punched their way through the melee and made it behind the Speaker's dais, where he hollered, "Stop!" The slugging continued.

"He said stop, dammit!" the first sergeant yelled, but the blows continued.

Then the captain pulled out his revolver, pointed it at the ceiling, and *Blam!*

"Now—everybody, stop!" he yelled.

There was still some pushing and pulling, so the captain looked up at his soldiers surrounding the room from the balcony and commanded, *"Ready!"*

The clickety-click of rifles cocking rippled around the room. Legislators looked up in disbelief.

"Aim!"

The soldiers pointed forty bayoneted guns over the railing at legislators looking back up at them from the main floor of the House.

N*ow* there was quiet.

"That's much better, gentlemen," the captain said. "Everybody *sit!"*

More armed soldiers came onto the floor and surrounded the crowd as sergeants yelled, "He said sit! That means in that chair."

When all the noise had faded, the captain turned to Mackey and asked, "What is the problem?"

"Mr. Wallace here thinks he's the Speaker. I was elected Speaker last week on a vote of fifty-nine to zero and am, by law, the Speaker of the House."

The Republicans murmured, "Yeah, he's the Speaker."

A Democrat stood, "Well, we just elected Billy Wallace Speaker this morning on a vote of fifty-seven to zero, so he's the Speaker now." The other Democrats applauded.

"You two come with me," the captain said, pointing at Mackey and Wallace.

They left the chamber and crammed into a small storage room behind the Speaker's desk. The captain said, "Mr. Wallace, you got any evidence your side elected you Speaker?"

"Yes, sir, here's the record of the vote. It was unanimous."

"Yeah, but you ain't the real Speaker," Mackey said. "I'm the Speaker. We voted on it last week. It was fifty-nine to zero. Yours was fifty-seven to zero, so we out-voted you."

"But that's because only Republicans voted," Wallace argued.

"Well, if we was both together, you would still have lost—by two votes."

"Well, once the Board of Canvassers downstairs finishes counting the Edgefield and Laurens races, we'll have you beat sixty-five to fifty-nine."

"No, they ain't, because y'all cheated."

"All right, all right," said the captain. "You two go outside. Both of you stand at the dais. No one sits. I'm going to decide how we'll do this."

The crowd in the chamber had grown restless by the time the captain walked out and yelled, "Here's what we're going to do. All you Democrats, stand up."

The white men were slow to rise.

"He said stand up!" the first sergeant bellowed. "Democrats, get up."

"Now," the captain continued, "you Democrats, get over on my left and stand in front of my soldiers. You Republicans, get up and stand over here on my right."

The captain watched as his sergeants yelled to maintain order. Satisfied with the division, he ordered, "Now, you Republicans, take your seats at these desks on this side of the aisle."

"You heard the captain!" the first sergeant yelled. "Get to your desks, sit down, and shut up."

The captain directed the Democrats to do the same on the left. Then he ordered extra chairs brought to the dais. He directed Speaker Mackey to move his chair and clerk chairs in front of the Republicans. Then he handed him the gavel said, "You are the Speaker for this side." As soldiers moved other chairs in place overlooking the Democrats, the captain said, "Mr. Wallace, you will be the Speaker of the Democrats on this side."

"I need a gavel," Wallace said.

"We'll get you one," the captain said, and then he yelled at the back door, "Corporal, get Speaker Wallace a gavel."

To the entire room, he said, "You listen to me, all of you. This is how we're going to operate. Mr. Mackey, you run your side of the House, and Mr. Wallace, you run yours. There will be no fighting. If that happens, I'll clear the whole room."

"You expect us to work while you got your Yankee soldiers pointin' their guns at us, *Captain*?" a Democrat hollered from the back of the room.

"Sergeant," the captain said, "call order-arms and at-ease."

"Or-derp, harms!" the first sergeant yelled, and the soldiers lowered their rifles in cadence. "At ease!" he yelled, and the soldiers relaxed.

"Now," the captain said, "they will be watching to make sure there'll be no more fighting."

He ordered a lieutenant up to the dais to take his place. "Lieutenant, you make sure nothing happens." He then turned to the members. "I'm leaving now to report to my commander. And since you are under martial law, you all know you must obey my orders. If you don't, I will clear you out of the building."

Since October, South Carolina had been under martial law after mobs of Negroes had killed whites and mobs of whites had killed blacks across the state. The riots broke out several months before the November elections—and then the election results stunk of stuffed ballots, stolen ballots, and gun-pointed harassment of black voters.

While the fight was underway in the House, a large group of angry whites was downstairs, shoving Negroes up against the staircase to get them out of their way. The Negroes pushed back, shouting, "You better quit now! I mean it! You goin' get hurt!" The noise was so loud that people in the upstairs lobby leaned over the banisters to see if a fight was breaking out below.

After a decade of Reconstruction and Republican government, these whites were in the Capitol to take back control of their state. They'd had enough of *equal* representation, *inclusion*, and women's toilets being *open to colored women.*

The man leading the bunch was Angus Merchant, a prominent farmer and rich banker from the Pee Dee area. He believed it was time to return control of the state to the proper white families of South Carolina. By "proper," Angus meant the old moneyed bluebloods who ran the state before federal officials had come and started this Reconstruction nonsense and forced people to obey laws passed by colored Republicans.

Angus was fussing for the crowd to be quiet as he pressed against the door. He wanted to hear what was going on inside. The state Board of Canvassers was certifying the results of the governor's race and the legislature.

The door opened, and a squad of Yankee soldiers marched out and raised their muskets. Despite Angus's protests of, "Now, wait a damn minute!" they pushed him and the crowd while chanting, "Get back, get back," and stomping in cadence. Negroes in the corner applauded.

A big white man tried to take a swing at one of the troops but cut his hand when the soldier blocked it with his rifle. The corporal saw what had happened and ordered, "Squad, halt! Fix bayonets!"

That angered the crowd more, and they started shaking their fists and shouting as the soldiers stomped and jabbed, forcing them to retreat.

The Negroes came out of the corner, whooping and clapping. They felt certain the election results would let them continue running the state. During their time in office, they had created a public school system and tax code and made hotels and restaurants open to everyone, regardless of race.

Angus Merchant had had enough of this Yankee-enforced colored progress, so he'd joined Wade Hampton's Red Shirts and made nighttime raids to discourage blacks from voting. Then he'd helped organize white turnout for the 1876 elections. Now he wanted to hear the results.

A loud knock sounded from inside the elections room. The corporal yelled, "Squad, halt!" Then he opened the door and stepped back to allow the chairman of the Board of Canvassers to step into the hallway.

The crowd moved forward with loud shushes of "Be quiet" and "Shh."

The chairman, a tall white man originally from Pennsylvania, cleared his throat and announced, "There are two issues the board had to resolve. One was the voting for the House of Representatives, and the other, the governor's race."

"Who won?"

"Shh, let him talk."

The chairman continued. "Upon examining the results in the races for the House in Edgefield and Laurens Counties, the board discovered there were more votes cast than voters registered."

Some in the crowd chuckled and poked.

"As a result," the chairman continued, "the board has unanimously agreed to set aside the entire Laurens County and Edgefield County votes and will leave those House seats vacant until the matter is decided by the court."

"So, what did y'all do about the governor's race?" someone yelled.

"In the race between Mr. Chamberlain and Mr. Hampton—"

"That's General Hampton, mister!"

"Initially, it appeared Mr. Hampton won by eleven hundred votes. However, the commission found the discrepancies I mentioned and set aside the votes of Laurens and Edgefield Counties. When the remaining ballots from across the state were then tabulated, the board found that the voters of South Carolina have re-elected Governor Richard Chamberlin over Mr. Hampton."

"Yes! Yes! Yes!" exclaimed a black legislator as his group shook hands, congratulating each other.

"That's a lie!" someone in the white crowd yelled.

"Yeah, and it's General Hampton, not Mr. Hampton! It's General Hampton!" someone else yelled.

"No, the votes the commission confirmed clearly show Governor Chamberlin is the winner," the chairman said.

"Yeah, but you commissioners are all Republicans!" yelled Angus.

"Yeah!" the crowd roared.

"You Yankees rigged this whole thing," Angus continued. "We aren't going to stand for this. It's not right to throw out all those votes."

A scuffle broke out, and after a few blows, Republicans ran upstairs and sent soldiers down to help the outnumbered squad. Using their rifles, the soldiers finally pushed apart the two groups. The captain ordered the crowd out of the building, informing everyone that those who didn't comply would be arrested or shot.

Angry at the results and the treatment they had received, Democrats poured onto the lawn and formed a circle around General Wade Hampton, who was waiting outside.

"They stole it, General. They stole it!" said Angus. He explained the results and then told Hampton he had enough supporters to demand another recount.

"General, don't give up on this!" a man yelled.

The crowd grew quiet as Hampton looked about and said, "The people of South Carolina have elected me, and as a citizen and soldier, it is my duty to follow their directives. I will not quit!"

The crowd erupted in hurrahs and applause.

To drive home that they weren't done with the election, Wade Hampton's backers marched him across the street and set him up in an office overlooking the Capitol. They declared he would run the state from there and, in the meantime, they would file a lawsuit challenging the ruling of the Board of Canvassers.

The dual House of Representatives tried to operate simultaneously in the same room for four days. Then the Democrats, tired of the noise and confusion, marched out in protest, went to the University of South Carolina, and set up their own version of the House.

With the Democrats away, incumbent Governor Daniel Chamberlain used a provision in the state constitution to get the Republican House to name him governor. For three months, South Carolina had two Houses of Representatives and, with Governor Chamberlain in his office and Wade Hampton across the street, two governors.

CHAPTER 5

THANK YOU, RUTHERFORD B.

Washington, DC, 1877

Angus Merchant was tired of the chaos. He wanted Republicans out of office—all of them. He rode a train to Washington to see if South Carolina's congressional Democrats could help. He was to meet them at a pub between Union Station and the Capitol.

Tired from the trip, Angus was dozing in a chair near a great fireplace open on both sides. A man in the next room laughed loudly, and Angus leaned forward, irritated, and looked through the fire. He saw a cluster of men smoking cigars and talking loudly.

"Must be Republicans," he muttered.

He sat back, winced, and fanned away cigar smoke as a young messenger approached.

"Is you Mr. Merchant?"

"Yes."

"Senator Butler told me to give you this." The boy handed Angus a note and stood at attention with his hand stuck out for payment.

Angus had him wait as he read the note. Then he reached into his pocket. "Here," he said and handed the boy some coins.

As the boy saluted and ran out, he looked at the note again. The senator would leave his office within the hour, and Congressmen Aiken and Ivins would go to the pub ahead of him.

Angus was putting the note in his coat pocket when two men stepped into the bar. They conferred with the tavern keeper and then walked over to Angus. One of the men said, "Mr. Merchant? I'm Wyatt Aiken, and this is Congressman John Ivins. Senator Butler asked us to meet with you."

"He just sent me a note. Please, take a seat. Would you gentlemen like something to drink?"

"Beer would be nice."

As Angus yelled for the tavern keeper to bring two pints, loud laughter erupted in the other room. He winced at the fireplace.

"Damn Republicans. Interrupted my nap."

"Mr. Merchant, you may know my second cousin," said Wyatt. "He lives in Haigler's Crossing. Thomas Upright?"

"At the drug store. Yes, I know Thomas. He banks with me. I'll tell him I saw you."

The barkeep was carrying in two pints when Senator Butler arrived. "You want a drink, Senator?"

"No, nothing, thank you. I'm in a hurry." The senator turned to Angus. "I think we know why you are here."

"Yeah, Senator, you heard they gave the governor's election to that Yankee Republican," Angus said. "General Hampton won, but the Yankees jimmied the results to let Chamberlain have it. And they are still lettin' colored slaves run the legislature."

He looked at the men. "Y'all know Chamberlain is from Massachusetts. He led one of them nigger Yankee regiments during the war. We were going to challenge the election in the courts, but when the Democrats left the Statehouse, the governor got the coloreds in the House to elect him."

"Can they do that?" asked Wyatt.

"Yeah, we checked on it. There's a provision in the constitution that allows the House to elect the governor should the popular votes be unresolved. That's why I came up here. You got to do something. We got to get Wade Hampton named governor."

The noise in the other room stopped. A few men bent down to listen through the fireplace.

Senator Butler looked at the fire and said, "You got here just in time. The president needs us Southern Democrats to certify he won."

There was some muttering next door. Then a few men walked around, shook hands with Angus and the others, and introduced themselves. They were congressmen from Georgia and Louisiana. The man from Georgia explained that the Democratic candidate for president won the popular vote but Rutherford B. Hayes won the electoral vote—barely—185 to 184.

"Ol' Rutherford B. needs our support to create a special commission to prove he's president. We've already told his people we ain't gonna do that unless he removes Yankee soldiers and officials from our states. We been filibustering to hold things up until he agrees."

"Is he?" Angus asked, looking at Butler.

"It looks like he will. We should know something tomorrow."

Butler was eager to end the meeting and excused himself. "Gentlemen, I'm running late and will need to leave. Please excuse us." He then turned to Angus and said, "Come, Angus, my wife has dinner for us."

The men stood. As Angus and Butler walked away, the congressman from Georgia asked the other congressmen, "Who is that man?"

"Angus Merchant," said Wyatt. "He was from one of the wealthiest families in South Carolina—actually, one of the richest in America until the war. His father, ol' man Cyril Merchant, went from rich to poor and from sane to crazy in the process."

"When?"

"Ten years ago."

"What happened?"

"Get some more beers, and I'll tell ya."

Wyatt fired up a cigar and took a couple of long draws as the tavern keeper brought in fresh mugs. "It was right after the Civil War."

*   *   *

As word of defeat flew through South Carolina, Cyril Merchant dragged two large bags out of the vault of his bank. An angry bunch of customers stormed in, demanding their money. One of them hollered, "You stole from us!"

Ol' man Merchant cried, "I'm sorry, I'm sorry." He was devastated. He'd built his bank from nothing, and now it was worth nothing, and these customers, the very people he'd helped, were acting as if he'd caused it. It was more than he could take.

He reached into a bag and cried, "You want your money? Here's your money!" He tossed Confederate dollars in the air and cried again, "That's all that's left. It's worthless. Everything is worthless."

The mob shoved him aside and ransacked the vault. They stole jewelry from some bins and rifled through others, but they found nothing of value save some coins.

"Where's the gold?" someone demanded. "There's supposed to be gold in here."

"The rebels took it," Merchant's bookkeeper tried to tell them. "When the Confederacy began printing its own money, rebel troops came in and took it to Richmond—at least, that's what they told us."

"You're lyin'."

"No, honest. They took the gold and left stacks of Confederate dollars like these."

A man jumped over the counter, snatched open cash drawers, and cursed. "There's no real money here, just this shit." He tossed bills in the air and vaulted over the counter.

"You want your money? Here's your money." Cyril threw money in the air and walked out the door, tossing money along the way.

His bookkeeper tugged his arm to keep him from the street. Cyril screamed, "No!" pulled his arm free, and then, laughing like a crazy man, threw Confederate money in the air as onlookers and bank customers formed a large crowd in the middle of the street. "Look at it," he cackled. "It's worthless. It's all worthless."

"My God, he's gone crazy," someone said as people came onto the street.

Cyril Merchant was one of the richest men in America—until the Civil War. His bank collapsed, his slaves burned his fields, and Sherman's army trampled over what remained. He was dirt poor, with no one to tend his ruined land. The losses savaged his mind, and late-night demons lured him out of his house well after his family was asleep. The first time it happened, he was barefoot in a dirty nightshirt, roaming about the empty fields, cursing his slaves by name, saying, "Damn you! I own you! Get out here. It's time for you to get to work."

His son, Angus, heard the noise, ran out, and guided him back by telling him, "It's too early, Daddy. They're still sleeping.

They'll be up in a couple of hours, so let's go back to the house and sleep some more."

Cyril kept walking out into his fields, and Angus would go out and bring him back. This went on for several weeks. Then what was left of a hurricane blew in from the coast. Angus thought the storm would keep his father from getting out that night. It didn't. The old man squinted, blinked, and spit at the rain as he stepped off the porch. By the time he reached the field, his nightshirt was soaked and stuck to him like adhesive. It made it hard for him to walk, and he groped about in the deep sand while blinded by the rain blowing against his face. He pulled at the shirt and cursed. It wouldn't let go. This set off crazed rantings for field hands to get to work and Yankee soldiers to get off his land. No one heard him howling or saw him struggle down the field, cursing at his nightshirt and trying to tug it free from where it had gotten stuck in his butt.

By the time he got to the river and climbed onto the trestle, he had to pee something fierce—but the nightshirt wouldn't let go. After twisting and tugging and finally getting it over his head, he lost his balance and fell into the roiling, muddy water, which sucked him under.

*   *   *

"The only sign that Cyril Merchant was at the river that night," Wyatt concluded, "was the dirty nightshirt a couple of boys found days later. It was hanging on a rusty bolt inside the trestle. His body was never found."

"Damn, that's a helluva story," said the Georgia congressman.

"Well, that's what I heard. Now you know why Angus Merchant is up here. He blames Abraham Lincoln, the Republican Party, and runaway slaves for his father's death. None of this would have happened had the North let us live the way we wanted."

The men in the pub nodded.

Wyatt continued the story, saying some of the slaves had come back after nearly starving to death. They told Angus freedom wouldn't feed hungry children and agreed to work the place as sharecroppers.

He finished his beer, stood, and said, "Gentlemen, I have to leave. I hope Rutherford B. agrees to what we want."

"I hear he's going to do it," the Georgia congressman said. "We should know something by tomorrow."

The men shook hands and left the pub.

*   *   *

Angus Merchant was in Senator Butler's office the next morning when a staffer told him President Hayes would remove troops from South Carolina and Louisiana the following week, and he was enjoying the good news and drinking coffee when Senator Butler returned from meeting with the president.

"I just left the White House," Butler said, beaming. "He has telegrammed Governor Chamberlin and General Hampton to come to Washington on the next available train. He told me he's going to tell Chamberlin he's removing federal troops. Chamberlin won't have any choice but to resign. I told the president we'll support his commission when he pulls the soldiers out. He's gonna do it."

"Wonderful," Angus said. "We're finally getting things back the way they're supposed to be. Now we got to fix the legislature."

"That should be no problem, Angus. With federal soldiers gone, you can run the coloreds out of the Statehouse. Ain't nobody gonna help them now."

*   *   *

After meeting with the president, Governor Chamberlin withdrew from office, and within a day, officials certified Hampton as the new governor. At the Statehouse, with no troops to protect them, Republicans resigned from office in droves, despite Wade Hampton's pledge to accommodate and work with black Republican legislators.

Over the next decade, Angus Merchant got his Democrat pals in the legislature to smear the credible achievements of black legislators. Baseless investigative hearings cloaked in formality were held. The goal was to overwhelm Negro achievements listed in the public record with questionable accounts and implications that black people, by their very nature, were dishonest. Evidence of malfeasance by a few applied to all.

*   *   *

Betsy took a deep breath and looked at the article. She thought for a moment and then decided it needed a pointed conclusion.

Folks, you need to know that there were newspapers that accepted the legislature's findings as truth when, in fact, they were lies.

They printed articles and editorials claiming Negroes were not competent to govern and must never again serve in public office. Years later, Governor John Gary Evans and his racist mentor, "Pitchfork" Ben Tillman, seized on this to push through Jim Crow laws segregating jobs and accommodations, and they got a new state constitution written that required voters to pay a poll tax, be literate, and answer questions about the constitution that you and I couldn't answer.

Betsy remembered Vernon telling her of working white people being taught racism, and this truth fueled her typing.

You and I have been duped. Lies about black people were told to us so often they galvanized the beliefs of many of us. We need to think about this, especially when it comes to how colored people are treated today. Now, coloreds have their beliefs about whites, some of which may be true, but some may not. It looks like both sides would rather stick to their beliefs about each other because it seems like false beliefs are always more powerful than the truth.

She pondered a bit about how folks would react to her story. Then she turned out the light, locked the door, and walked home. *Hell, somebody needs to tell them the truth. Might as well be me.*

CHAPTER 6

A WET NURSE

When Vernon read Betsy's copy, he smiled and then frowned. "Anything wrong with it?" she asked.

"It's damn good, but you might tone down that last part. I think Arthur's gonna make you change that . . . *if* he decides to publish it." Vernon pointed to the last paragraph on the page. "See this last part? It's your opinion."

"But it's the truth, Vernon."

"You know it's true, and I know it's true, but you're telling people what you want them to believe. You need to show them why it's true and let them make up their own minds. That's what we do. We print the facts and evidence. Opinions, we put on the editorial page."

"Yeah, but when you printed the truth about the mill and the strike, the people that run Haigler's Crossing turned on you and put you out of business. Vernon, we need to do a story about that."

"Well, maybe. But before we do, you need to know more about the people down there. The ones who run that place are a closed group. To get accepted, you have to prove you believe things they do and be from a family they consider suitable."

*　　　*　　　*

When his father disappeared after the war, Angus Merchant took over the family business. Angus used his bank to control the money, the people of the town, and his board of directors. The board gathered there monthly to approve loans and hear financial reports from the bank manager. One particular day, the manager was downstairs, holding up the board meeting. Angus was annoyed, and he tapped his heel impatiently. As the board laughed and joked, his irritation grew.

Somebody told a really good one, which lit off a roar of hoots and table slaps. Angus growled and then ordered his secretary to go down and get the manager "right now!" This was his bank, and he would not be delayed by one of his employees. And now his handpicked directors were carrying on like their meeting was a carnival show. They were descendants of the early families that had settled the town and made fortunes off the slave system until the war. The men on the board were just recovering some of the wealth their families had lost when slaves had been set free.

The conversations stopped when the secretary re-entered the room, and it resumed when she bent over and whispered in Angus's ear.

"You tell him to get up here now," he ordered. There was no more laughter.

"Is there a problem?" someone asked.

"It's Gedney Crowell. He brought in another check from that bank in London and doesn't understand we cannot let him draw on it until it clears. We go through this every month."

Angus despised Gedney. The men in the room didn't like Crowell, either. As if berating him was on their order of business, they took turns listing the things they disliked about him.

"Y'all heard he's calling himself colonel now." One man rolled his eyes and shook his head. "He was a lieutenant colonel during the war, although, for the life of me, I don't know how. Now he's claiming to be a full colonel."

The bank's manager came in and apologized for being late, and Angus called the meeting to order. When they were done, as everyone stood to leave, one of the directors asked the manager about Gedney Crowell's check. That started another round of Gedney Crowell put-downs as they walked out. This time, though, they included talk of Gedney's late wife, Clarice Ramseur, and that Catawba Indian woman he'd gotten to wet-nurse his baby.

Clarice and Colonel Gedney had been married just a couple of years when she died shortly after birthing Gedney Jr., their only child. The afternoon of her funeral, the Colonel shocked the locals when he hurriedly rode off from the cemetery and returned the next morning with a woman to wet-nurse his son. He'd learned of her from the funeral director, who'd told him an unmarried woman in North Carolina had given birth to a stillborn daughter just a week before. When Gedney found Charlene Brayboy, he promised she could stay at his house for free if she would care for his son. He set her up in a room right across from the baby's.

The first time she held Gedney Jr., Charlene cried for the daughter she'd lost. The Colonel watched and worried he'd made a mistake. Then he was reassured as Charlene heard Gedney Jr.'s happy sounds and began laughing through tears at the joy of the baby slurping her breast. After watching for days and getting assurance from Lorna, his housekeeper, the Colonel felt comfortable enough to travel overnight for business.

When he returned and asked how the night had gone, Lorna said she'd heard noises late that night like someone was in the kitchen, but when she checked, there was no one there. She said she later found Charlene upstairs in the baby's room, nursing Gedney Jr.

A few nights later, well after midnight, the Colonel woke up. He thought *he* heard movement and went downstairs and startled Lorna. "Mr. Colonel, you 'bout scared me to death. I heard that noise again. It sounded like someone in the kitchen. Did you hear it?"

"I did," he whispered. "That's why I came down here. Check the back door, and I'll check the front."

"Mr. Colonel, you check the baby. I'll check the doors."

When he entered Gedney's room, he found Charlene there, nursing. Her eyes were closed, and she was moaning as she rocked in and out of the moonlight. She slowly opened her eyes and smiled when the Colonel called her name and asked, "Were you in the kitchen?"

"No. I heard the baby and came in here," she said, and then she closed her eyes, sighed, and resumed as the baby smacked.

There were no more noise-in-the-kitchen episodes. The Colonel decided it must have been the house settling.

*   *   *

Charlene knew she'd done the right thing. There was wealth and comfort here and a baby and a place to live. Now, if she could only call up good feelings, maybe she could push away the sorrow of losing her daughter.

Over time, if she concentrated, she got better at pressing aside the anguish, regret, and sadness. Then, as the weeks passed, she noticed her feelings were not just nurturing, caring, mothering, emotional thoughts. Now her body was responding and encouraging her in the most pleasurable ways. Deep, warm, physical pleasures were rising, and they grew each time the baby was on her breast—she was getting aroused.

Over days and weeks, her thoughts moved into eyes-closed fantasies and rememberings. As the baby sucked, she daydreamed of lovers kissing and touching her special places. She wanted to feel more, but like a titillated schoolgirl, she wondered how far she should let her imaginings take her. The answer came late one night; the Colonel was away, and Lorna was asleep.

Charlene went to the baby's room, picked him up, and sat in the rocker. She lowered her gown, closed her eyes, and felt the baby's warm mouth on her breast. She rocked for some time and, as the feelings came on, decided that this night, she would give in to whatever her body wanted. She pretended the lips at her breast were those of a man she'd once loved. As she rocked and remembered and pretended, she became more aroused. Then she moaned, "Suck harder, baby. That's it. Suck harder."

What she experienced at that moment was wonderful. Surely, there was nothing wrong with it, she told herself. It must be okay; it took away her guilt. She wanted more good feelings and was determined to get them.

On Christmas Eve, Charlene Brayboy walked into the Colonel's bedroom, dropped her gown, and got in his bed. Two months later, they married in the big church at Haigler's Crossing. More curiosity seekers and gossips attended the event than well-wishers.

*   *   *

Nursing Gedney was fine when he was a baby, but when he was four, he was getting teased by his playmates for "suckin' on yo momma's tit." Complaints were also springing up inside the house, with Lorna's, "He too big for that," and the Colonel growling at the dinner table for Charlene to stop as Gedney grabbed at her breast from her lap. "Get his hands off you. He's not a baby. Gedney, stop it. You're too big to be doing that."

They were unaware that since that special night, Charlene had been cooing, "This is our secret, Gedney. You must never tell."

Now he was older and innocently believed her whispers. "Never tell Poppa or Lorna. It's our secret. Promise me you'll never tell."

"I promise."

Like a wife taking a lover, she lured him to her bedchamber whenever it was safe. "Come sit in Momma's lap," she would say while unbuttoning her blouse and lifting her breast. "Come taste Momma's love."

She needed this closeness. It stilled the dark voices wanting her to remember her dead daughter. That's why, when the Colonel was out of town and the voices came on, she would slip into Gedney's bed just after midnight, pull her nightshirt down, and say, "Come, baby, make your momma happy."

When it was over, she'd smile and say, "Thank you, baby. Now, what do you say?"

"I promise."

When Charlene returned to her room, the voices would be gone, and she could sleep.

As he got older, Gedney wondered if there was something wrong with what he was doing. His friends were teasing him, and he had to lie when Lorna asked him what he and Charlene were up to. Besides, he was six years old, no longer a baby.

Late one night, as he slept, Charlene eased into his room and quietly closed the door. Lorna was downstairs in her bedroom, snoring loudly. His father was away on business. Charlene dropped her nightgown, pulled back the covers, and climbed into bed. Gedney jerked awake and jumped out. "Momma, what are you doing?"

"I'm here to love on you, baby. Come taste Momma's love."

"No. It ain't right. I ain't no baby no mo."

"You come here right now," she hissed, "and do what I tell you."

"No! I'm a boy, not no baby."

"You come here right now, or I'm telling your daddy *you* are making me do it. I'm your momma. Do as you're told."

Afraid and conflicted, Gedney felt it wasn't right, but she was his momma and an adult, and he was taught he must obey adults, especially his parents. Besides, he had promised.

"C'mon, baby." She patted the bed. You'll like it."

Gedney got in and closed his eyes. To take himself away from what he was forced to do, he pretended he was somewhere else, playing with his friends. He was lost in his daydream when his mother frightened him out of it, saying, "That's it, baby. Suck harder. Oh, yes, that's it, oh, oh, God," as she shuddered and jerked.

She sighed and hugged him. "Thank you, baby. You made Momma feel good."

Gedney closed his eyes and turned onto his stomach to avoid seeing her.

Charlene picked up her gown and walked to her room.

Gedney lay there, scared, nervous, and confused. He needed to tell, tell his father, tell *somebody*, but he couldn't. He'd promised, and she *was* his momma. But now she was coming to him nekked, as his playmates called it, and he didn't want to look *'cause boys ain't s'posed to see they mommas nekked* and he didn't know what she'd do the next time. He wasn't supposed to know; he was a six-year-old boy, and he was scared because his momma was nekked and making him do something he didn't want to do. He got up and locked his door.

*   *   *

The first time they heard the voices, Gedney Jr. and a playmate were in the yard shooting marbles. They looked up; Charlene's window was open. The playmate raised his shoulders as if to say, "I don't know," and the voices from the window got louder.

"Must be Lorna," Gedney said.

"No, it ain't. Lorna out back talkin' wid Zeke."

The boys looked at the window and listened. Then the playmate huffed, "You gone play marbles or not."

"Yeah."

"Well, go on. Shoot."

Upstairs, Charlene was arguing with the voices in her head.

He's not your baby, Charlene. Your baby is dead.

"No, Gedney is my baby. He's my child. My baby didn't die."

No, he isn't. Your child is underground, in the dark. She's cold and crying for her momma.

The late-night noises in the kitchen resumed, usually at the onset of a full moon and when the Colonel was away. Charlene had fits of talking to herself about someone killing her baby as she walked about the house—sometimes with a butcher knife in her hand. Gedney would say, "Momma, it's me. You're safe. Just put the knife down." After he got her back to her bed, she would fall asleep and the next morning, would have no memory of what happened.

Weeks passed. Then Gedney heard a noise in the kitchen. His father was gone, Lorna was asleep, and the moon was out.

Gedney found his mother in the kitchen, talking to herself. "Momma, it's me," he whispered.

"Gedney, it *is* you. Let me hold you and nurse you, baby."

"No, Momma. You already did, remember? Come with me. Let's go back upstairs."

After getting her to bed and watching her until he was certain she was asleep, Gedney returned to his room. He took a deep breath and heard a whippoorwill off in the distance. He climbed into bed, thankful that the hot air had finally given way to an incoming breeze, pulled the sheet up, and fell asleep. He forgot to lock his door.

Two hours passed. He was on his stomach and hugging his pillow, dreaming. The breeze swished the curtains on and off his bed in rhythm with the whippoorwill off in the woods. He didn't hear his mother sneak into the kitchen, open the drawer, and grab the knife. She held it up to admire its gleam and then smiled and quietly said, "Now."

Creeping up the stairs, she eased into Gedney's room as the voices in her head said, *We told you we'd be back. Can't you hear your baby in the ground? She's crying. She wants you to know he put her there. He killed your baby. He killed your baby so you would be his momma. Your baby is crying for you. If you kill him, your baby will stop crying. Then we will go away, and your baby can rest.*

Raising the knife, she screamed, "You killed my baby!" and slashed. The knife snagged the curtains and slipped from her hand as Gedney rolled out. She stabbed and stabbed the bed with her fist. Then, exhausted, she fell onto it, laughing hysterically at her demons.

"See, I did it. You didn't think I could. I did it. My baby will stop crying, and you can't talk to me anymore."

She fell asleep, and Gedney and Lorna watched her until the Colonel came home.

When the Colonel learned what happened, he pulled Gedney onto his lap and hugged him, and they cried. "Gedney, she is not your mother," he said as he rocked his son. "I should have told you, and I'm sorry now that I didn't. Your real momma died just after you were born. It wasn't your fault. It wasn't anybody's fault. She came down with a bad illness and died. I should have told you."

The Colonel wiped away his son's tears. "You were a baby and needed a mother's milk. That's why I got Charlene. I thought she would be good for you. That's why I married her. But now

Charlene's sick. She has an illness in her mind. I'm going to take her away, where she can get some help. You must stay here with Lorna and Zeke. They will care for you while I'm gone."

Lorna packed Charlene's clothes and placed them in the buggy that afternoon and helped Charlene get seated next to the Colonel. She looked up as the Colonel said, "I may not get back until tomorrow. Likely, it will be late. Take care of Gedney Jr. and, if you can, help him understand about his real mother."

The Colonel turned the horse and headed down the driveway.

*   *   *

"He took Charlene to Columbia and had her committed to the state asylum for the insane," Vernon said. "He left her there and never went back."

Betsy was shocked. "He just left her there?"

"Yeah. Back then, if you had someone you wanted to put away, you could get a doctor to declare them insane and stick 'em in the lunatic asylum." Vernon leaned back in his chair.

"And so the story of this became part of the gossip to smear Colonel Crowell?"

"Yep, it even got splattered onto his innocent son."

CHAPTER 7

Excuse Me, Boss

It didn't help that Gedney Jr. was from the country. His playmates were colored, children of his father's sharecroppers. He played with them in the front yard, drawing pictures in the dirt or tossing maypops with sharp green sticks in the fields. He was taught how to make a sling out of an old shoe tongue and rawhide laces and played David and Goliath amongst the cotton bales in front of the house. Imitating his playmates, he'd give a cotton bale a hard look, staring down a Philistine giant. He'd growl, "Here, GO-liath, take this," and—*whap*—fling a rock against the bale, only to be challenged by his friends.

"You ain't kill 'em."

"Yes, I did. I hit him in the head, just like David."

"He ain't fell over."

"He too big to fall. 'Sides, we play-acting," Gedney Jr. would say, and then he'd fling another rock at the bale.

He absorbed the behaviors and dialect of his playmates and innocently carried that with him into a school filled with social barriers he didn't understand. The in-town kids of Haigler's Crossing were a closed society. They grew up from diapers to young boys and girls among friends within neighborhoods defined by class and standards of behavior.

When school started, the in-town children kept country kids away from their cliques as though something was wrong with them. What that "wrong" was, they didn't know, but it must have been dreadful, because they heard their parents complain. The tone their parents used told them country kids were bad.

The school promoted this belief, too. In-town mothers insisted their children be placed in classrooms with the best teachers and segregated from the others. But there were too many country kids to pack away separately, while town kids sat in rooms with empty desks. So, Gedney Jr. and others were placed with the townies. Teachers didn't like the arrangement, believing they must teach down to ignorant children, lowering the performance of their classes. The town kids picked up on their teachers' attitudes, which confirmed what they heard from their parents.

For several months, Gedney's teacher ignored his awkward dialect and mispronunciations, hoping they would change as he heard his classmates talk. They didn't. Just before recess one morning, she lost her patience over some goofy thing he said and yelled at him in front of the whole class.

"Gedney, the word is 'four' not 'fo,' and it's 'door,' not doh. Now, you practice that while you and your classmates go outside and play."

Embarrassed in the classroom, things were worse for him on the playground. The boys teased him, and the girls danced and skipped around him, singing, "Gedney says fo and close the doh. Step on his toe, and you'll make it soh."

The teasing got worse when Dupre Merchant overheard his grandmother say Gedney's stepmom was an Indian. Dupre told his pals, and they taunted Gedney with, "Hey, half-breed," and yips and hollers for weeks. Then, before school one morning, older boys shoved Gedney and Dupre inside a circle of them and began yelling, "Fight, fight, fight!" They watched the frightened pair dance and swat at each other until Gedney Jr. got lucky with a short punch and popped Dupre a black eye. The taunting stopped after that, but the resentment between Gedney and Dupre was forever fixed.

Years later, when they were adults, they almost came to blows inside the church after both their fathers died just hours apart— the same day. Dupre Merchant stormed into the church and was called down by the priest for interrupting his conversation with Gedney Jr.

"Please take a seat outside. Young Gedney and I are planning his father's funeral."

"My daddy's funeral is first!" Merchant yelled.

Gedney stood, clenching his fists. The priest stepped between the two. "Dupre, go to the sanctuary and sit down," he ordered. "I'll be finished here shortly."

"I don't care what you do with him, Reverend," Dupre said. "I want my daddy's funeral held first."

Dupre left, and then the priest closed the door and went back to his desk.

"Sit down, Gedney. You know Dupre is upset. You both lost your daddies, and both of you are filled with emotions. We need to calm down and take it easy." He took a deep breath. "Now, Gedney, your daddy was a good man, and I'm going to help you, but . . . you know how things are done around here. Your daddy didn't attend our church here much. Now, I know you can appreciate the position this puts the church in. Your daddy was a good man and all, and . . . so was Angus Merchant. He was a good man, too.

"And you may know, or maybe you don't, that the Merchants have been members of this church, well . . ." He looked at the ceiling. "Actually, the Merchants helped found this church, so . . ." He looked at Gedney. "They've been members here over one hundred years. And Mr. Angus here *was* chairman of our vestry. Dupre out there is our treasurer.

"Now, your daddy, Gedney Sr., uh, Colonel Crowell . . ." He smiled and paused. "He was a good man, and the church wants him to have a good service here, even though he wasn't regular. But I'm sure you know how things are around here, so the church will be available to you at four o'clock Thursday afternoon. Unfortunately, it's not available any other day or time. I'll be happy to officiate at your daddy's funeral, and we'll hold the service on Thursday at four p.m."

*   *   *

"You mean, the Merchants even controlled their church?" Betsy asked.

"Oh, yeah, they ran the whole town, including the church."

"Catholic?"

"No, Episcopal. It was the first church in Haigler's Crossing, so it is the oldest one over there."

"Then, when Angus died, his son, Dupre, took over running things?"

"Yeah, the power and influence he inherited went to his head. The son of a bitch was obsessive about it. That's why he ran me off when I wouldn't print what he wanted."

That's why we must write a story about what happened to you, Vernon. People need to know it."

Vernon brushed the suggestion aside and then grinned. "Let me tell you about the funerals. You won't believe what happened.

Angus Merchant's funeral began at eleven o'clock that Thursday morning. Men and women jammed into the church, crowding pews and fanning at the heat and humidity."

*   *   *

The rector worked through the Service for the Dead and then, wiping drippy sweat from his face, moved into an extensive homily praising Angus Merchant, his father Cyril Merchant— *May he be at peace, wherever he is*—Dupre Merchant, and the entire Merchant family. He noted their many contributions to the historic town and church, with the special family pew and stained-glass windows honoring famous Merchants back to the colonial period.

The funeral for Colonel Gedney Sr. later that afternoon was brief and chaotic. It took the undertaker a long time to find men to dig the grave. The weather was so hot that the men who'd dug Angus Merchant's grave refused to dig another one that day. Finally, the undertaker found some field hands, brought them to the cemetery and told them they had to get it done before the church service finished.

The priest read the Service for the Dead, briefly praised Gedney Crowell Sr. for his service to the Confederacy, and then cut the funeral short by claiming a thunderstorm was coming on. The small crowd filed out to the graveyard, mumbling and criticizing the three black laborers taking turns digging into the sandy soil.

The diggers had their shirts off and were blowing hard and sweating from the pace. One of them on the embankment said, "All right." He and his partner grabbed the shovel to pull the man out and then used it to lower the next one in.

The relieved man wiped the sand off his chest, looked in the hole, and said, "C'mon, boy—dig."

A white man—a *most important* white man—loudly wondered whether the coloreds were digging the hole properly. "These are field hands. Do they know what they're doin'?"

"Well, Ezra, why don't you go over there and ask them?" somebody joked.

"Hell, I will," he said and stepped to peek over. Just as he was saying, "You boys know wha—" a shovel-load of sand hit him in the face.

"Oh, excuse me, boss. I didn't see you comin'."

"Shit!" the *important man* sputtered and cussed as he spat and wiped the sand off his face while his friends laughed and hooted.

The men's wives told them, "Hush. This is a funeral, not a barbeque."

Finally, the hole was dug, and Gedney Jr. and his fiancé stood over it. The undertaker and three men hauled in the casket and lowered it into the ground. The priest stood at the foot of the grave, looking as if he had come upon an accident at a construction site. The men standing around had their jackets off, and they quietly cussed and stomped at the grass to get sand and clay off their shoes. Their wives glared at them and told them to stop. The man with the sand in his face was still spitting and wiping at the dirt.

The gravediggers were in the shade, sitting against a tree, passing around a water jar. They poked each other and grinned at the man swatting dirt. One of them muttered, "Excuse me, boss," and the trio snorted and hurriedly crawled around the tree, biting their rags to muffle their laughter.

After the service was over, the women chattered and chirped that the floral displays at the grave were gaudy to the point of being vulgar. They were shocked to see Adrianna Fitzpatrick standing beside Gedney Jr., holding his hand, and they spent weeks talking about Fitzpatrick and that awful funeral.

When the marker for Gedney Sr. was hauled through town to the cemetery, Dupre Merchant got upset when he failed to find a loophole in the historic church cemetery requirements to keep it from being set in place. It was bigger than the marker for his father, dominating the whole cemetery. Made from a huge block of red granite, it had a large rendering of a rebel flag on its face, crossed sabers etched across the top, and a bold inscription reading: "Gedney Crowell Sr., Colonel, CSA, Leader and Noble Son of the South." It was scandalous.

When the marker was set in place, Gedney Jr., who now called himself "Colonel," just to irritate the locals, smiled at the priest and said, "Thanks for helping with the funeral, Reverend. I was going to donate to the church, but then, well, Reverend, you know how things are done around here."

CHAPTER 8

SOMEONE IMPORTANT.

After being reared to believe he must aspire to be important, Gedney Jr. took his father's advice—marry someone that could help.

Adrianna Fitzpatrick was from a prominent family whose large plantation house wasn't far from his father's cotton fields. Young Gedney and Adrianna grew up attending school in town. Gedney was at university when Adrianna's father died, and she came home from Winthrop College to care for her mother. Not long after that, her mother died. The field hands all ran off, leaving Adrianna to fend for herself.

When he began courting her, Adrianna took Gedney to Charlotte, bought him new clothes, and forced him to talk without saying, "fo," "doh," "ain't," "they's," or "nigger."

"What's wrong with that? That's what they call each other."

"Gedney, we are not common. We don't use that word. The proper word is 'colored.' You need to talk properly and dress properly and be more like me if you want my friends to accept you."

Adrianna was determined to show everyone she could reshape the crude Gedney Crowell into someone respectable.

She hoped she could learn to love him, but she'd deal with that later. What mattered now was to return the Fitzpatrick mansion to its stately condition.

Their marriage was a big, fancy affair at the oldest church in town. By the time all twelve bridesmaids flowed down the aisle, it looked like someone had set loose a flotilla of hooped skirts, wide-brimmed bonnets, and floral bouquets. They filled the transept, spilled into the chancel, and crowded at the altar rail, almost pushing Gedney to the side, which made it look like they wouldn't have included him were he not the groom.

The newlyweds honeymooned in Charleston. Ten months later, Adrianna's home was restored to splendor, and she gave birth to their first child, Charles Wesley Crowell.

Marrying Adrianna Fitzpatrick enabled Gedney to associate with the better families of Haigler's Crossing. Their polite remarks made him feel he was accepted by them, when in fact, he wasn't. They were Adrianna's friends. Their conversations with Adrianna were warm and intimate, snuggled within some recollection of pleasurable childhood experiences. But with Gedney, they didn't waste time prattling. They addressed him in a tone that said, "You will never be one of us." Then, later among themselves, they snickered like schoolgirls that Gedney was too dumb to catch their meaning.

When Wesley was born, the ladies "oohed" and "aahed" and brought gifts. But when Amelia was born, their affection burst into adoration. Adrianna had given them a precious daughter, a lovely girl for the proper families of the community. To them, Amelia was more Fitzgerald than Crowell. She had to be. The Fitzgeralds were proper and good. And the Crowells? The Crowell's were . . . *common*.

The ladies did give Gedney credit for one thing. He restored the Fitzpatrick mansion to its antebellum splendor.

Over the next ten years, Amelia grew, playing dress-up and having tea parties with the children of her mother's friends. They were like little princesses, living in a world surrounded by magic castles. Then a scarlet fever epidemic moved onto the county as if laying siege.

Out at the Fitzpatrick mansion, it came in quickly, killed Wesley before anyone realized it was there, and put Adrianna in a state of delirium. The fever boiled her brain. Her tongue was so swollen that Gedney barely understood when she pointed behind him and waved Amelia off.

"What do you want, honey?" Gedney pleaded.

"Nnnnoo," she mumbled and flicked.

Gedney turned. Amelia was in the doorway. Paralyzed by fear, she was staring at her mother and noisily slurping three fingers stuck in her mouth.

Adrianna moaned and flicked. Now Gedney understood. He looked at Amelia and said, "Go downstairs and go outside with Mot" just as Adrianna grabbed his shirt, pulled him close and growled, "Shss her away."

Gedney stared in terror. His beautiful wife was mutating into a sweaty ugliness as this evil consumed more of her. Without changing his gaze, he yelled, "Amelia, go to Mot *right now!*"

Amelia flinched. *Why is Daddy yelling at me? He's never yelled at me before and why is Mommy's skin that color?*

Gedney turned and angrily shouted, "Amelia go downstairs." Amelia cowered and pulled the drippy fingers out her mouth. She smeared them on the bannisters when she took hold and slowly stepped down the stairs while pausing and looking back at her parents' bedroom. Out in the yard Mot was yelling, "baby come out the house." Amelia dawdled some more, looked back, sucked her fingers, took a couple of steps, hesitated, then ran when Mot yelled, "Amelia Jane Crowell, I mean it, get out here right now."

The next morning, Amelia was crying and bewildered as Mot and Clarence packed her belongings in a large trunk and hugged her goodbye.

"Why can't I stay?"

"You got to go, baby. Yo momma wants you to go," Mott said. "She 'fraid you catch the fever. Yo aunt Beatrice gonna meet you at the train to take you to Virginia, where you be safe."

At a time when Amelia needed comfort, Gedney Crowell could not hug her. He was afraid he might contaminate her with this thing that had taken his son and was killing his wife. He had Clarence take Amelia to the train, where she was met by her mother's sister, Beatrice Russell. Beatrice had arranged for Amelia to attend a girls' boarding school in Danville, Virginia.

Back at the mansion, Adrianna briefly came out of her stupor. She asked Gedney, "She gone?" She smiled when he said yes and then closed her eyes. Late that evening, Adrianna Fitzpatrick, the noble woman who had married a Crowell, silently passed away.

When the funerals were done, Gedney rode his horse deep into the woods, away from others, and cried.

Up in Danville, Amelia was kept in isolation for two weeks to ensure she wasn't infected. She had no one to hold her and let her cry or reassure her. Even when she was allowed to go to the dorm, her roommate didn't know what to do. She certainly wasn't going to hug her. Why? She hardly knew this girl.

Gedney had planned for Wesley to take over the family business. Now he couldn't, and there was certainly no way he could let Amelia. Women couldn't run a business. After agonizing for weeks, he decided the best way to care for Amelia was to earn as much money as he could. He took advantage of an opportunity that fell in his lap, kinda.

He was appointed tax collector for the county, which he thought was a good deal and made him sound important. But it caused a big uproar. The local powerbrokers hauled Senator Hiram White before them for an explanation.

"I had to," White complained. "No one else would take it."

"Well," one of them warned, "you better be careful he doesn't mess things up. He's ambitious, just like his daddy."

CHAPTER 9

SMALL DOGS START FIGHTS

It didn't take long for Gedney Jr., the new colonel and tax collector, to figure out he could expand his land holdings by taking advantage of his new job. With access to the city hall records, he discovered large tracts of property next to his were owned by Confederate widows who were several years behind in their taxes.

When word got around he was taking widows' property, people got upset. One winter morning, men showed up at the courthouse to do something about it. They jammed fists in heavy work coats and shifted and stomped to keep warm while talking among themselves.

They were farmers, men with wind-burned faces, thick, rough hands, and no-nonsense attitudes of right and wrong. Some smoked cigarettes. One spat tobacco, putting an exclamation mark on an important comment. There was no laughter.

The mules that had hauled the men in on wagons were tethered to hitching posts on the street. As they shook their harnesses, sweaty mist rose from their backs. Most of the men stood in clusters of three and five.

Behind the wagons, a man stood off by himself. A large bulldog sat beside him. Another wagon pulled up with a small, short-haired terrier seated next to the driver. Eager to pick a fight, the terrier climbed across its owner's lap and began a frenzied yapping.

The bulldog stood and eased closer to the wagon. The hair on his neck was up, and a low growl came from his throat. His owner yelled, "Jake, come back here!"

Too late. The terrier squeezed out of its owner's arms, leaped from the wagon, and ran at the much larger dog. The snapping and barking drowned out the men yelling at them to stop.

Then came high-pitched yikes and squealing. The bulldog had the terrier by the neck, and he violently shook the smaller dog. Someone kicked at the dogs as the bulldog's owner yelled, "Jake! Let him go!" The man kicked again, hitting the bulldog in the stomach, and with a loud cough, the larger dog dropped the yelping terrier, which jumped into the wagon and arms of its owner.

The dog fight started an argument.

"You son of a bitch, your dog almost killed my Dutch!"

"Well, your dog started it!"

Alarmed by the noise, the sheriff left his office and ran down the courthouse steps. "What's going on out here?"

"This man's dog almost killed my dog! Look at what he done, Sheriff, My dog's bleeding."

"His dog started it," the bulldog owner argued. He struggled with a rope as his dog jumped and snapped at the terrier in the wagon.

"Alright, y'all break this up. Go on home. Get away from here, all of you," the sheriff ordered the crowd, larger now because of the fight.

"What about my dog? He's cut."

"Take him to Dr. Hodge."

"Who's going to pay for it? His dog bit mine."

"Your dog started it."

"Take your dog to Dr. Hodge and pay for it yourself," the sheriff ordered. "And you, get your dog and get out of here. I don't want to hear any more arguing. And the rest of you people, get away from the courthouse."

"We came here for the tax sale!" someone yelled.

"There won't be a tax sale. Y'all go on home. Go someplace. Just get away from this courthouse. And you two, get your dogs away from here."

"No tax sale. We come to help Miss Alma save her property."

"There's no tax sale today," the sheriff repeated. "Colonel Gedney Crowell Jr. has paid off her taxes and bought Mrs. Alma's house."

"Gedney Crowell!!" the crowd yelled. They were furious. Gedney Crowell, the tax collector, had done it again. He'd taken land from another Confederate widow.

One of the men in the crowd looked at the sheriff: "We raised money at our church and told Miss Alma we was goin' to pay off the taxes she owed so she could stay on her place. Now this son-of-a-bitchin' crooked tax collector; that phony colonel, has stole her house from a poor old widow woman. It ain't right, Sheriff."

"It's all legal," the sheriff said. "He paid off her taxes. He told me he's going to let Miss Alma stay on the property."

Worried the crowd might try to push their way into the courthouse, the sheriff put one hand on his pistol, pointed with the other, and ordered, "Go back to work or go home. Just get away from here. There'll be no tax sale at the courthouse today."

Billy Hawkins stepped in front of the sheriff and motioned to quiet the gathering. "I'm announcing my candidacy today to run for the South Carolina House of Representatives. As your representative, I'll see to it that Gedney Crowell Jr. is run off from tax collector as soon as possible."

The crowd exploded into "hurrahs" and "yes-sirs."

"Gedney Crowell is a sorry-assed tax collector!" one man yelled.

"And he certainly is no colonel, either!" Hawkins shouted and pointed.

"Yeah!" the crowd roared.

"He's a liar!" another man yelled.

"You vote for me, and I'll run his ass out of office."

"Hurray!" the crowd yelled.

The bulldog barked and jumped.

Well, Billy Hawkins got elected and had Gedney fired from the tax collector job.

At this point, Gedney was making so much money that losing the job didn't bother him. He'd heard there was something going on nearby that was making millionaires overnight—textile manufacturing.

A couple of cotton mills in North Carolina had recently been built not far from his place, and he rode over to check them out.

He was surprised at the noise and heat inside the plant and fanned at the lint floating in the spinning room. It was almost as bad as being trapped in a furnace. He coughed and held a handkerchief to his mouth.

"Yeah, it gets thick in here at times," the mill owner shouted. "We pump steam in to try to hold it down and keep the fibers moist so we can better manage it. You get used to it.

"This is the spinning room. I'm not going to take you to the breaking room, where the bales are opened and carded. There's too much lint in there. It'll get all over your clothes.

"Come with me." He stepped to a huge door mounted on rollers and pulled on a chain above it.

Gedney was impressed by the door's size and thickness as it rolled open. They stepped through and climbed a wide staircase.

The noisy rumblings of the spinning room faded away as the door behind them closed.

"We can talk better here," the man told him. "I'm gonna show you the weaving room. Then we'll go to my office, where it'll be quieter. You'll find you have to shout or use hand signals inside the work areas of cotton mills. The machines are too noisy for people to hear. I'll show you.

"Stand back. let me get this door." He pulled on a chain, and a thick door rolled open, releasing a blast of rumbling noises that shook the floors. Clacking belts powered by overhead pullies ran to weaving machines, whose shuttles were slapped back and forth in dysrhythmic beats, preventing the whole building from collapsing in on itself.

Gedney swatted at the lint as he followed his guide. Puzzled weavers watched and then moved to appear busy as the mill owner led Crowell to the middle of the room. The boss weaver hurried over, concerned something was wrong, but he relaxed when the owner shouted, "I'm showing him the plant," and pointed back at Crowell.

Crowell's ears were ringing, and his feet were still tingling when he and the mill owner arrived at the main office. "Is it always this loud?" he hollered.

"You'll get used to it. You won't worry about the noise or lint when you see how much money you can make."

The mill owner had the bookkeeper show Gedney cost and revenue figures. The plant had turned a twenty percent profit in its first two years. Gedney was convinced he could make big money. All he needed now was to find investors to help build his plant.

As he rode away, the bookkeeper asked the mill owner, "Who is Gedney Crowell? Was he in the Civil War?"

"No," the mill owner said. "His father was. His father was one of those who believed that bunch in South Carolina who caused it."

CHAPTER 10

IT WAS THE YANKEES, NOT US.

Gedney had some money to build a mill, but he needed more. While he knew he shouldn't, he made the mistake of going to Dupre Merchant and his cronies for it. Gedney felt he should at least give the locals a chance to invest in something that would benefit the whole county.

Dupre and his buddies were meeting upstairs in the bank's boardroom the day Gedney decided to call on them. The portraits of Cyril and Angus Merchant scowled down at them as if warning, "Don't foul this up!"

Dupre was pushing the board meeting through its agenda of monthly activity and loan applications. He'd learned from his father that the best way to control the board was to move things quickly, as if he had other *important* things to do. This was how he showed them he was powerful.

Dupre was vain, sensitive about his image, and proud of the Merchant name. Why, his family had helped start the Civil War. *Well, it was really the Yankees who caused it. If they had left us alone, we wouldn't have fired a shot.*

The indoctrination of people like him was so thorough that despite experiencing the devastation *their families had caused,*

Dupre and others defended the war by exclaiming, *We didn't do it! The Yankees did it!*

Dupre had a particular hatred of Yankee soldiers. One of Sherman's men had ruined his aunt's face near the war's end. After leaving Columbia smoldering, Sherman's army looted its way up to Chesterfield County to teach those people a lesson for causing the war. Just ahead of them, rebel soldiers were in full retreat and set fire to the bridge at Cheraw as they stumbled toward North Carolina. This forced Sherman's army to bivouac and wait on engineers to build a new one. Over a week, Yankee soldiers destroyed a large plantation, burned the courthouse in Chesterfield, and accidentally burned the business district of Cheraw after setting off an abandoned confederate ammo dump.

At Haigler's Crossing, Dupre's great aunt saw Yankee soldiers torching businesses and worried they'd burn the whole town. She was standing in the street, yelling at them, when a sergeant rode up.

She grabbed his reins and pleaded, "Make them stop!"

The sergeant bellowed, "Let go!" slashed her face with his riding crop, and rode past. She fell, blinded in one eye, and was so disfigured by a puffy scar that she never married.

Raised on stories like this from the time they were learning to walk, Dupre and his friends had been bred to distrust those not from the South. They saw Yankees as people who may have been white but were really immigrants. Yankees seemed driven by some need to declare they were Germans, Hungarians, or some other ethnic appellation—but of course, never British.

During Reconstruction, occupying Yankee soldiers would irritate folks on the street with their, "You Irish?" or, "You're German, right?" Southerners never talked about ethnicity. There was no need. For Southerners, people were either white, colored, or some combination thereof.

The bank manager was finishing his report when there was a knock on the door. He opened it, and Dupre overheard a teller say, "He's downstairs."

"Who's downstairs?" he asked.

"Gedney Crowell. He wants to come up and meet with the board."

"Probably about that mill he wants to build," someone sneered.

"He's not on our agenda," Dupre said. "You men want to hear him out?"

"Hell, we know what he's gonna ask, and we already know our answer. What if we let him come up so we can get this over with?" There was head nodding and mumbling.

"Uh, Mr. Chairman, are you okay with Gedney, er, the junior Colonel Crowell meeting with us?"

They all laughed. Dupre scowled. "That son of a bitch . . . Yeah . . . okay. Thomas, go down and get him. Tell him to go around back."

The bank manager treated Gedney as if he were a sharecropper groveling for a pay raise. "Go 'round back and use the stairs off the alley. Knock on the door and wait until they tell you, *you* can enter."

Prideful and snobbish, these powerbrokers spoke of their ancestors often, a ploy to signal to others that *theirs were the better families*—they had the family histories to prove it. At times, they would condescend to hear from common white folk if the issue fell within the range of matters they found interesting. Coloreds were never allowed to meet with them. Their complaints were taken to a handful of colored shopkeepers and a preacher who served to mediate and communicate with the white leadership.

Eight men were seated around the table, and they finally allowed Gedney in. Dupre was at its head, tapping his fingers, impatient to get this over with.

He was gruff when he said, "Gedney, what do you want?"

Gedney cleared his throat, looked around, and, in a loud voice, began a formal lecture. Some of the men smiled and poked each other at what they thought was a phony colonel putting on airs.

"I am here to offer you an opportunity to join me in an enterprise that will change the economy of our county for the better. I plan to build a five-thousand-spindle cotton mill just outside town on land over at my place. The workers we hire will shop in town here, use your bank, and buy produce, milk, and hogs from local merchants and farmers. The whole community will benefit."

"When did you start caring about the community?" a man asked, though it was said more as a statement than a question.

"I have always cared about this town," Crowell replied formally.

"Hogwash!" Dupre said. He looked at the other men at the table and grinned.

"Yeah, you cared. You put that tacky monument up in the cemetery," a man said, and he looked around for approval from the others.

"That was for my father. He was the only colonel to come out of this area during the Civil War."

"He was never a full colonel. He was a lieutenant colonel," the man argued.

"All right," Dupre growled. "Gedney, we're wasting time here. What do you want?"

"I want you to invest in the mill I'm going to build. It will help our community grow. It'll help the county grow. That's what's happening over in Rockingham. I've been there. They have two mills and two villages going up. We can sell stock just like a corporation. You and I can invest in it, and we can all make money."

"Well, you say this will be a corporation; how much money you want us to put up?"

Gedney looked down as he said. "Forty thousand dollars." Then he looked back up. "We could sell stock at fifty dollars a share, and everybody could chip in. We could make this a community project, offer folks stock on installments at the bank here. This plant will be great for the county. In North Carolina, when mills go up, people move in and spend what they earn in the local community. Everyone benefits."

"And you want us to put up forty thousand dollars?" Dupre said. "How much are you going to put up?"

"I'm investing fifty thousand dollars."

"Hell, then you'll own the mill!"

"No, we organize like a stockholder company, with each investor having votes per shares of stock he owns."

"Yeah, but you would already have us outvoted."

"No thanks, *Colonel!*" Dupre said, and then he dismissed Gedney with, "You may go now."

Gedney tried to smile as he put on his hat. "Fifty dollars a share is a good price. We could help local folks buy stock on payment, and everyone would do good."

He touched his cane to his hat, nodded at the men, and, in a rebellious gesture, walked to the main door, slammed it shut behind him, and majestically strode slowly down the stairs.

"Manufacturing, shit. Manufacturing is what Yankees do," Dupre spat. "If he builds that plant, he'll be trying to hire our sharecroppers. We can't have that."

As Gedney rode out of town, he was frustrated he couldn't sell the locals his idea. While he was convinced it would help the community, he worried Dupre Merchant and his friends might interfere.

When he got back to the house, he stood in his stirrups and looked across his field. *That might work.* He sat, clucked the horse into a walk down a long row, and then squeezed it into a slow canter as he thought and smiled. *Yeah, it will work. I can clear these trees and build the mill at the river . . . in the next county.*

*   *   *

Vernon turned to Betsy and said, "Let's close up and get something to eat."

"But what happened next? Did he do it?" she asked.

"Yeah. There is more to this, but let's get something to eat. I haven't had anything all day, and I'm starved."

They closed the newspaper, walked down to a restaurant, and sat in a corner booth near the front door.

After dinner, the owner, Jimmy Theopolis, poured coffee and asked, "You want me to sweeten this for you?"

They said yes, and he pulled a half-pint of whiskey from his back pocket. "Here, but you got to keep it on the seat so nobody sees it. Leave the bottle and three bucks when you go."

As they sipped bourbon-flavored coffee, Vernon resumed his tale.

"Gedney Jr. picked up financial support from businessmen in the new county, and because they lived on the other side of it, they didn't know of his reputation as the tax collector, or the resentments held by those in Haigler's Crossing. Not long after he began clearing land, Crowell realized he needed help bringing his mill to life and looked north for expertise."

Betsy was wiping water condensation off the tabletop with a napkin. She looked up and gave Vernon a funny look. "Why would he do that?"

"Gedney didn't know anything about manufacturing, Betsy. He was a farmer. The people who knew manufacturing were up north. So, Gedney placed ads in Rhode Island and Massachusetts newspapers, looking for 'a man experienced in the establishment and operation of a cotton textile mill.' Well, the Colonel made the mistake of hiring a short man with a Napoleon complex."

Vernon asked Betsy if she wanted another snort. She said no, and he continued his story. "Gedney was unaware this little Yankee used his smarts to get rid of people who got in his way. He got them blamed for things he did. He'd been a selfish, conniving son of a bitch from the time he was a little boy."

CHAPTER 11

A MEAN LITTLE MAN

Up in Lowell, Massachusetts, workers sneered at a notice on their bulletin board. Sam Holden had named Lemuel Webster production superintendent of Holden Textile Manufacturing. The announcement was bad enough, but what stirred their agitation was the directive their new boss had written at the bottom of the page:

> Effective this date, all department managers and superintendents are to be addressed as Mister or Sir and not by forename or expressions implying personal familiarity.
>
> Mr. Lemuel Webster
> Superintendent – Production

Out in the weaving room, someone scrawled, "Little Napoleon," on the notice. In the warehouse, the workers struck through his title and wrote, "Little Lemuel," below his signature.

"Aye, Little Lemuel, that's him," the maintenance chief told their group. "I've been summoned to his office. His Majesty wants me to take the legs off his desk."

"For what?" someone asked.

"I dunno, maybe he's having to strain to see across it." The men laughed.

Later that day, the maintenance man returned, and a bigger crowd gathered.

"It wasn't just the desk. He had me shorten all the furniture in his office, including the chairs, except his, of course. I cranked his chair as high as it would go."

"Why?" someone asked.

"He thinks he needs to look important, and he can't do that if things around him make him look small, like he is."

"Little Lemuel. Our *new* boss."

This time, there was no laughter. Working for a little boy in little man's clothes who had to stand on equipment or boxes to look important was no fun.

Lemuel found the "Little Napoleon" note and snatched it off the bulletin board. Hopping onto a box, he yelled, "Get back to work!"

He glared at the women he caught socializing. The boss weaver saw it and ran to him from across the way, yelling, "Sir, what's the matter?"

"They're talking, not working!" Lemuel bellowed as he stepped off the box. He headed down an alley while holding up the memo. "They have time for this but not for work."

When the taller man tried to keep up, Lemuel quickened his pace to force him to run along beside him, and he yelled over his shoulder, "You make them pay attention to their work! If you can't, I'll find someone who can." Then he hurried away, not seeing the supervisor flip him the finger.

In textile manufacturing, when machines are set up and running properly, workers have to wait for them to finish their runs. So, they play games, sing, or socialize while waiting. Lemuel was fussing at them for doing what they normally did.

All over the plant, workers gossiped. Saying that even though Lemuel might be smart about equipment and operations, he didn't know squat when it came to people.

Lemuel Webster was born out of wedlock as a result of his mother getting raped. Despite what had happened to her, she was condemned as an unwed mother, sent away to a birth house, and then forced to surrender her baby to the Catholic Church under laws passed by the Irish Parliament.

At the orphanage where Lemuel spent his early years, he was recognized for being smart. He was promoted two full grades in a move that turned out to be a mistake. The bigger boys bullied him because he showed them up in schoolwork and made him pay for it on the playground with punches, shoves, and tripping. He was too small to fight back and often ran to the main building for safety as the boys chased him and called him a fraidy cat. Lemuel hid away in his secret place, a closet in the staircase near the headmaster's office.

Lying on old newspapers, he took out his special notebook and drew pictures, pretending he was someplace else. The stories he told himself grew into fantasies of having rich parents to getting even with the bigger boys. In the process, he discovered he could outsmart the others to make up for his lack of size. He drew up a plan and got smaller boys to help him beat the biggest bully in the orphanage, Frankie McCabe.

Early that morning, while the other boys were sleeping, Lemuel and his co-conspirators slid down the dormitory floor and quietly looped belts around Frankie and his bedframe. They strapped him down tight and beat him bloody with belt buckles and rocks.

The plans for the beating inspired Lemuel. He discovered he could outthink his opponents and learned that by outlining steps in his special notebook, he could get revenge, or anything he wanted, by using people.

There was such an uproar about the incident that the headmaster arranged to sell Lemuel to a workhouse as a chimney sweep. But before he could be taken away, a nun snuck him out of the orphanage and got him onto a ship to Boston. He was just ten years old at the time.

While on the ship, a German cloth buyer befriended him and took him to Lowell, Massachusetts, where he convinced Sam Holden to give the boy a job and a place to live at the company boarding house.

The first morning there, Lemuel was taken to Holden's office. Mr. Holden said he was glad Lemuel was settling in at the boarding house. There was a knock on the door, and a man wearing coveralls and a white shirt walked in.

"Ah, Charles, come in," Holden said. "Lemuel, this is Charles Daughtry. He's going to show you what to do. He is your boss here. And Charles, this is Lemuel Webster. I want you to use him as your new sweeper."

Daughtry gritted a smile. His boss was *ordering*, not asking him to put this boy to work. While he smiled and pretended to be happy, the anger churned in his head.

Six years, I been running the spinning room. I should decide who works for me. This boy is too little to do anything, even push a broom.

He thanked Mr. Holden and said to the boy, "Follow me."

They walked down a hall and into a small room. Loud noise rumbled from somewhere nearby. Daughtry pulled a chain, and a heavy door rolled open, unleashing the noise, as if the machines in the dark room were trying to shake themselves free of the thick wooden floor, which trembled and vibrated. The air was filled with lint and smelled of oil and metal. "C'mon!" Daughtry yelled, pulling a chain to close the door.

"This is the spinning room," he shouted. "Get that broom over there! Give it to me and watch." Daughtry pushed short strokes and then yelled, "This is how you do it. You put the lint you sweep up in that can down on the end. I want you to keep the alleys clean between all the machines in here. The whole room. Keep it all clean and put the lint in the cans. Here, you do it."

The broom handle was twice Lemuel's height and so thick it was hard to grip. Stiff bristles mounted on a wide hardwood base made the whole thing heavy and clumsy. Lemuel shoved and grunted to get it moving. He'd push, pick it up, and push again, collecting dirt and lint and, along the way, smearing oil from the machines that crowded his path.

"That's it. Keep going," Daughtry yelled. As he walked away, he complained to himself, *tell me who to work, huh?*

It took a while for Lemuel's eyes to adjust. The room was huge and filled with machines of a thousand moving parts shoving and pulling in disruptive rhythms. Overhead, steam pulsed at clouds of fluff, and thick belts flapped through pullies, carrying life to the mechanical monsters below. It was like being trapped in a hot cave filled with chaotic bats.

As he bumped against equipment in the dim light, men covered in lint and barefooted boys emerged from nowhere. One of the boys stepped onto his broom. Then, never looking at Lemuel, the boy made him wait while pretending to check some equipment. When he was done, he stepped off and yelled over his shoulder, "You better get moving before Daughtry sees you."

The routine of pushing the broom, eating lunch, pushing the broom, meeting Mr. Holden, returning home, eating supper, cleaning up, and falling in bed exhausted, continued for weeks. The work was so monotonous Lemuel often drifted into fantasies so real he was unaware of the noise and movement around him. Nor was he aware of the resentments growing among others over the attention Mr. Holden was giving him.

Employees who'd been there a long time resented it. The boy who'd stomped on his broom did it again, yelling over the noise, "Go tell Mr. Holden!" A doffer spat tobacco at Lemuel's feet and yelled over the noise in the room, "Boy, your feet are nasty! You better not let Mr. Holden see you."

One morning before he came in, someone removed the handle from Lemuel's broom and screwed a much shorter one into it. Lemuel looked and looked for the old one and then, worried Daughtry would yell at him for not working, began pushing the broom as it was. It was too short.

Stooping over until his face was barely off the floor, he was gagging from the stinking oil the machines slung at his face when laughter and whoops erupted down the aisle. Boys were slapping their thighs, and one pointed and said, "Damn, he grew overnight."

Charles Daughtry walked up and yelled, "What have you done to your broom?"

Lemuel pointed to the boys. Daughtry laughed and then walked over and yelled, "Get that long handle and don't be doing that anymore! This is a workplace, not a playground."

Someone slid the handle down to Lemuel and yelled over the noise, "We thought you needed something more your size, half-pint."

The boys shouldn't have done that. Back in his room that night, he took out his special notebook, thumbed through it, and found the plans he'd made to take care of Frankie McCabe. Lemuel smiled and then flipped to a blank page. He drew stick figures and wrote names beneath them. He had a new project. He'd get them.

He listed what the boys did each morning. The second hand would read a table of figures from a manual to tell the boys what settings to use for the yarn they produced. Then, once the machines were running, the boys left to play cards and checkers in the water house as they waited for bobbins to fill.

Lemuel looked at his illustration for a long time and then drew more pictures and smiled. The next morning, as he pushed his broom along, he watched the boys start their machines and enter the water house.

When he was sure no one could see him, he lifted his broom and held the oily bristles against the fibers coming off the first machine. He swept up more dirt and smeared fibers of another machine and then another.

When he was done, he moved on, pushing and smiling, knowing that behind him, machines were winding clean fibers over the soiled ones. No one knew . . . until cloth came off looms stained with oily streaks and dirt. There was yelling between the supervisors over it.

The boss weaver blamed Charles Daughtry for not maintaining quality control. Daughtry blamed his workers. He caught two boys playing checkers and fired one of them on the spot for mouthing back. Daughtry told Lemuel to put his broom down; he was promoting him.

That night in his room, Lemuel pulled out his journal and drew an X across the stick figure of the boy he'd gotten fired. He smiled and then drew a large checkmark over his plan. *I may be small, but I can outthink them.*

Sam Holden discovered Lemuel was very smart. He gave him manuals on textile equipment and was amazed that within a year,

Lemuel knew everything about spinning machines. Sam Holden had Lemuel to his house for dinner twice. He had other boys working for him, but Lemuel had come to him under unusual circumstances, so Holden felt he needed to take a personal interest in him.

Lemuel worked several years as a spinning machine tender until Daughtry, worried that Lemuel was showing him up with his mechanical knowledge, jimmied the settings on Lemuel's machine and blamed him for running off the wrong-sized yarn.

At the end of a shift, Sam Holden called Lemuel to his office.

"What settings did you use for the yarn?"

"These. See right here? That's what the tables called for, Mr. Holden. I've been writing them down each morning when the second hand tells us what settings to use. When the flaws showed up, the settings had been changed. Someone is messing with my work."

Lemuel met Mr. Holden at his carriage stop over several weeks and reported on production in the spinning department. Back at the boarding house, he took out his notebook and outlined a plan to take advantage of Mr. Holden's suspicions. He enlisted the help of another worker by lying to him, telling him that Daughtry was going to fire him, too.

They conspired to run off more wrong-sized yarn and get Daughtry blamed for it. Lemuel told the other worker that Sam Holden suspected Daughtry was behind the first bad yarn episode and all they needed was to do it again.

They noticed that some Tuesdays, about mid-morning, Daughtry would leave the spinning room to attend a supervisors' meeting. Whenever he left, machine tenders and doffers went to the water house to play checkers and cards. It was perfect. All they had to do was wait.

After Daughtry and others witnessed Lemuel's setup for the correct yarn one Tuesday, Daughtry left for his meeting. When the tenders went to the water house to play, Lemuel quickly shut down a couple of machines, changed the settings, and walked into the water house. His co-conspirator removed the correct yarn, put empty bobbins in place, restarted the machines, and then joined the others as if nothing had happened.

Sometime later, Lemuel went to the main office to tell Mr. Holden that the settings had been tampered with, but Holden was away. This was even better. Lemuel would get someone else to tell Mr. Holden what happened.

He gave a couple of bobbins to Holden's production superintendent and said he'd seen Daughtry tampering with the machines. The superintendent carried the bobbins to Sam Holden's office.

"Daughtry is doing it," he said. "Lemuel set up the machine with the correct settings in front of witnesses this morning. These are the bobbins with the correct-size yarn. Daughtry got someone to remove them, and then he tampered with the machines. If you go to the spinning room now, you'll find the machines are producing the wrong size."

Sam Holden was furious. He went to the spinning room, called the workers together, and shouted at Daughtry, "You tampered with the spinning machine!" Despite Daughtry's sputtering innocence, Holden shouted over him: "You're fired! Get out!"

Holden turned to the others and pointed at Daughtry as he was led away. "Because of him, we must make additional runs to get the right yarn, and we will be late getting our order out to our customer. There will be no more episodes of tampering with machines. Anyone caught doing it will be fired immediately.

"And another thing. You better pay attention and do what you are told to do."

Holden put his hand on Lemuel's back and pressed him to step forward. "Lemuel Webster is the new boss of the spinning room. I don't want any more problems with settings. If it happens again, I'll fire all of you if I have to."

Lemuel was seventeen years old.

Back in his room that night, Lemuel wrote three names in the "Devil's Workbook." At the top were two men who had helped Daughtry blame Lemuel for bad yarn. Below that, he wrote the name of the man who had helped him get Daughtry fired. He struck a line through the name at the top.

The next day, just as the men began lunch, Lemuel walked into the spinning room water house, pointed at the man whose name he had crossed off, and yelled over the noise, "You helped Daughtry mess with my machines. Get your stuff and get out. You're fired."

The men in the room began to mumble, and Lemuel stepped on a box.

"Let that be a lesson to all of you. If I ever catch any of you changing machine settings or trying to get me in trouble, I'll fire you on the spot."

Lemuel did two things that day. He got rid of one of the men who helped Charles Daughtry and demonstrated he had authority over the others. He liked it. He liked hurting people bigger than him.

A month later, he fired the other man who had helped Daughtry. A month after that, he fired the man who had conspired with him to get Daughtry fired. It was Christmas Eve. Lemuel didn't care; he didn't want anyone around who could jeopardize his job.

CHAPTER 12

LEMUEL QUITS

It was bad enough when Lemuel was plotting and scheming to get promoted, but now that he was head of production for the whole mill, he'd become a little tyrant.

The more Lemuel growled and hollered, the more the workers grew agitated and began getting back at him. Cloth came off looms with gaps, misaligned selvage, or sections tainted with small traces of machine oil. Doffers were removing spindles only half-full, forcing the spinning room to double the runs to supply the plant with the yarn needed.

Customers complained that Holden Mill was shipping them flawed materials. Webster became dogmatic about production and quality control.

The textile workers union took advantage of the resentment. An organizer met a group of workers in one of the millhouses one evening. "Here are cards. Give them to your friends and ask them to invite others to sign up."

"That's going to be easy," a loom fixer said. "Everybody in the plant hates that little son of a bitch."

By the time Lemuel and Sam Holden found out, it was too late. The plant was unionized. In addition to higher pay and shorter work hours, the union demanded only supervisors with direct responsibility be allowed to talk with and oversee the workers. They hoped that would keep Lemuel away from them.

When the plant didn't yield to their demands, the workers walked out in protest, and the plant was closed for three weeks. The strike was mainly about Lemuel.

This was no bother to him. He didn't trust people anyway. Getting shoved and punched most of his young life had twisted his personality into a tight protective knot. He was a short little boy of a man warning others not to mess with him.

People were either tools or impediments to his career. He determined this when first meeting them, usually while standing atop a box or machine. Lemuel would glare at them as if to say, *don't waste my time; I am important.*

Sam Holden reluctantly negotiated pay raises, reduced hours, and issued directives about supervision to end the strike. He needed to get his plant running again. New England mills now had competition from manufacturing plants that were springing up near cotton fields in the American South.

A couple of years later, Holden became frail and installed his Harvard-educated grandsons as vice presidents to prepare them to take over his company. It didn't take long before the grandsons complained that their production superintendent wasn't running the plant properly. Lemuel Webster was not family, and they had no intention of keeping him there.

The grandsons took pleasure in poking Lemuel's fragile psyche about his height, calling him a liar about his parents being rich and openly questioning his knowledge of textiles in front of his subordinates. The oldest grandson, Morris Coleman, was the worst.

"Lemuel, it's about time you showed up!"

"I was on the floor of the plant with the second hand and a loom fixer."

"When I call you, you come then. Don't wait until you feel like it."

"I was telling him how to replace the shuttle control to get the loom operating again."

"You're getting real good at making excuses!" Morris crossed the room with a sheet of paper in his hands and leaned over Webster. "I suppose you haven't seen these figures, have you?" He stretched the paper between his hands and held it high, forcing Webster to read the paper while looking almost straight up.

"But Morris, you can't compare our costs—"

"Morris? You don't call me Morris; you call me Mr. Coleman. I'm not your pal here. Lemuel, you work for me."

Lemuel mentally scrambled to understand where Morris was headed with this. He took a deep breath as Morris towered over him.

"These figures compare our prices with those of Southern cotton mills," he said. There is no way to use that to judge our plant's costs and outputs.

"Why not? It's our closest competition!"

"S-sir," Lemuel stammered, "Southern mills are right next to where cotton is grown. They don't have the shipping expense we have. Our cotton is hauled by trains from the South all the way to our mill here in Massachusetts. That adds to our costs. And Southerners work cheap; they don't have unions down there. Here we have the United Textile Workers."

Morris leaned forward, tapped Lemuel in the chest, and threatened, "Well, Lemuel, you were the reason our workers joined a union, and you're responsible for what is going on in the plant.

If you don't find a way to get our costs down, we'll need to find us someone who can!"

When Lemuel made it back to his office, his secretary was putting documents in a new desk. "What are you doing? What is this?" he demanded.

"They brought in your new furniture today."

"I didn't order new furniture."

"Oh, I thought you did. Mr. Coleman's secretary said you were getting new furniture. She said Mr. Coleman wanted everyone to have regular-sized furniture now. I thought you knew. Oh, and Mr. Webster, Mr. Henry Coleman wants to see you in his office right away."

That does it. I'll quit.

Later, Lemuel retreated to his house and, like he had as a little boy, hid away and crept deep inside his psyche, reliving each shove, push, or beating he'd gotten because of his small size. And now the one thing he was good at—his work—was under attack by two young men who had something he did not: a college degree and family ties to Holden Mill.

Seated at his desk, he opened his notebook and thought, *They're just like the rest of them. They're trying to get rid of me. I know more about textile manufacturing than they do. I know more about machinery and production than anyone in Lowell, Massachusetts. Hell, anyone anywhere.*

He was convinced his intellect and work were the most important things in his life, certainly more important than social skills.

Over several weeks, he outlined a plan and read newspaper articles and want ads referencing textile mill construction in Southern states. He replied to several, including an ad from a Colonel Gedney Crowell Jr. of South Carolina.

Webster was convinced Southern mill owners had little experience with manufacturing; they were farmers or merchants. They needed his expertise. After all, he was the smartest textile man in Massachusetts.

He felt he could stipulate that, as a condition of employment, he be given absolute control to operate the mill in the manner he chose. Better yet, he would find a way to own his own mill. Then no one could tell him how to run it. There would be no more *little boy* remarks. He'd see to that.

It was no wonder, then, that the day he got the Colonel's job offer, he loudly beat on Morris Coleman's office door, stomped in uninvited, and yelled, "You don't know what the hell you're doing, and someday, someway, I'll put you out of business, you incompetent son of a bitch!"

Then he slammed the door and walked away from Holden Mill.

CHAPTER 13

Is You Him?

After clearing out his bank account, Lemuel spent three days on a train that carried him through the major cities of the East Coast down into the steamy climate of South Carolina. Tired from traveling and sweating in heavy wool clothing, he was the only passenger to get off when the train reached his stop. It was getting dark.

The Colonel had written that he would send someone to bring Lemuel to his mansion, but when Lemuel stepped off the train, no one was there except for a man sitting on a bench some distance down the platform, and he wasn't moving.

As the train pulled away, Lemuel peeped into the windows of the darkened station, fearing he'd gotten off at the wrong stop. No one was inside.

The man on the bench stood, cocked his head, and stared at Lemuel, uncertain what to do. It was Clarence, the Colonel's housekeeper. At first, Clarence thought Lemuel had missed his train, because what he saw down the way looked like a young boy. Clarence slowly approached Lemuel.

"Is you him?"

"Who?"

"Mr. Webster?"

"Yes. Who are you?

"I'm Clarence. Colonel Crowell told me to come down here and get you. You *is* Mr. Webster, ain't you?"

"Yes, I am Webster. Please help me with my bags."

Lemuel had never seen a black man before, and Clarence? He'd never seen a grown man this small. As they rode along, they took turns staring at each other in the darkness. Clarence thought, *He sho' look young to me.*

When they turned onto the driveway leading to the Colonel's mansion, Webster saw the front yard was filled with cotton bales. "The Colonel's still growing cotton?"

"Yah, suh, he show is. The Colonel say he ain't ever goin' quit plantin' cotton. He goin' need cotton for his new mill. I hope he don't ever quit plantin'. My family need the work."

The Colonel came out the front door just as they drove up. Lemuel's short size and youth startled him. In their correspondence, he hadn't asked Lemuel his age and had assumed from his title that he was an older man.

After awkward introductions, the Colonel invited Lemuel into the house. In the light, he saw a short young man sweating like a steam bath.

"Here, let me get your coat," the Colonel said. "It's still hot down here. I'll take my jacket off, and we can both be comfortable. Let's go to the dining room and have dinner."

The Colonel was initially polite and formal over dinner. But when they began discussing the construction of his mill, he worried he'd hired someone who'd misled him.

"You say you've been working in textiles for fourteen years and you were superintendent of Holden Mills for three?"

"Yes, sir."

"How old are you?"

"What?"

"How old are you?"

"I'm twenty-four. Why?"

"You said you worked in textiles fourteen years and were superintendent of Holden Mills, and you tell me you're twenty-four years old?"

Lemuel clenched his jaw and, raising his voice to match the Colonel's tone, exclaimed, "I've worked in every phase of textile manufacturing, from sweeping floors to selling the finished product! I've set up spinning machines, repaired looms, hired and fired workers, and put down strikes. My last job there, I was superintendent of the whole operation," he lied. "I ran the entire mill for over three years. I know what I'm doing."

Still skeptical, the Colonel took Lemuel to a small room near the front of the mansion and had him unroll sketches of the layout of Holden Mill. Then he made Lemuel explain in detail the function of every department, and his voice grew louder each time he asked, "What's that?"

Sensing that the questions implied doubt about his competency—or worse, his size—Lemuel roared back, "Now, Mr. Colonel, *sir* . . . I'll show you how each of these illustrations come together to operate a full-sized cotton mill from one power source. I know what I'm doing!"

"How do I know you're not lying about this?"

"Lying? I don't lie, *Colonel.*"

"Where is your proof you can do the job?"

"My proof? My proof? Look at these diagrams; I drew them. See, that's my name in the legend here. What more proof do you want?"

"Give me the names of people up in Massachusetts who can vouch for you."

"Mr. H. M. Mickleberry at the Draper Machine Works or Abe Weinstein, who owns Modern Lady clothing. Mr. Mickleberry makes looms and equipment you'll need for your plant, and Mr. Weinstein bought cloth from the textile mill I ran. You write them, and they'll tell you I know what I'm doing."

The verbal pushing and shoving were so loud at times that the house servants were afraid to clear the dining room table. Lemuel didn't tolerate people implying he was a liar or beneath them.

Though still skeptical, the Colonel finally relented. He hoped Webster was truthful. He had no choice. There was no time to look for someone else in New England, and he certainly couldn't trust anyone in South Carolina to do what he needed.

"All right, Webster, I believe you for now. You can start work for me tomorrow."

"Thank you, Colonel. I know what I'm doing. I want a contract that spells out my role in all of this. I'll build you the finest mill in South Carolina, and if you let me run the mill the way it should be run, I'll make you richer than you already are."

"You prove to me you know how to build my mill, and then we'll talk about a contract."

Still wary of each other, they shook hands and drank a toast of brandy to seal the deal.

Lemuel moved into a sharecropper shack that night. The next morning, he'd begin overseeing the clearing of land and construction of a cotton mill, a mill he was determined to operate as he saw fit—and perhaps someday own outright *if* the chance came along.

CHAPTER 14

Labor-Management Issue

Early the next morning, Lemuel Webster found himself in the presence of dark-skinned men, descendants of slaves who had worked the fields for Colonel Gedney Crowell's father. Some of them were related to Clarence.

As Webster peered at the dozen or more of them, they stared back in puzzlement at the diminutive Irishman. Clad in a heavy wool jacket and pants, Webster was red-faced and sweating heavily. It was a steamy morning, thick with humidity long before the sun had climbed midway up the trees.

"These are your workers," said the Colonel as he rode up on a roan gelding.

"But Colonel, these men are Africans."

"Their relatives may have been called Africans when the tribal chiefs sold them," declared the Colonel, "but down here, we call them coloreds, and these men are your workers. They can fell trees, cut lumber into boards, lay brick, frame up the walls, and build the roof. They can even make the gears to connect to the waterwheel. I know this because I've watched them do it."

Webster was soaking in sweat, breathing hard, and even redder in the face. The Colonel cautioned him, "You better get out of that wool jacket and breeches, or you're gonna die out here when the heat comes up. It'll be real hot by two thirty this afternoon."

Before the day was half-through, there was a labor conflict.

Webster was singularly familiar with a manufacturing system. The workers Crowell had sent him operated on an agricultural system used for over two hundred years.

In manufacturing, workers begin at a designated hour, perform repetitive tasks in one place, and don't stop unless directed to do so or at a designated time. In Southern agriculture, workers are assigned projects to complete. They move at their own pace, take breaks for meals, and end their labors when the project is done, regardless of the day or hour.

Despite the Colonel's instructions of "do whatever Mr. Webster tells you," the men worked at the casual pace they were accustomed to, not at the rate and focus Webster expected. What upset Webster most was the joking and socializing among them as they went about their work.

Workers mustn't talk and joke and have fun. Workers are to work! Work is serious!

At noon that first day—dinnertime, as Southerners call the largest meal of the day—the workers just stopped working and walked off, leaving Webster to stammer, "Wh-where are you going?"

"We goin' to da house."

"For what?"

"Fo dinner. We goin' to da house fo dinner."

Webster went tearing off to see the Colonel, and when he found him, he was so worked up, he could barely get the words out. "This is insane!" *Pant.* "They won't listen to me." *Pant.* "I can't work this way!"

The Colonel worried that Webster's blunt way of talking would offend and labor issues might slow construction. He hired a black foreman to supervise the work, despite Webster's arm flapping protests.

"Webster," the Colonel firmly directed, "show Mr. Simkins your plans for the mill and how you want it built. The two of you can go out to the worksite and stake out the foundation. Speak directly with Mr. Simkins if any changes or corrections are necessary. There's no need for you to speak with the workers."

"But what am I to do?"

"You can work here at the house. I had a desk and some cabinets brought up from the basement and have set you up with an office in the parlor off the living room, next to my office. You and I will need to be conferring anyway on construction materials and machinery and how you plan to staff the mill when it's completed."

The Colonel wanted Webster close. He needed more time to be assured Webster was the right person.

Although frustrated by the lack of a contract and that he was no longer directly supervising the construction, Webster was delighted to be working in a new environment. He'd never worked in such opulence. His office was set up in the parlor near the front of the Crowell plantation house. It had heavily waxed, heart-of-pine flooring with Persian rugs scattered over them and a large bay window, making the room appear larger than it was.

The Colonel got Clarence to place a large, ornate mahogany desk in front of the bay window. Behind the desk was a high-backed oak chair on rollers. Webster could sit and swivel in the chair and watch the workers clear land for the mill's foundation.

Hung on the walls in the room were portraits of Crowells: Colonel Gedney Sr., Colonel Gedney Sr.'s father, Wesley

Crowell, and, on the center wall, Amelia, Colonel Gedney Jr.'s only living child.

Webster found himself looking up from his work and staring at the pale blue eyes and beautiful face. She seemed to overlook everything he did.

Beneath her portrait was a table he used to lay out drawings of the plant and maps of its location. One evening, he and the Colonel were at the table, discussing construction progress, when the Colonel noticed Webster looking at the painting of Amelia.

"She's my treasure. She's all I have left. Her mother and my son died of scarlet fever about ten years ago."

"She's very pretty,"

"She's finishing college this year; wants to be a teacher."

As Webster walked to his shack that evening, he thought about what he had heard.

What an opportunity.

*   *   *

"Damn, Vernon," Betsy said. "This Webster guy was going to scheme his way by using the Colonel's daughter?"

"Don't get ahead of me, Betsy. You need to know more about him. While he was a schemer, he was used to Yankee big-city ways and was having a devil of a time adapting to Southern culture. He had no experience in politics, particularly Southern politics. He'd also learn the hard way that his speak-directly-to-the-point manner could offend. He did not understand that Southerners were careful about expressing true feelings.

"As you were reared to say, 'Yes, sir,' and, 'Yes, ma'am,' under threat of getting your legs switched or hands slapped, Southerners are conditioned to believe being polite is more important than being forthright. They talk around things lest someone take offense that the remark is more about a person's character than the subject discussed. This template for behavior, demanded of everyone, grew out of the savage-tyrant, cultured-gentleman, dual personality of wealthy plantation owners. Dressed in finery, using proper etiquette, and speaking politely, planters would appear at formal affairs in genteel Southern mode right after hacking the ear off a disrespectful slave.

"Beneath this façade of propriety and civility," Vernon said, "lurked a determination to maintain control over the property and the society they felt belonged to them.

"To aid them, plantation owners created racism to control people. Sometime in the 1600's, a guy named Nathaniel Bacon in Virginia wanted to retaliate against Indians who were raiding his frontier settlements. He needed a large armed group to do it. But there weren't enough free white men to help. So, he put together a militia made up of white indentured servants and Negro slaves. They fought hard and ran the Indians off.

"This scared the crap out of the big plantation owners and the Virginia House of Burgesses. They feared that if slaves and white indentured servants banded together armed insurrections would break out.

"To prevent this, Virginia's legislature required non-slave-owning whites to serve in slave patrols to capture and discipline runaway slaves. In one Southern state a white man was sentenced to 29 lashes for stealing a pig, while the sentence for a Negro doing the same was 39 lashes. South Carolina passed a law requiring field-hand slaves to be under the supervision of white men, usually poor white men.

"Through laws like these poor whites were taught they were better than Negroes. Over time these perceptions grew into deeply held beliefs."

"So, racism was created for power and economic reasons and then it got turned into false beliefs that white people are superior to coloreds?" Betsy asked.

"Precisely," said Vernon, "and because of their bad beliefs some whites began committing the worst atrocities on Negroes while other whites silently approved." He lit a cigarette, took a deep puff, then continued, "The white elites controlled their slaves, their property and the politics in each of their states as you'll find out when you hear what happened when Gedney Crowell and Lemuel Webster met their new Senator."

CHAPTER 15

MEET SENATOR LAWRENCE

The people in the county next door enthusiastically bought stock in the Colonel's mill. With soil depleted from over farming and an economy still ravaged by the Civil War, investors were desperate to change things and hoped manufacturing would turn their county around.

Getting public support for the project was new to Webster. Why people in Haigler's Crossing opposed a cotton mill perplexed him. The plant would create two hundred new jobs.

He also puzzled over the control the legislature had over the business community. This came into focus the day he and the Colonel met with a civil engineer to draw a map of a spur to connect the mill to a nearby railroad.

"You'll need permission from the state to build the rail line and incorporate your business," the engineer said, "and that only comes if the county legislative delegation approves. Nothing happens in this state without their approval, especially when it comes to industry.

"You need to meet Senator Lawrence and get his okay. He controls the legislative delegation and appoints the commissioners that work for the county. Take someone the senator knows with you. That way, you'll have credibility when you talk with him. He's a good man."

The Colonel found that one of his investors was related to the senator and got him to arrange a meeting.

The investor told him his cousin was one of the few legislators favoring industrialization in South Carolina. "Senator Lawrence wants to help the state grow." He chuckled, "But he also welcomes these activities as a means to help himself financially. He's an attorney and is known to solicit 'retainer fees' from businessmen wanting him to sponsor legislation they need." He punctuated his statement with a wink.

They met in a committee room at the state Capitol. It was upstairs, behind the visitors' gallery overlooking the Senate chamber. Two thick doors protected the entrance, and inside, a long conference table sat in the middle, surrounded by heavy oak chairs. On the walls were paintings of former chairmen of the Senate Judiciary Committee. At one end was a larger painting of John C. Calhoun, South Carolina's revered champion of slavery, US senator, and seventh vice president of the United States.

After brief introductions, Senator Lawrence praised his cousin, closed the door, and invited the Colonel to talk about the project.

A loud chorus of "Aye!" interrupted from below. The Senate was in session and was voting by *ayes* and *noes*.

The Colonel told the senator his mill would be the first manufacturing plant in the county and the only one in that area of the state. It would employ two hundred people. The senator nodded and smiled as the Colonel asked Webster to show him what the plant would look like.

Webster pointed to illustrations detailing every phase, from opening cotton bales to finishing cloth. Included were references to how *he* was making Holden Mill productive and efficient and how *he* had plans to keep maintenance costs down.

He also dropped in anecdotes of his previous work experience, noting how he had advanced from a lowly spinning room sweeper to superintendent of one of the largest plants in Massachusetts. The senator was impressed and said, "This will be good for my county. Now tell me about this village you're building."

The Colonel unfurled illustrations of the street layout and held up sketches of the houses. The village would also include a mercantile store and schoolhouse.

"So, you're building this right on top of the county line?" the senator asked.

"Yes, the plant is in your county, but the mill village is going to be in the other, over here."

"I see. So, the village will be in Hiram White's County. It doesn't matter. I can still get the state charters you'll need so you can incorporate your town."

"It's not going to be a town, Senator. All of this will be the property of the mill, my property. But Senator, there is something you can help us with."

He had Lemuel unroll the map and point to the rail line they needed. The spur would be off the Waccamaw Railway route and would be used to ship in cotton and coal and haul out finished cloth.

The senator pointed at the map and told the Colonel he needed easements from landowners to allow the railroad to build the spur through their property.

"I believe I know everyone living along this route," he said. "I can also sponsor legislation needed for the county permits and incorporate your company."

"I like your project, Colonel," Lawrence said. "I don't have much time to work on it this afternoon; as you can hear, the Senate is in session, and I'm needed downstairs. But before we go much further, there is a matter you and I need to discuss in private.

"Cousin, pardon me, but would you and this Irish gentleman be so kind as to step outside?"

"Aye!" came up from the Senate floor as Lawrence closed the doors.

"We need to discuss my retainer."

"Your retainer?"

"To get you the railroad easements and local legislation, you'll need to be passed. You need to hire me as your lawyer. You pay me, that is, retain me to work for you."

Senator Matthew Lawrence was short and thin, but he carried himself like a seasoned commander. He pointed to the illustrations. "You say this mill is going to cost ninety thousand dollars?"

"Yes, and that doesn't include what the railroad is going to charge to build the spur. So, you're looking at one hundred thousand dollars total."

Lawrence pushed away from the table, stood tall, and sharply looked the Colonel in the eye, "My retainer will be nine thousand dollars."

"Nine thousand! Senator, that is too much. I can't pay that."

"You can't pay that?" The senator eased forward. "I'm the only lawyer in the delegation and the only senator in the county where your plant sits. I can assure you, no one else is going to write the legislation and get the permits you need unless I do it."

"It's too much!"

"You want me to ask Hiram White to do it for you?"

"No!" bellowed up.

"We're running out of time here. I've got to get downstairs."

"How about shares of stock?"

"I don't want shares; you may go broke. I want cash."

"Aye!" the voices shouted.

The Senator looked at the door, smiled, and turned to face the Colonel. "Since my cousin is a stockholder and I'm a public servant who wants his county to grow, I tell you what I'll do; I'll do it for five thousand dollars cash up front, and you pay me fifty cents for each bale of cotton that's shipped to your mill for the first two years you operate."

"Let me get Webster in here, Senator. He can tell us about the bales we'll need."

"Most of my colleagues in the Senate are farmers, Colonel. Some of them oppose manufacturing and are introducing bills to restrict where textile plants are located. You need me to block their bills. My retainer is a good offer. Besides, no one else from the county will do it, I can assure you of that."

When the Colonel took Webster aside to explain the senator's demand, Webster whispered, "This is extortion!"

"It is, but we don't have any choice. It's the way things are done in South Carolina. Now, calculate the bales we'll need the first two years."

Webster began writing figures on an envelope.

"Colonel, do you want to get this done or not? I've got to go downstairs."

"Okay, Senator, it's a deal. Five thousand dollars up front and fifty cents a bale comes to nine thousand two hundred and fifty dollars."

"That's more like it." The senator took the Colonel's hand. "A cotton mill will be good for my county."

He started to move but stopped. "You do have a check so I can begin today? Just make it out to the Lawrence Law Firm.

"The lady at the desk downstairs will have an envelope for you. Ask her to get a page to bring it to my desk." He looked at Webster. "And just in case you boys try to short me, I've got railroad friends who'll let me know how much cotton you get. Oh, and another thing, give my cousin here another ten shares of stock for bringing you here."

"Aye!" boomed the voices.

Lawrence smiled and walked his cousin out of the room.

After handing over the check, Webster and the Colonel left for lunch. Later, they went to a meeting of an association textile owners were forming near the Capitol. It was a new organization to beat resistance from farm area legislators who opposed textile mills in the state. The Colonel was named to the association's board.

Within a few weeks, Senator Lawrence got easements from families along the proposed route of the railroad spur. It was easy—he told them they had no choice, as state law required landowners to give the easements as part of the state's industrial development code. He also notified the railroad that *he* represented all the landowners along the route and the railroad was to directly pay him the right-of-way fees. He would see to it each family got their share.

Webster used his contacts with the railroads to get them to pay half the construction costs. He also persuaded the railroad to extend a telephone line to the mill. As to their part of covering the construction costs, Webster paid two thousand dollars, and the Colonel paid four thousand.

The Colonel thought Webster was helping. He didn't know Webster had arranged for companies supplying plant machinery to pay him a commission for each piece of equipment he bought—with the Colonel's money.

He never mentioned that when the Colonel invited him over for dinner to celebrate.

"I appreciate all you have done, Lemuel. You obviously know the textile business. I'm going to let you run the plant for me. I'll get Senator Lawrence to draw up a contract."

"Thank you, Colonel."

"I trust you, Webster. I have to. Don't ever betray my trust."

As the Colonel extended a hand, Webster took it, thinking, *You trust me? I don't trust you. I'm not family. You could fire me.* Then, looking the Colonel square in the eyes, he coldly lied. "You can count on me, Colonel."

"Good. Now, tomorrow we're going to town."

"For what? We already have the map."

"To get you some clothes. I can't have my mill superintendent walking around the community with clothes that make you sweat. That wool doesn't wear well down here. Besides, people are already talking about the clothes you wear. We can't have people talking about my mill superintendent. And another thing, it wouldn't look right for the mill superintendent to be living in a sharecropper's shack. You already have your office setup, and I have plenty of room here. I want you to move in with me until we can build you a better place than that shack. What say you to that?"

"I'd say living here would be a privilege."

"Well, you can move in tonight."

Webster's room was upstairs at the back of the house. It was the most luxurious bedroom he'd ever seen. A large four-poster bed rested between two windows, and on the opposite wall was a large chifforobe and chest of drawers and a mirrored dresser. There was a small round table with matching chairs in one corner. Webster sat at the table, took out his special notebook, and thought about what the Colonel had said. *Trust? Hmph.*

He smeared ink across the cover until it no longer read "Devil's Workbook." Beneath it, he wrote a new title, "Textile Equipment Notes."

Now, about this family and job thing. I have some planning to do.

*   *   *

Betsy had an ugly expression when Vernon paused his tale. "You mean this little shit wrote out plans for how he was going to get the Colonel's daughter *before* he even met her?"

"Yep, he used his notebook to figure out what to do about people. Dealing with people was the hardest thing in his life. Every time he trusted someone, they hurt him. So, he didn't trust people, he just used them. Hell he didn't trust *his own feelings*. Now he was faced with doing something he had no skills for and was mighty uncomfortable with - courting a woman."

CHAPTER 16

AMELIA

It was chilly when Webster left the mill and walked into the mansion. At the top of the stairs, an attractive young woman was smiling as if she'd found a Christmas present.

"You must be Mr. Webster."

"And you are Amelia. I've been staring at your portrait for months now."

"And you are a flatterer, Mr. Webster," she said as she descended the stairs and extended a hand.

Webster was flustered. "Nice to meet you, Miss Crowell," he said, shaking her hand hard. Then, worried he was doing it wrong, he let go and put his hands behind his back.

"Please call me Amelia. And what should I call you?"

"Just Webster, please."

"All right, Webster. My father says you're an expert in textiles."

"Well, my goal is to operate the finest mill in the country." He looked down, searching for things to say. "And to make your father richer than he already is. And of course," he looked up as if seeking approval, "to make me rich in the process, too."

He relaxed a bit, though he was still uneasy about what to do next.

"Oh, wonderful, a man with ambition. Not many men around here have ambition. Most of them are still making up tales about the Civil War. I hope we don't have much talk of that at the dinner tonight."

"Dinner?"

"Poppa didn't tell you about the dinner? He's invited some stockholders and legislators here tonight."

"He may have told me, but . . ." He looked down. "I've been busy with matters at the plant." He hugged himself and tried to smile. "He's not expecting me to attend, is he?"

"You must attend. Poppa wants to show off the mill. He said he needs you to answer any questions the stockholders may have." She squeezed his arm for emphasis.

He pulled away, still hugging himself.

"Then, if you'll excuse me, Amelia, I must prepare for this dinner."

He stepped into his office, closed the door, and exhaled. "Whew."

It was one thing to plan for meeting Amelia in his journal, but being near her felt awkward and, uncomfortable, and now there was this dinner.

Why can't I just work at the mill? I'm good at work. Now I have to go to this dinner and say nice things and do nice things among people I don't know, and the Colonel will want me to make a good impression even though I don't know what to wear or what to do.

I'd rather be fixing a spinning machine.

He appealed to Clarence for help. Among his new clothes, Webster had bought thick-soled boots to give him height. Clarence shined and brought a pair up from the kitchen and then laid out some striped pants and a white shirt with stickpins for buttons.

"Put them trousers on and wear that dark jacket in the closet. I got to get things fixed fo the dinner. You wear them clothes and put on that tie, and you will be just fine."

Webster managed the trousers and got into the shirt okay. Then he spent time combing his hair up and back. But when he tried the tie, he had problems. The color looked good, but the knot was awful.

He was going down the hallway to get Clarence's help when Amelia opened her door.

"Webster, you . . . Oh, my goodness! What did you do to that tie?"

"I don't know how to—"

"Here, let me."

Amelia began fussing with it. She was wearing a white formal gown with inlaid pearls and a silver necklace holding a pale blue gemstone that dangled just above her bosom. She was too close. Webster was looking at her bosom and worried over this new feeling stirring in him. He closed his eyes and took in her perfume.

"Webster? Pay attention."

He opened his eyes and noticed her lips. Strangely, he had this urge to kiss her, but then his old fears took hold of him. He wanted to run to the mill, where it was safe.

"There." Amelia stepped back and patted his chest. "You're a handsome man. Now, let's go win over Poppa's guests." She looped her arm in his, and they walked down the stairs.

"Miss Amelia, you look beautiful," Clarence said. "You and Mr. Webster is a handsome couple."

The Colonel stood near the front door and motioned for Webster to stand alongside Amelia at the foot of the stairs. Clarence was stationed near the Colonel, gathering coats and shawls as the first guests arrived. They were investors from the other side of the county.

Amelia was directing them into the piano room when there was a knock at the door. Clarence announced the arrival of Representative Lizenby Cathcart and his wife, Gladys.

As Clarence took Gladys's coat, she gave him a dismissive look and, over her shoulder, muttered, "Don't drag that on the floor."

The Colonel gestured for the couple to step into the foyer and then made introductions.

"Lizenby, I want you to meet Webster, the superintendent of my new mill. Webster, this is Representative Lizenby Cathcart. He lives in the area near our mill. And Liz, you and Gladys both know my daughter, Amelia."

Cathcart smiled and said, "Good evening, Amelia," but he didn't know what to make of Webster. More from an obligation of being polite than sincerity, he said, "Mr. Webster, it's a pleasure. This is my wife, Gladys."

Gladys looked down at Webster as if he were leprous—she never spoke, which paused the introductions a few uncomfortable beats. Her husband clumsily tried to break the silence but even then, the best he could come up with was a scornful, "You a Yankee, Mr. Webster?"

"He's no Yankee, Liz," interrupted the Colonel. "He's an Irishman but has lived in America most of his life. He knows his business. He was trained at one of the leading mills in Massachusetts."

"You don't say, Colonel—Irish?" Cathcart stared down at Webster. "One of those Europeans my family defeated during the Revolution. Who you gonna hire to work in this plant, Mr. Webster?"

"I intend to hire locally. That is, if a suitable source of operatives can be found."

"You're not hiring coloreds, are you?"

"We will be hiring white workers," the Colonel interjected. "If we hire coloreds, it will be for unloading and loading rail cars."

"Good," said Cathcart, still staring at Webster. "We need coloreds to work the fields."

Webster bristled at the slights. "Mr. Cathcart, I intend to hire whomever I deem suitable for this work, most likely women. They have the dexterity needed to handle fibers." He squinted and leaned toward Cathcart for emphasis.

Cathcart stepped back, irritated. Then, gazing down at Webster, he said, "Colonel, you need to let this little Irish Yankee know how we do business down here. We don't need nobody messing with our people, especially someone not from here."

"Now, now, Mr. Cathcart," Amelia cooed while stepping forward and taking his arm, "we've invited you here for a good time and good food. Let's not talk business tonight. You legislators take things so seriously." She led the Cathcarts into the dining room. "Come, Gladys. I'll introduce you to some of the ladies."

"I already know about these ladies." Gladys sniffed and, under her breath, observed, "There are some here I do not associate with."

The tension was interrupted when Clarence opened the door and loudly announced, "Senator Matthew Lawrence and his wife, Mrs. Lawrence."

The mood shifted. Deference to the senator and his wife bordered on homage to royalty, with comments of "Miss Nancy, how lovely you are this evening" and "Senator, your wife has dressed you well."

"You boys behave yourselves, now," the senator said. "This guy Crowell is going to industrialize our county, and we need to support him in it. And Lizenby, it looks like I showed up just in time. Are you trying to tell people how to run their business again? You must forgive Representative Cathcart, Colonel. He just got appointed chairman of the House Banking Committee and thinks he can tell people how to do things here. Lizenby, things are going to change in South Carolina; the old ways won't work anymore."

By dinner, the tension in the room created by Cathcart was forgotten, thanks to the senator. He initially deferred to the Colonel for introductions and announcements, only to seize the proceedings as if he were the host. He told tales, exaggerated for effect, that had the entire room roaring with laughter except for the Cathcarts. They just sat.

For Webster, the dinner was awful. The array of silverware was overwhelming. He didn't know what to do. The people were too polite. They smiled and asked him questions.

I'd rather be at the plant.

Amelia noticed. She cleared her throat to get his attention and then shook her head and motioned for him to remove the napkin he'd stuffed in his collar and place it on his lap.

Though the others were fixated on the senator, the signaling from Amelia to Webster didn't get past Gladys Cathcart. She had no interest in the senator's bombast anyway. She focused on Webster, compiling a list of his breaches in dining etiquette, which she periodically whispered to her husband.

Dinner ended with the men gathering in Webster's office for brandy and cigars. The Colonel had Webster unfurl his drawings of the plant and explain how each section would come together to comprise a five-thousand-spindle textile mill.

When he was done, the men were impressed, and so was the Colonel. Webster was comfortable talking about the mill, but general conversation, he didn't like.

After the guests left, the Colonel praised him. "Webster, you did real good. These folks are interested in manufacturing. They aren't like Dupre Merchant and his cronies."

"What about this Cathcart? Is he going to cause trouble?"

"He's a cotton farmer, and he just wants to make sure we don't take any of his field hands. His wife is Dupre Merchant's sister, and Lizenby owns some interest in the bank, but mainly he grows cotton. He is still upset that his grandfather lost almost all their land during the Civil War. They had a big place, but what he farms today is nothing like what his grandfather did."

"Do you men ever talk about anything other than business?" Amelia said as she walked in, and she kissed her daddy on the forehead.

"You made a big impression on the ladies tonight."

"Well, Daddy, now I want to play for Mr. Webster. He didn't get to hear me play."

"I, uh, would love to hear you play."

Amelia looped her arm inside Webster's and announced, "Daddy, I'm taking Mr. Webster to the piano room. You're welcome to come and join us."

"No, thank you, I've had enough. I'm going to bed."

At the piano, Webster complimented her playing but was uneasy being alone with her. The only women he'd been around were the ones at work.

Amelia began another number and then stopped. "Webster, we must find a way to get these people to like you. Southerners can be provincial."

"They're different from people I've known."

"Yes, they are. I've been thinking about how we could win them over. I think we need to start with the way you talk."

"What's wrong with the way I talk?"

"You talk like a Yankee. You talk fast and to the point. People around here don't trust people different from them, especially people from up north. There's still a lot of resentment about the Civil War."

"You mean like this Cathcart man?"

"Well, yes. Not as resentful as Mr. Cathcart, but still resentful. To win them over, let's work on the way you talk. Also, you looked uncomfortable at dinner tonight. What was the problem?"

Webster struggled to answer, afraid he'd say something wrong. Then he blurted out, "There were too many knives and forks. I didn't know which ones to use."

"You've never been to a formal dinner?"

"Once, on the ship when I came to America."

"And when was that?" she said as she stood and straightened her dress.

"About fourteen years ago."

"And you were how old?"

"Ten." Webster avoided her eyes.

"My goodness!" she said. "You were just a little boy." She placed her hand on his forearm. Webster carefully eased his arm free.

"I was traveling alone. My parents were rich." He looked at her from the corner of his eye to see if she believed him. "Then they died in a shipwreck, and I got sent to an orphanage. A cousin bought me a ticket on a ship from Ireland to Boston. That's how I came to America." Growing confident in his story, he smiled and looked at Amelia. Then he lied, saying that Sam Holden had sent him to college. When he finished, Amelia hugged him tightly. Webster stiffened.

"Does this make you uncomfortable?"

"I, uh . . ."

"Forgive me. I hug people I like and people who need a hug. I thought you needed a hug. And so, at dinner tonight, you were uncomfortable because you didn't know what to do? Is that why you ate so fast?"

"Well, yes."

"Was that the way you ate at the orphanage?"

"Yes, you had to eat quickly, or the food would run out."

"You poor baby." Amelia hugged him again. "Oh, I am sorry. I didn't mean to do that. It is okay, isn't it?"

"Well . . ." Webster stood stiffly. "I'm not comfortable with it."

"Okay," she said as she stepped away. "I see we have some work to do. You weren't having fun tonight because you didn't know what to do. We'll start working on that tomorrow at breakfast. Then we'll work on how you talk."

"I talk fine," Webster said.

"Not according to Southerners, and that's who we're trying to win over. You see, Webster . . I still don't like calling you Webster. What is your first name?"

"Please just call me Webster, Amelia. I prefer Webster."

"All right, Webster, we need to win over people like Gladys Cathcart because her cousin owns a bank. There may come a time when you and Daddy need a loan, and we don't need to be turned down because Gladys Cathcart doesn't like the way you talk."

She took his hand. "Now, it's late. We need to go to bed. Walk me to my room."

As they got to her door, she hugged Webster goodnight.

When he got to his room, Webster took a deep breath; it was over. He was confused, and he was mad with himself for feeling confused and he was sure as hell mad at those snobby Cathcarts for the way they treated him. He wondered if he'd made a mistake coming south. The people are strange with their *politeness* and *smiling* and their invasive *where did you grow up? who were your parents? and why did you choose to work for Colonel Crowell?* But what had him off balance were his feelings about Amelia. They were like the feelings he had when the nuns at the orphanage said they cared about him—just before they turned him away. Webster didn't trust feeling good about others. He only trusted feeling good about his work.

He removed his coat and sniffed. Amelia's perfume was on it. He smiled then frowned and tossed the jacket onto a chair. Looking out the window at the cotton mill, he fretted *why did I come here? Now I have to do things I don't like.* Getting people fired was easy, but this was different. If he was to get what he wanted he had to get someone to like him, and he didn't trust that because he didn't know how.

He made a note in his journal. *Make it about work.*

CHAPTER 17

MAKE YOU A SOUTHERNER

The next morning, Amelia called Webster to breakfast in the dining room.

"Even though we're having breakfast, I asked Clarence to set the table like it was a formal dinner. They taught us which knife and fork to use at the girls' school. I'll show you how to do it, so you won't be uncomfortable the next time we have dinner guests. First thing is to make sure any lady dining with you is seated before you sit. Now, come around here."

Amelia took Webster's hand and led him to her side of the table.

"Pull back my chair. As I sit, help me move forward to the table. Now, take your place. Just after you sit, take your napkin and lay it across your lap with the fold. See the fold I'm holding? Lay the fold in your lap against your belt. You never stuff the napkin in your collar. Look at your place setting. The bread, uh, toast, is on your left. Bread is always on your left, the meal is in the middle, and your tea, water, or wine is on the right."

"Last night, I didn't know which bread was mine."

"I saw you. You did fine. If ever you feel you don't know what to do, just smile, keep still, and do what the others do. In time, you won't need to, because I'm going to show you how to dine so you'll feel comfortable regardless of where you are. Webster, did you hear me?"

He was staring at the place setting. Amelia smiled, demonstrated the utensils, and got him to follow her examples.

After breakfast, he left to check on the mill. When he returned to his office, Amelia hurried in with some pencils and several sheets of paper and immediately began.

"Now we need to work on how you talk."

He pretended to smile. *I'd rather be at the mill.*

"I'll write out the pronunciation of the words, and you can keep these to practice on your own time. In South Carolina, we put the accent on the first syllable of a lot of words, especially nouns."

"Nouns?"

"The names of things and people and places. Now, here's a word that will show you what I mean."

She wrote, "McBee," and asked Webster to pronounce it.

"McBee."

"Not down here, it isn't," she said. "Down here, we pronounce it like this, MACK-bee. Try it."

"Mack-BEE."

"No, no, look at my lips. MACK-bee."

"MACK-bee."

"There you go. Here's another one. Look at my lips. MON-roe." Webster stared at her lips.

"Webster? Pay attention. MON-roe."

"Monroe."

"No. MON-roe! Look at my lips. MON-roe."

"MON-roe."

"There you go, MON-roe."

Over the Christmas holiday, the get-togethers expanded beyond pronunciation and dining lessons. Amelia spent time talking with Webster about his work at Holden Mill and shared her story.

"I was born here and grew up here. My brother, Wesley, was six years older. He and Momma died of scarlet fever about ten years ago. Daddy and I were lucky that we didn't get it. It was awful to watch them suffer."

"That must have been a very sad time for you."

"It was. They came down with it in the summer, and in a short while, they were gone. Momma was so worried I'd catch it that she made Daddy send me to a girls' school up in Virginia, and after that, he sent me to college at Converse.

"Momma died just after Wesley. She loved Wesley. She loved Daddy and me, too, but she loved Wesley. I was young when Momma died, and I needed to be so brave for Poppa. Oh, Webster, here I am crying. I can't help it. I know what it felt like for you to be alone in that orphanage. It reminded me of how alone I was when Momma died. I had no one to hug me. Webster, please hug me."

Webster felt that unease again. Standing very straight, he clumsily hugged Amelia and softly patted her back.

I don't like this. I'd rather be fixing something.

Amelia liked Webster because, like her, he had been wounded. She knew he was still formal and maybe didn't know how to be affectionate.

She delighted in asking him questions about the mill's operations, the people it would hire, and the economic and social impact on the area.

Webster liked it, too, because her questions were about work. He knew about work.

The happy experiences were short-lived. As Amelia's holiday neared its end, Webster's old fear of abandonment surfaced again. He stiffened when Amelia hugged him and kept most of their conversations to discussions about the mill and work. There was no more talk about feelings or her loneliness during her early years at the girls' school.

The day she left for the college Webster said his goodbyes shortly after breakfast. He walked to the mill to avoid seeing her leave.

The Colonel and house staff stood on the front steps of the mansion and waved as Clarence drove the tearful Amelia away.

Webster told himself he needed to focus on his work. He didn't like goodbyes.

CHAPTER 18

PRACTICE THE LIE

Amelia hadn't been gone long before Webster realized that if she were interested in someone else, he could end up an employee, with no chance of owning the mill. He was worrying over this when Clarence came into his office and handed him the afternoon mail. Included was a letter from Amelia.

"Shut the door, please, Clarence. I have important business correspondence, and I don't want to be disturbed."

Webster tore at the envelope, scanned each paragraph, and finally breathed; she'd sent more names to practice. He spread the other pages onto his desk and stood over them, looking for bad news. There was no mention of social events, classmates, or boys. It was about her classes. Webster slumped into his chair and then got mad at himself.

Damn it, now I'm worrying over a letter.

He tossed the sheets in a drawer and slammed it shut.

Courtship, shit! I'm going to the mill.

Up in Spartanburg, Amelia was struggling, too. She had a boyfriend, and it wasn't until the train ride back to school that she realized she hadn't thought of him while she was home. She went to her aunt for help sorting things out.

Beatrice F. Russell was married to a prominent banker in Spartanburg and well connected to upper society in the town. She'd developed a close relationship with Amelia and knew about the young man from the nearby men's college. Her aunt was her mother's sister and a graduate of the college Amelia attended.

She did what she could to discourage her niece's involvement with the boy. She felt he didn't come from a suitable background and certainly not from the proper family. Now she had an opening.

"So, sweetie, are you telling me your feelings for Jeffrey have changed?"

Amelia's eyes filled with tears. "I don't know what to think. Jeffrey is wonderful, and I love him, but he's dropped out of college and is working for the railroad now. I'm not sure, especially after meeting Webster. He's so smart and important. He is creating something good, a whole new way of life that will help lots of people, and he's handsome and listens. Oh, Aunt Bea, what am I to do?" she sobbed.

"C'mere." Beatrice hugged Amelia as she cried. "Well, if this Webster caused you to doubt your feelings toward that other boy, then maybe you need time to figure out what you want. You know, free of emotional entanglements."

When Amelia returned to her dorm, she wrote her young man a painful letter, telling him she was thinking about their relationship and had found their lives and interests were taking different paths, particularly since he'd dropped out of college. She hoped he'd understand she'd always remember the love they had, but she needed time to herself to decide what she wanted to do with her life.

She cried for two days and then stopped when she received a letter from Webster. She was unaware that he was also in a fret. He was having to do something he'd never done—court a woman.

Well, he needed to give her the impression he was courting her. For now, that would be easy—all he needed to do was answer her letters.

When she came home from college, now that would be a challenge. He would need to show her he cared for her and even be affectionate—and he didn't like affection and didn't trust caring.

Wait a moment. It doesn't matter if I love her, just that she loves me. He decided if he couldn't convince himself to love her, maybe he could teach himself to pretend he did.

Sitting at the table in his bedroom, he opened his notebook and began outlining a plan. He was certain she wanted to be a teacher and listed it as a topic in his notebook. Next to that, he added a reminder: "Buy textbook on organizing an elementary classroom."

He also guessed, since she wanted to help her father gain acceptance among the old families in the town, it would be important for him to continue practicing dining etiquette and the pronunciation guides. He would also resurrect his childhood tale that he was from a rich family and attended college in Massachusetts. That would be easy.

Next, he commenced the most uncomfortable part—the courtship.

He placed a pillow in the chair across the table and pretended it was her.

"Amelia, I am so proud of what you have accomplished. Here you've been away, on your own for many years, and look at what you have done. While I attended college, you have graduated. Why, most folks these days barely finish high school. And now you are coming home to take your place beside your father and me, transforming this area into a thriving, modern community." He held a corner of the pillow as if it were her hand. "Amelia, you are beautiful. You're the prettiest . . . Shit! I hate this!"

CHAPTER 19

A Hog Wallow

Vernon came in from magistrate's court, laughing as he made his way around the counter to his desk. Arthur came out of his office, headed for home, and Betsy told a caller, "Can I call you back in just a few minutes? Someone is at the front door, and we have just closed for the day." As soon as she put the phone down, Vernon said, "You won't believe what happened. This crippled guy gets hauled before the magistrate for stealing chickens."

Arthur grinned. "One-legged John the Baptist."

"You know him?"

"I don't know him, but I know *of* him. One-legged John the Baptist is a legend around town. So, they caught him again."

"Yeah, he got thirty days for his third offense, suspended if he promised to stop stealing chickens."

"One-legged John the Baptist?" asked Betsy.

"His name is Cecil Tanner," said Arthur, "but he tells folks he's One-legged John the Baptist. A train cut Cecil's leg off one night when he fell down drunk right next to the tracks. If he hadn't been near the AA club, he would have bled to death. A war veteran heard him hollerin' and ran out the clubhouse and used a belt as a tourniquet. The blood loss must have affected Cecil's brain, 'cause sometime after that, Cecil had a vision that the Lord had told him to go find Jesus and baptize him again. The town looks after Cecil. He's harmless, really, unless he hears the Lord tell him to feed his people. Cecil doesn't have fishes and loaves, so he steals a chicken. Usually, he gets caught in the act, and the chicken isn't harmed."

"And the town lets him do it?"

"Yeah, folks here know he's not right in the head, so they look after him."

"He's damn lucky he wasn't in Haigler's Crossing, 'cause those sons a bitches down there would run him out of town," Vernon said. "Hell, they ran me off. They run off anybody they don't approve of."

"I've already heard this one," Arthur said. "Y'all lock up. I'm going home."

Betsy and Vernon waited until they saw Arthur's car drive past the office. Then Vernon said, "Lock the door and get the bottle. I got the cups." Moments later, he poured a big drink, gulped it down, and with a "Whew, oh, yeah," began his tale.

"They ran off a blacksmith down there because he was a German Yankee. It got started when Dupre Merchant's board of directors were meeting to review the bank's activities of the previous month. Their manager, Tom Murphy, finished his report and noted the board needed to act on a foreclosure and had a couple of loans to approve."

*   *   *

Dupre looked at Murphy and asked, "Now, this Rainwater man. He's missed payments?"

"Yes, sir. I've been out to his house several times. He's got four mules. We could take two of them, sell them, and use the proceeds to cover his loan."

"Tell him I said for you to take three of his mules," Dupre grumbled. "We need to make an example of him. Otherwise, folks will think they won't have to pay us back. I worried about this loan, but you boys talked me into it. I should have turned it down. Now we got to find a buyer for three mules." *Damn these men. I knew better than to listen to them,* he thought. *The only reason they're on the board is because my daddy put their fathers on it.*

The meeting took up more loan applications and was interrupted when one of the tellers from downstairs knocked on their door. Tom Murphy barely cracked it open, and the teller whispered, "Mr. Murphy, Mr. Pegues is out here. He wants to speak to Mr. Merchant and the others."

"Tell him I said to go 'round back," said Dupre, and then he resumed the meeting.

A few minutes later, Henry Pegues was out of breath from the steep climb when he heard Dupre order Tom Murphy to open the door.

"What do you want, Henry?" Dupre barked.

"Uh, Mr. Merchant, that German has unloaded three hogs into the pen next to my back yard. They've trampled the grass into a muddy pit, and the smell is so bad we can't open the windows at the house."

A man at the far end of the table shifted in his chair and asked, "Who did this?"

"That German that moved here from Pennsylvania. He's gone to work as a blacksmith in back of Shumpert's store. You men have to do something. He's going to stink up the whole town once them sows start droppin' piglets. And that won't be long, either, 'cause that boar hog is already humpin' both of them sows almost day and night."

The men laughed.

Henry Pegues ran the local grocery in a building rented from Dupre. He reeked of tobacco, and his hands stunk of the mackerel he'd wrapped for a customer before coming to the bank. He was skinny, having smoked himself down to an emaciated state.

"Whew, how 'bout stepping back a bit," one of the men said. "You selling fish now?"

"Mackerel, salted mackerel. Sorry 'bout that."

The men laughed, and Henry stepped away from the table. He didn't think it was funny.

"Mr. Merchant, we don't need some Yankee coming in and making our town nasty. Please do something. We have to keep the windows shut, and our girls can't play in the back yard because that big Duroc is all the time a-humpin'. And those sows? They squeelin' like they're enjoyin' it."

There was more laughter, but Dupre didn't smile. He scowled at the table, looked up, and gave the others a hard glance. "Ever since Sherman, it seems like some Yankees have been trying to mess up our community. We don't need this, especially from some immigrant German."

Dupre asked Henry, "Did Shumpert rent him the house?"

"No, sir. That house belongs to Gedney Crowell. Remember, he took it away from Mrs. Hurt for back taxes."

"Crowell, that figures," said one of the men at the table. Phony colonel. He thinks he's as good as us."

"Mr. Merchant," Henry pleaded as he tapped the table to get the men to stop laughing, "y'all do something about them hogs, please. This summer heat is fierce, and we can't open the windows because of the smell gettin' in our clothes and even our beds."

Dupre never looked up. He dismissed Pegues with a terse, "Henry, I've heard enough. I'll handle this. I'll talk with Shumpert about this German Yankee, and I will talk to Gedney Crowell, too. It's time for you to leave. Go out the back way."

"Dupre," one of the men at the table said, "the village Gedney is building is in our county, but the plant itself is in the county next door."

"That son of a bitch. He must have hoodooed investors over there into giving him money.

"Crowell brought in a Yankee Irishman to build his plant. We got a German and now an Irishman living here. There'll be more of them moving in unless we stop this."

CHAPTER 20

Fixin' a Problem

Dupre Merchant had one thing on his mind—that German Yankee. At around ten o'clock in the morning, he walked out of his office. He was accustomed to getting his way through control of the money in the town or by sheer physical presence. When he was on the street, others knew where he was and noted where he was headed. This day, they saw him going towards Shumpert's Hardware.

David Shumpert was a fidgety, suspicious man, always worrying someone was trying to take advantage of him. Once a week, he argued with tellers about his bank balance and questioned every charge they applied to his account, even when it was just a penny or two.

He was so skittish of people trying to steal from him that he set things up, so customers had to dodge their way around a gauntlet of barbed-wire coils, chicken fence, and thick wooden posts inside his store. Things easily grabbed, like ax handles, rakes, and hoes, he kept in barrels at the back. Small things, like hammers, screwdrivers, and files, were locked in a closed display case at the counter, which also held his cash register. The place smelled of fertilizer, floor oil, and metal.

When Dupre eased around the wire and ducked the pots and pans hanging from the ceiling, he found Shumpert scooping nails out a keg and dumping them into one of the metal bins along the wall back of his counter. Because of the noise, Shumpert didn't hear Dupre come in, so Dupre cleared his throat and loudly announced, "Shumpert, I need to talk to you."

"What? Oh, hello, Mr. Merchant," Shumpert said as he turned and jammed the scoop into the keg. He smiled and wiped his hands on his apron. "How can I help you?"

The smile fell when Dupre gave him a serious look and said, "You and I need to talk about that German you got working out back."

"What's wrong with him?"

"First of all, he's stinking up the town with those hogs he's got. Secondly, he's a Yankee, a German Yankee. We don't need no Yankees living and working here after what they did to our town. You need to get rid of him."

"Get rid of him?"

"Yes, get rid of him."

"That German out back repairs plows and makes farm tools for folks around here. He even repairs equipment that your people bring in here, and you're tellin' me to get rid of him? Who do you think you are?"

"I said, get rid of him."

"You can't tell me what to do. That man's a good worker."

"Get rid of him."

"You may run this town, but you don't run my store. You can go to hell. Get out and don't ever come back!" Shumpert turned his back to Dupre and resumed scooping nails.

Dupre didn't like Shumpert partly because he was not native to the town. He had moved in from another county two years earlier and was just beginning to establish himself in the feed and hardware business. The main reason Dupre didn't like him, though, was because Shumpert's store competed with his own hardware store, run by Dupre's cousin.

"Son of a bitch," Dupre said to himself as he walked out. He didn't like being told no. "I'll fix him," he mumbled as he walked across the street. He stopped by the office of one of his moneyed compatriots before leaving for Gedney Crowell's place. The man was busy reviewing a financial ledger when Dupre walked in. "Walker, you own that building Shumpert is using?"

"Yeah. Is there something wrong with it?"

"Tell Shumpert to get rid of that German."

"Why, because of those hogs?"

"Well, that, but mainly because we don't need any Germans, Yankee Germans in our town. If he stays, more of 'em will want to come here. So, tell Shumpert to get rid of him."

"And if he doesn't?"

"Go up on his rent."

"Do what?"

"Go up on his rent."

"Dupre, I don't have anyone to replace him if he quits on me. You can't do this. I'll lose money."

"Go up on his rent."

"What if I don't?"

"Then I'll buy that note on your cotton crop, and you'll owe me instead of the bank. Don't mess with me, Walker. Go up on his rent."

"Dupre, you can't do this. I'm tellin' the others."

The two men stared at each other for a long minute. Finally, Dupre turned to walk out of the office. Before he left, he looked at Walker and said, "You do, and I'll call your note. I'm tellin' you, go up on his rent."

Walker knew he had no choice. He'd grown up with Dupre, and despite owning property and working sharecroppers himself, his wealth was nothing compared to what Dupre had inherited and then married into. And certainly, in this case, Walker had to comply with Dupre's demand. Dupre held the majority shares in the bank and could outvote the others combined, and he used that leverage to force most of the businessmen in town to do what he wanted.

When Dupre got to the Colonel's place, he was still upset over Shumpert's yelling and Walker's reluctance. He expected to get the same resistance from the Colonel, but the Colonel surprised him. "I'll get him to move the hogs," he said. "He's got enough land that he won't need to put them on the town side of the property. I think he put them out back to be in the shade."

The Colonel led Dupre into Webster's office. "Dupre, this is Lemuel Webster, the man who is building my mill."

Dupre smirked and thought, *My God, he's a small boy*, as he shook Webster's hand.

"Uh, let's all sit," the Colonel suggested. "Lemuel comes to us from Lowell, Massachusetts. He's worked in textiles over fifteen years and was superintendent of a plant up there."

"I thought he was from Ireland?"

"Originally, but I came to America after my parents died in a shipwreck," Webster lied, "and I have been here ever since."

As they talked briefly about the cotton mill, Dupre fidgeted, ready to get this over with. Webster showed him drawings of the plant and pointed to the construction site from the bay window of his office.

Dupre was rather curt when he stopped the presentation, saying he had to return to town to take care of some important matter. He rode back to town, irritated by the Colonel's pleasant willingness to take care of the hog problem. He was also upset that Southern custom had forced him to be nice to this *boy*. *We got to do something about that mill,* he thought. *But first, I need to fix this German problem.*

A few weeks later, David Shumpert's rent went up at his hardware store, and then, with no notice or explanation, the town's garbage service mysteriously stopped hauling away the trash from his business.

As the refuse piled up, Main Street merchants began advising their customers to avoid Shumpert's store because it was dirty, and a Yankee foreigner worked there. Shumpert began losing money. He complained to the mayor about the trash, only to be told that the pickup had stopped because he owed money on his business license.

Shumpert was certain he didn't. He ran back to his store and pulled up his business license receipt, and it was marked paid. When he showed it to the town clerk, she pulled up a notice of a new license fee showing his fee had been increased by a hundred dollars and payment was three months in arrears. She pointed out that interest charges were being applied, making the bill even higher.

Shumpert was yelling so loudly the sheriff came into the clerk's office. "What's the matter here?"

"They went up on my business license. She says I'm three months in arrears. That can't be. I always pay my bills, everything, on time."

The clerk showed the sheriff the notice. "See, he's three months behind. We mailed him the notice at the end of June.

"June? I never got your notice."

"We mailed it in June, Mr. Shumpert. You never paid it for three months, and then the town council voted last month to hold your trash pickup until you came in and paid your bill."

"I never got your bill. I paid my license fee right on time earlier this year. Now you are telling me I owe you a hundred dollars more?"

"Actually, you owe a hundred twenty-five dollars more because of the late fee."

"Why did it go up?"

"Because you added that blacksmith shop to your store."

"Nobody told me about that. I'm not paying this. I never received the notice."

"If you don't pay it, then we'll close you down," the sheriff warned.

Shumpert stomped out of the city hall, yelling, "It's about that German, isn't it? This town is run by crooks!"

Several days later, he fired the German and told him he needed to move to another town. Then he appeared at the town council meeting to appeal his business license fee.

"Everybody in town knows I pay my bills on time," he told the council. "I never got the notice the town was going up on it. Had I known, I would have paid it. However, since then, I got rid of that German and have closed down my blacksmith shop, so now I don't believe I should have to pay that fee."

After hearing from the town clerk that her office had mailed the notice back in June and Shumpert's red-faced denial that he'd never received it, the mayor intervened. "Gentlemen, I have a compromise that might satisfy everyone. First, we waive the twenty-five-dollar late fee. Then, since Mr. Shumpert operated the blacksmith shop for only three months, we reduce the original business license fee by seventy-five percent. Mr. Shumpert, if that is agreeable with you, you will only owe the town twenty-five dollars."

Shumpert said he still thought it was unfair, but he agreed to pay.

His business declined so much he had to close later that year because people stopped buying from him. After selling what was left of his inventory to Dupre Merchant's cousin, he moved away, still complaining the town had wronged him.

When Shumpert left town, Dupre Merchant beamed proudly as he walked into the town clerk's office. "Deloris, I have something for you. Thank you for handling Shumpert's business license matter for me." He handed her a box of candy with a twenty-dollar bill taped to the bottom of it.

"It was easy, Mr. Merchant. Thanks for the gift. Anytime you need me, I'll be glad to help."

To show his appreciation to Walker and further demonstrate his power to run things, Dupre got the bank to reduce what Walker owed the bank on his cotton crop by a thousand dollars. He told Walker it was a gift and should cover the loss of rent from Shumpert until Walker could find a new tenant for his building.

Henry Pegues gave Dupre a jug of bootleg whiskey and a pecan pie his wife had baked as a thank you for fixing the hog problem. Dupre was pleased. It was his town, and he was protecting it. Now all he had to do was fix things so cotton mills couldn't take away his sharecroppers. He didn't like cotton mills. Cotton mills were manufacturing, and manufacturing was what Yankees did.

*   *   *

"So, Vernon, this Dupre Merchant opposed the mill?" Betsy said.

"Very much so, especially when he saw what came to work there."

CHAPTER 21

HAFTA HIRE WHITE TRASH

When construction of Crowell Textile Mill was completed, there were complaints about the people coming to work at it. Just down the road from the mill, a meeting of the United Daughters of the Confederacy got underway. Dupre Merchant's wife made certain her remarks about the mill workers included the terms "unsanitary" and "linthead." She convinced her husband to get a law passed requiring workers to have physical exams to show they were free of communicable diseases before they could work in cotton mills. She hoped the law could be used to shut down the mill and force its workers to move away.

Dupre put the word out that he wanted no one from town working at the place. He'd foreclose on those who did and cut them off from any loans they might need in the future. Because of this, the Colonel was forced to hire recruiters to scour the countryside for anybody willing to work. He got upset when he saw what they had brought him.

"This was the best you could do? I gave you money, and you got these nasty hicks!"

"Sir, nobody from town wants to work in the mill. I found these people camped out in the country. They were all I could find."

The people, who had ridden up in wagons, stared at the Colonel. They were filthy. When the recruiter had come upon them, they'd been crawling out of dirt-floored shacks, squatting illegally in the woods.

They had no idea what manufacturing was and didn't care. What interested them was a chance to live in a real house with real floors and a good roof, and they were willing to do whatever this manufacturing thing was to get it.

They were ignorant and uneducated, lacked the basic skills of personal hygiene, and owned only the clothes they wore.

"You go back and get me better people!"

"Sir, I'll look for more, but I doubt they'll be any better than these."

A man sitting in the lead wagon—an old man wearing one shoe—snapped the reins, said, "Git up," and started his wagon out of the line in a slow turn back toward town.

He looked at his wife and said loud enough for everyone to hear, "Ain't nobody gonna talk 'bout me like that to my face. I'd rather starve. We goin' back to camp."

The Colonel told his bookkeeper to take the remaining families to the office. "Get their names on the books."

"We goin' get a house?" a woman asked.

"Yes, but go with Mr. Pringle here. He'll tell you what to do."

My God, what have I gotten into?

A few days later, another wagon with women and nasty children rode into town. People stared and mumbled.

Someone told a boy in the street, "Go get Mr. Dupre quick."

Moments later, Dupre Merchant ran out of his bank. He hitched up his suspenders, and waved his arms, and jumped in front of the wagon, hollering loud enough for the whole town to hear, "Where the hell you going?"

"To the mill. They is a mill around here, ain't it?"

"Go down that road over yonder. We don't want you in our town."

He walked to the courthouse and yelled to Tumpy Hendley, "Do something about this. They're making our town nasty."

Tumpy told him the millhands weren't breaking any laws. "They're on public streets. I'll go see the Colonel and get him to do something."

Back at his bank, Dupre complained to his cronies, "I knew this would happen. This mill is attracting the worst people. I don't want them coming in and messing up our town. Hell, our coloreds live better than these hicks."

Not only was the mill drawing undesirables, but the noise destroyed the peace of a community accustomed to quiet. The first morning the plant operated, it felt like some evil giant was roaring threats at the place. Above the window-shaking rumbling was a tone like an organ key stuck on G flat. You could hear it clear down to the eastern end of the river. It was incessant, stopping only when the plant shut down at the end of the day.

Some of the new employees were so terrified of the shaking and noise that they ran outside to get away. Their supervisors chased after them, yelling, "Come back, come back! It's safe!"

Willie Mae Timmons ran out, crying, "Please, mister, don't make me go back in there. They's devils in that place."

"It's a cotton mill," replied the supervisor. "There are no devils in there. Come back inside. I'll stay with you."

Staring in wild-eyed fear, Willie Mae sucked on a rag she twisted with her hands. Her supervisor tried gentle sweet-talk, but he lost his patience when she mumbled, "No, no, noo," and kept sucking and twisting.

"Dammit, woman, if you don't go back, you'll have to leave."

Willie Mae stared at the ground and sucked and twisted her rag.

Another woman who'd run out with her gently took her hand. "It's okay, hun. C'mon. I was scared, too, but we got to go back and learn our jobs. I'll stand next to you. We'll be alright."

The supervisor lost his patience. "I'll give you five minutes to come back. After that, I'm shuttin' the door, and you'll both be fired."

Willie Mae ran farther away, sucking on the rag and moaning, "No, no, noo!"

That evening, as her things were piled on the street, she told others she'd seen the devil inside the mill. "And when I wouldn't sell him my soul, he thowed me back to Jesus, praise the Lord."

Like Willie Mae, the others had come from farms where they'd worked outdoors at their own pace, taken breaks when they got tired, and stopped when the task was done, or the weather turned bad.

Now they were stuck inside ten to twelve hours a day, standing on shaking floors amid low lighting and humid temperatures, inhaling cotton lint. The place was alive with movement and noise so loud that yelling and hand signals were necessary—normal conversations were impossible.

The Colonel realized the emotional challenges these workers were going through; he, too, was shocked by the noise and heat. He told his supervisors to go easy but remind the workers they had access to food and were living in houses better than anything they'd had before and that working for the mill made that possible.

Webster had no empathy for them. The only thing he cared about was making them do what he wanted, and he had ways.

To live in mill houses rent-free, he required at least two people per household work in the plant. Widows with children could live there, provided the widow and at least one child worked in the factory. A boarding house was built for single women, and a schoolhouse was under construction, which Amelia would use to teach mill children once she finished college later in the year.

Webster convinced the Colonel to pay employees in scrip; mill money, he called it. Since merchants in town wouldn't take scrip, his workers would never need to leave the village. They'd get everything they needed from the company store on credit and . . . be indebted to the store and the mill.

Webster was happy. He could run the place like the orphanage, telling people when to get up, when to eat, when to go to work, and when to go to bed. But that wasn't enough. He wanted the mill. But to get it, dammit, he had to do something he was not good at, court a woman.

Back in his room, he kept practicing his pretending.

CHAPTER 22

MILDRED TURNAGE

It had been a couple of weeks since Vernon had told his story about the German Yankee, and Betsy was eager to hear about her aunt. They closed up the newspaper one evening and walked down to Jimmy Theopolis's restaurant. They sat again in a corner booth near the front door.

After dinner, Jimmy Theopolis poured them coffee and asked, "You want some sweetener?"

"Sure," Vernon said. "Leave the bottle."

As Jimmy walked away, Betsy said, "You were going to tell me about my aunt Mildred?"

"Yeah, Mildred came to work at the mill when they were first hiring. I talked with her during the strike. She was one strong-willed woman. The workers really looked up to her. She was tough, didn't take nothing off nobody. That came from what happened to her when she was about your age."

*   *   *

Mildred was a sharecropper's daughter. She managed to get an education despite growing up hard. Early in her life, though, she made the mistake of marrying a drunk. They were living in Union County, North Carolina, near Monroe.

Her husband, Jimmy Earl, went out with his drinking buddies one night, and when he got home, Mildred confronted him about it. She shouldn't have. Jimmy Earl cussed her out and grabbed his razor strap. She ran out of the house, and he stumbled onto the back porch after her, screaming, "Come back here!"

Mildred squatted and duck-walked to hide in the cotton field. Afraid he could hear her gasps, she knelt so close to the ground that she could see her breath blow sand away.

Keep quiet, she thought, panting. *Keep quiet! Damn it, don't breathe so much.*

Jimmy Earl yelled, "You don't love me!" Then he fell off the porch and passed out.

After waiting for about half an hour, Mildred eased back to the house, closed the windows, slid her dresser across the bedroom door, and went to sleep.

The next morning, Jimmy Earl pleaded, "I'm sorry. I'll never do it again." But Mildred kept him locked out and watched as he staggered down the road. It was Sunday.

She didn't see him stumble into the church down from the house. He was shaking and sweating and needed a drink. Crying and wailing from alcohol withdrawal, he asked the surprised congregants for forgiveness of his sins and gave his life to the Lord. He swore to God he would change.

The whole church came forward and laid hands on him as the preacher prayed, "Oh, Lord, save this sinner from the devil's drink. He's confessed and repented. Make him whole again." When they returned to their seats, Jimmy Earl staggered onto a back pew, and as he wiped dirt and tears from his face, he softly moaned, "Oh, Lord, help me. Help me."

After the service, men patted his shoulder as they filed out.

When he got home, Mildred was churning butter on the back porch. He shouted, "Sweetheart? Sweetheart, where are you?"

She didn't answer. She was sweating and flicking away gnats. Her arms and hands ached as she clunked the plunger. Jimmy Earl walked around, smiling at her.

"Here, hun, let me do it."

Mildred looked away, and Jimmy Earl moved around to face her. She turned again.

Jimmy Earl fell to his knees. "Mildred, I'm sorry. I've repented. I got saved at church. I'm born again. I promise I'll never take another drink."

She kept pumping and said nothing. Too often, he'd promised to do better only to start drinking again and chasing her out of the house. She didn't speak to him for the rest of the day.

As the weeks passed, Jimmy Earl didn't drink and was helpful and devoted to her. One morning, he came in from the field as she was preparing for laundry. He took the bucket, said, "Here, hun, let me do it," and pumped water to fill her washpots. Another time, he picked wildflowers and brought them home one evening in a bouquet.

But this re-courtship didn't last long. Jimmy Earl carried his body, mind, and soul deep into this newfound salvation. There he remained and mutated from an angry, alcoholic, abusive man into a book-worshiping, fundamentalist, angry, abusive man. This would have been harmless had he confined his faith to himself, but his new religion declared he *must* bring others to the Lord. As bad as he was as a drunk, he was even worse "born again."

Jimmy Earl believed God was in charge of everything and it was God who decided when the sun would shine, rain fell, babies were born, and people died. He believed bad things happened because people did things that displeased God or didn't believe exactly the way God required. He read that in the Bible and was certain of it because he'd been bad himself and had changed. He felt others should believe exactly as he did, especially his wife, and Jimmy Earl, in his normal abusive way, insisted she must.

He began complaining that her faith wasn't good enough. This was obvious to him when their first baby was born dead. It wouldn't have happened, he told her, if she'd believed as the Bible said. They fought over religion and their baby's death one long night, with Mildred yelling through tears and sobs, "I didn't kill my baby, Jimmy Earl Turnage! I'm a good woman!"

Mildred slept on the back porch for a week and told herself not to speak to him until he apologized. He never did. Jimmy Earl thought he was right.

The women at the church learned of the marital strain and began working hard on Mildred to take her husband back. They told her what she was doing wasn't Bible-like. She was supposed to be with her man, and Jimmy Earl was a good, godly Christian man who was now saved. They never let up. After weeks of pressure, Mildred decided to try it their way just to get them to shut up. She answered the altar call and pretended. There was a big celebration over it.

Mildred tried hard to be religious. Her days were filled with God. There was morning prayer, noontime prayer, afternoon prayer, night-time Bible reading, and more prayer. She tried to "let God be in charge," but she still couldn't understand why she couldn't get over her baby. It wasn't her fault. Why did God let her baby die?

"It's your faith," Jimmy Earl said. "If you believed exactly the way God wants you to believe, you wouldn't question what He has done."

Mildred's friends told her it was all a part of God's great plan, and when she asked what that was, they couldn't explain it, so they told her it was a mystery beyond what any human could understand.

As she continued to think on this, she wondered if God was punishing her for some sin her parents or grandparents had committed. The Bible said God punished others for the sins of their fathers, their fathers' fathers, or even their fathers' fathers' fathers.

Jimmy Earl told her that might be the reason. Maybe it *was* something Mildred's family had done, *certainly not his.* The Bible talked about God blaming whole families, so it *must be hers,* because everything in the Bible is true.

Jimmy Earl didn't like it when Mildred challenged him about that.

"Then why was it," she asked him, "that a book written by men and talks about men mainly blames what happened to men on women? See here? In Genesis, God asked Adam why he ate the fruit, and Adam said, 'That woman made me do it.' That ain't right, Jimmy Earl."

"Mildred, you don't question the Bible, because it's what God said. And according to His Word, men is to be in charge."

"Well, what about them men who ain't worth a shit? Is they supposed to be in charge?"

Jimmy Earl jumped to his feet. "Don't you blaspheme. The Bible says men is in charge, and . . ." He punched his chest. "In this house, I . . . am the head of it."

When Mildred became pregnant the second time, she felt she'd finally figured out the exactly exact, precise way God wanted her to believe, and He was blessing her for it. She read and prayed and read and prayed in blissful certainty.

Then she miscarried.

Jimmy Earl blamed her, "I told you your faith wasn't good enough. If it had been, this wouldn't have happened."

Mildred spent weeks in guilt, often crying while standing over the crib for a baby that almost was. If God was in charge and knew everything, then maybe He had found another something to fault her for that she wasn't aware of. Perhaps it was because she couldn't figure out how to believe precisely as He demanded, and He was teaching her a lesson.

That *must* have been it because God sent her a new pestilence: Jimmy Earl got sick with the flu then pneumonia.

Despite all Mildred did to make him comfortable, he screamed at her from his sweaty bed, "God is punishing me because I married such an unbelieving woman!" *Cough, cough.* "If your faith was better, I wouldn't be. . . Oh, Lord, help me! This hurts!"

The yelling got worse as the fever burned at his sanity. Four days later, Jimmy Earl Turnage, dehydrated and weak, lost consciousness and died.

For the first time in months, there was quiet. Mildred could hear the chickens softly clucking beneath her house. Emotionally exhausted, she quit trying to decode the enigmatic God of the Bible. *If He was in charge of everything—I really, really tried to do what Your Word said—then why did my babies die? And if Jimmy Earl got sober and was born again and doing everything the Bible told him, why was he still such an abusive shit?*

Mildred stopped going to church, stopped praying, stopped reading the Bible, and stopped talking about God every moment of the day. Once Jimmy Earl was buried and done with, she got mad. She walked out into the field one night and told God she wasn't so sure He really existed, but if He did, He sure was doing a lousy job. Besides, she'd tried his way, and her life was miserable. She told him she wouldn't bother Him anymore and for Him to "Goddammit, leave me alone!"

CHAPTER 23

AMELIA GRADUATES

"While your aunt Mildred struggled against these challenges," Vernon continued, "little Lemuel was plotting and scheming to get control of the mill."

"You mean Amelia?"

"Yeah. Webster was busy fitting the plant with equipment and missed seeing Clarence and the Colonel leave. When they returned a couple of days later, they had a wagonload of books, paintings, clothing, and Amelia. She'd graduated from college."

*   *   *

Unaware she was back, Webster was in the spinning room, talking with a mechanic, when the big door slid open, and there was Amelia, beaming.

Oh, no, not in front of the others, he thought and walked towards her, wiping his hands on a rag.

"Oh, Webster, I've missed you," she said and tried to hug him.

He stepped back and extended his hand with the rag in it. Embarrassed, he flung the rag aside and shook Amelia's hand as if greeting a man. Then he looked about. The workers were smiling at him.

"Let's go outside!" he shouted. "It's too noisy in here!"

As the door was closing, employees saw her hugging him.

"Oh, I have missed you."

"Uh, not here. Let's go up to my office at the house."

As they climbed toward the mansion, he didn't hear a word she said. "And Poppa told me what you were doing. He's so proud of you, Webster, and now we can be together, and you can help me with the school, and I can help you with your words and . . ."

Good lord, I can't think.

When they reached his office, she hugged him again. "Oh, I'm sorry, but it's just that I have missed you."

Webster took a deep breath, softly clasped her hands, and recited, "Amelia, I am so proud of what you have done, uh, accomplished. You've been away on your own for many years, and look at what you've done. While I attended college, you've graduated. Why, most folks these days barely finish high school, and you are amazing, and pretty, and you are beautiful pretty." He took another deep breath.

She was delighted. How thoughtful of him to memorize such compliments.

"And you are an amazing man. I'm so happy to be home." She hugged him again. "Oh, I'm sorry. I can't help myself," she said, beaming.

Webster stood stiffly. "Please excuse me, Amelia. I must make an important phone call in private. Please close the door behind you."

After she left, he exhaled. "Whew!" *In front of the workers?*

That night, he sat in a chair and held the pillow on his knee.

I can do this. It's important.

"Amelia, you are special. You are so talented and will be a wonderful teacher and help the children."

What else can I say? I don't like this. But I must do it.

He made a note in his journal.

After dinner each night, he went to the piano room to hear Amelia play, which was good because there was no hand-holding. When they weren't doing that, they were in the office, practicing his words. Each night, when he went to his room, he practiced holding and hugging the pillow.

Relax. It's getting better.

When Webster learned the Colonel had planned a dinner to celebrate Amelia's graduation, he left his office, closed his bedroom door, and sat at the table, practicing dining. He went through the routine several times, even rehearsing comments to guests. By the time he was dressed, the guests had arrived, and he rushed down, eased into line, and took a seat across from Amelia.

Just smile and pretend. See, she's smiling back.

The guests included friends of Amelia's late mother and some mill stockholders.

During dinner, there were animated talks and laughter about children attending college, which suddenly stopped when a lady asked Webster if he'd attended college.

Webster was smooth. "I wish I graduated from Lowell Technical Institute, but there were just too many duties when I was promoted to superintendent of Holden Mill. It was good training, though."

The Colonel joined in. "He comes from a good stock of Irish parents. It was a shame they were killed in a shipwreck, but Webster didn't let that hold him back. He's accomplished a great deal for someone so young. I hired him because of that."

The guests applauded when Webster announced he had a graduation gift for Amelia. She squealed as she unwrapped it. It was a textbook entitled *Organization and Functions of an Elementary School Classroom.*

As everyone congratulated Amelia, one of the guests asked her, "You are going to become a teacher at our school in town, aren't you?"

"No, I'm going to be teaching the children in the mill school Daddy and Webster are building." There was silence, cold, icy silence. Someone coughed.

Finally, a lady said, "Oh, we thought you were going to be teaching our children."

"The mill children need me. I'll be helping them. It will be good for the whole community."

The guests were shocked. After several moments of napkins pressed to lips and coughing, the talk shifted to the weather and the cotton crop. As soon as the group had finished eating, one couple stood, congratulated Amelia, and said that they had enjoyed the meal but now they needed to rush home to check on some livestock.

That was all the others needed. Couples stood in ripples amid comments about closing a gate or checking on their housekeeper's sick child.

When they left, the whispers among them became mumblings and, farther down the drive, loud talk. Southern etiquette required folks to be polite at dinner. Now there were no constraints.

The gossip crackled and snapped.

"How awful!"

"She went to college for that?"

"If Adriana Fitzpatrick had known her daughter would be spending days around dirty mill children, she'd have been mortified."

Inside the mansion, the Colonel observed, "They sure cleared out in a hurry."

Amelia nodded and then looked at Webster and said, "Let's go to your office. We need to work on your pronunciations."

As he sat at his desk, Webster asked, "Why do these people dislike your father?"

"They don't dislike Poppa. They were Momma's friends, and Poppa's, too."

"Yes, but those over in town, why do they dislike him so?"

"Well, there was that time when Poppa was the tax collector. Some folks didn't like him for that. But you'd expect that. I think the main reason was because of Granddaddy. Momma told me they were jealous when Granddaddy had money after the war. So, Webster, now you know why we must win over the people in the community here. I'm sure once they get to know you and see the good you and Poppa are doing here, they'll come around."

She looked at him. *What a handsome man you are. I would kiss you right now, but it might frighten you.*

CHAPTER 24

STOCK SHARES

In the evenings, Amelia invited Webster to hear her play the piano or practice pronunciations. She also took him to the schoolhouse to see her classroom. As the weeks passed, they were together nearly every night.

The Colonel noticed them, too. While he was happy that Amelia had ended her relationship with the boy from Spartanburg, he wanted her to develop an interest in someone prominent from the local community.

But she had no interest in any of the boys from town. "They're so wrapped up in farming, hunting, and fishing, Poppa, that they won't consider manufacturing," she told him. "Besides, they don't like the idea that I'm going to teach at the mill school. They think schools should be limited to those from proper families."

"She's like her mother," the Colonel told Clarence. "I guess all that schooling away from here was good for her. She didn't stay around here and get her thinking locked into some of the beliefs folks have here. She sure has a mind of her own."

Webster's rehearsing and pretending put him more at ease. When Amelia took his hands, he responded, gently squeezing hers as if holding the pillow. He found he could relax as she talked about the children she would teach and how important it was for them to learn.

Amelia assumed Webster's attention meant he loved children as much as she did. She was wrong. He didn't care about children; he just wanted her to think he did.

Surprisingly, Webster found there were times he wanted to hold Amelia and kiss her, especially after she hugged him goodnight and sent him to his room with her perfume on his shirt. He checked his progress in his notebook and hugged his pillow and shirt.

Amelia likes me. Keep working.

Late one evening, she brought a sheaf of paper and a couple of large pencils to Webster's office. She closed the door and pulled up a chair to sit close to him. Her eyes sparkled as she resumed her lessons in Southern dialect.

"Remember this word?"

"MACK-bee."

"That's right. MACK-bee. Wonderful."

"I've been practicing the words from your letters. I have all of them here in this drawer." Webster pulled open a drawer.

"My goodness, you kept all of my letters?"

"I treasure them, Amelia. You made my days happy."

"Wonderful. Now, let's try this word."

"Monroe."

"Remember, stress the first syllable," Amelia said, touching his arm for emphasis. "Webster?"

"Oh, yes, Monroe."

"No, first syllable."

"MON-roe."

"Look at my lips. MON-roe," she said, squeezing his forearm for emphasis.

"MON-roe."

"Okay, now try this word." Amelia pointed to a word on the paper.

"Converse."

"Well, yes, that's the way you pronounce it when you're referring to what people do when they talk with one another. But this is also the name of the college I graduated from in Spartanburg. Remember to put the accent on the first syllable. Try it."

"Con-VERSE."

"No, silly, look at my lips. It's CON-verse. Look at my lips."

"Amelia, I can't look at your lips. When I look at your lips, I . . . uh . . ."

She pulled him to her, kissing him and joyfully crying, "Oh, Webster, I've wanted to do this from the first moment we met. I've fallen in love with you. You are a wonderful man. You want to help Daddy make this community a better place. I love you, and I know that may frighten you, but I promise I'll never leave you, if you'll have me. Let's get married quickly, before you get too busy with the mill."

"Amelia, I, uh, love you, too." Webster smiled.

Six months later, they were married at the big church in town.

During the service, the guardians of custom sat in judgment over the event. They whispered, "Amelia's mother never would've approved of her daughter marrying a foreigner."

Beatrice Russell was maid of honor. What finally convinced her to accept Webster was when she learned Webster came from wealthy parents, had attended college, and now was the head of the biggest business in the county. That made him an important person. And to Beatrice Russell, important people were important. Besides, she told herself, even though he was a Yankee foreigner, Amelia marrying Webster was the best way to keep the family business in the family.

On his wedding day, Webster wasn't that caught up with the goings-on around the event. He was thinking of the Colonel making him a partner, which the Colonel did—sort of. He called Webster into his office and told him how proud he was with how he'd built and equipped the plant and how happy he was that he was marrying Amelia.

"I have something for you and Amelia," he said and handed Webster a certificate for five hundred shares of Crowell Manufacturing stock. "We're partners now."

Well, Webster and *Amelia* were his partners. The certificates listed both as owners of the shares. Webster was disappointed, and of all days, on his wedding day.

His wrestling with being emotionally close disappeared that night as he and Amelia fumbled and then felt the ecstasy of uniting for the first time.

He was even more at ease later that evening when Amelia initiated another union, leaning over him and moaning, "I love you, Webster. I'll never leave you."

It was at this moment that he felt safe enough to trust the love of his beautiful wife.

CHAPTER 25

SHARECROPPING WITH VIDA MAE

"Vernon, that makes me want to puke," Betsy muttered and then lit a cigarette. Vernon looked down at the bottle on the seat. He was smiling now, his eyes gleaming.

"You want another?"

"Oh, hell, yeah. I *need* a drink now."

"Jimmy," Vernon said, "bring us some more coffee." After pouring whiskey in the cups, he waited until Jimmy came and went, and then he resumed. "While Little Lemuel and Amelia were settling into being married, your aunt Mildred was doing a favor for a friend. She was washing clothes out in her back yard one morning when an emergency came up."

*　　　*　　　*

Mildred *knew* the smoke from the washpot was following her—*just to make you miserable, ha, ha, haa.* She hacked and coughed and clumsily felt her apron for a rag—not there.

Finally, there was a slight puff of wind. She took a deep breath, walked back to the washboard, grabbed a wet rag, and wiped her face. "Shit . . . soap!" she exclaimed and then felt for a bucket and splashed water in her eyes.

When she finally recovered, she held up the coveralls, blinked hard at them, and then slopped them into the rinse kettle. It was boiling one of her dresses and her late husband's underclothes.

Shit, why am I doing this? Vida Mae should be doing this . . . I'm the one who's a widow. If she wants 'em for her man, she can wash 'em.

After Jimmy Earl died, Mildred worked sixteen-hour days to maintain the farm just to keep a roof over her head. She and Clarence sharecropped for Morgan Hastie, a big landowner and banker in Union County, North Carolina.

After the funeral, Hastie let Mildred live on his place because she'd grown up there. Mildred's parents had sharecropped for him, and Jimmy Earl had come to live there when he and Mildred got married. They'd worked the place for several years until Jimmy Earl got sick.

Mildred was doing laundry to get his clothes out of the house. She wanted nothing to remind her of the misery he'd caused. She had promised them to Vida Mae Pressley, who lived on the farm next door and also sharecropped for Mr. Hastie, along with her husband, Boyce. They had one child, Matthew.

Mildred was stirring the washpot when she heard Matthew yelling and running towards her from the creek.

"Miss Mildred, Miss Mildred, come quick! Poppa's been hurt!"

"What?"

"A big limb hit Poppa in the head, and me and Momma can't get it off him."

Mildred pushed over the washpot, dousing the fire, stuffed rags in her pocket, and ran with Matthew. They jumped the creek, and Mildred stumbled up the embankment and regained her feet as Matthew turned.

"Hurry, Miss Mildred."

"Where is he?"

"Across the field, by the trees."

Mildred struggled to keep up with the boy. When she finally made it to the tree line, she heard Vida Mae yelling, "Over here!"

Bending over, out of breath, Mildred could only watch as Vida Mae desperately pulled at a branch to try to get the big limb off her husband's head. Mildred ran around the limb, still gasping, and tried to pull on the branch, along with Matthew, as Vida Mae yelled, "Heave!"

It wouldn't budge. Boyce Pressley's muffled groans were getting softer. He was lying in the dirt with the big limb pressing his head.

"You got an axe?"

"Here," Matthew said and handed it to her.

"Matthew, you and your momma pull on these branches. We need to make it lighter."

Mildred inhaled deeply and then swung the axe with a fury, flinging big chunks of wood in the air with each stroke. The first branch was cut away, and Matthew and his mother dragged it aside as Mildred attacked the next one.

By the time she'd cut free the smaller branches and they'd hauled them away, Boyce Presley wasn't making a sound. "Grab this log, quick. We're gonna lose him. Now, heave!"

They picked up the thin end of the branch and walked in a semicircle until the limb finally pivoted off the man's head.

"Matthew, go get the wheelbarrow and bring it here. Then you go get Mr. Hastie."

The women set Boyce in the wheelbarrow and bumped him over the field to the house. He was barely breathing when they hauled him onto the porch. They rolled him onto a quilt and waited two hours before Mr. Hastie was able to bring the doctor. Days later, Boyce Presley was dead.

Morgan Hastie paid for the funeral. He and a couple of his workers stood off to the side, leaning on shovels and waiting.

When the preacher finished, Hastie fired up a cigar, motioned for his men to fill the hole, and called over Mildred and Vida Mae.

He took a few big puffs and told the women he was making some changes.

"Mildred, you need to move in with Vida Mae. I got a man and wife and their boys coming to live on your place. I need them to work my crops. My men here can help you move your things this evening. Don't worry about cleaning the house. The new family will do that. You need to be out of the house tonight."

That was it, no discussion, no debate. Morgan Hastie owned the land, the houses, and the livestock. He let tenants have chickens, pigs, and cows and plant gardens, but he made all the decisions about who lived where, what crops were planted, and how profits were shared.

Mildred didn't have pigs and left the cow for the new family moving in. Her chickens were a different matter. They had no desire to move away and complained about it.

It took several minutes of chasing, squawking, flapping, and cussing for Hastie's men to corner them and tie all them up, save one hen, which flew over the fence. "Shit, let her go," said Mildred.

The chickens were tossed on the wagon, atop what little of Mildred's furniture would fit into Vida Mae's house.

She and Vida Mae talked about Morgan Hastie late that first night as they set up Mildred's bed. They wondered how long it would be before he found another family and forced them to move off his property altogether.

Not long.

Hastie showed up one evening about a month later and told Vida Mae he'd found a man and wife with three boys who could do the work he needed. He gave Vida Mae and Mildred a week to vacate.

*   *   *

"Damn, Vernon, they didn't have no rights?" Betsy asked.

"Shit, no. When slavery was abolished, the plantation owners just replaced slavery with sharecropping. Even got laws passed which locked sharecroppers into working for them. Most of the people that sharecropped might have been freed slaves, but they were still obligated to stay on the land. They knew it, and the plantation owners knew it. Your aunt Mildred and Vida Mae may have been white and weren't owned as slaves were, but they were treated just like freed slaves."

CHAPTER 26

DALTON THREATE SHOWS WHO'S BOSS

Vernon took a big sip of spiked coffee. "Oh, yeah, that's good. Gimme a cigarette."

Betsy lit one for herself and tossed the pack over.

"What did Aunt Mildred look like?" she asked.

"She was tall, busty, and had curly brown hair and deep brown eyes. She was pretty, somewhat heavy, with broad shoulders and hips. Despite her work as a sharecropper, she had nice-looking hands with long fingers." He lit a cigarette and puffed. "Vida Mae dragged your aunt Mildred to church, which was a good thing because the women there were talking about a new cotton mill across the river. They heard recruiters were in the area, looking for women to work in the mill, and that the mill would provide them free housing if they came to work.

"The housing part is what got your aunt's interest. She and Vida Mae found a recruiter who told them they'd better get over there fast if they wanted a free house. There were only three left. This sent them packing and begging a neighbor to come out from his fields that very day and haul them in his wagon. Only, when they got there, they found the recruiter had lied to them. There were plenty of houses available."

Vernon sipped some coffee, looked across the table and said, "Betsy, there's a lot to the story of your aunt and the mill. You want to hear it tonight?"

"Yea, tell me all of it."

Vernon yelled, "Jimmy put on some more coffee and, how 'bout bringing more of this." He held up the bottle then looked at Betsy, "OK, here we go."

*   *   *

When the head of spinning operations interviewed Mildred, he was impressed with her confidence that she could learn to do textile work. He was a Yankee named Otto Barringer whom Webster had brought in from Massachusetts. He liked that Mildred could read, as most of the women coming to the plant couldn't. But mainly, he was impressed with her grit.

"I did everything my husband did on Mr. Hastie's farm," she told him. "I can cut wood, drive nails, chop cotton, hitch up mules, and plow land! And while doin' all that, I did the cleaning, cooking, and washing, too."

The man laughed and smiled. "You're hired."

"What about a house? Do I get a house?"

"No, you can live in the boarding house. Regular houses are for families or if two people in the house work in the mill."

"My friend Vida Mae is trying to get a job here, Mr. Barringer. If we both worked in the mill, could we get a house? She's got a young boy."

"I don't see why not. Go to the office and see if they have a house for you. If that works out, then you go to the spinning room and tell Dalton Threate I said to put you to work."

Vida Mae got hired as a weaver, and she, Mildred, and Matthew moved into their new house that first day—rent-free.

Mildred's spinning room boss was a man named Dalton Threate. He had experience in textiles and a dark past. No one knew he came to Crowell Mill because he was about to be fired from a plant in North Carolina.

He beat his son with a belt one night in a drunken rage over a dog. The yelling and cussing were so loud the neighbors came out and saw his wife chase him off the front porch with a baseball bat. She screamed that she'd call the sheriff if he ever tried to beat one of her children again.

Word of the disturbance got to Threate's boss at the mill. He would have fired him, but Threate skipped work that morning and, with the luck of a drunk, happened upon a man looking for someone to run a spinning room at a new plant in South Carolina.

Threate promised his wife he'd do better. He would quit drinking, and they could make a new start at this mill across the river. She told him she'd have to think about it. "Dalton, you get mean when you're drinkin'. I'm tired of you tellin' me you gonna quit, and then you don't. So, for now, I'll just wait over here and see how you do. But I'm tellin' you, me and the children ain't goin' if you don't stay quit."

Threate moved to Crowell Village shortly after that. He promised himself he'd make a new start; he would do better.

He was tall, heavy, and hairy, with a big chest and belly. When he balled his fists, his arms looked like clubs. He wore bib overalls, along with dirty white shirts unbuttoned at the top and sleeves rolled to his elbows, which made the black hairs on his arms and chest seem to burst out of his body.

Although he shaved daily, his stubbled cheeks looked almost blue, and the hair on his head was so thick it didn't move when he stood in the wind. He wore white socks and oil-stained brogans that poked out beneath overalls cut too short. He also carried a deer-handled pocketknife and had a habit of pulling it out and flicking it open and closed when he was nervous or trying to bully someone.

In North Carolina, he was known to pressure employees to get what he wanted—especially sex from widows with dependent children. His forced liaisons were consummated in one-sided trysts among the cotton bales in the warehouse. Usually, these brief, "pull up your dress" ins and outs were initiated on the promise of better working conditions or promotion. Women who refused had a hard time. Now he was in a new place, and this new woman came to him. She was good looking.

"Are you Mr. Threate?"

"Yes."

"I'm Mildred Turnage. Mr. Barringer says I'm to report to you."

"Mildred, you ever work in a mill?"

"No, but I can learn."

"Well, from the looks of you, I think you'll make a good spinning machine tender. I'm the boss of the spinning room."

Threate stuck his hand in his pocket, pulled out the knife, and began flicking it open and shut. He looked at Mildred's bosom and said, "You a widow woman, ain't ya?" *Click, click.*

"Yeh."

"How long?"

"'Bout four months."

"So, you ain't been with a man for four months now." He smiled. *Click . . . click.*

Mildred crossed her arms. She didn't like what he was saying. "Mr. Threate, bein' a widow-woman ain't got nothin' to do with this job. I ain't helpless, and I don't need no man to take care of me. I'm a-livin' with Vida Mae Pressley and her son in a mill house we just got. I'm a good worker. I'll do a good job for you."

"Well, you make sure you do just as I te—"

"Mr. Threate."

A short man with bare feet walked up and looked at Mildred and then Threate. "I'm . . . Jimmy Presnell . . . Mr. . . . . Barringer . . . said I was to see you."

Threate's eyes never moved off Mildred. *I don't like your attitude, missy.*

He clicked the knife shut and turned.

"You ever work in a mill, Jimmy?"

"No, sir."

"Well, you gonna be one of my doffers if I see you can do it."

Another man and woman walked up and told Threate that Barringer had told them they were to report to him. Soon, a small group was around him.

Threate began explaining the various functions in a mill and gave them a brief overview of the spinning room. He took them over to the two machines that were called spinning mules. Mildred and Mrs. Hunnicutt would tend one of them, and two more ladies would tend the other. The men would be doffers, who removed full bobbins once the machines finished their runs.

Threate told the group to look at the machines while he went to the main office. When he returned, he would explain how the machines worked and what he wanted them to get done that morning. In the payroll department, he asked the clerk if she had a woman named Vida Mae Pressley listed in a mill house with Mildred Turnage. He smiled upon learning she was a weaver and she and Mildred shared one of the new houses. Vida Mae had a son named Matthew.

Threate walked down to the weaving room floor and asked someone to point out Vida Mae. He stuck his hand in his pocket and, shouting over the noise, demanded, "I need your boy."

"What?"

"Your boy, Matthew. That's his name, ain't it? Matthew. I need Matthew to work for me."

"Matthew? Why do you . . . They said he could go to school!"

"I want your boy today!" Threate had his knife out. *Click, click.*

"They didn't tell me nuthin' 'bout needin' him to work."

"They told you wrong." *Click, click.* "I need your boy this mornin'."

"Who are you?"

"I'm Dalton Threate, and I'm the boss of the spinnin' room."

She pointed at the office and yelled, "They told me my boy could go to school! This ain't right. Besides, I don't work for you. I work for Mr. Oxley."

"I don't care if you do work for Oxley. You want to keep your house?" *Click, click.*

"Me and Mildred is both working in the mill, which means two of us in our house is a-workin' in this plant. So . . ." She looked down. "I don't think my boy has to work for you." She looked up. "Only two people in the mill house needs to work in the mill, ain't that it?"

"No, that's at *least* two people. It don't mean *only* two people. I know about your boy—Mildred already told me, and Mildred works for me. So, you let me have your boy now, or I can have the sheriff throw your stuff out in the street before your shift ends!"

He was bluffing. He felt if he yelled and looked angry, he could pull it off. As a new employee, Vida Mae was uncertain about arguing. Threate took advantage of it.

Vida Mae struggled. "Mister, this ain't right. They told me Matthew could go to the mill school. Now you tellin' me he has to work for you. You can have him, but you can't have him today. You can have him tomorrow morning; he ain't a-goin' today."

"I don't tolerate people talkin' back to me. I'll let it go this time 'cause we're just settin' this mill up. I'm the overseer in the spinning room. That makes me one of the bosses in this here mill.

"Have your boy in the spinning room tomorrow morning before startup!"

Threate turned and walked away. *That'll teach Mildred Turnage. Click, click.*

When they walked home that afternoon, Mildred got upset.

"He said I told him about Matthew?"

"He said you told him me and Matthew was livin' in the mill house with you, and now he's sayin' Matthew has got to work for him. It ain't right, Mildred. They told me Matthew could go to school."

"He told us he was goin' to the office. He never said he was looking for Matthew. I don't trust him. When I met him, he was givin' me dirty looks and talkin' nasty. We need to be careful. If you talk to him, Vida Mae, make sure they's other women around to hear what he's a-sayin'."

After supper, Vida Mae got into an argument with Matthew over a haircut. She made him sit on the back porch with a towel around his neck, and despite his protests of "Momma, I don't need no haircut," she said, "Sit . . . still," and whacked away and then clipped him a burr cut.

"I ain't lettin' you go crawling under no spinning mule with your hair getting caught. Them machines is known to cripple and kill children. You be careful tomorrow."

What troubled her was that Threate had told her she had to do what he said, even though he wasn't her boss.

I woulda asked my boss man if I did, but I didn't want to risk me and Mildred getting run off from our jobs on our first week. Now, after they told me Matthew could go to school, they telling me he can't because they need him to work. It ain't right.

"There—that's better. Now, go out in the yard and shake that towel."

CHAPTER 27

LEARNING THE SPINNING MULE

The next morning, Vida Mae walked Matthew into the spinning room, made sure Mildred was near, and yelled over the noise, "This here's my only son, Dalton Threate. Don't you ever mistreat him or make him do something that ain't safe!"

"I told you not to talk back to me." Threate reached for his pocketknife.

"You ain't my boss man. I work for Mr. Oxley. Don't you ever cause my boy no harm!" She pushed Threate aside and walked out, wiping sweat from her face with a rag.

Mildred tried an appeal.

"It ain't right, Mr. Threate. He's barely ten years old and should be in school. Me and Vida Mae is working in the plant. So that's two of us."

"Let me tell you something, Mildred Turnage. I'm the boss of this spinning room, and I can do whatever I want. You better shut your mouth right now!" The knife clicked open and shut.

Mildred walked back to her machine and said to herself, "Damn it, I'm workin' for a man . . . again. He ain't worth a shit!"

"Don't none uh you ever try to talk back to me!" Threate yelled.

"Missus Hunnicutt, you and Missus Turnage get on the back of the mule and start threading the roving through them rollers. You got a thousand strands to thread. Pull them out and then feed them through them guides and down to the bobbins. I want you to get finished by nine thirty so we can start spinnin'."

Mildred and the Hunnicutt woman, still new and uncertain of their jobs, reacted to Threate's yelling with awkward, hesitant movements, which drove Threate into a craze.

"Pull that yarn on through! We ain't got all day. You acting like you don't know shit!"

Two men mumbled that Threate was using strong language in front of women.

"What are you two doing?" he demanded as he clicked his pocketknife.

"We're waiting for you to tell us what to do."

"Waiting for me? Goddammit, get to work!"

"Don't take the Lord's name in vain and don't cuss me!" one of the doffers yelled.

"Don't talk back to me. Help these women. We're late."

Matthew hid behind Mildred. No one moved. Then Threate yelled, "Everybody get to work!" Then he walked over to the other machine, yelled at those workers, closed his knife, and slipped it into his side pocket.

At Mildred's machine, the man Threate had yelled at told his group, "Let's get this done. I don't want him back here, yelling and cussin'. I'm afraid of what I might do."

Even Matthew pitched in. He stood on a small crate and pulled roving off the feeder one end at a time. Then he passed it through the rollers to Mrs. Hunnicutt and Mildred. Within an hour and a half, the group had the first machine set to go, or so they thought.

When Threate returned, he moved down the machine. From time to time, he stopped, pulled out some roving, and, with a grunt, turned to no one in particular and said, "Fix this. This is wrong." Once he was certain the changes were made, he yelled, "Stand back!" and pulled on a big lever, sending a power belt over a spindle and bringing the spinning machines to life.

They looked like two giant spiders skittering back to back, defending against predators. Tension arms took roving spewing out from rollers and stretched it, filling the room with webs of cotton. As if satisfied, the machines stopped and, like they were covering flies, wound fibers onto a thousand bobbins before moving back to repeat the cycle again and again.

Threate took Matthew to the back, handed him a long-handled brush and small burlap sack, and yelled over the noise, "Watch how this machine opens and closes. As soon as the mule starts rollin' out, I want you to slide in on your hands and knees and sweep into your sack any lint that's come loose.

"You see that yarn getting' wound on them bobbins? Listen to how it sounds. You hear that?"

"Yessir."

"As soon as you hear that, you get out quick, because the machine is fixin' to close up. You'll get squashed if you don't."

Matthew watched the machine open and close a couple of times and then dove beneath the web. He got yelled at.

"What are you doing? There ain't no cotton under there yet. Get outta there."

"I thought you wanted me to dive in each time?"

"Not unless you see cotton on the floor. You got to check all the way down the room. Cotton will get stuck on the frame, too. Watch the machine and then practice going in, sweeping, and gettin' out."

Matthew plunged beneath the webbing, crawled between the rollers, and came out just as the bobbins were winding. He held up a puff of cotton and said, "Look, Mr. Threate, I got some."

"Good, you keep doin' that, boy. You're a natural."

The two machines ran without stopping into late morning. By that time, Threate had returned with two more boys he'd forced their mothers to give up. He got Matthew to show them how to dive in and crawl out before the machines closed.

"Pay attention," Threate warned. "Keep your machines clean, and get out quick, like a rabbit."

By day's end, the spinning room had processed enough roving to create warp and filling yarn. It would be carried to the slashing room to be prepped for weaving. In just a couple of days, the mill would be making cloth.

CHAPTER 28

UNCLE HENRY

David Oxley worried that his workers were so ignorant, he might never get them trained. They certainly didn't talk like him, and they couldn't read, so he couldn't give them manuals to study.

He felt he was in some strange land, a foreigner among unkempt illiterates, tasked with turning around a whole culture. He wondered if it could be done. He was head of weaving and finishing and had come down from Massachusetts with Otto Barringer.

For their part, the workers were struggling to keep up with what this fast-talking Yankee was trying to tell them. Oxley shouted over the noise, "If you do as we teach you, you'll never live in poverty again." Some were skeptical. Some were hoping he was right.

He held up a strand of fiber and asked what it was.

"Strang."

"Strang?"

"String," a woman said.

"It's not string. Well, you could call it that, but here in the mill, we call it yarn."

"Yarn? Why you call it yarn instead of strang?"

"Everything in the mill, everything that's done, has a name. You need to learn the names so everyone will understand what you're talking about. Now, what is this called?"

"Yarn!"

"That's right. Here in the weaving room, thousands of strands of . . ." He held up the strand.

"Yarn!" the workers chanted.

"Right. Thousands of strands are wound on the roller on the back of the loom. Each one is pulled from the roller, threaded through these heddles, and wrapped around the roller in front. We call all these fibers the warp. Fabric is created when strands of fiber, called filling, are woven left and right over and under strands of warp. We call those strands the weft.

"This is real important!" he yelled as he held up a shuttle. "This is the shuttle. Inside it is a bobbin with filling wound around it. As the shuttle gets batted across, the filling unwinds off the bobbin through this hole and goes through the warp."

The women clustered around to hear over the noise. Some dabbed rags on their sweaty faces and swatted at cotton lint floating in the air.

"Over time, bobbins run out of yarn and empty, which causes problems. You need to replace bobbins *before* they run out. Otherwise, you'll have to shut your loom off to rethread it."

Oxley pulled out an empty shuttle, popped out the spent bobbin, and demonstrated how to thread yarn off a fresh bobbin and suck it out a small hole in the shuttle.

"It's like kissing—use your tongue to find the hole. See? Then, snap the bobbin in the shuttle, tie the yarn onto the weft, place the shuttle back in its slot, and restart the loom."

A short, old, skinny woman hollered, "We gone be sucking them yarns through them shuttles behind one another?"

"If you try to thread it by hand, it'll take too long. So, you must suck the yarn through this eyelet. There's nothing wrong with it."

"Some uh the women in here dip snuff."

Women puckered and frowned.

"Just put a rag in your apron and use it to wipe the shuttle. The point is, don't let your bobbin run out, and you won't need to do that."

Out in the opening shed, Otto Barringer looked at three men to see if they could wrestle cotton bales onto hand trucks. They would haul the bales into the shed to be opened and placed into machines to blend cotton fiber. The work required strength, dexterity, and endurance. They would be moving five-hundred-pound bales from the warehouse into the room where they were opened.

Two of the men were well muscled. One was tall; the other was stocky. The third was a slender, white-haired colored man of dark complexion who told Barringer he'd been "on Mr. Colonel's place all my life. I was born right down the street yonder. I ain't never lived no other place but right here."

Barringer was skeptical. "Well, let me see how long it takes you to get that bale over there, put it on the hand truck, and take it to the opening shed."

The man pushed the hand truck against the bale, reached across the handles, and, with a grunt, tipped the bale back and pushed the hand truck beneath it with his foot. He let out another grunt, pulled the bale onto the hand truck, and pushed it through the doorway.

Barringer was impressed. "What's your name?"

"Uncle Henry."

"Whose uncle?"

"I'm everybody's uncle . . . Thass what they call me, Uncle . . . Henry."

"Well, Uncle Henry, how many times a day can you move bales like that if I hire you?"

"I can move as many bales as you need me to move."

"You're hired. I'll pay you a nickel a bale. I see you smoke a pipe."

"Yass, suh."

"Well, don't ever smoke that pipe, or the rest of you strike a match or smoke anything inside the breaking room. It'll be filled with cotton lint, which is highly combustible. Any man striking a match or smoking in there will be fired on the spot. Do you understand?"

"Yes, sir."

"Now," Barringer said to the tall man, "let me see what *you* can do."

Trying to show he could work faster, the tall man tried to kick the hand truck beneath a bale. It bounced to his left. He tried again.

"You won't get it that way," said Barringer. "Do like Uncle Henry did. Tip the bale forward. Then push the hand truck beneath it."

"Shit," the tall man said. "This thing's heavy." He struggled and needed the assistance of the stocky guy before finally getting it into the shed.

The stocky man had no problem but was breathing heavily by the time he got his bale inside.

"All right, I guess you'll do. The three of you will be responsible for taking the bales I select into the opening room. I'll tell you which bale goes where. We'll be blending the cotton according to its grade."

He said they would also assist Colonel Crowell's field hands with unloading boxcars into the warehouse when cotton came in from the South Carolina Lowcountry.

When the first train arrived, Barringer placed a standing desk next to the scales outside to record the grade, weight, and location of where the cotton was grown. After watching him, Uncle Henry began reading aloud from the tags as each bale was hoisted onto the scales.

"This here is middling cotton, boss. It come from Murdaugh farm, in Orangeburg County."

Barringer checked the tag. "You're right. Where did you learn to read?"

"From my church. We read the Bible every week. Near 'bout everybody that go to my church know how to read."

"You keep reading those tags and tell me how much each bale weighs."

While Uncle Henry stood at the scales, the others were sweating and breathing hard as they pushed bales into the warehouse.

Shorty Thomas turned to his partner. "Would you look at that? We got to be careful, or we gonna end up working for a nigger!"

"That bale weigh fo hunnert and a little less ninety-eight pound," Henry said. "It dry, too."

CHAPTER 29

FILLED WITH THE SPIRIT

Despite the long hours, workers found millwork had an ebb and flow. Setups kept them busy, but once the machines were running, they could relax and socialize in the water house or sing, as some ladies were doing in the weaving room one morning.

Vida Mae was singing alto as the women chorused, "Gimme that ol' time religion. It's good enough for me."

"Yay, that was a good one."

The second hand hollered, "What's goin' on here?"

"We're just singing, Mr. Warren."

"You're s'posed to be watching your looms."

"We're checkin' them, Mr. Warren," said Vida Mae. "We're stayin' on the floor rather than wait in the water house."

"Out here, we can sing and still watch our machines while waitin' for them to finish they runs."

"Well, I guess it's all right. Just be careful," Warren said, and then he walked from the room.

"Let's sing 'Rock of Ages,'" someone said. "Myrtle, you start us off."

Downstairs in the spinning room, Matthew and other boys were off in a corner, playing mumblety-peg with a pocketknife.

They'd learned there were long periods before cotton lint of any size would build up on the floor or frame, and it wasn't necessary to crawl under the machine every time it began its outward run.

Mildred spent her *waitin' time* in the water house, knitting and talking with other ladies until the spinning machines finished. "This is a lot better than sharecropping."

"Oh, Lord, yes," a woman replied. "When we was sharecroppin', they was always something to be done. In the mill, once we get things runnin', we can take it easy."

Mildred was thankful she and Vida Mae had come to Crowell Village. She told the other ladies how happy she was about her mill house. It was new, built solid, and there were no cracks in the floor. One of the ladies agreed.

"Lord, I know what you're sayin.' When we was sharecroppin', the floors had cracks so big you could see the chickens peckin' dirt."

When the mill shut down for the day, Mildred caught up with Vida Mae as she was going out the front gate. They talked as they walked down the road toward their house.

"This is a lot better than the Hastie place."

"I like it, too, hun. The work is fun, and we been able to talk and sing while we work. Why, already they's a group of us singin' harmonies so good we sound like a church choir."

Vida Mae was still talking about singing hymns and how good life was in the mill when they finished supper that evening.

"Mildred, this here place is a good place. People help each other out. I got a lady to mind my looms today while I got our groceries, and Mr. Robinson told me he's gonna come with his mule tomorrow to plow our garden. The hours is long, but the work ain't that hard. It's better than sharecroppin', and even Matthew likes his job."

"Matthew should be in school," Mildred said. "I had to get on him today about pullin' pranks on other boys."

"I know. I wish he was, too. But this work is fun, and the women I work with are nice. Let's get these dishes done. Brenda Quick is havin' prayer meetin' at her house this evenin', and I want you to go with me to meet Roberta Bouknight. She's the one who hepped me today."

"You and Matthew go. I think I'll stay here and straighten things up a bit."

Brenda Quick had held prayer meetings at her house every Wednesday night for weeks. What had started out as three or four women sitting around the kitchen table, quietly reading scripture, had grown into a noisy crowd so large it filled the kitchen and spread into one of the bedrooms. Mill houses had only four rooms.

What was drawing the crowd was Roberta Bouknight, a friend of Brenda's. Roberta was a widow of two years who'd become the preferred preacher of sorts to her mill worker friends. Twice she'd been so filled with the spirit that she'd fallen trance-like into Holy Ghost preaching. It was so captivating that ladies felt the Holy Spirit touching them deep in their souls.

Word quickly spread around the mill that there was a woman, a widow woman, preaching the way God intended for preachin' to be done. Roberta was strong. She shredded the religious formality of mainstream preachers, who, cloaked in their robes, delivered tepid, orthodox sermons quietly ladled to bored but spiritually hungry congregants.

Here now was someone who connected to mill people because she demonstrated she was unencumbered by the rules of the church and free to shout, cry, plead, fall on her knees, and call out to God and Jesus like the children of Israel had done. Roberta Bouknight was an authentic Christian, filled with the Holy Ghost.

Anticipating a big crowd, Brenda Quick made room by taking down her bed and flipping bed rails, mattress, and all on its side against a wall.

It was early spring, and rising humidity made everything sticky and warm, so Brenda opened the front and back doors and every window of her house to give air to the women standing nearly against each other.

"Tonight's lesson," she told the assembly, "is from the book of Daniel: when Daniel got tossed into the lions' den."

As Brenda Quick read the lesson, the attendees nodded, already familiar with the story. She closed the book and announced that Roberta Bouknight would talk about her faith, how it was like the faith of Daniel.

Roberta stood, closed her eyes, and swayed gently as she softly said, "Oh, Lord, oh, Jesus, I know You hear me. You said You'd always hear me. Well, tonight I pray You hear me, and You also hear these other ladies and they children, Lord."

"Amen," the crowd said, placing it as an exclamation to each line of her prayer.

"Lord, I come to You tonight"—*Amen*—"like Daniel thowed in a den of lions, Lord." *Amen.* "I come here tonight for all these ladies here and they childrens, too, Lord." *Amen!* "I'm a-pleadin' with You, Lord God, Lord Jesus, come down tonight and save me, a poor widow woman who struggles daily to feed her childrens and keep a roof over they's head and who, like Daniel, has been a faithful, prayin' Christian."

Frightened by Roberta's animated shouting, young kids buried their faces in their mothers' dresses, gripping tightly with their little fingers.

"I feel the spirit rising in me, Lord. I can feel it. I know you will help me and my children, glory to God. I know that if You saved Daniel, glory to God, you could save a faithful, poor widow woman. Oh, Lord, I feel the power . . . I feel . . ." Roberta fainted and was caught by a large woman and dragged away and placed on a bed in the other room.

Children began crying and were hushed by mesmerized mothers.

Matthew whispered, "Momma, what happened to that woman?"

"She's filled with the spirit."

"She's play-acting," a girl next to him said.

"She's filled with the spirit," Vida Mae demanded.

The two children gave each other mistrustful looks and eased from the noise as another woman claimed, "I feel it, too. I feel the holy spirit touching me, oh—"

She collapsed and was dragged back to the bed. Two more women shouted and fainted and were dragged off.

The crowd broke into cheers of "Praise God" and clapped so loudly that neighbors crossed the street.

Matthew and the girl escaped to the front-porch steps just as a neighbor shouted, "Y'all cut out that noise. This here ain't no church; it's a neighborhood where people sleep. We got to work tomorrow. Go home and go to bed."

Matthew and the girl walked down the steps.

"Them women were scary," he said. "Do you have to shout for God to hear you?"

"I don't know 'bout that, but . . . if you ask me, them women was a-play-actin'."

CHAPTER 30

MADE IN GOD'S IMAGE

People in the town were still complaining about the noisy mill. At the UDC meeting, most of the conversation was about the workers coming out of the plant with cotton lint stuck to their hair and clothes.

Frances Merchant told of seeing mill children peeing next to the roadway in front of mill houses. "That child just pulled up her dress, squatted, and did her business right there, as if she had no thought of using the outhouse around back. She didn't have any underpants on, either."

"Frances," a lady said, "they do that all the time. They run around barefoot and dirty, peeing whenever the urge hits them. They either don't know any better or just don't care. I bet they don't."

"Something needs to be done. I don't want my children catching anything from these nasty hicks."

"They won't be attending school with our children," Frances said. "Amelia Crowell, uh, Amelia Crowell Webster—her mother never would have approved of her marrying a foreigner. Anyway, Amelia has opened a school in the mill village, and the mill children are going to school there."

"I hear they use children to work in the mill."

"The little children go to Amelia's school, but those eleven years old and up work in the mill."

"Before they let them live in one of those mill houses, they ought to make them pass a test on how to keep themselves and their children clean, how to keep a clean house, and how to use an outhouse, too."

"They could be bringing consumption into our community. Remember when Crowell's wife and son died of that scarlet fever epidemic several years ago? We don't need any more of that."

"My husband is already working on Billy Hawkins to pass legislation that'll take care of that," Frances declared.

It was Senator Lawrence who told the Colonel and Webster that Hawkins had introduced two bills in the legislature affecting textile manufacturing and the state's public schools.

One required workers engaged in manufacturing to pass a physical exam proving they were free of communicable diseases before they could be employed. The second bill required the state board of health to adopt regulations requiring schoolchildren to pass a similar health examination before being admitted into South Carolina public schools.

"There is strong support for both bills among legislators," the senator said. "And they will likely be passed into law."

Amelia told Webster her mill students didn't bathe, wore the same clothes every day, and didn't know the importance of keeping clean.

"I spend time each day explaining how and why they must keep themselves clean. But unless their mothers are taught this, not much will change. Why don't we provide classes to these women in homemaking and housekeeping?"

"Homemaking and housekeeping?" said Webster. "We're just starting to teach them spinning and weaving, and now you want me to train them on how to be a homemaker, too? They need to concentrate on learning their jobs."

"What would happen if someone from the state board of health came here and found some of our workers had diseases? They could shut the mill down," she warned.

Realizing she was right, Webster instructed his foremen to schedule one hour of homemaker training each Thursday and Friday during the last hour of the shift, beginning immediately.

The training was held in an open space just off the spinning room. Supervisors set up a heavy table with wash pans, dishes, and scrub boards on it, next to which was a small, coal-fired cooking stove. Next to the stove was the framed outline of an outhouse, including the box and seat. Additionally, there was a black, soot-stained clothes washpot on the floor.

Amelia opened the proceedings, explaining she and her father valued each worker and the need for everyone to understand how important cleanliness was to every household.

The workers felt they were being talked down to by this just-out-of-college schoolteacher. They also resented having to listen to the Colonel's black housekeeper, Thomasina Ratliff, explain the sanitary way to prepare food as well as the need to train children to use the outhouse.

One lady stood and said, "I ain't lettin' no nigger tell me how to cook and clean." She was confronted by her foreman, who told her she was still on the clock and to sit down.

Thomasina yelled, "I ain't no nigger!" She placed a hand on her hip, pointed an accusing finger at the woman, and shouted, "I'm a human bein', just like you. I'm made in God's image, just like you. I can read, I can write, and I teach the Bible to my children. My children ain't no niggers; they made in God's image, like yo childrens. They can read, and they can write.

They keep themselves clean, and they don't pee in the street like yo children do."

The women were shocked.

Thomasina was tall, slender, and dark-skinned, with expressive black eyes and graying hair that set off a beautiful face. She had large hands and used them to mime each task covered in her lecture. Her delivery was predicated on talking loudly, as if volume could force the reluctant gathering to accept what she was saying.

"Listen to me. I know how to keep from getting sick or my children from getting worms—my children ain't never had no worms—you wash yo pots and pans and dishes in hot—not cold, but hot—soapy water. Soapy water," she said as she pretended to wash, dip, and then wring a rag in her hands.

"When you cook your food, you cook it all the way through. Don't eat raw meat. If you keep wiping your pans with a dirty rag and cold water or feeding your babies meat that ain't cooked till it's done, yo babies' bellies will swell up," she said. "And another thing. Don't just feed yo family cornbread and fatback. You got to feed them fruits and vegetables, too. You feed them just cornbread and fatback, and they get plegra. I know what I'm talkin' 'bout. I seen field hands wid plegra. I seen one die from it." She flashed her palms.

Several women began glancing at the clock.

"Here's another thing," she said, pointing at the women. "Make sure your cook pots are clean. You cook with dirty pots, everybody in your house get sick, so make sure they clean. And don't leave no soap in your dishes or pots. You leave soap in yo pans and dishes, yo whole family will get the runs, which brings me to this. You know what this is?"

"An outhouse," the women said.

"Everybody in my family uses the outhouse. Don't nobody in my family crap or pee in the street. We ain't niggers. I been hearing 'bout yo children peein' in the street. When you go home tonight, first thing you do is to tell yo children to use the outhouse. You tell yo children to quit peeing in the street. Otherwise, they'll get sick, and the whole neighborhood will get sick, and the mill will shut down."

Thomasina ended the meeting by wagging a finger and saying she'd be back the next evening. "And I'll show you how to wash your children's clothes, so they look clean instead of looking like a bunch of dirty field hands. My children's clothes is clean, and you can keep yo children's clothes clean, too. I'll show you tomorrow evening."

The mill workers stood and looked at their supervisors, their eyes asking, *Is it time?* Then they filed out of the room. No one spoke until they got past the gate.

"They got no call to talk to us like that!"

"Who they think we are? We're white women, and our children are white children."

"They think they better than us."

"My children don't pee in the street. I switch 'em if they wet their pants, but my children don't pee in the street."

"It's bad enough for them to be training me how to run my job, but now they're training me how to cook, wash and clean, and take care of my children."

It wasn't long before the legislature passed laws requiring school children to be tested for contagious diseases, and a new law requiring textile workers to be tested, too.

Crowell Mill was shut down for three days while the state health inspector checked workers and school children. It was the first mill in the state to be checked. Representative Billy Hawkins had seen to that.

CHAPTER 31

GOOD FEELINGS CAUSE BAD THINGS

Having won a victory over the health inspections, Frances Merchant turned her gossip to Amelia Webster. Amelia was pregnant, and word of it flashed through the UDC meeting.

Frances made sure the conversations rehashed the old comments of how Amelia's mother would never have approved of her marrying that little Yankee foreigner who was wrecking their community. She openly wondered what kind of child could possibly come from such a union.

For Webster, Amelia's pregnancy was both joyful and troubling. Before he married, he never knew what a naked woman looked like, much less a pregnant woman, and now his wife was going through changes that confounded him. He was happy they'd have a child, but at the same time, he was afraid he'd done something that threatened Amelia's health, or even worse, her life—her life that connected him to his mill.

What would the Colonel do? What would happen to me?

These selfish fears swirled within him at a time when he was beginning to feel comfortable with the idea of actually loving Amelia. He needed reassurance, but what could he do? He had no friends, and within himself, he had no means of generating self-assurance about anything other than his work. The attitude of their neighbors didn't help.

Those few old families willing to call on Amelia gushed praise on her for becoming a mother. They didn't say much to the Colonel about becoming a grandfather and coldly addressed Webster, as if under some Southern obligation to speak to him. Even Aunt Beatrice was formal when she came to visit.

Webster was furious at the slights and often retreated to his office, announcing to visitors that he had important work he must get done.

Amelia had a difficult pregnancy. Her doctor cautioned against her teaching at the mill school, but she insisted, despite feeling weaker each day. She went straight to bed after school and took a nap so she could join Webster and her father at dinner. The last few weeks, she was too weak to leave her room and had dinner brought to her bedside.

Rather than devote himself to caring for her, Webster isolated himself to avoid thinking he might lose her. She was getting weaker each day.

On the afternoon of her delivery, he ran from the house, terrified by Amelia's painful labor. He began to calm down as he stood on the vibrating floor inside the plant, amidst the familiar noise, smells, and sights of the weaving room. As he gasped for breath puzzled workers stared and talked among themselves, wondering what had frightened him so.

Finally, Clarence came from the house and yelled happily, "Mr. Webster, you got a baby boy!" Amelia had barely survived the seven hours of labor, but finally, Charles Wesley Webster had been born. He weighed six pounds, three ounces. The doctor announced that Webster and Amelia had a fine, healthy boy but cautioned they should seriously consider having no more children.

Despite the joy Webster felt over the new arrival, he began closing the door to his office to avoid thinking of Amelia's health. He told the household workers he didn't want to be disturbed, as he had important business to attend to. He even told Amelia the mill was entering a critical phase and needed his constant attention.

She didn't believe him. After a few weeks of this, one morning, she entered Webster's office, placed Charles Wesley in his lap, and walked out, announcing she had "things to do at the school" and Webster needed to "look after his son."

Webster was petrified. He didn't know what to do with a baby. He had a mill to run. He loudly called for Clarence. "Get Thomasina in here. I need her now."

He was taken aback when Thomasina said, "Mr. Webster, Miss Amelia told me not to do nothing with that baby. She told me Mr. Webster need to learn to care for the baby, and Mr. Webster, I goin' to do just what she told me. Caring for a baby ain't nothing. People been doin' it since Eve birthed Abel."

"What do I do?" Webster asked, holding Charles like some fragile vase.

"Hold him and hug him, gentle-like, not too tight."

"Like this?"

"Thass right, gently, just like that. Now coo to him, Mr. Webster."

"Coo?"

"Softly like, like you singing him a lullaby."

Webster cooed. Charles sighed and gripped his father's shoulder with his little fingers as he was hugged.

"Now, Mr. Webster, lower him down, cradle him, and look into his eyes."

Webster looked at the pale blue eyes sparkling back at him and began to sniffle.

"Mr. Webster, you just keep on lovin' him. The only thing greater on Earth than the love of a child is the love of your wife, and the only thing greater than that is the love of the Lord."

Webster's tearful emotions swirled, collecting specks and tads of the few warm feelings from his past. Then, as he looked at his beautiful creation, the good feelings spun down into his memory's foreboding chasm.

It's like . . . it's . . .

"Take this child, Thomasina! Tell Missus Webster I have important work to do. I don't want to be disturbed. And *close* the door when you leave."

CHAPTER 32

JOHNNIE FAYE ESCAPES

About this time, a young girl in North Carolina decided she'd run away from home. She hoped a job at Crowell Mill would mean a better life where a Prince Charming would sweep her up and carry her to happiness.

Johnnie Faye Laney pulled the pillow over her head and scrunched beneath the covers. "When I get away, I won't hafta listen to this anymore."

Even with the pillow, she could hear the bed squeaking and headboard slapping in her mother's room next door. She grabbed the quilt and wrapped it and the pillow around her head, but her hands couldn't press away the sound of her mother's, "Oh, Lord, I know this is a sin . . . Oh, Lord, honey, *give* it to me . . . *give* it to me, honey . . . Keep goin'!"

Johnnie Faye had promised herself she would cry about this no more, but because of what she was about to do, the noise next door was too much. Her big-girl dam burst into little-girl sobs when she heard her mother's *yes, yes, yes!* for the last time.

"Mommy never hollered like that when Daddy was alive. My daddy would never do that to her."

Johnnie Faye believed men should be like her daddy—handsome, kind, loving, and gentle—like the men in her storybooks.

But this stepfather of hers, he was the evil handsome princes fought against. He was mean and conniving and, like other villains, forced her mommy to do something she shouldn't, even if her cries *did* sound like she was enjoying it.

Johnnie Faye wiped away tears, telling herself, *Tomorrow I won't be bothered by him anymore*, and went to sleep.

She was sixteen years old and maturing into a young woman, but her beliefs about men and women were little-girl fixations with fairy tales.

When things were bad, like when she came from school, where she was teased about her *froggy butt* shape, she often ran to the back corner of the pasture and climbed the chinaberry tree. Then, opening a book, she got lost in tales of chivalry and beautiful princesses carried away to forever and ever and ever happiness.

Here was her place to daydream about her handsome prince . . . her daddy. She could still feel him pulling her up in the saddle and getting her to cluck and tell the horse to "get up" as he held her in his arms. He called her "Princess" and kissed the top of her head.

As the years passed, her daydreams and fantasies became longings to find a man just like him. She knew there was someone who'd be loving to her and protect her from the teasing at school and verbal abuse her mother and stepfather hurled at her.

Well before sunup, Johnnie Faye got her suitcase, took her daddy's picture, and packed it with her clothes, shoes, and hairbrushes. She was doing a final check when she remembered her books, stuck them in the suitcase, shut it, and clicked the latches.

She leaned out her window to quietly place the suitcase on the ground. After a final look at her bedroom in the only home she'd ever known, she crawled out the window and walked barefoot toward the Hamlet railyard two miles away. She was heading to happiness. Now all she needed was to find a boxcar loaded with cotton, headed for Crowell Mill.

It was still dark and hard to see when she heard the yard man cussing at a stuck boxcar door. She ran down the train, passing up open cars, until she found one a good distance from the man. She pitched her suitcase up as hard as she could, but it bounced off a cotton bale in the doorway. She squatted and checked to see if the yard man had heard the noise. No problem. He was several cars up, cussing at another door, but he was working his way towards her.

She grabbed the handle, reared back, and, spinning like an athlete, slung it high. It sailed inside.

Now, get in quick.

She grunted, pulled herself in, and hurriedly climbed up over bales. Then she lay across one in the corner and tried to slow her gasps.

When the yard man slid the door shut, she was trembling. It was dark, scary, and dusty and smelled of burlap and cotton. She snuggled her suitcase for comfort and took a deep breath. Regardless of what happened now, she was on her way. She'd made the right decision, particularly after what her mother had done to her.

Years back, her mother dragged her to a Pentecostal church to find a miracle cure for Johnnie Faye's dying father. That's what her mother said she wanted, but it didn't take Johnnie Faye long to figure out her mother was after a man to replace her daddy. And she complained, "No, no, Mommy, let me sit next to you," after her mother told her to scoot over to let the strange man sit between them—again. They were late getting to the church that night, and the service was well underway.

Her mother gave her a hard look. "Sit down and be quiet. This is the house of the Lord," she said as the praising, waving, and shouting went on around them.

Johnnie Faye was horrified when the man held her mother's hands and prayed and demanded that Jesus cure this poor woman's sick husband. It was confusing. Here he was, praying and pleading, but he was holding her mother's hands, her *married* mother's hands.

All Johnnie Faye knew was that despite the noisy pleadings and praying, she could only watch helplessly as cancer ate away at the one person who loved her. She was frightened that night when her precious daddy called her "Princess" and kissed her for the last time. By morning, he was dead.

The whistle blew twice, and the locomotive lurched, sending jolts rippling down the train. Johnnie Faye's boxcar jerked, and her head bounced against the side. She rubbed it a bit and then hugged onto her suitcase as the train accelerated. Its rhythmical clicking and clacking reminded her of last night—she hated those sounds.

I'm gonna marry a nice man someday. And he'll be gentle and love me, and . . . he won't make me do things like that.

As the train jostled along, she thought about how smart she'd been to listen to those women at church talking about this new cotton mill in South Carolina and how it was looking for women to work there. She'd pretended to look at a hymnal as one of the women called her husband over. He worked at the Hamlet rail yard.

"Mac, tell Eunice about that new mill."

"We built a spur line to the plant and have already shipped several loads to them. It's called Crowell Mill. We s'posed to ship more cotton to them next week."

Johnnie Faye smiled as she remembered that night and how she'd leaned over the pew and pretended she had a school project. She'd gotten Mac to tell her how trains were put together, and in his explanation, he'd told her where the cotton load would be.

There was a lot of yelling, bumping, and clanking when the train arrived at the Crowell Mill siding. By the time the boxcars were uncoupled, Johnnie Faye was coughing and sneezing something fierce.

The dust and lint inside the car were so awful that she crawled over bales, desperate for fresh air. Her eyes ran, snot dripped out her nose, and she coughed so loudly she startled Uncle Henry when he flung open the door.

"Chile, what you doin' up there?"

"I want to work in the mill." She coughed and coughed.

"Work in the mill? Git down out that train. You coulda got killed in there. Go 'round front to the office."

After wiping her face and dusting off her clothes, she put on her shoes, toted her bag to the office, and was hired.

Dalton Threate walked her to Mildred Turnage's machine and, over the noise, yelled introductions. "Mildred, this here is Johnnie Faye Laney. She's goin' to help tend your frame. Missus Hunnicutt musta quit, so Johnnie Faye is takin' her place."

Right away, Mildred liked Johnnie Faye and wanted to know more about her.

"So, tell me why you ran away," she said as they walked home that first day.

After hearing Johnnie Faye's story, she said, "Good Lord, no wonder you ran off. C'mon, hun. Let's get your things fixed at the boarding house. Then you can come and have supper with us and meet Vida Mae and Matthew."

After the meal, Johnnie Faye tried to help with the dishes, but Vida Mae said, "No, you and Mildred go sit on the back porch. Me and Matthew will get the dishes—it's his turn anyhow."

Mildred grabbed the light hanging down from the porch ceiling and switched it off. "We don't need this. It attracts bugs. Johnnie Faye, I don't blame you for runnin' away. Tell me your plans. What do you want?"

"I want to live and work in a nice place, and someday I'd like to marry a nice man and have a family. You had a family, didn't you?"

"Well, I tried, but both of my babies died. Then my husband died."

"I'm sorry."

"We didn't have no doctor. For a long time, I thought it was my fault. My husband did. He blamed me. Then he got sick and died. Jimmy Earl was never good to me." Mildred stared into the darkness. "I . . . don't want to talk about this no more."

There was another pause. Then Vida Mae hollered from the kitchen, "Y'all want some cake? I baked a fresh one."

The next day, Mildred explained what work in the mill was like. She cautioned Johnnie Faye to be careful around Dalton Threate. "Don't ever get alone with him. You make sure someone else is around when Threate's with you."

She painstakingly trained Johnnie Faye on the spinning mule and was pleased with how quickly the girl picked it up. Mildred stood close to her to talk over the noise and watched the boys crawling and sweeping up cotton fibers beneath their machine.

Johnnie Faye was concerned the boys might get hurt and often yelled at them, "Careful there! Get out, get out!" and watched them scramble away.

She liked Mildred and was touched by her kindness, but what she wanted right now was to change her look to become more attractive. She liked where she was and what she was doing. She would never go back to where she had been teased and derided, and she told that to a North Carolina deputy sheriff who came to the mill to take her back to her mother. The deputy had tracked her down after her mother had filed a missing person's report.

"I got a job, and I live in the women's boarding house," she yelled to him over the noise. "I'm legal age, old enough to be working. I ain't goin' home, and you can't make me."

Mildred joined in, shouting, "Johnnie Faye is doin' a good job at this mill. Her boss man likes the work she's a-doin', and everybody here likes her. She's old enough to make decisions on her own. If you don't believe her age, the payroll department can prove it."

The deputy shouted back that he was going to the office and, if he were satisfied with what they had told him, he would have no further business with Johnnie Faye. He said he'd include in his report that she was of legal age and had no desire to return to her parents.

As he walked away, he thought, *How can they work in that? It's so noisy you can't even think.*

CHAPTER 33

A BIRTH, A DEATH

Webster and the Colonel drank toasts to their latest sales reports and were laughing and joking when Amelia said goodnight and went to her room. Crowell Textile Manufacturing was one of the leading cotton mills in South Carolina.

Earnings were so good the early years that the mill bought back all outstanding shares. The mill is solely owned by the Colonel, except for the shares he'd given Webster and Amelia.

Tonight's celebration was another Christmas-like experience, as combined sales and production figures brought more positive news. There was more brandy. The Colonel congratulated Webster on his excellent work and handed him a bonus check. They smoked cigars and talked some more, and then the Colonel went to bed. Webster looked out the window at his mill, smiled, turned out the light, and walked upstairs.

When he got to the bedroom door, he got a whiff of Amelia's perfume. It was the fragrance he'd smelled on his coat that first time she'd hugged him. When he entered, the room was dark except for the moonlight flowing through the windows. The sweet fragrance around him was alluring.

"Lock the door, darling," Amelia cooed. When he turned from the door, she giggled and said, "Come see what I have for you." She flipped off the covers, sat up, and wiggled her finger. She was naked.

Webster got his shoes off and opened the chifforobe to hang his clothes. Amelia purred, "There's no time for that, honey. Get undressed quickly. Please come. I want you in me."

Nine months later, Jacob Fitzpatrick Webster was born, just a few days before Colonel Crowell felt the stabbing pain of a heart attack and collapsed face down on a boggy side road one rainy morning. The Colonel died that afternoon. He left all his possessions, the mill, and all the buildings and houses of Crowell Village to Amelia.

Weak from the lengthy childbirth and torn between the joy of her new son and death of her father, Amelia was barely able to attend the service in the church and had to be taken home to rest.

At the gravesite, Webster pulled Senator Lawrence aside. "Amelia will need a document to protect her estate."

"I can prepare a will for her. What should it specify?" the senator asked.

"First, prepare a separate document in which Amelia desires to make me a full partner in Crowell Mill and all its properties by giving me a fifty percent share in the company and its holdings provided her by her father's estate. Also, include that she designates me the sole operator of everything and leaves me—only me—the right to determine who my successor shall be. Put in the will that she leaves everything to me should she precede me in death, and then at my death, to our sons."

"We will need to discuss my retainer."

"I don't see that as a problem. Oh, and another thing, Senator, I want to change my name. Make it Charles Lemuel Webster. Can you take care of that for me?"

"I will be happy to . . . Charles."

Within a week, Senator Lawrence visited Webster and Amelia, saying he had papers Amelia needed to sign.

Weak and depressed, Amelia was still in her bed. "Why do we need to do this now?" she protested, but she reluctantly signed and initialed several pages, including an extra page Lawrence had included.

He explained, "Simply says you have read and understood the contents of the above documents. It's just a legal formality."

Webster doubled Lawrence's retainer.

The day the papers were filed, Webster shut the door and danced around his office like a little boy who'd won a prize. It felt the same as when he'd beaten Frankie McCabe and gotten Charles Daughtry fired.

Now it was *his* mill. He had absolute control, and never again would anyone tell him what to do or how to operate it.

He was also determined to settle an old score. In his notebook, he wrote the names Morris and Henry Coleman, Sam Holden's grandsons. Then he called Abe Weinstein, owner of Modern Lady Apparel, one of New York's largest manufacturers of women's clothing. Weinstein and Webster had developed a friendship when Webster worked at Holden Mill.

"You want me to tell you what Holden Mill's prices are when they negotiate to provide me cloth?" Weinstein asked.

"You just tell me what they're asking, and I'll beat their price."

"Why? Mr. Holden was good to you.

"He was," said Webster, "but his grandsons are running things now, and I know I can beat their price."

"How?"

"I don't pay shipping costs for raw cotton, because our cotton is local. And my workers aren't unionized, so my wages are lower. You just tell me what they've bid, and I promise I'll beat their price."

Shortly after that, Crowell Mill became the almost-exclusive fabric supplier to Modern Lady Apparel.

Amelia never recovered. She declined a little each day. Another teacher was hired to assist her and, on some days, had to run the school by herself. Amelia tried to devote time to Charles Wesley and Jacob, but some days, she had no energy to do anything but lie on the couch in her bedroom.

Webster got Thomasina and the doctor from a neighboring town to attend to her. It wasn't that Webster didn't care—he did—but as Amelia got weaker, his old fears of losing someone came out, and the only way he knew to tamp them down was to focus on work.

He also used work to keep from spending time with his sons. They reminded him of Amelia, and he was uneasy about becoming emotionally attached to them, especially after his experience when Charles Wesley was a baby. It infuriated him when his work was interrupted by some act by his boys, especially his youngest son.

Jacob Fitzpatrick Webster was vain, spoiled by a childhood of having his way, and as headstrong as his father. Unlike his brother, Charles, who was of normal height, Jacob was short and small, and he was sensitive about being teased.

One morning, soaking wet after being bucked off into a pond by his pony, Jacob was laughed at by his playmates. Humiliated, he ran into the big house and got one of his grandfather's pistols from a cabinet. Then he marched outside, grabbed the pony by the halter, stuck the barrel against its head, and shot it dead in front of his horrified playmates and Thomasina's oldest boy, Isaac, who pleaded, "Please, Mr. Jacob, don't shoot dat pony."

"Don't none of you ever laugh at me again!" Jacob said, holding up the gun as he wiped the blood from his face and defiantly stared at the boys.

Amelia was bedridden with shock. Webster was furious. Within a week, over Amelia's weak protests, he sent Jacob off to a military boarding school in Virginia in the hopes he'd receive the discipline needed to change his behavior.

The years there were turbulent. Jacob was nearly dismissed several times for acting out. He turned into a bully. Even the bigger boys avoided contact with him.

To fill the void of Webster's focus on work and the absence of Jacob, Amelia devoted her time to Charles. She limited her teaching at the mill school to two days a week to have the energy to review his schoolwork and occasionally walk to the stables and watch him ride. She rarely left the house, and her husky voice sounded as if she had fluid in her throat.

Webster asked—more like ordered—the doctor from the nearby town to ride over and check on Amelia every week. The results were always the same, "No improvement," after which Webster would announce, "No interruptions, as I have important work to do," and close the door to his office.

When he wasn't working at the plant, he spent time with the textile association in Columbia. They were still working legislators to push back against the farm communities opposed to mills. The association members praised Webster for his work and elected him to the Colonel's seat on the board. They noted it was Webster who had turned Crowell Mill into one of the leading textile companies in the United States.

Webster felt at long last he was being recognized for something he cherished—his work.

CHAPTER 34

PRETTIEST GIRL I'VE EVER SEEN

Johnnie Faye Laney stood in front the mirror in her room, she disrobed and smiled. She'd lost weight. Her stomach and thighs were smaller, her bosom had become more prominent, and her auburn hair, with its widow's peak, framed a pretty face and brown eyes that drew people to her. She was happy.

No more froggy butt. I . . . am a woman now . . . ready for my handsome prince.

The next morning, as she made her way through the mill gate, she giggled when she heard one of the men whistle and say, "Damn, she's filled out."

She was busy tying on her apron and didn't notice the men in the water house watching from the breakroom window. Egged on by others, one of them was giving a running commentary of how good she looked and what he'd do to her if he ever got the chance. They laughed. Then Mildred saw them.

Damn men, I'll stop this shit!

She ran toward the water house. The men saw her and dove for the toilets.

"That's right. Run and hide, you sonsabitches; I saw what you was doin'. Johnnie Faye is a young girl. She ain't no mill hussy you can hump in the warehouse. Don't ever let me catch you a-lookin' and talkin' nasty 'bout her again, you bastards. You ain't worth a shit."

"Damn, that woman can cuss," one of them said. "Don't ever make her mad."

Mildred may have stopped the leering from the water house, but she didn't stop their talk nor their looking. Dalton Threate noticed Johnnie Faye's changes, too. He wasn't the only one. So did Mervin Hutson, the cotton waste scavenger paired with Matthew to crawl beneath Johnnie Faye's machine.

Mervin was forced to work in the spinning room because of his sister. She was new to the job and had made the mistake of meeting Dalton Threate in the warehouse, innocently thinking he was going to show her something about work. Clicking his knife, Threate tried to kiss her and told her to pull up her dress. When she hollered and ran off, Threate went to the office and got Mervin's name and put him to work just to teach her a lesson. He saw to it Mervin lived hard for what his sister had done.

It took a while for Mervin to adjust to his new boss and this new job that had him crawling beneath the spinning machine. Then he discovered Johnnie Faye Laney. His early thoughts of *She sure is pretty* grew to *I wonder if she ever thinks of me?* and then to *I wonder if she knows how much I love her?*

He was speechless the morning Johnnie Faye put on her apron and asked him, "Tie this in the back for me."

"Um, how do I do it?" he clumsily asked, holding the apron ties away from her dress. He was afraid to touch her.

"Just make a bow, like you're tying your shoes."

"I ain't got no shoes that tie."

"Here, let me show you," she said, reaching back and touching his hand. "Let go."

"Huh?"

"Let go of the strings." She turned to face him.

"Oh, uh . . ."

"I'm going to tie it in the front. You see, you just make a loop on each strand and cross them and tie them together like this."

"Um, uhh," he mumbled, afraid to look into her eyes. A voice inside his head screamed, *Are you crazy? Don't look at her bosom! You ain't s'posed to look at her bosom!*

He looked down, and the voice shouted again. *Don't look at your feet! Your feet are nasty!*

Oblivious to Mervin's dilemma, Johnnie Faye untied the apron, turned her back to him, and said, "Tie it in the back so the strings don't get caught in the machine."

"Oh! Uh, lemme see, uh . . ." He fumbled and tied a loop too big on one end because he was afraid to touch her.

"Come on now, pull it tighter."

"Like this?

"That's good."

The next morning, Mervin was in the spinning room early. He'd washed his feet and slicked his hair and stood waiting. When Johnnie Faye came in, he said, "Good morning. Here, let me tie it for you."

Fixing Johnnie Faye's apron became a ritual for several days until Threate walked up in mid-ceremony and yelled, "Mervin, get under that mule! Johnnie Faye, you fix your own apron!"

Things settled down for a while until the men noticed Dalton Threate spending more time around Johnnie Faye. From a distance, it looked like they were lovers whispering to each other. Threate leaned against her to talk over the noise and smiled as she innocently turned to speak as if whispering in his ear.

"Ol' Threate's sure hanging around that machine," one of the doffers said with a laugh. "Must be something wrong with it."

"They ain't nothing wrong with that machine. Threate hangs 'round 'cause Johnnie Faye is on it, and . . . I don't think Johnnie Faye minds it so much."

Mildred didn't like it. She was convinced Threate was after Johnnie Faye. *No boss man should do that to no grown woman, much less a innocent girl.*

Whenever she thought Threate was talking too friendly, she would yell across her frame, "You gonna be movin' yer wife and kids down here, Mr. Threate?" If that didn't work, she'd call him over with some question about the spinning machine she already knew the answer to.

She made a point of cautioning Johnnie Faye, "You be careful about talking with Threate. He's a married man with children."

"Mildred, he's only tellin' me how I can do my job better." Starved for male attention, Johnnie Faye didn't mind, even if he was older, and so what if he *was* her boss?

Threate's instructional talks became more informal and then intimate. He began using seductive tones and phrases, complimenting Johnnie Faye's appearance and work. One afternoon, he checked to see if anyone was watching. Then he leaned in until his shoulder was touching hers, put his lips close to her ear, and, over the noise, told her he had a secret.

"This machine is like a woman, a pretty woman like you. This machine opens herself to let the roving slide inside her and transforms it into yarn to make cloth. It's like a woman receiving a man's seed and turning it into baby."

Johnnie Faye closed her eyes and sucked a breath through her teeth. As her heart beat fast, she moaned. Threate walked away, smiling and clicking his pocketknife.

Mildred saw the reaction and was convinced Threate was talking dirty.

Johnnie Faye was so enchanted she was unaware of the young man watching and fantasizing from beneath the yarn.

Mervin Hutson was so absorbed in the forbidden pleasures he saw that he lost track of where he was. Stupefied, he didn't hear Matthew's "Get out, get out!" and almost got trapped. Matthew snatched him away just as the machine closed. He dragged Mervin to the window and gave him a good cussing.

Brushing Matthew off, Mervin shouted, "You ain't my boss! I can run my job. Anyway, I'm older than you."

While this was playing out, next door in the breaking room, Shorty Thompson found Hubert McLain. "Look what I got. This is gonna take care of our nigger problem."

"A burnt match?"

"I'm gonna lay it on the floor over yonder so Mr. Barringer sees it first thing when he comes in this morning."

"A match on the floor ain't gonna prove nuthin'."

"I know, but I also got this, too. Uncle Henry tore it off his tobacco. I found it just now out in the yard. All I got to do is lay this tag 'longside the match, and Mr. Barringer will know Henry done it."

"Shorty, it ain't right. Uncle Henry ain't harmed you or me."

"You want to be working for a nigger? You see how Mr. Barringer gets him to read them labels on them bales. He'll have him writing in the record book and bossin' us around if this keeps up. Barringer is a Yankee, and Yankees don't know 'bout niggers the way we do. I ain't workin' for no nigger."

"I ain't goin' along with this. I don't like it."

"You just keep quiet. When Barringer sees that match and that label, he'll fire ol' Henry on the spot."

"I ain't gonna lie, Shorty."

"You won't have to say nuthin'. This here label and match will do all the talkin'."

CHAPTER 35

I Got Your Toe

By this time, Crowell Mill workers had gelled as a community. They were sensitive to the lint-head comments by people in town and often talked of protecting themselves should they ever need to walk over there, which they rarely did. Most of their time was spent working and living in the village, which seemed alive with people planting gardens, raising chickens, or watching children play.

Neighbors shared vegetables, milk, butter, sewing machines, and household tools. They looked after each other at work and developed a system to cover for one another during downtimes when waiting for their machines to finish their runs.

Vida Mae pulled Roberta Bouknight aside one afternoon. "Keep a lookout for Mr. Warren. I got to go to the store to get stuff for supper. Miss Bitty is gonna watch my looms for me. I won't be gone long."

She snuck out and walked to the company store. Along the way, she convinced herself it was okay to leave the mill.

I got twenty looms. Most of the time, they run by they self, with no attention. I believe I could leave 'em all day and come back in the evenin', and they'll be runnin' just fine. I ain't goin' do that, but I believe I could.

While she was away, the second hand came onto the weaving room floor. Roberta waved and hollered to pull him aside to keep him from noticing Vida Mae was missing. "Mr. Warren, does this shuttle sound right? It don't sound right to me."

One of the sweepers waved his broom to get another weaver's attention, pointing towards Roberta and Warren. The weaver shut off a loom, called Warren over, and asked if she should call the loom fixer.

Workers used deflection and deception on supervisors to help those taking advantage of rest-time when not needed at their looms. They also helped slower workers keep up.

The signaling and deception continued until Vida Mae returned. She ducked down an alley and found Miss Bitty, the matriarch of the weaving room. She got up close to speak over the noise and asked if the boss weaver had asked about her.

"He was here, but he ain't asked. He's gone to a meeting at the big house."

"Oh, Lord, I hope he didn't see me on the street. Thanks for watchin' for me."

"Brenda Quick is doin' a Bible readin' over at the windows," Bitty shouted. "Check your looms. I'm goin' over there to get some air."

As Bitty walked away, Vida Mae complained to herself about the heat. *My Lord, I thought it was sticky outside. It's worse in here.* Steam pulsed from a valve over her head. *And they pumpin' steam in here, claimin' it keeps the lint down and makes the yarn easier to work. Everything here is about the mill. Ain't none of it about us.*

She pulled out her blouse and fanned herself. After checking her looms, she walked over to the ladies gathered at the windows. She thought it was nearly a sacrilege for Brenda Quick to have to yell to get the Word of God out over the noise, shaking floors, steam, and lint.

Downstairs in the spinning room, Johnnie Faye Laney dabbed her face and chest with a damp rag. She pulled off her scarf, checked—*no one's lookin'*—and pulled her blouse out of her skirt to fan herself with the front. It was steamy hot.

She didn't see Mervin staring through the fibers at the woman he loved; the spinning mule had opened on its outward track.

Johnnie Faye tied the ends of her blouse in a big knot just below her bosom, exposing her belly and back. Satisfied no one was watching, she cupped each breast to adjust her bra.

Mervin was absorbed in titillating wonder. He forgot where he was. That's when Johnnie Faye saw him. "Oh, my God, Mervin, get out!!" she yelled and stood on tiptoes to see over the rollers. The mule was closing. Mervin twisted away safely except for his foot. The wheel had it by the toe.

He kicked at it, but the wheel rolled on as if it wouldn't let go until it finished cutting him for getting in its way. Mervin hollered and then jerked at the screams from above. Johnnie Faye's hair was caught in a roller, and it was dragging her headfirst into the machine.

"Stop! Stop it! Oh, God, stop it!" she cried and then fell back. Blood poured from her scalp and down her neck. Matthew shut down the machine just as the roller spewed out a flat, bloody mat of skin and hair.

Mervin was on his back, hollering and grabbing his foot. Johnnie Faye wailed as she desperately jerked at the tail of her blouse and held it against her head.

Mildred ran over and yelled, "Gimme that!" Then she pulled off the blouse and pressed it hard against Johnnie Faye's raw wound.

Matthew took off his shirt and wrapped it around Mervin's foot. "Here, hold on to this!"

Other operators shut down their machines and ran to see what the squalling was about. Doffers walked up and, finding Johnnie Faye almost naked, turned so as not to see her breasts.

"Git me some clean rags!" Mildred yelled. The men continued to look away.

"One of you, git an apron." A man turned, and Mildred yelled and pointed, "Go get me an apron! Over there."

Dalton Threate ran up. "Mervin, you caused this. I told you to pay attention . . . but you wouldn't listen."

The man returned, and Mildred yelled, "Dammit, gimme that!" She snatched the apron away, wrapped it around Johnnie Faye's chest, and said to Threate, "Here, tie this on. The rest of you, go get me some clean rags." The men stood dumbfounded as Mildred ordered, "Git me some clean rags, and be sure to fold 'em! You can look, but you can't do nothin'. You ain't worth a shit."

By now, Mervin was sitting up, squeezing his foot with the shirt. "Oh, Jesus, this hurts. Jesus, help me."

"Serves you right. I told you to pay attention!" Threate hollered.

One of the boys ran up. "Mervin, I got your toe."

Unaware of the calamity next door, Otto Barringer was in the breaking room, giving hard looks at Shorty Thompson, Hubert McLain, and Uncle Henry. "Any one of you been smoking in here?

"Somebody left this match and label on the floor."

"Mr. B," Uncle Henry said, "dass de top off my tobacco pouch, but I throwed it down in the yard. I don't know how it got in here. I know better than to smoke in here."

"You men know what I said. If I ever—"

"Mr. Barringer!" A boy ran up. "There's been an accident in the spinning room. Mr. Threate told me to get you."

Barringer, followed by the others, pulled open the heavy door and found the spinning room shut down and Johnnie Faye Laney and Mervin Hutson both yelling and crying, "Oh, God, oh, Jesus, this hurts, it hurts so!" and, "My toe, it cut off my toe!"

Seeing his boss, Dalton Threate yelled at the other tenders, "Get your machines running! We don't shut everything down because of some accident."

"Get me some kerosene, somebody!" Mildred shouted. "Hurry up; she's still bleeding."

"What happened here?"

"It's that boy's fault," Threate said, pointing at Mervin as he rolled on the floor. "This woman's hair got caught in a roller; it pulled part of her scalp off. The boy over there got his toe cut off."

"Hurry up with that kerosene!" Mildred yelled. "We got to stop this." As she pressed on Johnnie Faye's head, she looked at her big boss. "Mr. B, these men here can't do nuthin'. I asked them to help, and they just stood like they was helpless—they ain't worth a shit!"

One of the boys ran up with a small can.

"Is that kerosene?"

"Yes'm."

"Mr. B, you take that can and get over here. Once I move this rag, you pour some of that kerosene on. Wait, before you do, let me get another rag to keep it out of her eyes. Better yet, Johnnie Faye, lean over this way so we can just pour it in your hair and not on your face."

Mildred took off the rag. "This is gonna hurt, hun, but we got to do it. All right, Mr. Threate, pour it on."

Johnnie Faye's screams could be heard clear to the weaving room.

"That's good," said Mildred. "Now, Matthew, hand me that folded rag. Johnnie Faye, sit up."

"Here, Mr. B, hold this rag against the scraped-off place real tight. I'll tear up this blouse and make a strap to wrap her head to hold this rag in place."

Tearing strips, she said, "Matthew, put this under Johnnie Faye's chin and tie it against this pad on her head. Put two of 'em on it. While you do that, I'll go look at Mervin's toe. Somebody, bring that kerosene and more pads."

Mildred told Mervin to let go of his foot. She removed the shirt and poured kerosene on the stub. Mervin hollered, and Mildred yelled, "Keep still! You gonna be all right. It only took part of it."

Barringer leaned in. "Here, let me see." He turned to Threate. "Where's the nearest doctor?"

"In town."

"Get a buggy and take this boy and that woman right away, and when you get back, you come tell me what happened."

CHAPTER 36

It's Pure Nastness

Mildred Turnage became a hero, even to the men she yelled at. That is, except for the doffer who quit after workers criticized him for not helping.

At Mildred's house, neighbors dropped off cakes, pies, canned vegetables, and other foodstuffs at her back door—several times anonymously.

Although Brenda Quick had criticized Mildred for not attending her prayer meetings, she now lifted her up in prayer. "Oh, Lord, we is so grateful to have among us a strong woman like Mildred Turnage to help us during our times of need."

The responses touched Mildred. She came to see the workers as family. They respected her and turned to her for guidance and leadership. She grew even closer to Johnnie Faye Laney, the daughter she'd never had. Mildred was happy she'd come to the mill. Her life was filled with goodness, and she didn't need no man to help her either.

The praise annoyed Dalton Threate. He saw Mildred as a threat and tried to think of reasons to fire her, but he couldn't. Even if he could, he felt he needed the approval of his boss before he could act.

The accident upset Webster. To him, it was as if the whole mill were at risk. He called David Oxley and Otto Barringer off the plant floor to meet with him in Oxley's office. Workers could see through the office windows that Webster was yelling and very animated.

"He's chewing them out real good. What did they do wrong?" someone asked.

After being yelled at by his boss, Barringer turned on Dalton Threate. He told Threate he was personally responsible for the production and safety in the spinning room and responsible for what happened there. He didn't accept Threate's lengthy argument that Mervin had been warned about paying attention and his daydreaming had caused the accident.

"You didn't train him properly, and you could have fired him before this accident, but you didn't. I hold you responsible for that, Dalton Threate. If it ever happens again, you'll be out of here fast!"

Shaken by the criticism, Threate fired Mervin Hutson and yelled at his employees for trivial things—except Mildred Turnage.

There was another incident, this time in the weaving room. David Oxley's second hand had a labor problem.

"What happened?" Oxley asked.

"She shut her loom off," said the second hand while pointing to a tiny, old woman. It was Bitty, and she was standing at her loom, ready for a fistfight.

"She won't turn it on."

"I turned it off, Mr. Oxley!" Bitty yelled. "That woman a-runnin' this loom before me dips snuff."

"So, what's the problem?" Oxley asked.

"She was a-suckin' on this shuttle before me."

"So?"

"Look what come on my rag when I wiped it!" The worker held up a faded green cloth smeared with a dark brown stain.

"It looks like she wiped her ass!"

"There's nothing wrong with it," Oxley said. "It's okay."

As other women approached, curious about the yelling, the older lady became emboldened. "Mr. Oxley, I ain't a-suckin' on no shuttle after some nasty-mouthed snuff-dipper! I mean it now, I ain't-a-goin' to do it. I know how to run my job.

"It ain't right to make me or the rest of the women here suck on some shuttle behind some snuff-dipper. It's pure nastness!"

The women applauded. Some yelled, "Amen!"

Oxley gave her a stern look and pointed at her loom. "You turn your machine on right now, or I'll turn you and everything you got out on the street by sundown."

Looking around, he yelled above the noise at the other women, "And that goes for the rest of you, too! Don't you ever shut your loom off because you don't like the way things are done here. I mean it! I'll put you all on the streets. Now, get back to work!"

Burning a stare clean through Oxley's eyes, the old woman picked up the shuttle, wiped it with a clean rag, sucked the yarn through from the bobbin, and, with great drama, loudly spat on the floor in Oxley's direction. She tied the yarn on, placed the shuttle back in its tracks, and slammed her loom on, all without changing her gaze.

Webster ordered Barringer and Oxley to draw up a list of safety rules for the whole mill. Each employee was required to know them whether they could read or not. The first rule required women to tie their hair up in scarves and keep their blouses tucked in their skirts. There was also no smoking in the mill, except in the water houses or while outside. No machinery was to be shut off unless needed to prevent failures in the yarn or cloth.

Learning the rules was like learning their work. Those who could read would teach those who couldn't. Lessons were held every morning at the beginning of the shift, with workers reciting each line until they could do so from memory.

Barringer met with Shorty Thompson and Hubert McLain and resumed his inquiry into the match and tobacco label on the floor of the breaking room.

"I didn't do it. I swear on the Bible I didn't do it," McLain said.

"Me, neither," lied Shorty Thompson. "That nigger done it. That's his tobacco."

"Don't you ever call Uncle Henry nigger!" Barringer said, lowering his voice to a growl. "I can't prove you two put that match and label on the floor, but I believe Uncle Henry knows better than to smoke in here. And I know neither of you like colored people. That likely was your real reason for blaming Henry. If this happens again, I'll let both of you go."

"I didn't do it," McLain said. "And I don't lie!"

Later, McLain slammed Shorty Thompson against the warehouse door. "Listen, you little son of a bitch, I'm not losing my job just because you don't like a colored man. You try something again, and I'll whip your ass and then tell Mr. Barringer what you done. You don't think I won't. Just try me and see."

As if to make two points, Barringer directed Uncle Henry to read the new safety rules to Thompson and McLain each morning at the beginning of their shifts. For them, the first rule was "No smoking in the breaking room."

Barringer then announced that from then on, Uncle Henry would be in charge of offloading cotton, the warehouse, and the breaking room. Shorty Thompson smoldered and pretended to smile.

In the spinning room, Mildred Turnage watched Threate yelling at the scavenger boys about paying attention. From the expressions on their faces, she felt they were more afraid of the yelling than hearing what he was saying. The next morning, she called the boys together and said she'd made up a poem that would help them when gathering cotton waste from under the spinning machine.

"Listen to me," she said. "This could save your life." She sang:

> *Dive in quick as the mule moves past.*
>
> *Sweep up the cotton and get out fast.*
>
> *Don't be slow or lose your toe.*

The boys loved it.

"Every time you go under that mule," she said, "I want to hear you a-sayin' that poem out loud. I'm gonna come by to check on you, and you better be sayin' it the whole time you're under there." She drilled them over and over each morning until the rhyme was memorized.

In short order, the boys modified the slogan and, in a gleeful chorus as they dove beneath the spinning machines, chanted:

> *Dive in under as the mule moves past.*
>
> *Get out fast or lose your ass.*

Each day, the boys' chorus grew louder, as did their laughing and giggling at getting away with something their parents wouldn't approve of.

Meanwhile, Mervin Hutson was learning to walk without putting too much weight on his injured toe. He changed the bandage every evening, as the doctor advised, and his toe was healing nicely. It still hurt, though.

Since he was out of work, Mervin's mother forced him to go to the mill school rather than have him "idling around the house." She wanted Mervin to be better than her, and she knew getting an education offered him more opportunities than she had.

Mervin hated school. He couldn't read well and was uncomfortable trying. At school, every student had to read. He thought people who could read had a special gift he didn't have, and every day, school told him the students who could read were better than him.

He blamed Dalton Threate for making him go to a place he hated. Mervin believed Threate hated him for loving Johnnie Faye, and that's why Threate had fired him.

Finally, his mother got worn out by his daily complaining. "Enough!" she hollered and let him go back to work as a sweeper in the weaving room.

After the accident, Johnnie Faye Laney hid in her room for two days, embarrassed by the huge bandage on her head and nearly sleepless from throbbing pain. Threate told Mildred to tell Johnnie Faye he would "have to give her job to somebody else if she didn't come back to work right away."

"I can't go back in there. Look at me!" Her face was swollen, and her left eye was purple. As Mildred removed the bandage, Johnnie Faye cried, "Look at it! I ain't got no hair up there. I look like someone hit with a tomahawk!" The wound was red, oozed oil, and stung from the air.

"Johnnie Faye, you got no choice," Mildred said while sponging witch hazel onto her skin.

Johnnie Faye hissed and sucked air through her teeth. The scalp had been ripped away from the hairline above her left eye, down her temple to just before her ear. It was ugly. Mildred knew it was ugly. She bandaged Johnnie Faye's head and wrapped it in a scarf, saying, "There, it doesn't look too bad."

"Too bad??!! Look at me! I look like a circus freak! I got a giant lump on my head like a gourd."

"Come on, hun. I'll sneak you in the side door. Ain't nobody gonna see you. Them boys won't be watchin', 'cause I got them payin' attention to runnin' their jobs. Come on, now. You can do it."

Johnnie Faye reluctantly went back to work, feeling self-conscious. Her scalp was tender for a long time and throbbed, especially in the afternoon as she got closer to the end of her shift. She cried every night while staring in the mirror as she cleaned and re-bandaged the big clump of hairless scalp.

How can any man find me attractive now?

A new man named Wilbur Parker was hired in the spinning room to replace the doffer who quit.

Wilbur thought he'd found paradise when he came to work for the mill. He was no longer trapped in a life of sharecropper servitude, and his children no longer had to work the fields—they could go to school. His wife, Sallie, worked in the weaving room. They had three daughters, Jewell, Opel, and Pearl.

Parker had worked on a farm owned by a man in North Carolina and had left for Crowell Mill right after laying out tobacco beds. The man wanted to sue, but North Carolina didn't have the laws South Carolina had, which protected landowners from sharecroppers walking off without completing their obligations. There was a big stink about it in the North Carolina legislature, which took up the issue and quickly adopted new laws shortly after Wilbur Parker got his job at the cotton mill.

The boys in the spinning room liked Wilbur, especially when he and another doffer raced one another to see who could be first to replace full bobbins with fresh ones and set up the machines for another spinning run.

Matthew often bet on Wilbur to finish first when the doffing contests sparked nickel bets. He would push the cart, and Wilbur would doff as Matthew yelled, "Go, go, go! Keep going! You're gonna win!"

Most of the time, Wilbur won, except when the pains in his chest left him panting for breath and holding the bin to stay up.

A few times, Matthew thought Wilbur was going to tumble over headfirst. "Are you all right, Mr. Parker?"

"It's okay. I'm all right. It don't happen often. Lemme catch my breath."

By this time, Webster had hired a man named Higgins to be Crowell Mill's company doctor. Higgins, a graduate of the Wake Forest Medical School, was to serve everyone living within the mill village, including children. He was also permitted to take in other patients as long as they came to his office at the mill. He smoked.

Dupre Merchant was relieved. He didn't want mill people coming to town to see his doctor. Back when the accident had happened, he'd gotten into a heated argument with Dr. Hodge over taking care of Johnnie Faye Laney and Mervin Hutson.

"You shouldn't be treating those hicks. You need to take care of our own."

"You're crazy, Dupre. I'm a medical doctor. I am bound by oath to care for people, and it doesn't matter where they're from, what kind they are, or who they are."

Dupre stomped off and considered using his bank to force the doctor to do what he wanted. But then realized he shouldn't. Dr. Hodge was highly regarded and might tell others.

As he made his way up the street, Dupre saw Rudell Thomas with a small crowd of coloreds gathered around him in front of the bank again. Rudell was selling newspapers out of a small homemade cart.

"Y'all get away from here. You're blocking my bank," Dupre ordered, "and Rudell, you go someplace else to peddle your papers."

He was still muttering and fussing when he entered the bank and climbed the stairs to the board room. A few minutes later, his cronies came in to review the bank's monthly activities.

He looked around the table. "Any of you know what that colored boy Rudell Thomas is selling out on the street?"

"It's a colored newspaper from somewhere up north," someone said. "The Railway Express man says Rudell shows up the same time each month when the train stops here on the way to Atlanta. The porters hand over two or three stacks of papers, and Rudell pays them and hauls the papers to town."

Dupre hmphed and then called on Tom Murphy to give his manager's report. When Murphy was done, he passed out more papers the board needed to act on a foreclosure. They also had a couple of loans to approve. When they were finished, Dupre adjourned the meeting still grumbling about Rudell Thomas.

CHAPTER 37

HITCH 'EM UP

Matthew and the other boys were arguing in the water house over which doffer was fastest. "Wilbur Parker can beat your man any day," Matthew whooped. "He's so fast he could do it one-handed."

"Could not."

"Could so."

"Well, if you're so smart, why don't we make this a real bet?"

"Okay, how much?"

"Twenty cents."

"I ain't got twenty cents."

"How much you got?"

"I got a dime and a nickel."

"Lemme see it."

After establishing the wager, which was the highest one ever in the spinning room, the boys went to the doffers and told them of the bet.

"Mr. Lowery, I'll give you five cents if you beat Wilbur."

"I ain't doin' it for five. I'll do it for ten, but I ain't doin' it for five."

"Mr. Parker, you okay with that?"

"Yeah, I'll do it for ten."

The boys got Mildred Turnage to officiate. Matthew and the other boy took up positions at the bins. Mildred stood at the end of both machines and hollered, "One, two, three!" Both doffers shut off the machines and, in a flurry, were lifting full spools and replacing them with fresh bobbins. The boys cheered and yelled as they pushed the bins along.

They were about halfway down the machines, and Matthew was yelling, "Keep goin'! You're winning!" when Wilbur sucked hard, clutched his chest, and fell into the bin.

"Mr. Parker, Mr. Parker, are you all right?"

Mildred ran up and yelled, "Wilbur, can you get up?"

He didn't move.

"Here, help me turn him over."

As they tried, the bin tumbled, and Wilbur clonked onto the spinning room floor—dead. His face was purple, and his eyes were clamped tightly shut from the pain.

Mildred told one of the boys, "Go get three aprons. We need to cover him up."

By the time Sallie Parker learned that her husband had died, a crowd had formed. She ran into the room, yelling Wilbur's name, fell across his body, and sobbed.

Mildred was comforting her when Dalton Threate came in. He ordered everyone except a doffer and Matthew to go back to work.

Looking down at Mrs. Parker, he said, "Sallie, there ain't nothing we can do for him since he's dead. So, get off him so we can move him out. I'm sorry, but we still got work goin' on. The rest of you people, get to work. We got orders to fill."

Threate turned to the doffer and Matthew and said, "Pick him up and put him on that table in the room over there. Here, let me help. Mildred, bring those aprons so we can cover him up."

Wilbur's body lay in the room for a couple of hours. Dalton Threate stayed on the spinning room floor to make sure his workers tended their jobs. He let Mildred stay with Sallie Parker, mainly to keep her off the floor so she wouldn't talk to others.

Barringer came in, bawled Threate out for being disrespectful, and ordered someone to go get the funeral home man. The undertaker didn't like mill people, so he took his time getting there. When he finally arrived, Sallie Parker told him she had no money. He said he wouldn't take Wilbur's body until he got paid. When he threatened to walk, Mildred cussed at him real good.

"Somebody oughta whip your ass, you son of a bitch. You ain't worth a shit!"

Barringer interceded, got the mill to pay the funeral man, and told Sallie they'd add the cost to her bill at the company store.

Even after getting paid, the funeral director didn't like it. Just before the coffin was closed at the church, he motioned for the pallbearers to stand. There were confused and passed uncomfortable looks to one another before filing to the casket. Then they clumsily unfolded a thick burgundy cloth to screen the casket from the Parker family and congregation.

One of them whispered, "Is this what you want?"

The funeral director nodded. Then he moved behind the pall, reached inside the coffin, and began removing clothing from the corpse and loudly stuffing it into a paper bag.

"Why are they taking Poppa's suit, Momma?

"That's not his suit, baby; your poppa never owned no suit. That's a funeral home suit. The only clothes your poppa ever had were the ones he wore to work on the farm and in the mill."

"They took his clothes off?"

"No, baby, I made them put him in his overalls. Then they put the funeral home shirt and coat over that. I wasn't gonna let them bury him nekked."

The casket was closed and sealed. Then two men placed the burgundy pall over it, and the preacher did the service. When he finished, the funeral director put the grocery-bagged funeral home clothes on top, took hold of the casket, turned it, and began pulling it to the front door.

"Three of you, get on each side and take a hold of it when we get to the door and walk it into the hearse."

The indignity of the clothes removal inside the church was worse at the gravesite. The solemn ceremony was abruptly halted by the funeral director, who stepped in front of the preacher mid-sentence and, in a firm voice, said to no one in particular, "We got to fill this hole now before this rain that's a-comin' gets here."

Mildred was on him with a fury. "You got no right to treat Wilbur Parker like that. That was shameful. You ought to apologize to Sallie, and these people here, too."

"It's beginning to rain; we have to get it done." He turned and said to his laborers, "Fill that hole."

Sallie Parker was still in shock over Wilbur's death, and now she was worried she might never be able to pay down the debt she owed the mill. She also worried it wouldn't be long until her boss came and demanded that one of her daughters work in the mill. She wanted her girls to stay in school. If she refused, they could be thrown onto the street, and the total debt she owed the mill would come due.

A few days after the funeral, her boss told her she had to put one of her daughters to work in the mill because of a complaint by Dalton Threate. Threate didn't care that Wilbur Parker had died. He cared that his spinning room was short-handed.

Crying and near panic, Sallie found Johnnie Faye and Mildred in the water house. "My girls is too young to be a-workin' in the mill. I want them to stay in school. Johnnie Faye, you talk to him. Threate likes you. Don't let him put me and my girls out. We got no place to go."

"I got an idea," Mildred said. "Johnnie Faye, you could move in with Sallie."

"That might work. I've wanted to move out of the boarding house, and I could help keep house and cook, and look after your girls, too."

"Yeah, you could tell Threate you was helping Sallie meet the mill requirement and he needs to hire a man because a man would be a better doffer than girls."

"That's a good idea. I can give you the girls' bedroom, and they could move in with me. But how we goin' to get Threate to do it?"

"I know how," Mildred said. "Johnnie Faye, I been a-tellin' you to pay no attention to ol' Threate. He's a married man, and he wants only one thing from you. This here will prove it. This is the only time I'm a-gonna tell you to flirt with him, 'cause you're too young to be a-doin' this, and we're a-doin' this only because we need to help Sallie. Come here."

Mildred unbuttoned the top of Johnnie Faye's blouse. "This will get ol' Threate's mind off-a Sallie's girls. Hitch 'em up! When he comes by you, take big breaths and do your shoulders like this and let him get a good look. Then tell him he needs to hire a man to be the doffer and you is goin' to move in with Sallie."

It worked. Threate kept looking, talking, and hanging around, fascinated by the rise and fall of Johnnie Faye's adornments. He was nearly speechless, agreeing, "Uh-huh, uh-huh," each time Johnnie Faye made a suggestion.

Later, he told Sallie Parker, "If Johnnie Faye moves in with you, I'm satisfied with it. I'll find me a man to replace your husband."

The first night in the house, Sallie Parker's youngest daughter, Opel, stared as Johnnie Faye removed the bandanna from her head. The accident had left a shiny white scar about the width of a ruler running from Johnnie Faye's hairline to just above her left ear. It had a jagged edge as if scarred by fire.

"Does that hurt?"

"No, it doesn't hurt. It just looks ugly."

"Is that why you keep it covered up?"

"Opel, what are you doin' in there?" her mother called from the kitchen.

"She's okay, not bothering me."

"Can I touch it?"

"No, I don't want anyone touching it. It looks ugly."

"Will your hair grow back?"

"No, the doctor said it won't ever grow there."

"Well, you could let your hair grow long and comb it over to cover it. Then nobody could see it."

"How do you know this?"

"Momma told me. When I asked her about you always wearing a scarf, she told me you were letting your hair grow long so you could comb it over that place where you got hurt."

"Well, that's what I plan to do."

"Miss Johnnie Faye, you're pretty. I bet, when you let your hair grow long, nobody will know it."

"We'll see. But right now, it's ugly. And these scarfs make me look ugly."

"If you was to tie your head up with pretty cloth, I bet you'd be more prettier."

"What a wonderful idea. Get your momma's scissors, and you can help me. I got an old dress we can cut up. We'll see how that works."

After sewing the remnants into turbans, Johnnie Faye tried them on. Opel beamed. "You do look pretty. It's a lot better than them rags."

"Thank you for suggesting this, Opel. It does look better."

When women in the mill complimented Johnnie Faye, she began experimenting with different materials from the company store. To look more mature, more alluring, she kept the top of her blouse unbuttoned and got called down by Mildred, who yelled, "Stop it! You're too young to be dressin' like that!"

Johnnie Faye didn't care. Her handsome prince might appear.

It wasn't long before men resumed whistling and Dalton Threate was back. He leaned close to her ear and said, "I'll come by sometime to see if you and Miss Sallie need anything done around there." He liked it when Johnnie Faye squeezed his arm and said thanks.

He needed something to feel better. His wife and kids had moved in, there was the accident that boy had caused, Wilbur Parker had died, and Barringer was after him. It was more than he could bear. That's all the thought of drinking needed. It bubbled up and argued with the *don't do it* in his head. *Get a drink,* it told him. *You'll feel better.*

He went to a bootlegger and bought a bottle of brown whiskey. Then he walked into the woods and took the first drink he'd had in two years.

His mind told him it was okay. Then the liquor said, *Get another one. That's right, a big one. Feels good, don't it? Yeah, get another.*

Soon his thoughts . . . his being . . . were secure in the warmth of bourbon's embrace. He was safe—safe from Barringer, safe from his wife, safe from his problems.

Besides, he wasn't hurting anyone. Why, he was merely standing alone, drinking by himself in the woods, in the shadows—looking through the bedroom window at Johnnie Faye Laney.

CHAPTER 38

FORCED MARRIAGE, FORCED HOME

Webster and Amelia's eldest son, Charles Wesley Webster, graduated from the Citadel, down in Charleston, near the top of his class and was a company commander at the military school for men.

An engineering major, Charles was hired by the new electric utility bringing power to the city. He married the daughter of a prominent judge and was ushered into a family of pedigree and wealth. He and his wife were expecting their first child by the time his brother, Jacob, enrolled at the Citadel as a knob, as first-year cadets were called.

Whereas Charles followed the rules, Jacob was incorrigible. At the Citadel, Jacob fought back against the hazing and discipline upperclassmen imposed. He was constantly walking off demerits and threatened with dismissal by the school's commandant. He completed his second semester with grades just above failing and was finally kicked out after getting the daughter of the school's chemistry instructor pregnant.

Webster called Senator Lawrence for help. "He got this girl pregnant. Amelia insists he marry the girl, but I don't want him to. Mainly, I don't want her or her family thinking they can use this to gain an interest in my mill. What can we do?"

"I've got a friend," Lawrence said. "He's the senator from Charleston, a Citadel graduate, and knows the important families down there. Let me see what he and I can come up with."

A couple of days later, Lawrence called Webster. "All right, here's what we can do. Ravenal Anderson has arranged for Jacob to work for the county supervisor up in McClellanville. He and I agree that Jacob should marry this girl."

"No, I won't permit it."

"No, no, Charles, just listen a minute. This girl's family wants her to be married before the baby is born. They want to protect their family name and their daughter's reputation. Senator Anderson met with them, and they have agreed for him to represent their interests in this matter. He's a lawyer.

"Here's what he and I have worked out. Jacob marries this girl, she continues to live with her parents, and Jacob works for the supervisor up in McClellanville until the baby is born. At that point, you pay his wife on the condition that she renounces any claim to your company as part of a divorce settlement."

"How much?" Webster asked.

"Senator Anderson says it will take twenty thousand dollars to make this work."

"Twenty thousand? That's extortion."

"Charles, if you want this done, trust me, this is what it will take. Ravenal says he will prepare the agreement as part of a mutually agreed-upon divorce between Jacob and this girl, which will happen right after the baby is born. Ravenal already has a judge lined up to grant the divorce."

"I don't want them living together."

"They won't. She'll be with her parents, and Jacob will work for the county supervisor in McClellanville. The divorce agreement will specify that in exchange for the twenty thousand dollars, she agrees to give her child her family name, not yours, and to never file suit on her or her child's behalf against your company."

"How do we know Senator Anderson will keep his part of this bargain?"

"He's a longtime friend of mine, Charles. He's trustworthy. Besides, he doesn't get paid until the girl gets her money. His fee will be fifteen percent of whatever she gets."

"And how much do you want, Matthew, to make this happen?"

"Two thousand. I can make it happen for two thousand."

Webster summoned Jacob home to the mansion and yelled at him despite Amelia's pleading to be nice. "You listen to me, Jacob Webster. You either do this, or I'll see to it you never inherit anything from your mother or me. Do you understand?"

"Yes, sir."

"Now, when this divorce is over, you're moving back home and will work in the mill, where I can keep an eye on you!"

"Charles, please," Amelia pleaded and then gasped for air. She leaned against the door frame and took deep breaths. "He's . . . our son. There is no need"—she sucked in big gulps—"for you to yell at . . . I"—*cough, cough*—"need some water."

"Are you okay?"

Amelia waved Jacob away and walked from the room. "I'll"—*cough, cough*—"be all right."

"Jacob, take care of your mother. And close the door," Webster ordered. "I have work to do."

Amelia's health was slipping again. For some time, she had difficulty breathing and a cough that dogged her and could be heard throughout the house.

Between Jacob, Amelia, and the mill, Webster felt it was more than he could handle at times. *Be tough*, he told himself. *You're tough—concentrate on the mill.*

Gossip about the pregnancy flew through the community. Ladies in the town embellished tales of Jacob's behavior.

"He was so spoiled. Why wouldn't you expect him to believe he could do anything he wanted? And that poor pony."

"Webster never spent time with his boys. It's a wonder Charles Wesley turned out all right, and now Jacob so badly."

After the marriage, birth of a daughter, and divorce, Webster brought Jacob home and put him to work as a management apprentice.

"Barringer is your boss now. You do what he tells you to do. I expect you to learn everything about the spinning department, and I mean everything, from opening bales and blending cotton to making warp and weft yarn.

"You foul this up, and I'll see to it you'll never get anything! Nothing!"

As if to underscore where Jacob stood, Webster made him live in one of the sharecropper shacks on the other side of the big house.

CHAPTER 39

THERE, TAKE THAT

Dalton Threate tried to make amends with Sallie Parker. For weeks, he kept coming to the weaving room, asking her if she was all right and promising, "If you or Johnnie Faye need anything, you just ask."

He was there one afternoon, looking for David Oxley, when Sallie waved at him from across the room.

"I'm glad I saw you," she yelled over the noise.

"What's wrong?"

"I need your help at my house. Got a couple of windows with broke latches."

"I'll come by this evening. Right now, I got to find David Oxley. He told me to see him about some special fibers he needs."

That evening, Sallie's daughter, Opel, was sitting on Johnnie Faye's bed, watching as Threate opened a jar of glue and pulled a match out of his pocket.

"You gonna burn something?"

"No. I'm gonna stick it in these holes where the screws come loose . . . see? I put some glue on it and then stick it in this hole and—*snap*—break it off. Then, where the hole was too big for the screw, there's more wood for the screw to tighten up against. That way, I can make these latches snug-on tight."

"Opel, don't be botherin' Mr. Threate!" Sallie yelled from the kitchen.

"She ain't bothering me none. Now, where's that other window?"

"In our room next door."

"Oh, wait!" Sallie yelled. "Lemme get in there. I got to move some of the girls' stuff so you can get to it."

While Sallie and the girls were moving and bumping things around their bedroom, Threate stepped into the kitchen. Johnnie Faye was drying dishes.

"I got your window fixed."

"Thank you, Mr. Threate." She looked at the dishes, feeling like a schoolgirl doing something she shouldn't. She couldn't stop herself, though, and began panting like when he leaned against her in the plant.

Threate smiled and moved around, touching the dishpan, causing Johnnie Faye to look at him. "Call me Dalton," he whispered. "Outside the plant, call me Dalton."

"Well, thank you . . . Dalton."

She pursed her lips, took a deep breath, sighed, and smiled nervously. "I'm glad you got that window fixed. I've been worryin' that some peepin' Tom may be outside."

"Have you seen anyone?"

"I ain't seen no one. It's just a feeling I been havin'."

"Well, you let me know if anyone is ever out there. I'll take care of it."

"I moved my girls' stuff, Mr. Threate!" Sallie yelled from the bedroom. Then, as she walked into the kitchen, she said, "You can get . . . to . . . the . . . window now," as if she'd interrupted something private.

After the repairs were made, Sallie and the girls stood on the back steps to say goodbye. Johnnie Faye was on the porch, still curious about her feelings in the kitchen.

Threate was looking at Johnnie Faye the whole time when he said, "Miss Sallie, I put some sticks and glue in them holes to make the screws tight. Don't be messing with them latches until that glue sets up. I can come by and check on it for you." He reached into his pocket, pulled out his knife, and began clicking it.

"Girls, say, 'Thank you, Mr. Threate.'"

"Thank you, Mr. Threate," they chorused.

He smiled at them. "It was my pleasure. Goodnight, ladies."

"Goodnight, Dalton."

Threate smiled as he walked away.

Sallie turned to Johnnie Faye. "Dalton?"

"He told me to call him Dalton away from the plant."

The next morning, in the water house, Mildred Turnage exploded. "You called him Dalton? You let him in your bedroom?!"

"Where did you hear about that?"

"Sallie told me."

"He was just fixing a latch on my—"

"I don't care what he was fixin'. I told you to stay away from him. He's a married man, and the way he looks at you—well, he looks at you with plain nastiness in his eyes!"

"Mr. Threate likes me. He makes me feel more . . . more mature. I'm tired of being thought of as some child around here. I ran away from home because of that. I'm a woman! He treats me like I am a woman. And besides, you ain't my momma."

"You might be a woman, but you ain't growed smart yet."

Mildred grabbed Johnnie Faye's blouse. "You keep this buttoned, and ol' Threate will leave you alone. He's s'posed to leave you alone. He's a married man."

Johnnie Faye walked onto the floor, looked across the spinning frame. With a defiant glare, she unbuttoned the top of her blouse, cupped her breasts, and stared as if to say, *There . . . take that!*

Lord, help, Mildred thought. *That child don't know what she's a-doin'.*

CHAPTER 40

You'll Like It

Dalton Threate left home to get away from his nagging wife and those noisy kids.

I come home for quiet, and what happens? Those kids are loud, and she's a-yappin' at me like I done something wrong when I ain't done nothing.

He took the bottle hidden beneath the back steps and walked away from the house to do some thinking. He looked at the bottle, briefly thought he shouldn't, and then took a big gulp. The whiskey burned his throat, and he wheezed loudly as his mind told him, *It's okay. Get another one. Get a good one.*

Alcohol removed the barriers that normally governed Threate's behavior. This evening, it made it easier for the dark things deep inside him to come out into the night.

Take another drink, yeah that's good. Now, go to the woods. You like the woods, Dalton. You can think in the woods.

Threate saw Sallie Parker and her daughters walk out the back door and head toward Brenda Quick's house for a prayer meeting. He hid in the shadows and took a big, big drink. The lights were still on inside. She was home.

Go ahead, the whiskey murmured. *She wants it.*

He eased around the side of the house and, from the dark, looked into Johnnie Faye's window. She was holding a dress up against her throat and chest and looking at it in her mirror.

Threate took a slow pull on his bottle and stared. The thought of *go home*—a brief flicker of rationality—was burned away as liquor-fueled desire ignited.

Go ahead, the whiskey told him. *She likes you.*

Carefully laying his bottle next to a tree, he walked to the back steps, took out his pocketknife, and used it to *tap, tap, tap* on the screen door.

"Who's there?" asked Johnnie Faye as she walked into the kitchen.

"It's me, Dalton," he said, clicking his knife open and shut.

"Dalton?"

"Yes, me." *Click, click.*

"What are you doing out there?"

"I came by to check them latches." *Click-click, click-click.*

"Well, Sallie's not home."

"I just need to look."

"I guess it's all right. Come on up."

"It won't take a minute," he said, walking through to Sallie's room. He unlocked the latch and pushed the window up. Then he pushed it shut again, relocked it, and said, "That one works good. Now let's see 'bout your room."

Threate called Johnnie Faye to stand with him between the bed and the window to look at the repairs. He closed and reopened the window, smiling as he noticed her holding her breath and then gasping slightly.

"These screws came loose," he said. "See? I put matchsticks and glue in the holes, and it's now good and tight."

He closed his knife and slowly rubbed Johnnie Faye's forearm. "The window works fine now."

Johnnie Faye sucked air between her teeth and squeezed his arm. Threate gently hugged her and lightly kissed her lips. She lightly kissed him back.

She was trying to decide if this was okay. Something in her wanted to go on, so she kissed him again. Threate moaned and pulled her tightly, pressing his lips against her mouth and sliding his tongue inside. Johnnie Faye gasped. Threate tasted of strong whiskey.

This is going very fast, she thought, pushing back a little. *He's a married man,* she heard Mildred's voice warn.

Threate pushed her onto the bed, kissing her along her neck and just below her jaw. Meanwhile, Mildred's voice was growing louder in Johnnie Faye's head.

He wants only one thing from you!

Johnnie Faye was gasping. She didn't know what to do. She wanted to continue, but then she didn't. Threate pressed his lips against hers, moaning and pushing his tongue inside her mouth. He tasted awful.

She turned away. "Don't do that, Mr. Threate. Don't kiss me like that."

Threate breathed heavily as he rolled onto his side and grabbed her breast. "Call me Dalton."

"No, stop, Mr. Threate! Please stop," she begged.

Threate fumbled inside her blouse to lift her bra. "Come on, now, Johnnie Faye, you know you want it."

The strong smell of whiskey and Threate's breathing and grunting were frightening her.

He wouldn't stop. He looped his arm around her neck and clicked the pocketknife open. She lay still, her eyes open in terror as he held the blade against her throat and drunkenly growled, "You just be still, now. Once you feel it, you're gonna like it."

"Mr. Threate, please don't!"

"Shh!" he said, lifting her dress and clumsily feeling his way inside her panties. Then, with a few violent jerks, he pulled them off.

Johnnie Faye felt naked and helpless. Threate had her pinned to the bed. Letting the knife fall to the floor, he held himself up and fumbled with his overalls. Then, holding Johnnie Faye down, he pressed into her as she yelled, "No, no, stop! It hurts!" Threate grunted and grunted, thrusting into her while she yelled, "Help, somebody help me!" After more grunts and thrusts, he shook and quivered in a drunken, eye-rolling spasm and collapsed on top of her.

Suddenly he was knocked onto the floor. It was Matthew Pressley from next door.

When Matthew and his mother had first heard the noise, they had walked onto their back porch. At Johnnie Faye's cries for help, Matthew had run over and dived onto the bed.

"Get off me! Let go of me!" Threate hollered.

"Mr. Threate?" Matthew said when he realized who he'd tackled.

"Johnnie Faye, get up and get back of me!" Vida Mae yelled. "You get outta here, Mr. Threate!" She held an iron skillet over his head. "Get out of here now, or I'll knock the shit outta you!"

"She wanted me to do it," Threate said as he frantically tried to pull up his pants.

"I did not," Johnnie Faye sobbed. "I told him not to."

"She brung me in here and pulled me onto her bed and told me she wanted it," Threate lied, still fumbling with his pants.

"I did not. He pulled a knife on me."

"This knife?" asked Matthew.

"Give me that," said Threate. "I was usin' it to check the window. She got me in here, tellin' me she wanted me to check the window latch I fixed. Give me my knife, now!"

"I'll give it to you," said Matthew, closing the blade, "but you gotta leave here right now Mr. Threate!"

As Threate ran out, Vida Mae held Johnnie Faye tightly. "We gotta get you to Dr. Higgins. Matthew, run down to the doctor's house and tell him me and Johnnie Faye is on our way down there and Johnnie Faye has been raped."

When Sallie Parker and her girls got home, little Opel found the bloodstain on Johnnie Faye's bed. She nearly scared her mother to death when she ran into the kitchen, yelling, "Somebody's killed Johnnie Faye."

Sallie sent her girls out to find Mildred.

After seeing the bloody sheets and talking to Matthew, Mildred ran down to Dr. Higgins's office just as the doctor was sending Johnnie Faye and Vida Mae home.

"We got to get the sheriff," Mildred said.

"Now, there's no call for that," the doctor cautioned.

"Did you examine her?"

"Yes," he said as he lit a cigarette. His fingers were stained with nicotine.

"And she was raped?"

"Well, she'd had sexual relations, her first sexual relations, she told me. Says she's been raped. But there are times when young girls change their mind, especially when there's blood after the first time." He drew deep on the cigarette, tilted his head, and blew out smoke.

"You just like them men in the mill, Dr. Higgins. You ain't worth a shit," Mildred scolded. "Vida Mae, get Matthew to go get the sheriff. Then go get Mr. Barringer. I want him to know about this before Threate tells him a lie."

"I was raped, Mildred!" Johnnie Faye sobbed. "You got to believe me! I was raped by Dalton Threate."

The sheriff reluctantly arrested and charged Dalton Threate and then released him. A few weeks later, the case went to trial.

Despite the testimony of Vida Mae Pressley and Matthew, both the solicitor and Threate's attorney attacked Johnnie Faye's "so-called" claims at trial that she'd been violated.

Using Dr. Higgins's professional opinion that "young women often change their minds," they questioned and then assaulted Johnnie Faye's morality, lifestyle, and dress.

Threate claimed he was tempted by Johnnie Faye and it was she who'd pulled him onto her bed. "After all, she dressed seductively and rubbed on me at work. She was even in a bad accident at the plant, which she caused because she was trying to seduce me. I was trying to be helpful to her," Threate lied.

"She told me some peepin' Tom had been 'round her house and she needed the latch on her bedroom window fixed. When I got there, nobody else was there. We was alone in the house. I was checkin' the window I'd fixed and had my knife out. That's when she pulled me onto her bed and was a-rubbin' all over me. I shouldn't have done it, but I couldn't help myself. She caused it. Told me she wanted it."

"That's a lie!" Mildred yelled.

"Quiet in the court!" the judge yelled, rapping his gavel.

Johnnie Faye's sobbing at her treatment stopped her testimony. Each time, the judge ordered her to stop crying and "Speak up!"

"I didn't cause it," she said. "He pushed me down on my bed even when I told him I didn't want to. He pulled up my skirt and held a knife to my throat. I couldn't get up; he was too heavy!

Then he violated me. He is my boss man at the plant, and he violated me. Matthew had to wrestle him off me."

"Yes," Threate's attorney said, "we heard Matthew earlier, but what I want to know is, what did you do to get Threate to get on the bed with you to begin with? You seduced him. Didn't you?"

"No, I didn't. He forced himself on me. I didn't cause it."

"Threate's already told us that at work, you unbuttoned your blouse, rubbed on him, and talked dirty. You lured him to your house that night when you knew nobody else would be there, didn't you?"

"No, I didn't."

"You got him into your bedroom on the pretense of fixing your window. Then, after you seduced him to have sex with you, you yelled rape!"

"No, no, no, I did not seduce him!"

"Yes, you did, didn't you?!"

"How could I seduce him?" she yelled and snatched the turban off her head. "Look at me!"

"Put that rag back on," the judge demanded.

"Look at me!" she said to the jury, lifting her hair away and revealing a shiny white scar. She sobbed loudly as tears ran down her cheeks. "How can any man want to love me when I look like this!"

"I can!" a voice cried from the back of the courtroom. It was Mervin Hutson.

"Order!" yelled the judge.

"I love you, Johnnie Faye. You're still pretty to me."

The jury—all men—was out twenty minutes. Then they came back and found Dalton Threate—*not guilty*.

Over in town, Dupre Merchant complained, "See, that's what happens when people move in who are more like animals than humans. I'm glad my daddy isn't here to see what this mill is doing to our community."

Webster ordered Barringer to fire Dalton Threate. "There have been too many problems in that spinning room. I want him away from my mill. And Barringer, see to it that he and his family are out of their mill house by the end of the week."

Barringer wanted to fire Johnnie Faye, but Mildred intervened.

"Ol' Threate tried to claim Johnnie Faye stirred him up and he couldn't help himself. That's what all men do. Don't punish Johnnie Faye for somethin' she ain't done. She's been punished enough . . . and them jurors? They just like Threate. They ain't worth a shit!"

CHAPTER 41

DEPRESSION

Dupre Merchant stormed into his bank, locked the doors, and pulled down the shades. One of them flappity-flapped back up. "Dammit!" he cursed, and after three more flappity-flapped "Dammits!" he finally got it to stay.

"All you ladies, stop what you're doing. We're closing up. Gather your things and leave out the back way."

His manager came out. "Is there something wrong?"

"Tom, you stay with me," Dupre said then ordered, "you ladies, just leave everything where it is, get your things, and leave. I'm closing the bank today and will send word to you when we open again."

The ladies were mumbling, and one screamed as Dupre yelled, "Get out, now!"

"Is there a run on the bank?" the manager asked.

"I'm trying to keep that from happening. A crowd just hit the bank in Cheraw and Bennettsville, and I just saw a bunch of farmers pull up near Front Street."

"Open this door!" a man outside hollered as he rattled the door. "Open up! I know you're in there."

Soon, more men gathered, and they began yelling. The ladies ran up the stairs. "Be quiet!" Dupre yelled. "Go down the back steps and walk out the alley. Go home. Don't stay downtown."

The ladies took off running when one of them said, "Run! They might take us hostage."

Dupre turned to his manager. "Here, help me." He tugged at the heavy check-writing stand and slid it against the front door. Then, grunting, they shoved a big desk against it.

From outside, a man yelled, "Damn it, we know you're in there! Open up!"

Tumpy Hendley ran across the street from city hall and hollered at the crowd, "What's going on here?"

"They got our money, and they won't let us in."

"Y'all just calm down. It looks to me like you're trying to make a run on the bank. Merchant is probably trying to protect your money by closing the bank for the day. Come back Monday. He'll probably be open then, but right now, if you run in there now, some of you might get your money, but others may not. Just go on. Get out of here."

An economic downturn was invading the South. The World War I boom was over and this local downturn was a prelude to what was coming, but the rest of the country was too drunk to care. They were intoxicated on rising stock prices, a new music called jazz, and illegal whiskey sold in speakeasies to defy Prohibition.

Dupre told his manager to lock the vault. He didn't want another mob doing what they'd done to his grandfather. On Sunday night, he and his brother backed a truck into the alley, lugged gold out of the vault, and hauled it away to a barn in back of his farmhouse. The bank closed for a week.

The shutdown had the whole town upset and not just the bluebloods. Rat-bait Presnell and Freddie Hatcher spent three alcohol-fueled nights roiling themselves into a stew about them being as good as anybody else and having the right to get at their money. They lived in shacks behind the train depot.

"It ain't much, Freddie, but it's mine. Gimme that bottle."

When the bank didn't open on Wednesday, the drinking got worse, and so did their thinking.

"I know how to get in there, Rat. I put the roof on that place. All we got to do is sneak up the alley and jimmy the door. There's a big wooden bar across it. I can fix a piece of flat iron, lift it off, and we can walk right in."

They drank and smoked and got so caught up in laughing and drinking about what they were going to do that they passed out on Rat-bait's porch. Sometime after midnight, their liquor levels dropped to *wake up, I need another*, and they sat up, peed, took a big drink, and set off to get their money back. They snuck into the alley and tiptoed up the creaky steps, giggling over what was about to commence.

"Rat, get on my shoulders and use this."

It took about ten minutes. Freddie Hatcher whispered, "Hurry up, Rat." There was a loud *clunk* as the crossbar hit the floor. Then he huffed, "Get down. Your feet smell so bad I'm 'bout to thow up."

The two went through the board room and down the stairs inside the bank. After rifling through a couple of empty drawers, Rat-bait found treasure.

"Freddie, this one is full of money. There must be three, four hundred dollars in here."

"We only gonna take what's ours. Gimme fifty-three dollars. That's how much I got. How much you got in there?"

"Thirty-seven."

"Well, you get thirty-seven. Hold it up so I can see it. Okay, that's all you get. Come on. We got to get out."

It didn't take Tumpy Hendley long to track down the thieves and sweat them into confessing they'd buried the money in their back yards. They were put on trial and admitted to breaking into the bank, but each testified he took out only what was in his account and no more. The jury met for less than ten minutes and found them not guilty. Rat-bait Presnell and Freddie Hatcher were heroes.

*   *   *

At Crowell Mill, the downturn had Webster in a sweat. During the war, he had his mill operating three shifts to meet demand. He was forced to raise wages to keep employees from skipping out to work at better paying mills. Now, the demand was gone and he had to get his costs down, hoping to ride it out until sales picked up.

He rescheduled shifts, reduced days worked, and cut pay. Workers, panting at their machines, were angry at being driven hard to work more for less and suspicious of the job cuts they knew were coming.

In Washington, DC, mill owners banded together to form an association to get favors from Congress. They lobbied for favorable tax treatment and export agreements after Britain put a tariff on American fabric shipped to England.

Webster attended his first meeting there and, at a banquet ran, into his old nemesis, Morris Coleman, Sam Holden's grandson. Morris was in a financial fix. His mill was losing money, and he was mad that Webster was the cause of it.

Drunk on bourbon, Morris found Webster dining at a table of other manufacturers. "You!" he yelled. "You're trying to put me out of business!"

The people at the table were shocked.

"After all my grandfather did for you, and now you're trying to put us out of business!"

"Morris, take it easy," one of the guests suggested.

"No, let him talk," said Webster.

"He's drunk!"

"I know. Maybe he'll speak more truthfully drunk than he did when I was running his mill for him."

"You little son of a bitch! You've been undercutting my prices. I ought to whip your ass!" Morris circled the table.

Webster stood and stepped in close, causing Morris to step back. Webster squinted, trying to look tough. "I'm beating your price because I know how to run a mill and you don't!"

"Gentlemen, stop this right now!" one of the men ordered. "Morris, you've had too much to drink. You need to leave here right now! And Charles, sit down!"

"Nobody is going to put me out of business!" Morris slurred and staggered from the room.

Webster watched him go. "I'm just offering my cloth at competitive prices."

"His mill has gone down since Sam Holden died," someone remarked.

"Morris is angry because our Southern mills can make cloth cheaper than he can," Webster argued. "I'm not trying to put him out of business. I'm just trying to be competitive. After all, this is a free enterprise system."

The men grinned at him, and one of them said, "Free enterprise system? There ain't ever been a free enterprise system, Charlie. Businesses have always steered the system in their favor. That's why we're in Washington tonight. You conspired with Abe Weinstein to rig the system in your favor. Morris Coleman, and the rest of us, lost orders for cloth because of your scheming. Free enterprise ain't ever been. It's always been rigged, and Charlie, you just proved it."

Angry at being lectured to and derisively called "Charlie," Webster promptly left the table, returned to his room, and packed for the train ride back to South Carolina.

On the return trip, he reviewed the notes he'd made from presentations on textile production. He'd heard mill owners complain they were stuck with high-pay employees and little demand for cloth. He knew Crowell Mill was in the same straits and was determined to do something about it.

He planned to reduce his workforce to get costs down, but he immediately ran into opposition from Amelia.

"You can't put them on the street. They have no land to farm—they won't be able to feed their children. You can't do this. They have no place to go."

Webster didn't concede. He called in his bookkeeper and Oxley and Barringer, and they meticulously reviewed scenarios to cut their workforce and wages.

The cuts dominated conversations among mill employees. They couldn't understand why, after being driven so hard and given raises during the war, their pay was being cut and work hours increased. Talk of it took over the prayer meeting at Brenda Quick's. One lady complained, "They done made lots money off us, and now they cutting our pay to make even more."

"That ain't true," Johnnie Faye said. "The mill's losin' money, and they got to cut our pay to keep from losing more."

"They tried to say that over at the plant, Johnnie Faye. I don't believe it. They done lied to Mervin, so he'd get you to tell us a lie."

"No, you're wrong. Mervin told me it was a fact the plant was a-losin' money. He told me, unless they was a increase in sales, they gonna hafta lay people off, or even shut the plant down. If that happens, then where we gonna be? We won't have no place to live."

"I don't believe you, Johnnie Faye. I was makin' twenty-five dollars a week when he was a-drivin' us to death. Now I'm makin' twelve and doin' twice the work. He just don't want to pay us nuthin' so he can make more."

"That's not true."

"Johnnie Faye, ever since you married Mervin and he was named second hand, it seems you spend a lot of time speaking up for the mill. I always wondered if you was a-tellin' the truth about what Dalton Threate done, and now you tellin' us this."

"That's a-goddamned nuff!" Mildred yelled.

"Mildred, your language!" said Brenda. "This here is a prayer meetin'!"

"I don't give a shit," Mildred replied. "I know for a fact Johnnie Faye was raped. And some of you's husbands let ole Threate get away with it. You ought to be ashamed."

"Mildred, you gonna hafta leave. I don't allow that kind of language in my house, especially on prayer meetin' night. Go on, and take Johnnie Faye with you, too."

"Damn women," Mildred complained as she and Johnnie walked away. "I was sorry I come here, but now I'm glad Vida Mae made me. Them women keep makin' up stuff they want to believe—they wouldn't know what the truth was if it slapped them in the face. They ain't worth a shit!"

CHAPTER 42

JESSIE SCORES A HIT

It didn't help when two industrial engineers were brought in from New Jersey. Webster wanted to apply Frederick Taylor's "Principles of Scientific Management" to the system he and his bookkeeper devised. He believed there must be some way to get costs down and productivity up.

Other mills were trying the same, only to find their workers walking out in protest. In Ware Shoals, millhands turned off their machines and stormed the local hotel in the hopes of getting hold of the engineers who were about to do time studies on their work.

Webster decided explaining why changes were being made might lead his workers to think they could negotiate with him. Rather than risk it, he put engineers in the plant, unannounced.

A man named Destazio, carrying a clipboard and wearing a white lab jacket, walked into the weaving department. He was short, chubby, had brown curly hair, and wore a tie. Workers were suspicious of men with ties.

Without even a hello, he stood behind Brenda Quick's oldest son Jesse and began timing each of Jesse's movements as Jesse tended his looms.

Jesse Quick worked in the mill since he was a boy. He was tall, slender, and pale, and unhealthy. The years in the plant had sweated and shrunk his body away from the inside of his clothes. He had a bad cough from breathing lint.

Nearly every evening, Jesse was seized by spasms that sent him stumbling down the steps and out into his back yard. Bending over, with his hands on his knees, he'd cough and spit, and at times, he couldn't breathe.

Despite knowing that millwork was costing him his health, Jesse Quick was proud. He was the best weaver at Crowell Mill. So, it was no wonder he looked at Destazio and shouted over the noise, "What are you doing back there?"

In a clipped New Jersey dialect, the engineer yelled, "Just keep doin' ya job like ya supposed-ta!" and made notes in his tally sheet.

Alarmed at the man's abrupt tone, Jesse turned and yelled, "You writin' 'bout me on that there paper?"

"Get back to woik. Ya wastin' time!"

Now Jesse couldn't do the things he normally did without thought or hesitation. The more he tried, the more his brain repeated, *Ya wasting time!*

"Whadda ya doin' up dere?"

"I'm a-runnin' my job; I'm the best weaver in this here plant!"

Jesse's worrying wouldn't turn him loose. This ill-mannered *whadda ya doin up dere* Yankee, wearing a tie, was standing behind him, writing things about him on some papers and wouldn't leave him alone. When he heard his brain say, *Whadda ya doin up there?* one more time, he told himself, *By God, I'm gonna stop this.*

Blam—the roundhouse right caught Destazio above the eye and sent him skidding down the alley between several looms. Papers flew off the clipboard, zig-zagging their way to the floor.

"Jesus fuckin' Christ!" Destazio yelled. He tried to get up, and Jesse hit him again.

"Don't you blaspheme Jesus, and don't you cuss me, you goddamn Yankee!"

Jesse reared back to hit Destazio again, but Mervin Hutson stepped in front of him.

"Jesse, stop! This man's trying to help."

"He ain't a-heppin' me. I know how to run my job. I'm the best weaver in this mill. He come in here and started yellin' at me about how to run my job. I know how to run my job."

Mervin helped the engineer to his feet. "Get your stuff and follow me to the spinning room." To Jesse, he said, "This man is hired to find ways to do our jobs better."

"Nobody asked me! Nobody asked me nuthin'. You keep him away from me. I know how to run my job."

Mervin handed the engineer over to Matthew Pressley, telling him, "I think you need to call all your people together and explain what Mr. Destazio is doin' here so they won't be no misunderstanding."

Matthew looked at the engineer and grinned. "Damn, buddy, somebody cold-cocked you. Can you see out that?"

"I can fucking see good enough," Destazio said as he spat on the floor and wiped at the lint and grease smeared on his jacket.

"Don't be talking like that in here. We got women workin' here."

"Just let me do my fuckin' job, buddy!" Destazio yelled, wiping his nose with his sleeve.

Matthew grabbed him and pulled him close. "I said, you don't use that goddamned language in here, you eye-tal-yun Yankee. You say it again, and I'm gonna whip your ass!"

Destazio pushed Matthew's hands off and walked away.

"Where you goin'?"

"I'm lookin' for Oxley, I can't woik like this!"

Barringer and Oxley walked up to the big house to meet with Webster about the Yankee problem among the mill workers. Webster first wanted to know if either of them had told their employees they were going to talk with him about the problem.

"No," they replied.

"I've told you before, you work for me. You don't work for the employees. I don't want them thinking, anytime they don't like something, all they need to do is talk to you, and you'll come to me about it. Is that clear?"

"Yessir."

"Now, what is this Yankee problem?"

"These engineers are unaccustomed to Southern culture," Barringer said, "especially Southern politeness. That Italian guy, Destazio, was hit by one of the men in the plant today. He just walked up, no introduction, no explanation of what he was doing, and began a time study of one of them. He refused to tell the worker why he was there and ordered the worker to do his job. He got hit when he started using some rather rough language."

"We need to terminate the man who hit him," Webster said.

"Sir, if we do that, we'll create serious problems among all the workers."

"I can't have employees hitting someone just because they aren't polite."

"It was more about the language he used. He said, 'fuck' and took the Lord's name in vain."

"Tomorrow morning, at the beginning of the shift, you call everybody together by departments. Introduce the engineers and explain why they're doing what they're doing. Tell them the engineers are looking for ways to make their jobs easier. Tell them their pay is going to be based upon how much they produce.

Make it plain that's the way things will be done, and if there are those who don't like it, they can leave."

Barringer and Oxley called their workers together. They tried to explain that the time studies were important, but the workers weren't listening. They were busy snickering, and erupted into howling laughter when Destazio was introduced. His left eye was swollen and purple.

Someone in the back of the group yelled, "Welcome to the South."

When the productivity figures came in, Webster got Oxley and Barringer to rank employees from most productive and cooperative to least.

Layoffs were announced on a Friday afternoon, and the plant was shut down for the weekend. When it opened on Monday, it was running just one shift.

Senator Lawrence prepared court orders and got a judge to issue eviction notices that gave terminated workers one week to vacate mill houses.

Hiram Rangle was one of those who got laid off. He was convinced the mill was making plenty of money and vowed not to leave his mill house. Hiram was religious. He prided himself on being the head of his household and saw his opposition to the eviction as a way to demonstrate he was obeying the Word of the Lord.

He tied his three small children to one of the columns on his front porch and then stepped onto the lawn with a big stick to wave away the sheriff.

"It ain't fair. They worked me and my wife half to death when the mill was running full, and now they says they don't need me no more. You can tell that little midget Yankee I ain't a-movin'."

Hiram's children were crying. His wife pleaded, "Please don't throw us out!"

The sheriff leveled his shotgun. "Stand aside, Hiram. Don't make me use this!"

"No!!" the wife screamed, and she ran into the yard and fell at the sheriff's feet. Clutching his leg, she begged, "Don't shoot my husband."

"Get off me, woman!" the sheriff growled and bumped her with the shotgun butt.

"Don't hit my wife!!" Hiram drew back to swing.

The shotgun blast splintered Hiram's stick and blew off the tips of two of his fingers. The force flipped him onto his back, and he rolled on the ground, wailing.

"I told you not to do this! You left me no choice!" the sheriff yelled.

Hiram's wife tore her dress and wrapped it around Hiram's bleeding fingers.

"I could have killed you, but I didn't," the sheriff said as he walked to the front porch. He cut the rope off the children, and they ran to their momma and daddy.

The sheriff ordered two field hands, "Go in the house and put everything they own out on the street." Addressing the startled neighbors, he yelled, "Someone get some kerosene to stop the bleeding! Now, I don't like having to do this, but I got a court order that means I must put Hiram and his family out. Let this be a lesson to everyone. I have other court orders, too, and I will do everything necessary to carry them out."

While Hiram's wife tried to calm the children, Hiram rolled on the lawn, still crying and moaning in pain. The whole community was agitated.

Even Amelia was distraught. "Webster," she gasped, "that was cruel. There was no reason to shoot that poor man. "He . . ."

She struggled to catch her breath. "Excuse me, he"—*cough*—"was only trying to protect his family."

She bent over; red in the face, and sucked for air through her mouth.

"What's the matter with you?"

"I've been short of breath for a couple of days now." *Cough, cough.* "It'll get better. Let me get some water."

"A couple of days? You've had that for almost a year, and it's getting worse. I'm getting Dr. Higgins to check on you every week. You hear me? Every week!"

"Webster, you must look after these workers," she wheezed. "They have no place to go."

"I'm sorry the man got shot," he said, irritated with her coughing. "We gave him fair warning weeks back. He didn't make any pla—Amelia, go to Dr. Higgins, now. And close the door. I have important work to do."

Webster's old fear of losing someone was back.

*   *   *

Over in the town, Dupre Merchant summoned Tumpy Hendley.

"What's this disturbance in the mill village?"

"I got court orders to evict some of the workers."

"All of them?"

"No, just the ones I got orders for. Webster is laying off workers."

"Yeah, well, I don't want them coming here, looking for work or places to stay.

"Dupre, I can only do what the law allows me to do."

"Yeah, well, you better be finding a way to move them on, or me and my boys will be looking for a new sheriff."

CHAPTER 43

WEBSTER, THE LITTLE TYRANT

The time studies continued, and each employee's movements were analyzed. Additionally, records were kept of the time workers spent in the water house on bathroom breaks, how long they spent at lunch, and the time they socialized with others when their machines didn't require attention.

The industrial engineers used the most productive workers to demonstrate how to perform jobs. Others were taught to mimic the best movements and their equipment setups until the practices became common.

Webster reduced his workforce further. He was desperate. *If only sales would pick up.* But they didn't. The few orders he got were small, not nearly what he needed.

He was reviewing mill data and fretting over what to do one morning when Thomasina frantically beat open the door to his office, yelling, "Mr. Charles!"

"I told you never to—"

"It's Miss Amelia! She turnin' blue!"

Webster ran upstairs to the bedroom. Amelia grabbed him by the shirt, pulled him close to her face, and died while desperately trying to tell him she couldn't breathe. Her blue corpse stared, mouth open, as if calling for help. He pried her fingers away from his shirt, sat on the bed, and sobbed.

Then he stopped. That was the last time he would ever cry. Looking at Amelia's pleading face, he got angry. It was as if some new, malevolent spirit seized him. He screamed at the company doctor, "You could have done something! You didn't do anything, and now she's gone. She's gone!"

"She was too weak. It was her heart. There was nothing I could do. She was just too weak."

"You're fired. Get out!"

Thomasina tried to calm Webster down. "Mr. Charles, yo yelling ain't makin' things no better. Now, you go back down to yo office and let me and the doctor clean Miss Amelia up. She ain't in pain no mo. Go on. We'll take care of things up here."

Webster was shaken. At the funeral, he sat like a wounded animal and pushed away gestures of condolence by well-meaning people until no one wanted to be near him.

He told Charles Wesley, "Go back to Charleston," and yelled at Jacob, "Get out! I don't want to see you in this house."

Webster sat alone at the gravesite for what seemed like hours, muttering, "Never again—never!" He shifted into angry-little-man mode, beginning his days with looking for reasons to yell at people, often over trivial things.

At the house, Clarence and Thomasina busied themselves to avoid him. Barringer and Oxley couldn't. As they walked up to Webster's office each morning, they would speculate on who would get chewed out and over what.

After gathering data, Destazio gave his report. "Your plant is operating at sixty-three percent of its potential output. You could improve productivity significantly in the weaving room."

"What do we need?" Webster asked.

"Put electric motors on every loom. That way, when a loom is shut down, you shut down only one instead of the five to ten looms operating on the pulley system. Next, assign your best workers more looms to operate and get rid of the slow ones."

"How many looms could they operate?" Oxley asked.

"They are currently capable of operating thirty-six to forty looms each, maybe even fifty."

"We could cut our payroll by half. That's a big savings," Webster said.

"And," Destazio said, "you could recoup that productivity you're currently losing."

Webster wanted to immediately cut employees and increase the looms each weaver tended. Oxley argued for a phase-in.

"Oxley, I'm not going to tell you again that you work for me, not the employees," Webster said, growing angry.

"Charles, uh, Mr. Webster, I know for whom I work. But think about it this way. We'll need time to install the electric motors. While that's underway, we can begin adding more looms for each weaver to operate and develop a plan to reduce the number of workers. If we do it suddenly, it might cause unrest among workers in the whole plant. We don't need them banding together or joining a labor union."

"There'll be no union at my plant," Webster declared. "You tell the workers, if they try to join, I will replace them with coloreds who will work cheaper and be glad to live in the mill houses. I expect you to keep up with the productivity of each of your employees and report to me each week how they're improving. I will hold you accountable for that. Is that understood?"

"Yes, sir."

"Now, here's what you are to do. Make the changes in phases."

Barringer looked at Oxley as if to say, *Your idea?*

Webster told them they were also to alert the workers there would be further layoffs. That would give them time to make plans. Everybody would be informed and shouldn't complain if they get laid off.

On their way back to the mill, Oxley was annoyed by Webster's demands. He muttered that Webster must think it was going to be easy for people to accept losing their jobs and the homes they'd lived in for years.

"And he's not the one who's telling the employees they're getting laid off," Barringer said. "He's giving us the dirty work." He kicked at a rock in the driveway. "He's gotten mean since his wife died. I don't like what he's become." He kicked another rock.

Sallie Parker maintained a low profile to avoid being noticed. Johnnie Faye had moved out of Sallie's house when she'd married Mervin Hutson, and now there was only one person working out of Sallie's house, though the mill required two.

A conspiracy helped keep the matter quiet. Mervin was promoted to second hand in the weaving room and was Sallie's boss. He didn't press the issue, and Sallie never brought it up. She wanted her girls to remain in school, and that was okay with Mervin.

It worked well until the new data and productivity system came on. Webster noticed in the reports there was only one adult in Sallie Parker's household working in the plant. He yelled at Oxley that his lack of awareness had cost the mill productivity.

Oxley yelled at Mervin Hutson, "You knew this?"

"Yessir."

"I oughta fire you, but I'm not. We've got a schedule to maintain. You tell Sallie Parker this morning that she either puts her daughters to work in the mill today or loses her job and the mill house. That's all of her daughters, not just one of them."

Sallie had just gotten her looms running when Mervin walked up and, over the noise, shouted, "Sallie, they found us out. If you don't put all your girls to work, they gonna throw your furniture on the street this morning. Plus, Mr. Oxley told me they'll make you pay off the balance on your husband's funeral expenses and any other debts at the store. You ain't got no choice. I'll send someone to get your girls out of school."

"Can't I get them?"

"No, you got to tend to your looms. I'll bring them in here, and we can decide where they're gonna work. I'm sorry, but that's the way it's gonna be."

Sallie Parker thought she had been managing things well, but now it had all fallen in. Her daughters were pulled out of the schoolhouse and brought to her in the weaving room. She told them they had no choice. Jewell was assigned to the drawing-in room, Pearl the spinning room, and little Opel was allowed to work alongside her mother in the weaving room.

To make the point that he was in charge, Webster ordered Oxley to send the industrial engineer to time Sallie Parker's work again and report the results directly to him.

Sallie tried her best but thought it ridiculous when the engineer stood outside the water house and timed how long it took her to use the toilet or get a drink of water.

She stopped socializing and kept moving around her looms, looking for broken ends to appear busy. Now the only time she talked was with Opel, who was trying to learn how to operate a loom.

Opel stood on a box and watched as her mother said, "See here, hun? This yarn broke loose and is leaving a opening in the cloth. See that line up yonder? We got to tie up these broken ends, check to make sure it holds, and then start the up loom."

Opel coughed and hollered, "Momma, it's so dusty in here! I can't hardly breathe."

"It's okay, hun. You'll get used to it." *Lord, Jesus, please protect my youngin'.*

As Sallie and Opel walked home from work, Sallie worried about her daughters not being in school. She was certain an education would help them have a better life. *But with things the way they is, I can only hope.*

"Here, hun, let's go in the store. I got to get groceries."

When they finished shopping, the manager wrote the price of Sallie's groceries on the back of a paper bag. Opel looked on, mentally tabulating the numbers like she had been taught at the mill school.

"That'll be four fifty, Miss Sallie. You want to pay now or put it on your account?"

Opel tugged on her mother's dress. "That ain't right, Momma. It should be four thirty-seven.

"What?"

"It ain't right. It should be four thirty-seven."

"It's right, Miss Sallie. It's four fifty. You got money to pay now, or do you want me to put it on your account?"

"I ain't got no money."

"It ain't right, Momma. It should be four thirty-seven."

"It's right, little girl. I added it right, and it's four fifty, and that's what I'm a-puttin' in the book."

"No, no, it ain't right, Mr. Broadway. It's four thirty-seven. I can prove it."

"Let Opel add them figures, Mr. Broadway. She's finished third grade, and she knows how to add."

Opel copied Broadway's numbers in a new column alongside his and began reciting her calculations as if she were in school.

"And nine and eight is seventeen, and carry one is three, making the cents thirty-seven, and one and one and one and one is four. See, it's four thirty-seven. It ain't four fifty. My numbers is the same as yours, Mr. Broadway, but you added it wrong. It ain't four fifty; it's four thirty-seven."

"Maybe you made a mistake, Mr. Broadway," said Sallie. "You weren't tryin' to cheat me, were you?"

"No, no, it's four fifty. I wasn't trying to cheat."

"Lemme look at them numbers, Broadway," Mildred said as she stepped into the store. "Opel, you add them numbers up out loud, and I'll check your work."

Opel recited again, concluding, "And nine and eight is seventeen, and carry one is three, making the cents thirty-seven, and one and one and one and one is four. See, it's four thirty-seven."

"Broadway, you trying to cheat this woman because she can't figure?"

"No, I musta made a mistake. I won't trying to cheat. I'll write four thirty-seven down in the book. See?"

Mildred studied the entries next to Sallie's name.

"You son of a bitch," she said and snatched away the book. "You been cheatin' her all along!"

"No, I ain't. Give me my book!!"

"Hell, no!" Mildred scanned the numbers.

"Sallie, every entry he charged to you in this book ended with a zero. They ain't no entries ending in thirty-seven cents or forty-two cents. They ain't no way every time you shopped your bill added up even. He's been adding something extra in the book to steal from you."

"Broadway," Mildred glared, "I'm telling Mr. Barringer about this, and I'm gonna tell everyone I see to make sure they check behind you because you is a cheat!"

Barringer carried the complaint to Webster, who fired Broadway after Webster's bookkeeper found a pattern of even numbers in all the entries.

Opel became a hero at Brenda Quick's prayer meeting. Even Mildred was praised for getting Broadway fired.

"I had a feelin' he was cheatin' me," one woman complained, "but I couldn't prove it."

"We was a-gettin' cheated 'cause we are ignorant about arithmetic and can't read," Mildred said. "We need to study on it so no one can cheat us no more."

"Why don't we start a learnin' club?" someone suggested.

"We could meet up at my place on Thursdays," Mildred told them. "Y'all bring your children's reading books and arithmetic books, and we can practice reading, writing, and 'rithmetic. We'll call it the Three R Club."

Soon the group grew too large for Mildred's house and moved to the schoolhouse. Some men started attending. Opel and other children taught adults how to read and do math.

Meanwhile, things were changing at the mill. Webster sent Jacob and Matthew to Draper Manufacturing to learn how to set up and operate the new spinning machines. They were faster and so easy that young boys could run them, which was exactly what Webster wanted.

Barringer recommended Jacob for the trip. He was impressed with Jacob's knowledge of plant equipment and mentioned that to Webster.

Mildred was transferred to the weaving room. She was told she had one week to learn how to operate a loom. She wasn't the only one getting harassed.

In the past, managers had casually moved through the departments and subtly encouraged employees to pick up their pace. Now there was no more singing or gossiping. Things were serious—and personal.

Pick clocks and other devices were used to measure individual output against standards set by industrial engineers. This enabled Webster, Oxley, and Barringer to analyze the output of each employee on a daily basis.

Webster used this information in his morning meetings to badger Oxley and Barringer as they reviewed the previous day's output. He enjoyed catching them off guard.

"What's going on with this Wilma Thompson?"

Oxley fumbled to locate her name on the production chart. Then he mentally raced to determine how to phrase his answer, only to be cut off by Webster.

"You don't know, do you? It's plain she's not keeping up."

"No, sir, I don't know why."

"Damn it, find out! Your job is to keep production up and find out why when it isn't, and I expect you to fix it. You're responsible for weaving, not me!"

CHAPTER 44

Great Depression –
The Stretch-Out Begins

Orders for fabric stopped completely when the New York clothing industry shut down. Owners were waiting to see what would happen next across town in the financial district. The stock market crashed on Black Thursday, October 24, 1929.

Unregulated, speculative stock buying with no money to pay it back had created a phony market. When it collapsed, it pulled everything down with it. There were runs on banks, factories closed, and growing numbers of people were out of jobs.

Abe Weinstein called Webster.

"You've heard about Morris Coleman?"

"No, what has he done now?"

"He's dead—jumped from the roof of his mill. He has a wife and three kids."

"You didn't cause him to jump, Abe. Morris did that on his own."

"Well, I helped you undercut his prices, which affected his business, and now he's dead. I don't want to do business like that anymore. From now on, Webster, your company will submit bids like everyone else. No more special contracts."

"I'm not responsible for Morris Coleman's death. I just have a better way of doing it cheaper."

"From now on, Webster, you speak to Mr. Bumgardner. He'll handle your orders with my company. I don't want to have anything to do with you."

"Go ahead! I don't need your business anyway!"

Webster slammed down the phone and kicked a trash can across the room.

Thomasina ran in to check on the noise, and Webster yelled, "Get out!"

The mill shut down for a month; Webster laid off more workers. When it reopened, it ran four-day, sixteen-hour shifts among two groups to share work among as many households as possible.

Those not laid off ran more machines, worked at an exhausting pace, and drew lower pay. And they got docked for defects in fibers and fabric, despite complaining the machines were running too fast.

Webster was convinced his new system would enable the mill to operate until sales improved. The workers came to hate it. They called it "the stretch-out."

Vida Mae complained about it in the water house. "They got me runnin' thirty-five looms when I used to run twenty."

Webster fired David Oxley after growing tired of a lack of improvement in the weaving room. Oxley, shaken that he was being turned out during the Depression, complained, "How could you do this to me? I helped you build this company."

"You failed!" Webster said. "You didn't stay on your supervisors to get the job done. I don't tolerate failure. Now, get out!"

To replace Oxley, Webster hired a man from Graniteville to take charge of weaving. Charlie Prickett had worked his way up from sweeper to loom fixer and then to boss weaver at Graniteville Manufacturing, one of South Carolina's largest textile companies.

Webster told Prickett, "I got rid of one man because he wouldn't stay on his employees. I don't want to do that again. Do you understand?"

"You needn't worry about that with me, Mr. Webster. I'll see to it they do what you want."

On his first morning, Prickett called in Mervin Hutson and the other second hands. "I see that these three women ain't meetin' their production quotas. You tell them they got one week to get up to speed or I'm throwin' them out by Sunday. Just remind them that they's plenty of workers waitin' outside the gate, and ol' man Webster has told me, if he has, to he'll hire niggers who'll work cheaper and turn the mill village into a nigger town."

Prickett fired Wilma Thompson at the end of his first week to show Webster he was up to the job. Webster was impressed.

The firing shook the Three R Club. "He warned her when he first come in to work," said Mildred. "Then he let her go the end of the week, even after she'd made her quota. I helped her; she was always a little slow, but she was makin' it up. She was trying."

Other women complained. "He tells me and Jesse we have-ta take over Wilma's looms as well as ours now. Jesse's runnin' forty looms, and they got me runnin' thirty. I can't even sit down. Don't have time to get a drink of water."

"I hear tell that mill hands at other plants are goin' on strike over this stretch-out."

"Maybe we need to go on strike."

"They'd just hire them spare hands standing at the front gate," Mildred cautioned. "We need to be a-heppin' each other on our jobs. If you get behind, get someone to hep you catch up. If you're caught up, hep somebody who ain't. We all in this thing together."

On the other side of the mansion, in his sharecropper shack, Jacob Webster was isolated, shunned by his father and viewed suspiciously by workers who went out of their way to avoid him. He was stuck in a community that offered no social interaction, much less friendship. To fill his evenings, he studied trade publications and manuals Draper Manufacturing gave him.

On the work floor, he spent hours observing how the new machines operated, and he used Draper's tables and mathematical calculations to make minute adjustments that improved output.

Otto Barringer noticed the improvements and pointed them out to Webster during his meetings. "Look at these numbers. Jacob's got us running ahead of schedule now," he said as he stood at the drop-leaf table.

After debating whether to continue, Barringer mumbled, "Jacob told me he'd like to see you, sir."

"Well, it's about time these figures improved, Barringer. I'm tired of having to point out things to you that you should see yourself. And another thing, don't be telling me what I ought to do about my family."

"Sorry, I wasn't suggesting, sir; I just thought you'd like to know what he said."

"You may go now. When you see Jacob, tell him to come by some evening when it's dark. In the meantime, stay on your workers. They could be doing better, and you're responsible for that."

"Yes, sir," Barringer replied and walked away.

A few evenings later, Jacob knocked on the door at Webster's office.

"Come in, Jacob. What is it you want to talk with me about?"

"I just wanted to see you, Father."

"I don't have time for a social visit."

"I came here to tell you I can make the looms run faster. I've read the manuals, and I've looked at the settings Oxley and the new man, Prickett, are using."

"Oxley was too soft on his workers." Webster frowned. "The workers can run a lot more looms than they're complaining about. I've got the figures to prove it."

"I can speed them up, Father. And I think we can do it without losing time due to breakage. The yarn we're running now can handle faster speeds."

Webster liked what he was hearing. It reminded him of his days reading machine manuals to Sam Holden.

Next, he made Barringer fire most of the adults in the spinning room and replace them with young boys. He'd gotten the idea from mill owners who'd found ways to get around South Carolina's child labor laws. The state had set the legal age for employment at twelve.

The mill owners told him to hire a few twelve-year-old boys and list them on the payroll as employees. Then, as a condition of their job, the boys would be told to bring their younger brothers or other boys with them to work as helpers. Webster could save money by paying the older boys low wages with a little extra to pay their brothers or friends.

"If any inspectors show up, hide the young ones and show the inspectors your payroll records and the older boys."

"What about their parents?"

"The parents are so desperate they won't tell."

The decision to hire boys was easy. The new spinning machines required much less attention than the old spinning mules. Most of the time, they ran on their own. This left the boys with extended time for play and to get in trouble.

When they weren't shooting marbles or playing mumblety-peg, they'd hide underneath machines and tug on the trousers of unsuspecting workers or pull the spring back to the toilet door and let it whang as someone was trying to do his business. If they weren't doing this, they took naps.

The spinning machines were so large it was difficult for Barringer to see his young workers. He was nearly crazy, shouting, "Get down off there!" "You goin' to get hurt!" and, "Put that back!"

Barringer tried to tell Webster he thought it unwise to hire boys too young to be around dangerous machinery. One boy, he said, was just six and so small he needed help getting his clothes fixed after going to the toilet.

Peanut Tillman would shuffle out of the water house and onto the spinning room floor, fumbling with his union suit with his coveralls around his ankles, needing an older boy to help him.

Webster told Barringer that even though he and Jacob had made improvements, their production wasn't nearly as good as it could be, and he must do more.

As the criticisms mounted, Barringer realized he was about to be fired. He was the highest-paid employee in the whole mill. He planned his move.

After contacting Oxley, he found a job at a North Carolina mill and then quit on a Thursday morning. Webster had chewed him out for not making production. Barringer unloaded.

"You're not the same man I knew when we first worked together. You're like some little Napoleon, strutting and yelling. You may own this mill, but you tricked your way into getting it, and now you bully people to get them to do what you want.

"Gimme my pay. I'm sorry I ever came here."

"Get out! Nobody talks to me like that!"

Webster summoned Charlie Prickett to his office. "You know somebody who can run the spinning room the way I want it?"

"I know just the man, Mr. Webster. He'll whip your spinning room into shape in no time."

A few days later, Webster hired Prentice Coker, a man with a mean streak. He'd lost an eye in a fight as a boy, had a quick temper, and wore an eye patch as a warning for others not to mess with him.

His first day on the job, he called the boys in the spinning room together and yelled at them just to let them know he was their new boss and meant what he said.

"They ain't gonna be no more mumblety-peg in the spinnin' room. This here is a workplace, and I expect every one of you to be a-standin' and watchin' your machine, even if it don't need tendin'."

Then Coker nearly scared Peanut Tillman to death. The six-year-old shuffled out of the water house, looking for help with his coveralls, and came face to face with his new boss. Peanut's pants were around his ankles.

"What are you doin' like that?! Hitch up them coveralls. Don't you ever come out onto the floor lookin' like that!"

Peanut wet himself. He shambled into the water house and turned in circles, crying in frustration, grabbing for the coverall strap he just couldn't reach. One of the older boys came to help him.

They all told their parents that night what their new boss had done. Most were shocked to learn Barringer was gone.

"Did Webster fire him?"

"No, I heard tell he just quit. Nobody knew anything until this new guy Coker come to the spinnin' room."

CHAPTER 45

PEANUT GETS CAUGHT

Things settled down in the spinning room for a couple of weeks as the older boys helped Peanut Tillman with his pants. Then, on a Friday morning, he made a quick dash to the water house. There was no one to help. After he did his business, he shuffled onto the spinning room floor with his coveralls around his ankle, struggling to button his union suit and whining.

Wham! Coker was on him.

"Damn you, little pissant. I told you not to ever come out here and do that no more!"

To prove he was boss, Coker picked up the terrified boy, hung him by his ankles out the second-floor window, and yelled at him, "You gonna do that again?!"

"No, please, I won't do that again! Please don't drop me!"

"I oughta drop you."

"No, please, I won't do it no more."

"I oughta drop you, but I ain't!" Coker pulled the terrified boy back into the spinning room.

"Now, hitch up them pants and get to work!" he thundered. "All of you, get to work!" Then he strode from the room. That was Friday.

On Sunday morning, the sheriff of Anson County, North Carolina, found the body of a one-eyed man with an eye patch floating in the North Carolina side of the river. There was talk among millhands that the killing was proof there were some things workers wouldn't put up with. They were developing a collective discontent over how they were getting treated and had begun talking about what to do about it.

With Barringer gone and Coker dead, Webster needed someone to run the spinning room. He summoned Jacob to his office and tried to tell him what he wanted, but then he shifted into angry frustration over what was happening in the plant.

"Hanging a child out a window, no wonder the workers killed him. Jacob, *you* must get the spinning room—the whole plant, for that matter—settled down."

"I've got just the idea, Father. We can turn what happened to that boy to our advantage."

Jacob had read engineering studies showing more savings could be had if mills reduced the time workers were on breaks, eating meals, or using the toilet. Engineers called these activities wasted time because they didn't produce anything. "We could recoup some fifty minutes of wasted time per employee per day, Father. Here's how. We give workers sandwiches and drinks so they can eat while they work. If we got the food out the company store, we could use that Tillman boy to deliver it to the workers from a cart. We can put a memo out that he is getting promoted and announce that the mill will provide workers dinner. That way, we'll be demonstrating the mill cares about this boy, and the others, too."

Jacob also suggested that his father include in the memo new rules about bathroom and lunch breaks. "Put it in writing. That'll show them we mean business."

"You get this boy and make arrangements with the company store, and I'll write the memo," Webster directed. "Now, if you're going to be in charge of the spinning department, you can't be living in a sharecropper's shack. You can move your things into the house here."

"Thanks, but I think it would look better to the workers if I were to move into Barringer's old house. That way, they'll think of me as the head of the spinning department and not the boss's son."

Peanut Tillman began his new job that very day. He pushed the cart the workers would later call the "dope wagon," after a term they used for soft drinks. He surprised Jesse Quick as he made his way down a long alley of Jesse's weaving machines. It was lunchtime, and Jesse was hot and sweaty.

After coughing into a rag, he asked in a wheezy voice, "What ya doin' boy?"

"I'm bringing you your lunch, Mr. Quick."

"I ain't asked fer no lunch. I ain't got time to eat." He coughed.

"No. Here's a sandwich. And I got you a soda drink, too."

"How much?"

"It don't cost you nuthin'. The mill is givin' it to you. I got promoted to lunch wagon tender. They told me to bring everyone here a sandwich and a drink. You can eat your sandwich and keep right on workin'."

Jesse took a long gulp of his soft drink and then bit into a bologna and cheese sandwich. *Damn mill—give me a sandwich and a drink? They got me runnin' fifty looms; no wonder they don't want me stopping to eat.*

Mildred Turnage saw the lunch cart rolling towards her and thought it was some new automated device until she saw Peanut's head bobbing behind it. The cart was almost as tall as he was, and the boy pushed with a grunt to get it rolling. Peanut used a Coke crate as a step so he could reach inside.

She smiled. "Are you sure you can handle that?"

"It ain't heavy once I get it goin'. I got a promotion, Miss Mildred. I'm now the lunch wagon tender. They's a sandwich and a drink in here for you." He plopped the box on the floor and stepped up. "It don't cost nuthin', neither."

He smiled, handed her a sandwich, and snapped open a Coca-Cola. Then he wiped the fizz off with a rag and handed it to her.

Mildred thought it was nice of the mill to give her a sandwich. Then she realized, *Every time I think they bein' nice, it becomes plain they doin' it 'cause they want somethin'.*

At the end of the shift that first day, the boss weaver brought everybody together and told them the mill would provide dinner from that time forward. But, he said, there would be no more thirty-minute dinner breaks. Workers could eat and tend their looms at the same time.

Workers groaned when he told them they were allowed only two bathroom breaks per shift and for only five minutes each. Those not abiding would get their pay docked. Anyone who took extra time off would be let go.

The plant was operating one shift, twelve hours a day, three days a week. Mildred, Jesse, and the others were mumbling the plant was making them work longer hours on a short schedule to produce as much cloth as they did on a regular one, with or without a free sandwich. The boss weaver posted a memo on the bulletin board announcing Peanut's promotion and the new company rules.

The next day, someone scrawled, "This ain't fair," on it.

CHAPTER 46

Mildred Writes FDR

The Depression ground on through South Carolina. There were more bank failures. Textile mills and other plants ran abbreviated schedules. In Columbia, Governor Ibra Blackwood parroted the Hoover administration's claim that tax cuts and reduced government spending would fix the economy and prosperity was just around the corner.

It was a conservative mantra used until the public got tired of bread lines and homeless camps, called "Hoovervilles." Franklin Roosevelt was elected in a landslide. By this time, twenty-five percent of American workers were unemployed.

Roosevelt quickly pushed the National Industrial Recovery Act through a willing Congress. The law suspended antitrust laws so industries could collaborate to set prices at levels enabling plants to stay open and keep people working. The Fair Trade Codes also protected workers by prohibiting industries from firing or demoting workers trying to organize labor unions.

The codes roiled textile owners. Webster had no desire to stop undercutting the market price for cloth and didn't care what the codes provided for workers.

Senator Lawrence called him to warn that rumor mills at the Statehouse were talking of a big push by the United Textile Workers to organize mill hands in South Carolina.

Webster wasn't worried. He felt the isolation of his plant away from areas with lots of mills was a buffer that would enable him to operate his company as he saw fit.

He was unaware his workers listened to a Charlotte radio station reporting on strikes at North Carolina mills and were already talking about strikes themselves.

They also heard Franklin Roosevelt's fireside chats and believed their new president was talking directly to them. The Three R Club believed it so much they got Mildred to write the president a letter.

President Franklin Roosevelt
White House
Washington

Dear President Franklin D. Roosevelt,

We is writin' you on behalf all the workers here at Crowell Mill at Haigler's Crossing in South Carolina.

They was a time when Colonel Crowell and Mr. Webster treated us workers like human beings and paid a decent wage and let us live in mill houses. Since this depression, they have fired lots of workers and made them move out they houses. Some of them had no place to go. Some moved in with families.

Then they worked those of us they kept on nearly half to death with this stretch-out, which is making us run twice the number of machines we was running before. And they threatening to kick us out of our houses if we don't.

Mr. Webster is now treating us like we was slaves. We don't get no break for lunch no more. We have so many machines to tend we barely have time to go to the bathroom, which they don't let us go but two times a shift.

We know you got a lot to worry about because of this depression, but please help us down here. We're tryin' to do the best we can but can't never seem to catch up.

God bless you, Mr. Roosevelt.

The Three R Club
Crowell Mill, SC

A month later, Vida Mae Pressley ran out to her back yard, yelling, "Turn your radios on! Turn your radios on! The president is talking 'bout us."

Franklin Roosevelt was holding a fireside chat to explain how his National Industrial Recovery Administration was going to work. Roosevelt used the textile industry as an example.

The president said he'd received thousands of letters from textile workers complaining of long hours and being overworked as a result of the stretch-out. He noted he was creating a Cotton Textile Board to help workers and mill owners alike.

Mildred Turnage gleamed. "He got our letter. The president read our letter."

She teared up as Roosevelt said:

It is probably true that ninety percent of these cotton manufacturers would agree to eliminate starvation wages, would agree to stop long hours of employment, would agree to stop child labor, would agree to prevent an overproduction that would result in unsalable surpluses.

But what good is such an agreement if the other ten percent of cotton manufacturers pay starvation wages, require long hours, employ children in their mills, and turn out burdensome surpluses?

The unfair ten percent could produce goods so cheaply that the fair ninety percent would be compelled to meet the unfair conditions.

Here is where government comes in. Government ought to have the right, and will have the right, after surveying and planning for an industry to prevent, with the assistance of the overwhelming majority of that industry, unfair practices, and to enforce this agreement by the authority of government.

The so-called antitrust laws were intended to prevent the creation of monopolies and forbid unreasonable profits to those monopolies. That purpose of the antitrust laws must be continued, but these laws were never intended to encourage the kind of unfair competition that results in long hours, starvation wages, and overproduction.

"Glory to God, praise Jesus, the president read our letter!" shouted Brenda Quick, holding her arms over her head as she danced in her back yard. "Thank you, Lord, for President Roosevelt."

A crowd gathered behind Mildred's house and spread down the block.

"She done it! Mildred done it! Thank God for Mildred Turnage!" someone shouted.

"At last," Mildred cried, "we got a president who knows about us and cares about us!" She picked up Opel and hugged, kissed, and danced with her.

"Opel, you hepped us get the Three R Club goin'. Without you, we'd a-never got the club started, and we'd a-never knowed to write the president. You are precious!"

On the other side of the mill, Webster heard the broadcast. Jacob came running in, nearly out of breath.

"Did you hear what he said?" Jacob gasped.

"I heard . . ."

The telephone rang. It was Senator Lawrence.

"You heard the president?" Lawrence asked.

"Yes, and I don't like it."

"I'll get my staff to review his proposals, and we'll advise you on what to do next. I've spoken with other mill owners, and they're working on plans to squash what Roosevelt's doing."

At a time when textile workers believed the president was going to help them, mill owners were pressing Congress to do everything they could to block the president—and they were doing it while publicly claiming they were trying to be supportive of Roosevelt's plans.

Webster hung up the phone and looked at Jacob, who said, "Father, I believe I can help you run the entire plant. I've worked in every section, and I think you could use some help right now."

Webster stood, looked down at his desk, took a deep breath, and then looked up and smiled. "You've made some good improvements. I appreciate what you've done. I think you realize how important this work is to me. I think you could run the whole plant, too. I'll need you to spend some time with me, learning how to set up contracts and deal with the buyers."

He extended his hand and said, "You've done a good job. Keep it up. I need you to help me find ways to reduce our payroll and get our prices down. I don't like what I'm hearing from this new president. Roosevelt sounds like he favors the workers over the mill owners. I don't like that."

CHAPTER 47

FIXING WHAT THE PRESIDENT DID

Senator Lawrence found the Cotton Textile Board would be patterned similarly to Roosevelt's National Industrial Relations Board. He called Webster.

"The president wants all mills to have committees of workers and employers to resolve problems over work conditions. If the mill committee can't fix them, the matter is to be sent to a state committee and, if needed, on up to the national board in Washington to make a final decision."

"We won't have a committee at my plant," Webster fumed. "It's my mill, not the government's. Nobody is gonna tell me how to run it."

Jacob nodded. He sat in a chair in the doorway, listening in on a telephone in the hall and making notes.

Lawrence explained there were new federal regulations establishing a forty-hour workweek. Word of this made Webster tap on his desk rapidly as he grew more upset by what he was hearing.

"He wants Northern mills to pay a minimum wage of thirteen dollars a week for forty hours of work and for Southern mills to pay twelve dollars a week."

Webster jumped up and yelled, "Hell, I'm losing money on what I'm paying now. I'll go broke at twelve dollars a week." He thanked Lawrence and then hung up the phone. "This thing is a mess."

Webster called his bookkeeper to his office and began instructing him to change the payroll ledger to make it look as if each employee had gotten a raise and was being paid twelve dollars a week. "Make it look like we made the change just after the new regulations went into effect."

"Sir, we'll go broke."

"I know that. We're not raising their pay. This will be the set of books we'll show federal officials if they ever come here to check. You keep the actual figures in a separate book."

He said to Jacob, "Go to the plant and bring me back three workers you can trust to keep their mouths shut."

When Jacob returned, he had three worried-looking employees with him: a man named Blanchard; his wife, Reva; and Reva's brother, Thomas.

"Father, these are the workers I mentioned."

"Have you explained what we want?"

"No, I thought you—"

"You're their boss. You tell them."

The workers were frightened now. Reva Blanchard fidgeted with her apron as her husband wiped his face with a rag. They thought they were being fired.

"I brought you here to tell you we're giving you each a pay raise. As of this week, your pay will be twelve dollars a week."

The trio's mouths fell open. Reva hugged her husband, and her eyes gleamed with tears as he said, "Uh, thank you, Mr. Jacob. We need the money right now. And also, thank you, too, Mr. Webster."

Webster nodded, and then Jacob warned them, "There is one condition. You must tell no one you're getting a pay raise. We can't raise everyone's pay, and we don't want your friends getting resentful, which they'd do if you tell them your pay has been raised while theirs hasn't.

"We'll be raising the pay of other employees, too," Jacob lied, "but they'll be told the same thing. We won't tell you who they are, because, if word of this got around, some folks would be upset. One thing, though, if people from the government come to check on our plant, we may need you to meet with them to talk about the pay raise you and others are getting. If that happens, we'll come and get you. Now, do each of you promise to keep this a secret?"

The three employees smiled and nodded.

Jacob asked each one, "Do you promise?"

They all said yes.

"This is a good deal for you. But if any one of you tells someone, or anyone, anywhere, we'll fire you. You won't have any money, and you'll have no place to live. And if you try to get a job at another mill, we'll tell them you cannot be trusted. Is that clear?"

"Yes, sir!"

"Now, go back to work. Don't be smiling when you get out on the floor. We don't want people guessing you got a raise. And if anyone asks why you got called here, you tell them I was fussing at you and said you need to improve your production. Is that clear?"

"Yes, sir!"

From the window, Webster watched the three employees walk down the road to the mill, talking among themselves. He turned and smiled. "Jacob, you did great."

When they got back to the plant, Reva Blanchard pulled on the chain to open the weaving room door. All the weavers turned to see.

Four women and a few men scurried up. A woman fanned cotton lint from in front of her face and yelled, "What did he want?"

"He bawled us out in front of Mr. Webster," Reva lied. "Said we weren't meeting production."

Her brother Tom added, "He said we wuz gonna get fired if we didn't catch up. They gonna fire others, too, so y'all better mind how your machines is runnin'."

Others gathered around them, and the door opened again. It was Jacob. "Get back to work!!"

The group scattered.

Jacob walked over to Reva's brother and made a big deal of shaking his finger at his face and yelling, "I told you not to say anything! If you tell anyone, you'll get fired!"

"I didn't tell them nuthin'. I just told them they'd better get their production up, and that's all I said."

"Good! You do that!" Jacob yelled, and then he walked across the room. The weavers stared at their machines, afraid to look at him for fear they'd be bawled out next.

CHAPTER 48

THE BIG SHAM

At the Three R Club, workers complained more about the stretch-out, lack of breaks, and new work schedules that had most working only three to four days a week.

"Roosevelt says they s'posed to pay us twelve dollars a week. I heard that on the radio. And they ain't allowed to work us more than forty hours in a week, too."

"They workin' me twelve hours a day now, and only three days. That's to keep them from payin' me twelve dollars. If it weren't for my wife and kids all workin', we couldn't afford to eat."

"They breakin' the law."

"We need to write the president."

Mildred drafted another letter. Weeks passed and then months with no response. The club members began talking again about going on strike. They were encouraged by reports from the Charlotte radio station that, during a Labor Day march in Gastonia, some twenty thousand textile workers walked off their jobs. The governor of North Carolina had been forced to call out National Guard troops to keep order.

In the South Carolina Piedmont, there were more than eighty strikes in one year over low wages, part-time hours, and the stretch-out.

Mill owners wouldn't budge. They shared information about strike leaders and used their political influence to place men friendly to mill owners on the Cotton Textile Board.

Workers, still believing the federal government was going to help them, didn't have a chance. They believed Roosevelt would force the board to halt the stretch-out and reinstate workers fired for joining unions.

It never worked that way. At a hearing in Greenville, a worker testified, "They got me tending forty looms now. I hardly have time to go to the bathroom, much less eat dinner. The mill is bringing me a sandwich, so I won't need to leave to eat. I was doin' better operating twenty looms. I can operate twenty. Forty looms is more than I can do."

The company lawyer put up an industrial engineer to rebut the worker.

"The data we gathered on this gentleman clearly showed he could operate forty looms. When he was running twenty, there were long periods when he had nothing to do. I observed him socializing a lot with other workers who were also operating twenty looms.

"This man can operate forty and still have time for bathroom breaks and lunch, provided he properly maintains his equipment. Here's the data on this man." The engineer handed up papers to the grievance committee.

The committee chairman looked at the data and then turned to the worker and said, "Do you have any data that would disprove what the engineer has presented in sworn testimony?"

"I ain't got no data. All I know is, me and the other workers in our plant is being overworked."

"I'm sorry, sir. If you can't provide evidence to refute the engineer's testimony, then we have no basis to direct the mill to make any changes."

Frustrated at being rebuffed, workers turned to the United Textile Workers union for help and began threatening strikes.

Late one morning, a mill owner in another town telephoned Webster with alarming news.

"I just called the governor's office," he said. "We got problems across the state. My contact says labor unions are moving in, trying to organize workers."

"How does he know?"

"They get information from the sheriffs. In Ware Shoals, over a thousand workers walked out again in protest of time studies. They are still on strike, and the owner there has asked other mills to send him some strikebreakers. You let me know what you hear about mills up in your area."

"Thanks, I'll see what I can find out." Webster hung up the phone, turned, and looked out at his plant.

This is my mill. He nervously tapped an arm of his chair. *I built it, and I'm gonna keep it.*

The more he thought, the angrier he became. He stood and paced, and began shouting, "*I* was the one who hired the workers and gave them good jobs! When they came, they were filthy, barely had clothes, and I taught them how to keep clean and keep their houses clean. They don't appreciate what I've done for them. I'll run all of them off and start over. There won't be a union at my plant!"

Clarence heard the shouting and reluctantly looked in the room.

"Mr. Charles, was you callin' me?"

"Uh, no, Clarence . . . uh, yes. Go tell Jacob I want to see him and that new Prickett guy right away."

CHAPTER 49

THE UNION

Outside the gate, a new man had been hanging around for days. He didn't say much. The others thought he was hoping to be hired on as a spare hand. However, the stranger wasn't looking for a job. He was there to listen.

He kept hearing the name Mildred Turnage come up. He heard how she'd stopped the bleeding when a worker's hair had been caught and gotten the company store manager fired after a little girl caught him cheating workers.

After sundown one steamy evening, he walked behind Mildred's house. The cicada choruses were rising and falling in the trees.

Mildred and Vida Mae were in the kitchen, putting up supper dishes, when Schwartz tapped on the screen door. He could hear the women talking loudly, almost shouting. He tapped harder, and they stopped.

"Who's there?

"My name is Schwartz."

"What do you want?"

"I'd like to talk with Mildred Turnage."

"For what?"

"About the mill."

"Are you from the government?"

"No, I'm from the United Textile Workers of America."

"You a union man?" Mildred asked as she walked onto the back porch drying her hands with a towel.

"Yes, ma'am. I'm a field agent of the UTWA. I want to talk with you about how we can help you and your neighbors get more pay and better working conditions."

Vida Mae walked onto the porch, holding a pot she was drying, as Mildred said, "You ain't from the mill, are you?"

Schwartz pulled out a Labor Department form stating he was an authorized agent of the United Textile Workers of America and held it against the screen door. Mildred looked at it and then glanced off her porch to see if any of her neighbors were about.

"Come up. It would be better if we sat in the dark. Vida Mae, cut that light out. This is my friend Vida Mae Pressley. She and her boy, Matthew, live here with me."

"I wanted to talk with you only."

"We live here together. She's my best friend. Anything you say to me, you can say to her. We'll keep it quiet."

"Pleased to meet you, Mrs. Pressley."

"Come in. We can talk a little louder in the kitchen. We just come in from the plant, and our hearing ain't good yet." A small oscillating fan was whirring softly. "It's cooler in here anyway. I swear, I think August has got to be the hottest month."

"The fan feels nice," Schwartz said as Vida Mae pulled back a chair and motioned for him to take a seat.

"I know what's been happening to you and your friend here in the mill. I want to talk with you about how we can make things better."

Vida Mae wiped a corner of the table. "You want us to go on strike?"

"Not unless we have to. We need to organize first."

Schwartz explained how the UTW got better pay for workers in Massachusetts and forced the mills to end the stretch-out up there.

He said he'd already signed up 1,400 mill workers in Ware Shoals and was planning to get other workers to join up, too.

"Why did you come here? We're a small plant," Mildred said.

"Over in North Carolina, there are six mills with over four thousand workers. If we can be successful here, it'll make it easier to get workers in North Carolina to sign up."

"Why did you come to see me?"

"I've hung around the mill for nearly a week, and almost every day, someone talked about you and how you help others. I figured, if you could provide that kind of leadership, you might be willing to help the workers get better pay and end the stretch-out."

Vida Mae looked at Mildred. "That's true, hun. The workers trust you."

Mildred frowned. "This stretch-out is a-killin' us, and the mill's been a-hirin' children to run the spinnin' room. Children should be in school.

"Everybody is working hard, but it's us weavers that are sufferin' the most. You want us to go on strike?"

"That may not be necessary. If we get the workers to join the union, the mill will be forced to arbitrate, and we could get you better working conditions and better pay. We won't strike unless we have to."

Schwartz told them the National Industrial Recovery Act allowed workers to organize unions and the mill couldn't do anything about it if the workers followed the right procedures.

He cautioned them to get people they trusted to help recruit members.

"Mr. Schwartz, most of the workers is ready to go on strike anyway. We've talked about it at our Three R Club meetings."

"It's best you don't talk about this in a meeting," he cautioned. "When word gets around about meetings being held, mills plant friendly employees as spies. We've already had cases where owners found out who was talking with our field agents and fired them."

He said the mills were gambling that the Labor Relations Board wouldn't intervene. Some mills developed blacklists of pro-union workers to send the message that workers risked not getting a job anywhere if they got involved in union activities. So, he cautioned, they must be careful about how they got people to sign up.

"They can't fire us for talkin' with you, can they?"

"Not for talking with me outside of work, but they can fire you if you're not doing your job. So, don't talk with anyone about joining up while they're working unless you're certain no one can see or hear you."

Schwartz handed them cards. "We got to get at least thirty percent of the workers to sign these. The cards go to the national labor board, which can order the mill to hold the election.

"If we get fifty percent to sign up, then the union goes in automatically. The cards still go to the labor board. The union, of course, uses the cards to compile the list of workers joining the union at this plant."

"They's two hundred fifty workers in the mill," Mildred said. "So, we need seventy-five to have a vote and one hundred twenty-five to put the union in without a vote."

"Actually, we need one hundred twenty-six to put the union in without a vote," Schwartz said. "A majority is one vote more than fifty percent."

"It ain't goin' be no problem gettin' a hundred twenty-six people to sign up, Mr. Schwartz. They all ready to go on strike."

Schwartz told them to find ten people they trusted. "Get them to sign the cards and give them back to you. Then you give them ten cards each and ask them to go find ten workers. You collect the cards. Then give them to me. Now, this is most important: you cannot give out cards inside the gate or inside the plant. You can give them out only in public, like on the street or at their houses. You can't do it in the plant. You make sure you explain that to all the people giving out cards—no cards in the mill. It's best to go to their homes and give them out."

Mildred and Vida Mae smiled at Schwartz.

"This'll be easy, Mr. Schwartz. You like pound cake?"

"I certainly do."

After thanking them for the cake, Schwartz walked down the steps and away from the house. Vida Mae and Mildred giggled like schoolgirls planning a prank. They made a list of ten workers each would contact. The giggling stopped when both agreed they would avoid talking with the Blanchards, especially Reva's brother Tom. Mildred was suspicious.

"They's something fishy about his tale. Jacob Webster took them out of the plant, all the way to Mr. Webster's house, just to bawl them out? He coulda done that in the mill. They could be spies."

"Maybe what we ought to do, Mildred, is like what Schwartz said, you know, talk to the others outside the plant."

It was late that night when they stopped their planning and went to bed.

Mildred lay on her back, listening to Vida Mae's soft snoring from the next bedroom. She thought of Schwartz telling her, "Nearly every day, someone mentions Mildred Turnage and how she helps other workers."

For the first time, her life meant something. *I have a family.* In the trees behind the house, the cicadas were singing, and Mildred smiled. *I'm gonna do this for my family.*

CHAPTER 50

RUDELL THOMAS STIRS THINGS UP

Rudell Thomas grew up hearing horror stories about white people. He heard his grandmother tell of how a plantation owner chopped toes off her granddaddy for stealing eggs to feed his sick wife and how whites burned black houses and killed black children. He overheard his mother and her friends gossip about what the white folks did in the houses they kept and why, when white folks ever misplaced something, it was always *the colored help stole it.*

He longed for the day when Negroes had their own communities and wouldn't need white people, white money, and, worst of all, white police.

That's why he spent one Saturday a month selling copies of Negro-owned newspapers in front of Dupre Merchant's bank. White officials despised them for publicizing editorials and accounts of atrocities carried out by lynch mobs and white police all over the country. The stories they ran created the impression it was happening everywhere, every day, every hour, despite some accounts being months or years old.

Rudell got called out by a local black preacher for spreading hate. "Rudell, you know nothin' like that is happenin' here. We ain't Mississippi or Tulsa. Why you want to stir people up?"

"People need to know how white people are treatin' us!" Rudell yelled as a crowd formed around them at the bank's front door.

"Rudell, they is good people in this town, good colored people and good white people who mean us no harm."

"If they so good to us, then why won't they hire us to work over at that cotton mill? They workin' white women and white children now. They won't work us 'cause they 'fraid we goin' to rape some white woman. I read that in the paper."

"What paper? You ain't read no such thing in our paper here."

"Well, it did happen."

"Where?

"It was in Mississippi, but it might as well be here."

The crowd was starting to grumble. Dupre Merchant stormed out of his bank and yelled, "What are you people doing? Get off the sidewalk. People can't get in the bank. What's this all about, Rev?"

"Uh, nothin', Mr. Dupre. Rudell and me was discussin' something about Mississippi."

Dupre turned to Rudell, "How many times do I need to tell you to stay away from my bank? Those papers you peddle are lies. They need to be outlawed. Now, go on, or I'll get Tumpy over here to run you off."

"Rudell, do what he say. Go on home."

"I'll move, but I ain't goin' home. I got a right to tell our people what's happening to them."

"You just be sure what you tellin' them is the truth, Rudell." The preacher turned to the crowd. "Y'all move along. Go get yo shoppin' done and then go home. And tomorrow be sure all of you be in church."

Rev. Bernard Robinson was a carpenter who built and repaired houses around the town. He'd taken over his daddy's church after his father had died and was so effective in his preaching he quickly doubled the congregation, turning it into the biggest colored church in the area. He was one of three Negro men who served as the unofficial spokesmen for the colored community at Haigler's Crossing.

While things were stirring in the town, out at Crowell Mill Village, Mildred and Vida Mae found most workers eager to sign union cards. There were some, though, they couldn't convince. Betty Jean Snell was one of them.

Betty Jean was feeding chickens in back of her house when Mildred approached her.

"Them are some pretty chickens you got there, Betty Jean. I bet they give good eggs, too."

"They ain't bad. They take less work than a garden. What do you want, Mildred? I got to fix supper."

"I come to talk with you about what's happening in the mill."

"If you want to talk about that union, save your breath. Me and Herman have already talked about it and decided we want no part of it."

"But Betty Jean, the mill is working you and Herman to—"

"That don't matter. At least we got jobs. Other folks ain't got jobs, and Herman said for me to stay out of this union talk."

"Where did he hear about it?"

"They was a couple of men talking about it in the water house yesterday. Herman told them not to count on him. They mentioned you was involved with some Yankee Jew in town, stirring things up."

"That man is tryin' to help us."

"Well, me and Herman don't want no part of joinin' no union."

"All right, then, don't. All I ask is that you and Herman not talk with anyone about what we're doin', especially your bosses."

"We ain't talking. Just don't drag us into it."

There were similar results out in the breaking room. Hubert McLain was feeding layers of cotton into the picker machine when a man who worked in the carding room walked over and started talking about the union.

"Yeah," McLain said, "that's all well and good, but I don't want to have nuthin to do with no union. I got a job here, and I aim to keep it. Now, move along. I want to finish this bale so I can go cool off."

Outside, the man found Shorty Thompson sitting on a cotton bale on the porch. Shorty had his shirt off and was wringing sweat out of it as the man came up. Shorty told the man he'd think about joining. Then—never one to miss an opportunity to promote himself—he went to his boss and told him mill workers were trying to organize.

By that time, it was too late; 193 workers had signed cards. Crowell Mill was unionized—or so they thought.

The day Mildred and the union representative went to Webster's house, Thomasina turned them away, forcefully declaring, "Mr. Charles say he ain't meetin' wid you. He say, if you don't get off he property, he callin' de sheriff!"

Schwartz tried to explain that Webster would be violating labor laws, only to face an even more forceful Thomasina.

"All I know is, Mr. Charles told me to tell you to get off the yard. If you don't, he goin' call de sheriff!"

Back at the mill, Charlie Prickett and Jacob Webster blocked Mildred from entering the plant. She was fired and told she must move out of her mill house by the end of the week.

Mildred and Schwartz insisted that the union had formed under federal regulations and she couldn't be fired for helping organize it.

Jacob told her, "We don't care what those Yankee laws say. You're fired for disrupting our mill. And another thing, you can tell Vida Mae Pressley she and her son are fired, too!"

"For what? They didn't do nothin'," Mildred complained.

"That's right. They didn't do nothin'. You all live in the same house, so don't try to tell me they didn't know anything. They're fired, too!"

The next day, there was a cascade of mill hands shutting off machines and walking out of the plant. They stood outside the gate, four deep in the sun, fanning and wiping their faces. Webster saw them from his office. He called Senator Lawrence for help.

"They're outside the fence right now. Get the governor to send me some National Guard troops up here!"

When Lawrence telephoned, new Governor John G. Richards was frustrated. "You are the third legislator to call me, Matthew. I have no troops to send you. All of them are already posted at strikes in Ware Shoals and Greenville. This thing is spreading much faster than we can handle. We're trying to come up with something, but right now, I don't know what to tell you."

Webster told Lawrence he was desperate. "We've got to do something. I have new orders to fill, and the workers have got my plant shut down. I'll lose what little money I'm making."

"Can you get other workers to come in?"

"I've had three mill owners say they can lend me some, but if their workers go out, they can't help me. This could shut down the whole industry."

Outside Mildred's house, the crowd was angry and helpless. They watched deputies pile Mildred's, Vida Mae's, and Matthew's belongings onto the street. Workers quickly divided the furniture and took it into their homes for storage.

"It ain't right, Sheriff! You know it ain't right!" someone yelled.

"This here eviction notice is legal, and I got to enforce it," the sheriff responded.

"It may be legal, but that don't make it right."

Despite Webster's threats that striking workers would be put out of every mill house in the village, the workers stayed away. They believed, any day now, President Roosevelt would order the Cotton Textile Board to force Webster to recognize their union and negotiate new terms for employment.

Nothing happened.

CHAPTER 51

DALTON THREATE COMES BACK

A farm family down the road from the village took in Mildred. Johnnie Faye Hutson tried to get Mildred into her home, but her husband was adamant. "I'm management. I'll lose my job, and we'll be put out. She can't stay here."

Vida Mae and Matthew went to a sister's house in North Carolina.

Webster made calls to nearby mills and got support. He notified Senator Lawrence he had a hundred non-union workers coming to run his plant. "I need National Guard or law enforcement to escort them inside. The strikers will try to keep them out. It's going to take guns to keep them back."

"There are no National Guard troops available," Lawrence said, "but the governor has issued an order permitting mills to appoint special constables to assist.

"I'll write you up something to give the sheriff, notifying him you're hiring security guards. We'll tell him three busloads of non-union workers are coming in next Thursday and he needs to protect them."

Webster got Jacob to look for constables. Jacob first tried men from the town. No luck. Dupre Merchant had put the word out

319

that no one would help. He was hoping the strike would put the mill out of business.

At a country store near the North Carolina line, Jacob finally found some men drinking beer. They got excited when he said he'd pay them ten dollars a day.

"I know that plant inside and out," one of them bragged.

"Who are you?"

"Dalton Threate. I worked there several years till a woman got me fired."

"If her name was Mildred, we just fired her for trying to organize our workers. We're gonna need more than just you men. I need each of you to get one or two more to help. They need to be people you trust. Threate, you take charge of this. Be at the plant by six o'clock tomorrow morning. I'll show you what to do. Do you have guns?"

Most nodded yes, and a few raised hands. One said, "I ain't got no gun, but I can get one."

"All right, bring your guns and get your friends to bring their guns, too, and plenty of bullets. We don't expect trouble, but all of you will be acting as special constables, so you need to be armed. And another thing, don't a-one of you take a drink tomorrow. If you show up drinking, I'll send you away. You be sure and tell them that."

It was dark when the gunmen showed up. Jacob stood close to each one, checking their breath. He wrote their names on a form Senator Lawrence gave him that stated the men were appointed as special constables under orders from the governor.

Next, Jacob checked the pistols and shotguns. "I hope you don't need these, but you may use them to protect the company property or for your own safety. At eight o'clock, three buses will bring in strikebreakers. You are to escort each bus up to the gate, where the workers will get off and walk inside. Once the last worker gets off, you come inside the gate, and we'll lock it shut. There's some coffee and biscuits on that back table for you, so y'all just stand at ease now. I'll line you up before the first bus comes."

The men gathered around the table, eating biscuits and talking quietly. There was no joking or laughter. When asked about working at the mill, Dalton Threate told them he'd been supervisor of the spinning room.

"They laid me off because of an accident a young boy caused. It won't my fault, but I got blamed for it because of that woman. She's a loudmouth."

At seven thirty, Jacob returned, lined up the men, and had them check their guns again. He told Threate, "I need you to take two men with rifles upstairs and man the windows overlooking the front gate. The rest of you, just stay in the line here. I'll take you outside and show you where to stand. You'll be making room for the busses to come in."

Up in the village, striking workers began leaving houses and congregating in pockets in the street. They bunched up when Mildred and the union man drove up.

Schwartz cautioned them, "Don't anybody throw a rock or stick or anything. This is a peaceful demonstration. We're just going to stand together and block the gates to keep strikebreakers out."

Mildred pointed toward the town and said, "I been tellin' you we better than what them folks over in town say we is. We make the cloth which becomes the clothes everybody wears in America. Hell, we made uniforms for our soldiers. If'n it weren't for us, them uppity women over yonder wouldn't have no dresses and they children no school clothes. We ain't hicks, and we damn sure ain't lint-heads."

The crowd applauded. Then someone yelled, "Look!"

Men with shotguns and pistols filed out the main gate just as a bus carrying strikebreakers slid to a stop.

"C'mon!" Mildred hollered and ran towards the plant.

Workers strung out behind her. The crowd came to a halt when the security guards leveled guns at them. Some of the strikers bent over, hands on their thighs, trying to recover as their cotton-mill lungs struggled for oxygen. For a moment, the crowd was still, uncertain what to do next.

Then third-floor windows went up at the plant, and men with rifles leaned out.

"Dalton Threate!" one of the strikers shouted, and he pointed at a window. "I figured it would be just like you to show up!"

There was some movement among strikers to let Mildred step forward.

She looked up at Threate. "It looks like old man Webster will stoop real low to try and break our strike. He hired him a rapist." Turning to face the crowd, she said, "It ain't right Webster shut us out. We got the law on our side. All we got to do is hold on until Roosevelt's people come here and *make* Webster recognize our union."

There was a big cheer.

Threate whispered, "Somebody needs to shut her up."

The bus pulled away, and the crowd surged forward, backing the guards against the fence. Another bus pulled up, was blocked by the crowd, and then drove off.

A door opened, and strikebreakers came out of the mill. They stood in a line behind the fence, unarmed. Jacob Webster stepped in the doorway and began handing out picker sticks, which the men passed along the line. Used to bat shuttles back and forth, the picker sticks, with their metal tips, were perfect clubs.

The strikebreakers began slapping the clubs against their palms, daring the crowd to start something.

That was all it took. The mob exploded into cursing, spitting, and fist-shaking as they pushed toward the armed guards trapped against the fence.

The gunmen were jumpy and swung guns from one person to another in wild-eyed panic. One of them hollered, "Get back! I mean it, get back! I'll shoot you dead!" A shot was fired . . . then another and another and another and another.

The crowd ran away, shrieking, and the bullets kept coming.

Mildred Turnage was shot in the back and fell face down in the street. Vida Mae hollered, "I saw you shoot her, Dalton Threate!" and ran to Mildred. She rolled her over, crying her name and holding her. Mildred opened her eyes and tried to say, "Don't let them." Then she died.

Vida Mae looked up. Her son, Matthew, was running towards her. She watched a bullet blow off the top of his head, and what was left of him flopped onto the street. She let go of Mildred, stared at Matthew, and screamed . . . and screamed . . . and fainted.

Some of the crowd began running back to try to help those who had been shot. Seven bodies lay on the road in pools of blood.

Two buses pulled up, and more strikebreakers ran through the gates. Some of them grabbed picker sticks.

The sheriff came up and ordered, "Everybody get back. I don't care whose side you're on. Everybody get back." He sent a deputy to get a doctor.

Meanwhile, in town, the fire bell rang and rang until Dupre Merchant ran out of his bank and shouted, "Get to the fire department and find out what the hell is going on!"

Someone yelled, "It's over yonder! Look, near the colored church."

A small group of colored men who saw the smoke ran to the fire department, shoved white men aside, and jumped on the truck. They told the driver, "Get goin'."

They were yelling and pointing as the firetruck sped down the street. Their church was smoking. By the time Bernard Robinson got there, the fire had been put out. The sanctuary was safe. The fire had burned the broom closet and part of a Sunday school classroom.

"Lord, it's good you boys got here when you did."

"Rev, if we waited on them white men, the whole church coulda—"

"It was white men who did it!" a voice shouted.

The crowd turned. It was Rudell Thomas and another man, running up the hill from the river. "Get the sheriff! They gettin' away!" He turned and pointed. A couple of men ran towards them, and Rudell gestured and pointed while his friend ran back to the river with them.

Rudell ran up the hill. "It was two white men, Rev. They run past me and Caleb, jumped in a boat, and started paddelin' hard across the river. Then we saw the smoke, ran up to the church, and hollered for someone to get the fire truck. Then me and Caleb ran back to the river. We was gonna try to catch them, but they was too far to the other side. It was two white men. We need to get the sheriff."

"You didn't try to put the fire out?" Pearson asked.

"It was goin' too much, and we hollered for someone to get the fire truck. We lit out for the river to catch them white men who done it."

"You sure it was white men, Rudell?"

"Yessir, it was two white men."

"What did they look like?"

"White. They was two white men."

"You sure of this, Rudell?"

"I can't believe you said that Rev. Ain't no colored man gonna set fire to no colored church. It was two white men. Let's go to the river. Caleb will vouch for it. Somebody go get the sheriff."

Tumpy Hendley couldn't help; he had a massacre on his hands, with seven bodies lying in the street. He turned to the crowd and said, "Get some sheets or something to cover them up." Then he entered the mill and ordered Jacob to shut down the plant and line up all the security guards.

The initial storyline among them was that all of them had fired their guns in the air as a warning. "You all fired in the air? Shit! You all fired into the air, and seven people got killed? You ain't getting by with 'I shot in the air'!"

The sheriff got his deputies to divide the guards into different locations in the plant to interview them separately. He then went outside to find witnesses who could corroborate what he and his deputies had seen. He was certain he had a solid case to charge all the guards.

The next day, Dupre Merchant came stormin' into Vernon Covington's newspaper, red-faced and demanding Vernon publish stories saying that the workers were communists. He wanted him to criticize old man Webster for creating this mess by building a cotton mill. Vernon yelled that nobody was going to tell him what to put in his newspaper. Dupre kept screamin' he'd put Vernon out of business if he didn't do as he said.

Vernon shoved Dupre out the door, yelling loud enough to be heard by everyone on the street, "You can't tell me what to print! My newspaper tells the truth."

Dupre walked to his bank, cussing. Rudell Thomas was back on the sidewalk with a crowd of coloreds, who listened raptly as he told them, "It was two white men. Me and Caleb seen 'em."

Dupre said, "Rudell, and the rest of you, get away." Then he walked into the bank, slammed the door, and told his manager to get the local morticians on the telephone. He spent the day threatening foreclosure on any funeral home in the county if they embalmed the bodies or planned funerals for the slain textile workers. The morticians told him they had no plans to do so, because mill workers wouldn't have money to pay for funerals anyway.

The United Textile Workers union met with victim families and paid the costs for the bodies to be taken to some North Carolina funeral homes nearby.

The solicitor who held the inquest into the shootings was one of the early investors in Crowell Mill. He'd made a lot of money when the mill had bought back his stock. He didn't tell anyone about this and didn't disqualify himself before he called the hearing. He advised the grand jury that although Tumpy Hendley had been on the scene, the mill was outside the sheriff's jurisdiction. For that reason, he limited the number of witnesses the sheriff could call and then, on his own, selected a few non-union workers to testify, too.

Despite the testimony, the grand jury recommended just five of the security guards be held for trial, including Dalton Threate. The others were ordered to appear as witnesses.

"You can't do this," Tumpy complained. "We have witnesses who saw them murder those workers. What you've done is unlawful and unfair."

The solicitor warned him, "Keep quiet or face opposition the next time you come up for re-election. As a matter of fact, some of the leading businessmen have already asked me to help them find someone who can replace you. You better keep quiet."

"It ain't right," the sheriff said. "Them people was murdered."

A week later, a jury of white farmers handpicked by the solicitor declared the gunmen "not guilty."

Dupre Merchant was happy with the verdict but thought something should be done about the union. He went to Columbia to meet with Billy Hawkins, who, thanks to Dupre, was now a state senator.

Hawkins set up a meeting with senators from the Piedmont, where most of the state's textile mills were located. They had been meeting in private during the strikes to see how they could stop the union.

Dupre told them the business community was upset. "This union stuff is communist, and if we don't keep 'em out, we're gonna end up like Russia."

One of the senators said, "Several of us are already talking about it, Dupre. That strike crippled my part of the state, and we're trying to find a way to fix unions, so this doesn't happen again. But it's likely gonna take federal legislation to fix it."

"Why?"

"Roosevelt got Congress to pass federal laws saying workers can join unions. We can't pass state laws prohibiting them without being in violation of that. Right now, outside of the South, there ain't no support for changing it in the Congress."

A senator from Greenville spoke next. "The angle we're working on is not to outlaw unions but tinker around with what they can do or who their members are. We are looking at a way to prevent unions from having closed shops in South Carolina. In a closed shop, those who voted against the union still have to join and pay union dues, even when they don't want to."

"That ain't fair," said Dupre.

"I know. We are looking for ways to write a bill that says that those voting against the union have a right to work at their jobs without being a member. We aren't done with it yet. We got some of the smartest men in the legislature working on it."

"It would be best if we could fix that federal law of Roosevelt's first. But we can't because of the union control of Yankee congressmen.

"Up north, those people have had unions a long time, so the voters up there think unions are okay. They have no problem electing congressmen the unions support. Down here, except for the textile workers, most people don't know what the hell labor unions are. That gives us an opportunity. Right now, we can tell our people anything about unions, and they'll believe it, especially if we scare them."

"Yeah, Dupre, white folks here already think Yankees love coloreds and believe they're as good as you and me. All we got to do is tell our people that labor unions are Yankee organizations that want colored men working alongside white women. Then, even if the lintheads keep trying to form unions, the rest of the people won't support them and will elect people like us, and we'll still have control."

"Gentlemen, this is impressive. But how do we get the word out?"

"We're already working on it. We got businessmen talking about it among themselves and in their Sunday school classes. We've got preachers giving sermons that labor unions are communist, and communists don't believe in God or Jesus. Newspapers are beginning to report that unions always lead to violence and threaten our communities."

"Hell," Dupre said, "I just ran off a liberal Roosevelt-supporting newspaperman from my town. I foreclosed on him and put him out of business. Now the next newspaperman that comes in will hafta believe as we do, or we'll put him out of business, too."

"Dupre, we got white people believing the Civil War was about states' rights and not so much about slavery. If we can do that, we can convince them that unions are evil. If they start believing it, then we'll have no more worries about unions in South Carolina."

CHAPTER 52

THE BIG FUNERAL

Webster kept the mill shut for two weeks and starved workers into returning. He required them to sign contracts stating they'd never organize or discuss the shootings.

There was national outrage over the killings. Northern newspapers condemned them, called them murder. Southern papers disagreed, saying the shootings wouldn't have occurred had the textile workers not been on strike. They also ran editorials blaming the workers and Yankee immigrant unions for the deaths.

The United Textile Workers union convinced the victims' families to let it hold a service for all of them in a field down the road from the mill. Ten thousand people showed up.

Flatbed wagons were pulled together to form a stage for the president of the UTW and other officials to speak. Johnnie Faye Hutson sat up front, looking at the stage, crying and tearing at tissues she pulled from a box.

The union leader concluded his remarks by urging those attending to fight for the rights of textile workers "so that these fallen servants will not have died in vain."

Johnnie Faye stood, shook her fist, and, choking back sobs, yelled, "My best friend believed you, union man! My best friend believed Mr. Roosevelt would help us. My best friend believed the Cotton Textile Board would treat us fairly. All of us believed you. And what good did it do? People got killed, and Mildred got shot in the back! And even now, we can't get no justice. Why? 'Cause the mill and the politicians rigged it. The system is against people like us in South Carolina. People here think we millhands ain't good enough to have no rights. You and all them others up there, *and Mr. Roosevelt* in Washington, you can all go to hell—you ain't worth a shit."

CHAPTER 53

How the South Stayed Locked into Bad Beliefs

The gory shooting and bloody death of Mildred and Matthew damaged Vida Mae's thinking. It was like a blunt-force injury to her brain. For weeks, she sat in a rocking chair at her sister's, hugging Matthew's bloodstained shirt and screaming when someone tried to take it from her. Tired of this, her brother-in-law eased the shirt from beneath her pillow one night while she was asleep. He walked outside and buried it in a just-plowed field.

For years now, Vida Mae has been seen out in the field some nights with a shovel, poking in the dirt and moanin', "Matthew, come back. I'll take care of you, baby."

*   *   *

Betsy McCall stubbed out her cigarette and looked at Vernon. "That's a hell of a story. And you got run out of business—"

"For tellin' the truth," he replied.

The two of them sat a long time, quiet.

Out on the street, the stores were closed. People were heading home, and streetlights were coming on.

"How did we get this way, Vernon?"

"We're like . . . newspapers are like . . . those streetlights pushing against the darkness of ignorance and beliefs. It's difficult to change opinions once they harden especially when we have to fight against those with the resources to tell things untrue over and over. The false information gets accepted; usually because it fits what folks want to believe. The Dupre Merchants of the South blame unions for what happened despite what the mill owners did to their workers. Just like the Civil War myth, they will keep at it until the lies they tell about unions become accepted as common knowledge."

"But what if we tell them the truth?"

"We can try, but you can't make people accept something they don't want to hear. They've been raised on bad information so long it is not only part of their beliefs; it is now part of their culture. That goes for coloreds as well as whites.

"Some of them prefer to believe people like Rudell Thomas and blame all white people for their troubles, rather than examining facts and evidence. Some coloreds are even changing the history of slavery to do that. Their version of begins with the Middle Passage, slaves already on ships. That way they can avoid revealing that Africans conspired with Europeans and for hundreds of years captured their own people and sold them out of African-owned markets in the Atlantic Slave Trade. That's no different than what white Southerners did about the history of the Civil War.

"Things in the South could be different if textile workers and other working-class whites joined up with Negroes. They would be big enough politically to challenge those in power, but they won't. The racism and misinformation both sides grew up on gets in their way. They have no idea that what they believe is used to hold them back.

"So here we are, people holding onto bad beliefs even with evidence they are half-truths, falsehoods, or deliberate lies."

"Can we stop it?"

"Not as long as there are people whose fortunes or political power depend upon keeping us divided. Bad beliefs affect our ability to trust and abide by our system of self-governance. If we continue down this path, someday our distrust of each other will put our very democracy at risk."

EPILOGUE

The myth of the Lost Cause is true. Generation after generation of South Carolinians were taught a lie that the Civil War was never about slavery, but about states' rights, unfair federal laws, and regulations. That Confederate soldiers gladly went off to war to defend their homeland is partially true, but most soldiers were drafted into service by the Confederate government. Greenville County, South Carolina, became known as the Black Hole because of the number of men hiding out to avoid service.

While the story of what happened inside SC Statehouse was fictional, South Carolina did have two House of Representatives and two speakers for a few months as a result of the 1876 elections. President Rutherford B. Hayes pulled federal troops out of the South Carolina Statehouse. This forced Governor Chamberlain to resign and let General Wade Hampton become governor. Jim Crow laws adopted a decade later remained on the books for generations.

The inclusion of slavery is based on research, including articles by Dr. Thomas Sowell and Dr. Henry Louis Gates. However, it should not be regarded as an attempt to diminish the cruelty of American chattel slavery and the subsequent Jim Crow laws, segregation, and harm caused to slaves and their descendants in America.

The story of Webster's mother being sent to a convent is based upon a 2009 report published in *The Guardian* about the treatment of out-of-wedlock mothers in Ireland during the 1950s and 1960s.

The National Industrial Recovery Administration (NIRA) and Cotton Textile Board failed to live up to textile worker expectations. Mill owners used their DC influence to dominate the board. They ignored the law's intent, developed self-serving standards, and began "stretching out the stretch-out," as historians James Leloudis and Kathryn Walbert wrote in their book, *Like a Family* (UNC Press). The owners "effectively turned the minimum wage into the maximum most workers could earn and laid off thousands of additional hands."

Frustrated by the failure of the Cotton Textile Board and NIRA to resolve wage and labor disputes, members of the United Textile Workers union called for a national strike in September 1934. Hundreds of thousands of workers, mainly in the South, walked off their jobs.

Strikers were killed in South Carolina, North Carolina, Georgia, and Alabama. In North Carolina, National Guardsmen even bayonetted strikers in one incident.

The story about the strike at Crowell Mill is based upon a real event, the shootings at the Chiquola Mill in Honea Path, South Carolina, on September 4, 1934. Seven workers were killed by special constables hired by the superintendent of the mill, who was also mayor of Honea Path. He ordered funeral homes not to prepare the bodies of the victims. The shooters were acquitted. The mill hired back striking workers on the condition that they never mention labor unions and never discuss the shootings. The Honea Path code of silence remained for some sixty-two years, as Frank Beacham reported in his book, *Whitewash*.

Nearly six months after the national textile workers' strike, the U.S. Supreme Court struck down the National Industrial Recovery Act. The National Cotton Textile Board disappeared as well. Writing for the majority, Justice Hughes held that Congress had, in effect, delegated legislative power to the president, making the act unconstitutional.

The workers who led their local strikes thought that under the federal NIRA, they'd be able to return to their jobs, and they were shocked to find that not only were they terminated, but they were blacklisted from working in other textile plants, and there was nothing they could do about it.

They felt betrayed by union leaders, who, after promoting the walkouts, suddenly called for an end to the strikes on the promise that a new, neutral federal board, including a UTW representative, had been created to arbitrate worker grievances. The workers had been sold out. The new body did little to arbitrate between labor and management.

The violence and public outcry over the Chiquola killings and other strikes helped spur passage of the Wagner Act in 1935, which created the National Labor Relations Board to conduct union elections, and the Fair Labor Standards Act in 1938, which established a minimum wage and regulations affecting overtime pay and child labor. Out of these laws came reforms that vastly improved the lives of American workers.

The failure of thousands of Southern textile workers to form labor unions led Francis Gorman, an officer of the UTW, years later to comment, "Many of us didn't understand then, as we do now, that the government protects the strong, not the weak, and it operates under pressure and yields itself to that group which is strong enough to assert itself over the other."

The story of whites getting told that labor unions are evil originated in efforts by newspapers, the SC Chamber of Commerce, the SC Textile Manufacturers Association, and other business groups from the 1930s to the 1970s. As a result, most white South Carolinians believe labor unions are bad despite most of them having little knowledge of what unions are. Even today, most folks are unaware that the forty-hour workweek, overtime pay, medical care for job-related injuries, and other benefits are all the result of working men and women striving for fairness via labor unions almost a hundred years ago.

Acknowledgement

Thanks to Allison who told me to keep going despite what she read of my initial draft and my talented brother Van for his help with phrasing, grammar, and support. Thanks also to my nephew Kevin who kept my records straight. Thanks also to the South Carolina Writers Association for their inciteful recommendations, Frank Beacham for his account of the 1934 Chicola Mill killings in his book Whitewash, Walter Edgar for his book South Carolina a History, and the numerous authors of books about textile workers in the Palmetto State. Lastly, a thank you to the staff at Write Publish Sell for turning my manuscript into a book.

ABOUT JERRY DEAN PATE

Jerry Dean Pate is a retired trade association president and executive. He spent some thirty years lobbying the Congress and state legislatures on behalf of the telecommunications industry and electric cooperatives. He holds a BA in Journalism and Master of Public Administration degrees from the University of South Carolina.

A South Carolina native, he also worked twenty years in radio and television as a reporter, writer, producer, news anchor and news director covering the state legislature, the Civil Rights, and women's movements from the mid 1960's onward.

Pate grew up in a small SC town, was raised on false beliefs about the Civil War and as a child participated in the annual march to a Confederate Monument to praise those who fought for the South. He was taught American Exceptionalism as part of the country's WW-II propaganda and was unaware the *America is the Greatest* history imparted to him and other school children never said anything about the trail of tears, nor the near genocide of Native Americans.

His views about what he was taught changed as he began reporting on the civil rights movement and saw how bad beliefs and attitudes about women, African Americans, textile workers and labor unions affected his state.

He witnessed the rise of Christian Conservatives as a political force and watched the Republican National Committee dupe black Democrats into giving Republicans control of Southern state legislatures in exchange for drawing minority-majority legislative districts. As a result, Republicans are empowered to adopt the most egregious laws knowing Democrats can do nothing to stop them.

As today's Americans retreat into separate communities fueled by disinformation and false beliefs, he worries Americans are losing their ability to govern their country. His book provides examples of what happened to mislead people in the past and hopefully will serve as a warning for what can happen if we continue to believe in things that are untrue.

CPSIA information can be obtained
at www.ICGtesting.com
Printed in the USA
JSHW040103010722
27490JS00002B/8

9 781955 119276